THE HIGH MOUNTAIN COURT

THE FIVE CROWNS OF OKRITH

AK MULFORD

To my mom. Thank you for always telling that little girl with the notebooks full of stories that one day you would be holding her published book! (Please don't read Chapter 23 and 24...)

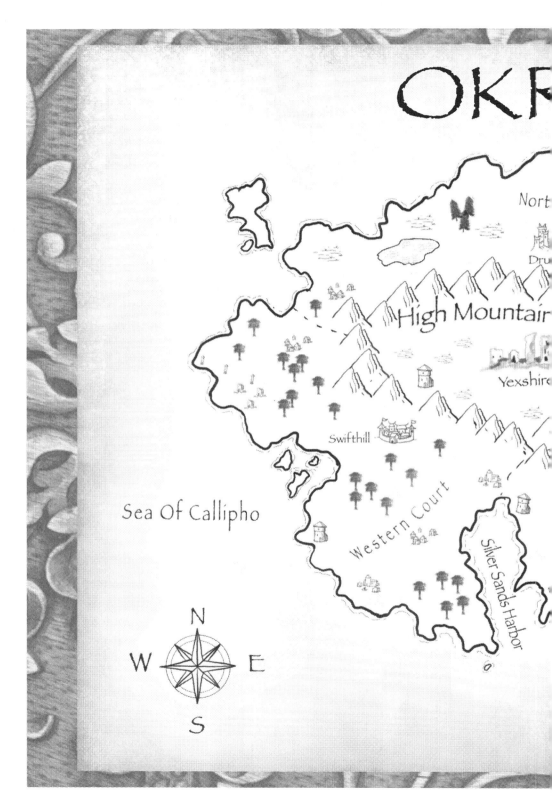

CHAPTER ONE

A black cat wove around her legs. Remy released a long-suffering sigh. Now the entire tavern would know she was a witch.

A glass shattered on the floor behind her as two tavern patrons pulled daggers on each other. The sounds of their drunken brawl echoed through the room. Remy didn't even flinch. With her weathered brown boot, she shooed the cat away. She did not fear daggers or tavern spiders or the anger of drunken men. She feared being seen. For if any one of these tavern patrons knew she was a red witch, they would all be clambering over each other to cut off her head.

How many gold coins was the Northern King paying for red witch heads these days?

She set down another heavy wooden chair in the Rusty Hatchet tavern. The smell of dirt and stale beer swirled around her. It was the smell she knew as home. A handful of other tavern workers dotted about, readying for the evening rush of locals who would flock to the tavern for its strong drinks and spiced meats.

Remy swept up after the slow trickle of midday travelers. She stole a sidelong glance toward the bar, where two of the tavern's courtesans sat, bored. Josephine and Sabine chattered away to the barman, who was listening, doe-eyed, entrapped by their beauty.

Remy looked with jealousy at their delicate embroidered dresses that flaunted their figures. She wished she could wear those beaded necklaces and teardrop earrings, wished her guardian, Heather, would let her paint her face and line her eyes with kohl. She wished she could stand out, but that was, in fact, the opposite of what they wanted with their constant efforts to keep Remy hidden. Soot stained her warm brown skin. She tied her loose black curls in a messy low bun and kept her whole demeanor intentionally unremarkable.

Swapping out the full bucket with an empty one, Remy looked up at the droplets leaking from the thatched roof. Despite its rundown appearance, the Rusty Hatchet was far better than the last tavern. Remy and her brown witch companions had been at the Rusty Hatchet for nearly a year, and it was the best tavern they had worked at in a long time.

Taverns were the only places left that would hire witches anymore. Heather insisted they move taverns every three years. They kept funneling themselves along the chain of backcountry taverns along the foothills of the High Mountains. Remy tried to convince her guardian that the ones closer to the Western Court coast would be nicer. Heather insisted that the ones closer to town would have more fae customers and it wouldn't be worth the risk.

In their realm, fae were at the top, ruling each of the five courts of Okrith . . . well, four courts now that the High Mountain Court had fallen to the Northern Court King.

An energetic voice piped up from behind her. "Scrubbing pans or scrubbing sheets?"

She looked over her shoulder. Fenrin was the same age as Remy. She had known him since they were twelve. He was an orphaned brown witch. Both Heather and Fenrin were brown witches, the coven native to the Western Court. Heather had found Fenrin living on the streets and offered him temporary shelter. But now, seven years later, he was an inextricable part of their makeshift family.

Fenrin was tall enough to draw attention in a crowd. Eating twice as much as Heather and Remy combined, he couldn't seem to gain an ounce of weight. Built like a stork, he was still impressively strong despite his lean limbs. He had a mop of straw-colored hair and ocean blue eyes.

"I'll serve the food." Remy craned her neck up to him.

"There's lots of folks from out of town here tonight," Fenrin said. "Better to work in the back."

Remy's shoulders drooped as she dusted her hands down her cream-colored apron. She once would have argued with Fenrin about staying hidden, but she didn't anymore. The likelihood of one of those travelers being a witch hunter was slim—that was the benefit of living in seedy little villages, but Remy listened to Fenrin. She had made so many mistakes over the years. Mistakes that had them fleeing towns in the middle of the night, and all to protect Remy's secret: she was a red witch.

When King Vostemur of the Northern Court slaughtered the High Mountain fae, he also slaughtered the native coven of red witches. The witches scattered across the courts, driven into hiding to avoid the witch hunters, who made a living off the witch heads they brought to the Northern King. So few red witches remained now, the only ones she knew of were the property of the royal fae who protected them from the Northern King's wrath, but the free red witches were either well-hidden or dead. Remy had not heard any gossip of a witch-slaying in years. Maybe she was the only one left.

"Pans," she said with a resigned huff. She was about to get more stains on her clothes whichever task she did. These were the choices Remy made: pans or sheets, mopping or dusting, cooking or serving.

She would rather scrub grit and grease than face whatever stained those sheets. Remy had learned more about bedroom habits from washing tavern sheets than anything Heather had ever taught her. Everything else she had learned from a cobbler's son and the tales of courtesans, though Heather tried to keep Remy away from them. Witches needed to keep to their own.

The humans and the fae couldn't be trusted, a fact which Heather reminded Remy of every day. There was a new hierarchy to their world. That hierarchy changed after the Siege of Yexshire, the mutinous slaughter of the entire capital city of the High Mountain Court. It happened when Remy was six. Now, red witches were at the bottom of the barrel.

"You always pick pans," Fenrin grumbled.

Remy couldn't help but smile. "I just know how much you love scrubbing dirty sheets, Fen."

The roar of drunken laughter echoed through the tavern. That black cat still mewled at the witches' feet. Fenrin frowned at the cat.

"Go harass one of the humans," the brown witch said, rolling his eyes as he pushed open the kitchen door.

Remy rubbed an acrid balm into her sore, cracked hands. Scouring pans had left its mark. Luckily, Heather was a skilled brown witch. Remy's guardian had a potion, elixir, or balm for every malady under the sun. Many humans would seek out Heather in secret and trade coins for her remedies. Between their tavern work and selling potions on the side, it was enough to keep their group of three afloat and pay for their frequent moves.

"Ale!" Remy heard a deep voice shout from the front of the tavern.

Matilda, the matron who owned the Rusty Hatchet, came bursting through the swinging double doors to the kitchens.

The white-haired, heavyset woman groused to herself, cursing whichever patron had screamed. She chucked a rag over her shoulder and grabbed a tray of clean, dried glasses, hefting it easily. She tilted her head to the four plated dishes on the kitchen table.

"Remy, can you give us a hand?" she asked, exasperated. "Those plates to the loud assholes in the corner booth."

"Yes, Matilda," Remy said.

Matilda sagged with relief, as though Remy's response was an act of kindness and not obedience. Remy liked Matilda. She was the nicest matron Remy had met so far. Matilda gave her staff fair wages and fair breaks. Remy was off for the night after the pans, but she heard the bustle of a full tavern and decided to help, ignoring Fenrin's warning. Staying on the good side of the tavern matron was worth the extra few minutes of work.

Remy grabbed all four plates, balancing two on her left forearm and one in each hand. Using her hip, she pushed open the wood door.

Clamorous banter and the merry tunes of a fiddle and drum greeted her. She made her way past the bar full of cheery, drunk locals. Pushing her way through the throng of standing patrons, she did not let a single pea roll off the four plates she carried. Remy had been serving boisterous crowds in taverns since she was a child. She passed the musicians, casting a sideways glance at the fiddle player. He wore a dark tunic over his broad shoulders and a cap that covered his red hair. Like most of the people in this town, he was a human, not a witch or fae. There was no visible difference between humans and witches, apart from when the witches wielded their magic. The eerie glow of magic gave them away, each radiating with the colors of their home coven: blue, green, brown, and red.

The fiddle player gave Remy a wink, a blush creeping up her neck. She was glad Heather and Fenrin had already retired to their attic room so that she could enjoy the fiddler's attention. Though Remy had learned many times over the years that the affections of a half-intoxicated man meant nothing.

She moved toward the far corner booth below the stairs of the Rusty Hatchet. The hair on her arms stood on end. Her face chilled in an invisible breeze. A thread of power hung in the air; there was magic in the tavern tonight. With enough time and stillness she could probably discern which people they were, but Remy was too tired. She wanted to serve this table and then go to her bedroll in the attic above the stables.

The lamp that normally shined above the booth was dark. The candle on the table did not flicker with life either. The four men in the corner sat in darkness. Remy could only just make out their shapes. It was not unusual, this sitting in darkness. Many a secret deal happened in back booths. Perhaps they were politicians and thieves, or sheriffs and scoundrels. She did not care to know their business, and she would not attempt to peer under their hoods.

"Your food, gentlemen," Remy said, serving their plates.

As she backed away from the table, a hand snaked out and encircled her wrist. A jolt of lightning buzzed through her veins at the warm touch. The man who held her wrist flipped it over and placed two silver *druni* in her palm.

Remy looked down to the waxing and waning moons printed on the witch coins. The currencies of Okrith were all muddled together, but each race had their preferences. Fae preferred gold pieces, humans preferred coppers, and witches traded in silver *druni*. Perhaps these men were witches.

"We asked for ale," another man spoke out from under his hood. She expected a deep, gruff voice, but it was rather lighthearted for someone hiding under a hood.

Remy didn't take her eyes off the shadowed face of the man who still held her wrist. She clenched the coins in her palm, trying to stare through the darkness to his face.

"If you want your ale, then you should tell your friend to release me so I may fetch it," she said through gritted teeth.

The man who held her wrist leaned forward, bringing his torso more into the light. With his free hand he grabbed his hood, pulling it back to expose his angular face, golden sun-kissed skin, and wavy chestnut hair that fell into his gray eyes. He was the most handsome man Remy had ever seen. Unnaturally so. Remy's power buzzed through her again. The magic wasn't witches in the tavern, it was the power of a fae glamour.

Remy froze.

Before her sat a fae male glamoured as a human. Here. In the Rusty Hatchet. The humans of this town didn't take kindly to fae being amongst them, but the humans didn't sense magic the way that witches did. To them, these were merely human travelers and nothing more.

Remy looked to the other three hooded figures, allowing her eyes to peer deeper into the darkness. She suspected the other three must be fae too. Remy bit back the gasp that wanted to escape her throat. She schooled her face, hoping they could not scent her fear.

"Apologies," the striking fae said, releasing her hand. "I only wanted to tell you . . ." He paused to swipe one long, tanned finger across her cheek. It took everything in Remy not to flinch.

He showed her the soot smudge on his fingertip. She rubbed her cheek.

"I thought you'd like to know." Remy's eyes snagged on those lush lips pulling up at the corners. He was watching her, looking at her mouth. Gods, she blushed when a fiddling human winked at her, but this . . . this fae was something else. It was hardly her fault she wanted to ogle him.

Remy couldn't hold his stare, though. Those depthless smoky gray eyes promised to entrance her.

"Thanks," she said, looking to the floor.

"My pleasure." The male's voice was a deep rolling wave that made Remy's toes curl in her boots. "Have a good night, little witch."

Curse the Gods. He knew.

The fae male knew she was a witch, at the very least, and if she lingered much longer this infuriatingly gorgeous problem might discern what kind of witch she was.

This was the difficulty with the fae. This was why Remy avoided the sneaky, charming bastards like the plague.

His cunning face missed nothing, though Remy refused to reveal she knew he was fae.

"Y-you too," Remy said.

It was not a crime to be any other kind of witch . . . only a red witch. Heather claimed to be her mother, so as long as Remy did not linger with these fae, she should be okay. She looked toward the shadowed male who spoke before. "I'll fetch your ale at once."

Spinning, she disappeared into the crowd. She rushed past the musicians, ignoring the fiddle player's gaze this time. She plunged into the kitchens and out the back door. Remy braced against the damp wind as she rushed straight to the stables. She scurried without breaking into a suspicious run. She had to find Heather. Remy was sure the brown witch would want to leave at once. Fenrin was going to be furious. They'd been at this tavern for less than a year, and they had to flee again.

Remy darted up the two flights of creaky stairs and burst through the low attic door. Heather glanced at Remy's face and jumped out of her cot.

"What happened?" her guardian asked, even as she reached for her worn-out pack.

"Fae males, four of them—" Remy panted in Mhenbic, the witches' native tongue. "I just served them their meal. We should have some time."

"Four. Shit." Fenrin grabbed a bundle of dried herbs hanging from the ceiling without standing up from his stool and slammed the handful on the table. Half-made potions and elixirs covered the table's surface, along with bowls of foraged mushrooms and seeds, and a crate of small, empty brown bottles and corks. "I liked this place too."

Even with his muttered cursing, he'd already started to pack the witch goods. Only what fit in their leather hiking packs would come. Heather had two bags for her potions, and Fenrin normally hefted them. They always assumed Fenrin would be the strongest. Remy didn't correct them.

"They called me a witch," Remy said.

Fenrin cursed again.

"That means nothing," he hedged. "We're all brown witches here." He said it like the walls were listening. Maybe if he said it enough times it would become true. He would not acknowledge who she was, even in the attic.

Heather produced two silver druni from her bag and passed them to Remy.

"Only a witch's goodbye," she said.

Remy thought about grabbing her bow leaning against the doorframe, but that would make her stick out like a sore thumb. It was a worn, old bow, but it still worked well enough for hunting rabbits, and Remy was an impressive shot even with an impractical weapon.

Remy rushed back down the stairs. She would barge into the kitchens to grab the usual traveling fare: a few pieces of bread and a hard block of cheese. It would be enough to tide them over.

The three of them had made a quick art of moving after years of practice. Sometimes it would be a slow, calculated move, but other times they would flee in the night. They fled a lot more when Remy was little and she did not have as much control over her powers. But they had bolted from the town before this one too when Remy's first and only boyfriend had discovered her powers. Remy didn't think she could really call Edgar her "boyfriend", but Edgar had tried to kill her by the end of it. Going in to serve those fae when Fenrin had told her not to was just another mistake on her long list.

Remy barreled back down the stairs and across the courtyard, back to the tavern.

Blessedly, the kitchens were still alive with scrambling staff, and Remy was still in her grease-stained work clothes. No one looked at her twice as she grabbed a few apples and shoved them in her pockets. Next, she snagged some bread, cheese, and sticks of dried meat until her pockets bulged.

She knew exactly what to grab and where it would be. She sized up the food pantry the day that she arrived in any new tavern. As she darted out the back door, she dropped the two druni into Matilda's ledger, more than enough payment for the food. The coins would be their only goodbye. A witch's goodbye, they called it. Matilda wasn't a witch, but she employed a lot of them. She would see the two silver coins and know they fled.

Remy scurried back up the stable stairs. She sensed the stillness in the attic above her. Heather and Fenrin must have finished Remy's packing too.

Good.

As she dashed through the attic door, she realized her mistake.

Heather and Fenrin sat bound and gagged on the floor with three hooded fae looming over them. Heather's eyes widened when she saw Remy, and she tried to scream even through the gag.

Remy knew what she screamed: "Run!"

Remy turned without a second thought and whirled right into the fourth fae male, the one who had grabbed her wrist from earlier.

"Hello again, little witch." He smiled down at her.

CHAPTER TWO

"You have no right to bind my friends," Remy spat out. "Witches are free in the West."

The fae male had not yet shown his hand. Fenrin was right; the fae could assume they were all brown witches. They may be traffickers looking for some cheap money. If that were the case, showing her red magic would be a death sentence.

"You are as cunning as you are beautiful, little witch," the fae looming before her said with that charming, deep voice.

His eyes swept over her face, as if assessing her beauty. Remy couldn't help the flush that crept up her cheeks. He was truly stunning, this fae, like no one she had ever seen before. Tanned smooth skin swept over high cheekbones, and he had a strong, stubbled jawline. A whole head taller than Remy, he blocked the entire doorway with his large, muscled body.

Remy tried not to fall victim to the male flattery. So, this was the game he wanted to play.

She recast herself to fit his ploy: not the fighter, not the fool, but the vixen. Sabine and Josephine were not only skilled in the art of the bedroom, they also were experts in the art of the hustle, and Remy was a quick study.

11

She allowed her eyes to sweep over his body with an arched eyebrow. She wanted it to look like she was indulging in his form, but she was assessing her opponent. Remy had been sizing up strangers her whole life.

It was clear that this fae was a warrior. Not only in his muscles, but in his stance. He wore carefully selected leathers. Well-cared-for blades belted to his narrow hips, and Remy could tell there was a secret dagger hidden, sheathed, in the ankle of his boot.

Her gaze purposefully lingered for a beat on his full lips before sweeping back up to his entrancing gray eyes. She smirked up at him.

Remy swept a stray hair off her face and tucked it behind her ear.

"Cunning indeed," he said.

"If you have come for our brown witch services, I don't see how tying up my mother and brother will garner you their aid," Remy groused.

The fae warrior glanced over her shoulder to where Heather and Fenrin sat bound on the floor. Remy looked nothing like either of them. They both had fair complexions, and Remy had rich brown skin. Heather's hair was a coppery red, Fenrin's a straw blond, both pin straight, and Remy had thick loose curls the color of midnight that fell to the small of her back. Clearly not related by blood, Remy raised her chin at the fae, defying him to contradict her.

"Besides, you don't seem like the type to be seeking a love potion," she said with that coy smirk again. The male's eyes danced with surprise. "So, I can assume you've come to take us to the North and sell us into servitude. If that is the case, I can assure you a brown witch will gain you not a single piece of gold, barely enough to cover the cost of dragging us there."

"What is your name?" the male asked with a toothy grin.

"Remy," she said.

"Remy." He paused, as if savoring her name.

"And yours?" Even at a head shorter, she still leveled him with a look.

"You do not recognize me then?" he said with a flicker of surprise.

A devious grin spread across his face. "I suppose a backcountry witch would not know my visage."

Remy's stomach tightened. He was not merely a fae male, then, but an important one. Her fingers twitched to use her magic.

"Allow me to introduce myself. My name is Hale Norwood, Crown Prince of the Eastern Court."

Remy's stomach dropped. She had heard his name before. Of course she had. He was the eldest son of the Eastern Court's King Norwood. Rumors said he was born a bastard but given a royal title anyway. They said he was a reckless warrior prince. He had taken over villages and scourged through towns in the name of his father, the King. No one knew where the Bastard Prince would pop up or what havoc he would wreak. Now here he was, in her tiny attic, all the way in the Western Court . . . and that could not be a good thing.

Remy dropped into a quick bow. "Your Highness." The prince's lips curved. Remy was certain now he saw through her. "Are you seeking the services of the brown witches?"

The prince rubbed the stubble of his chin, assessing her. "I am not seeking the services of a brown witch at all." Those lead-colored eyes lit up as he added, "But you can help me, can't you, Red?"

Shit.

The game was up.

Vixen be damned, time to be a fighter.

The prince advanced. Remy grabbed her bow beside the door and swung it with all her might. The wood broke over his muscled bicep in a pathetic snap.

Cursing the Gods for her broken bow, Remy cast out her magic. She blasted the door behind the prince, who stumbled and cleared the doorway. She bolted past and leapt down the stairs, willing her magic to slam the room's door behind her and hold it fast.

Hold, hold, hold.

Her magic felt the force of the four fae warriors trying to kick it down.

She urged her legs forward, faster, out into the street. Stealing a look over her shoulder, she spotted no one chasing her yet. She whipped her head back around and ran face-first into the hard chest of the fae prince. He laughed as he caught her from falling. She looked up to the open second-floor window above her. He had jumped? She had forgotten how strong and swift the fae were.

The prince gripped her forearms as he implored, "I am not here for your head, witch. I need your help."

Remy instantly processed his words. Lies. They must be. None of it made sense. She tugged at his grip. Kicking his leg, she freed a hand, but he caught her fist and spun her around, trapping her arms and pinning her back to his chest. Remy cast her magic again, crimson red glowing from her pinned hands as she levitated a nearby bucket. The bucket flew over, colliding into the prince's head. He swore but did not release her as she stamped on his foot.

"Dammit. I am serious, Red. I need your help and I cannot let you go until you hear me," he said, struggling to hold her, and then cursed again. "Gods, you are strong."

She willed a broom to attack him, but he was expecting it this time. He released one arm to catch the broom in the air. Even one enormous arm was enough to pin her to him. But his grip was weaker, and when Remy lifted both of her legs, it forced the prince to bend forward to accommodate the sudden weight. She hadn't expected that he would release her, but he lowered her just enough, just enough to grab the dagger sheathed in his boot. Before he realized what she was doing, she plunged the dagger into his outer thigh.

The prince yelped and dropped her. She sprang into a sprint, willing her magic into a maelstrom of debris. Buckets, barrels, and spades whizzed behind her.

She tore across the ground toward the forest's edge behind the tavern. She pushed that speck of extra magic into her thighs, increasing her speed. But the fae had speed unlike any other, and she could hear the prince crashing after her.

The stab wound to his leg had done nothing to slow him down. Fae healed too quickly, Remy thought with despair, racing through her options and coming up short.

This would not be the way she would die.

As Remy breached the threshold of the forest, she dug into her power. She summoned all the magic left in her and directed it toward the giant pine tree in front of her. With an ear-splitting creak, the enormous tree bent. She pushed more, her hands shaking with the effort.

Come on. A little more. A little more. Yes!

Feeling the tree give, she heard the heavy swish of branches as she dashed under it. The massive boughs just missed her as the deafening crash shook the ground. Wind whooshed at her back. Still she did not stop. Her legs burned.

There was a river not too far into these woods. She'd jump into it. The fae had a supernatural sense of smell, but it could only work so well. If she swam down river, it would be a challenge to know where she emerged. She had to get to the river.

She prayed they would not punish Heather and Fenrin for hiding her. But that was the deal they had made with each other long ago. If ever there was a question of what she should do, Remy had promised to run.

Always run.

Remy's ears filled with the crunching of leaves beneath her feet and her panting breaths. Her lungs reminded her with every stride that she was out of shape. She needed to run more often and maybe learn some hand-to-hand combat too.

As her mind wandered to her future escape training, she heard the swift movement of air. She ducked to the right, praying she was fast enough. She felt for her well of magic. The felling of the pine tree had drained her untrained power.

The running behind her was louder now. She didn't dare a look back.

Faster, she willed her legs. In her panic, she summoned another flare of her magic. A crackling shield bent branches out of her way, and they snapped back behind her. She forged on, breathing so heavily her throat burned. The footsteps were right behind her.

A hand reached for the crook of her arm. Remy wrenched it away but forgot to cast her power to the branch in front of her.

Shouting out half a curse, she ran headlong into the unyielding wood.

She fell hard.

Those mesmerizing eyes shone over her as the prince panted. He reached down and pressed a thumb to Remy's temple, wiping away a droplet of blood.

"Are you all right?" His voice blurred like something muffled on an invisible wind.

Remy tried to scramble up, but the ground swayed beneath her. The prince's arms shot out and caught her before she fell again. He hoisted her to her feet as she struggled.

"I told you, I won't harm you," he said, his voice cooling her like a winter's wind. He stood straight, not a flicker of pain on his face, even though his trouser leg was soaked in blood. Remy didn't feel the slightest hint of remorse. Fae healed so rapidly the wound would be gone in a few days.

Remy didn't trust him for a second either. She willed a branch down to hit him on the head, but it was no more than a light smack.

"Who *are* you?" He laughed. His eyes filled with surprise and something like a begrudging admiration.

"I am no one," Remy said as she fought the darkness that clouded her vision and threatened to pull her under.

"I highly doubt that, little witch." The prince grinned.

Remy watched those shining eyes widen as she released a breath.

The darkness claimed her.

Remy heard scuffling sounds echoing through the cavernous hall before her eyes opened. They weren't in the attic above the stables of the Rusty Hatchet. No, they were in a ruin of some sort. Her head throbbed. The blurring of her vision was abating. It looked like an ancient stone cathedral. Half of the roof had crumbled inward. The windows opened out into the night air except for the small hints of stained glass in the corners.

She looked over her shoulder to see the prince. Hale was his name, Remy remembered. He crouched before an ornate stone hearth. It had recently been lit, judging by the hungry flames licking up the stack of logs.

Across the darkness of the hall, Remy heard shuffling and then Heather's voice.

"Remy!" she shouted and rushed over.

Fenrin appeared quick on her heels. They both looked unscathed, their hands unbound. Remy didn't understand why her head still remained attached to her body or why Heather and Fenrin were here, unharmed.

Her copper-haired guardian knelt next to Remy, fretting over her like a child. She reached a hand to the swollen lump on Remy's forehead and spun towards the prince.

"What did you do to her?" she accused.

"Nothing," the prince said, shrugging. He craned his neck back to look at Remy and with a cat-like smile, said, "She did that all herself."

"Bastard," Remy hissed.

Heather stifled a gasp. She grabbed Remy's arm in a silent warning. Remy rolled her eyes. He was the Bastard Prince of the East, after all.

"Very original, Red." Hale's lips thinned and his eyes narrowed at her.

"Don't call me Red," Remy snarled.

She didn't like this prince talking about her red witch magic. Even if they were in a ruin in the middle of the forest, there was no telling who else might hear.

"Then don't call me 'bastard'," the prince rumbled back.

"Kids, kids." A feminine voice called from across the darkness.

A fae female appeared from the doorway. She was tall and lithe with a long white-blonde braid that swayed behind her as she walked. Her cloak opened to show her fighting leathers and a sword strapped to her hip. Two more fae appeared behind her, a male and a female.

Remy blanched. "You have two female soldiers?"

17

"You don't believe females make good fighters?" The second one laughed as she entered the room.

The blonde fae neared Remy. Her large blue eyes glowed in the firelight.

"Says the little witch who nearly escaped a fae prince and felled a giant pine tree with her magic alone." She spoke in a warm, velvety voice. "No one here will underestimate you because you are a woman." She extended her hand, her braid slipping over her shoulder. "Carys."

Remy took the fae's hand. She had a powerful grip.

"Remy," she said.

"Those two are Talhan and Briata, the Twin Eagles." Carys nodded to the other two fae who had taken off their cloaks across the hall and were unbuckling bedrolls from their packs.

It was easy to tell they were twins, even without their moniker. Both were tall and muscular, the male slightly taller and bulkier than the female. It was clear why Eagles was their nickname; not only for their short, brown hair and hooked noses, but it was their eyes that completed the likeness. They had golden eyes, a remarkable, unearthly yellow. Remy shuddered when they gazed her way. They were attractive in the way all fae were, but their striking features would make anyone do a double take. No wonder they had kept their hoods up in the Rusty Hatchet.

The Twin Eagles gave Remy a nod and carried on with what they were doing.

"I have many more than two female soldiers," the prince replied, "but these three are my best fighters, so I selected them to accompany me on this mission."

"And what exactly is this mission?" Remy asked.

Heather put her hand on Remy's arm again. *Don't push them*, she told Remy with her eyes.

The prince dusted off his hands and sat, turning his back to the fire. Carys passed him a skin of water. He took it from her with a tip of his chin.

"We are looking for Prince Raffiel," Hale said as if it were nothing at all that he was looking for the eldest child of the fallen King and Queen of the High Mountain Court.

Fenrin was the one to laugh this time, but when the prince gave him a look, Fenrin turned the laugh into a cough. Fenrin had never seemed so young compared to the warrior prince who sat across from him now.

"You are hunting for a ghost . . . Your Highness." Fenrin added the title at the end with haste.

"Are you so certain of that?" Hale asked. "I knew Raffiel as a boy. We are the same age."

Remy's heart twisted at that. He had known him. She had known him too, long ago, when she was a little girl. She did the math. That would make Hale twenty-eight.

"I'm sorry you lost your friend, Your Highness." Heather added a touch more gently.

"I do not believe he is lost," the prince said, scanning Heather's face. "You have heard the rumors as well as I, I'm sure. There have been whispers of Raffiel's appearance all around this continent."

"Whispers," Remy said.

"Tell me, then, little witch," the prince said, turning his gaze on her. "If all the High Mountain Court are truly gone, why can't the Northern King wield the Immortal Blade?"

Silence stretched out between them. That was the question. With all the High Mountain Court presumed dead, the Immortal Blade was free from its blood bond with them. Any fae should be able to take control of the sword. It was a kingmaker, a death blade that, when mastered, could level entire armies in one fell swoop. The blade could kill from a distance, too, without even coming into contact with the recipient of the blow. It was a ferocious magic. While it did not give everlasting life, like its name promised, it made the owner of the blade untouchable in battle. No sword could slay them. If the Northern King created his own blood bond with the blade, it would start a slaughter the likes of which Okrith had never known.

"The High Mountain bloodline carries on," the prince said, confidently. "Many people have claimed to have seen Raffiel flee the flames of the Yexshire slaughter."

Remy shuddered and tried to push the images out of her mind: the palace burning, people frantically pounding on barred doors, others leaping from windows. Some escaped only to be cut down by Northern soldiers the second their lungs breathed fresh air. Remy still smelled the smoke, still heard the screams, and still felt the weathered hands of Baba Morganna, the High Priestess of the red witches, pulling Remy away from the bloodshed.

"That was thirteen years ago," Fenrin said. He shifted closer to Remy as he spoke. Remy realized the prince noted the movement, even though the only visible sign was his jaw clenching. "King Vostemur himself has been hunting endlessly for him, and yet he has not been found . . ." Fenrin didn't finish his thought: *what makes you think you will succeed when the most powerful man in the world has failed?*

"The Northern King may be powerful," the Eastern Prince said, "but he is also arrogant. Raffiel may be glamoured as a human or a witch for all we know."

Carys chuckled as she sat beside her prince. Remy glanced at the two of them and wondered if they were together. She shook the thought from her head.

"We have no interest in hunting down Raffiel, and so he should have no reason to hide from us. Indeed, we want to help restore him to the throne. Why wouldn't he reveal himself to his true allies?"

"Why would he think your words mean anything after thirteen years of waiting?" Remy said.

The blow struck true. She saw it on the prince's face. Over a decade had passed, and the Eastern Court had done nothing to stop King Vostemur as he tracked down every last High Mountain fae and red witch.

"The wrath of the North was too great at first," the prince hedged. Remy laughed bitterly. "Vostemur had raised the largest army the world had ever seen. He destroyed the strongest fae court in Okrith. Did you really expect us to turn that bloodthirsty army toward the East?"

Remy frowned. The Northern King would have leveled any opposition. Bowing to his power was a strategy for survival. Still, she begrudged the East, South, and West for their inaction. Even with all three of their armies combined, it would not have been enough to stop the Northern Court thirteen years ago.

Remy didn't care. If her people were going to burn, then so should they all.

"His armies dwindle," Carys said through the shadowed quiet. "There is not enough coin or conquest to keep an army that size. Many of Vostemur's legions have disbanded, and he has turned his energies inward. If he cannot find Raffiel, then he seeks to undo the blood bond on the Immortal Blade."

Heather gasped. "Can it be done?"

"The blue witches enslaved to the Northern King are trying. The King has been using the bodies from his red witch hunts to manipulate the magic." Carys's eyes slid to Remy as a sort of apology. She was speaking of Remy's people. "But we know the remaining red witches are gathering."

The prince held up his hand to cut Carys off, and she paused.

"We would tell you where they gathered if we thought it inclined you to help us." His eyes swept over Remy. "But I fear with that knowledge you would run off to your coven and leave us behind."

Remy's hammering heart crept into her throat.

"The red witches are gathering?" she gasped.

CHAPTER THREE

Her whole body felt frozen by the power of Hale's proclamation. If the witches were coming together once more, that meant there were enough of them left . . . and they were finding each other. Remy squinted into the darkness, grappling with that thought. The red witches had scattered to the wind, all seemingly hunted down. Remy had wondered for a long time if she was the only one left.

"Yes," Hale confirmed, watching as Remy's mind whirled. "Baba Morganna leads them still."

Remy's chest crumpled inward. It couldn't be true.

"Baba Morganna is alive?" She wrung her hands. She had seen a mountaintop fall onto the High Priestess of the red witches. She was certain that the falling rocks had killed her. But maybe her six-year-old memory was incorrect. "How can you possibly expect me to trust what you say?"

"A courtier friend of ours has seen her with his own two eyes," Hale said.

"That means nothing," Remy said. "Your friend might be working with Vostemur."

"Bern can be trusted. He has . . . ties to the High Mountain Court.

He would never betray them," Hale assured her. His lips tilted up at her as he spoke his next words, as though he had been waiting to at long last release them. "But Bern said to tell you to use that red candle in your bag if you do not believe him, Little Sparrow."

Blood drained from Remy's face. *Little Sparrow.* It was the nickname Baba Morganna used to call her as a child. It was true, then. She was alive. She could use her red witch candle to call on the High Priestess to confirm it . . . but then the candle would be spent forever. It was too much information for it to be a lie. She would use the red candle if she ever came to doubt them, but if the red witches were reuniting, it changed everything. Remy had hoped all these years that the High Priestess had survived, but to have it confirmed . . . she clenched her hands to keep from crying.

"You still haven't explained *why* you need me," Remy said, schooling her shock, staring down the prince once more. He smirked at her hard look.

"Your magic links you to the High Mountain Court. You can feel their magic and all objects made by it," he said. He swept his wavy hair off his forehead.

"If you know the red witches are gathering, why not just go to them? Their combined powers are much stronger. They would be better able to help you," Remy said. "I didn't even know of such stirrings."

"I doubt your coven would trust or help me," Hale said. "But it is not Raffiel himself that I need your help to find."

Remy's leg tapping paused as the prince continued.

"Red witch magic is in the Immortal Blade, yes, but also in its two sister talismans: the *Shil-de* ring and the amulet of Aelusien."

Shil-de was Mhenbic for "eternal shield." The red witches made the ring to protect the wearer, making them indestructible. The ring passed through many hands over the years, and no one knew where the ring was anymore.

The ancient High Mountain fae stowed the amulet in Mount Aelusien. They imbued the talisman with witch magic, and whoever wore it could access the powers of the red witches. So many people had died on the slopes of Mount Aelusien in their quest for the amulet that the mountain now bore an ominous name: the Rotted Peak.

"You want *me* to help you find them?" Remy raised her eyebrows to Fenrin and her friend laughed. This prince was delusional.

"I already have an idea where the ring is," the prince continued, "but I need a red witch to authenticate it. And to survive the Rotted Peak, I need red witch magic too. I plan to take the talismans to the red witches in the hopes they tip off Raffiel. Even if the witches won't give up their prince's location, the talismans in our possession should draw him out. He can defeat the Northern King with the amulet and the ring. He could end this war before it begins."

"And if risking life and limb for these talismans doesn't draw him out?" Remy hedged.

Heather continued her fussing over Remy, producing an ointment from her bag. The brown witch applied it to Remy's bruised forehead, her healing magic glowing a faint brown around her fingertips. Remy winced at the stinging tincture, swatting Heather's hand away. The wound would disappear soon enough on its own.

"Then the Eastern Court will have two powerful bargaining chips in the inevitable war with the North," the prince said with a disconcerting level of nonchalance. "The Immortal Blade will struggle to cut across our lands if faced with those talismans' protection. We will offer safe haven to the red witches in the Eastern Court and rally the other Courts to our side if we must."

"You speak as if the war between the Courts is certain," Fenrin muttered.

"We've already had skirmishes with those cocky Northerners at the Eastern border," Carys said. "You think Vostemur will ever stop? His ambition is endless. He will not be satisfied until he is the only ruler in all the land."

Hale nodded. "We have a window to make our move while his attention turns toward the blade."

"And what do we get out of this arrangement?" Remy cut in. "So far it seems you have abducted us from our home and threatened us."

"I told you tying them up was a bad idea," the female Eagle,

Briata, called from across the room. She spoke in a low, enticingly gruff voice that made Remy's eyes snag on her striking features once more.

"Yeah, nothing like abduction to really breed trust, Hale," Talhan added with a snicker.

The prince scowled at them, but his warriors only grinned back. It was strange to hear these soldiers talking back to their prince. They spoke like they were friends, not just his loyal servants.

"Maybe you should take a walk, Hale," Carys added, leaning in to speak to the prince in a whispered voice that Remy could barely hear. "Let me talk to them."

"I can handle this," Hale whispered back.

Remy had to school her face from registering that she heard.

"Well, handle it better, then," Carys hissed.

Remy liked this warrior. She liked the Twin Eagles too. They had charisma like all fae but were strangely humorous and informal too. Were it not for the fact they were fae, and that they served the Bastard Prince, Remy might actually like getting to know them.

"She asks a fair question," Carys said louder, clearly intending for the witches to hear. "Why should she help us?"

"Besides seeing her prince, the one she swore to serve, returned to his rightful throne?" Hale's lips pulled up into a smug smile as he looked at Remy. She squinted at him. The red witches pledged their fealty to the High Mountain Court, but it was a low blow to ask this much of her. Was her fealty enough to go hunting for two lost talismans?

The Eastern Prince seemed to read her reaction. "We can safely return you to them. I suspect it will be the safest the three of you have been in thirteen years."

It was Heather who considered him then. She may have been affectionate, but she was still a witch, not a human, and that made her shrewd. Heather and Fenrin would not be able to get Remy to the red witches alone. Remy had narrowly missed being captured or killed several times and that was in small country towns. If they were to travel out into the Courts, she needed more protection than two brown witches. Remy knew she needed to get to Baba Morganna the instant the High Priestess' name was spoken.

Heather gave a thoughtful nod. She was the leader of their little unit, and so it was her decision. Either she seemed to believe that the prince offered them protection in earnest, or she didn't trust the prince but still felt allying with him was worth the risk. Regardless, Remy knew Heather would do anything to ensure her safety.

Remy felt like she had been sleeping for thirteen years, only to be awoken into a panicked run. All her patience flew from her body. She was desperate to get back to the red witches.

She rubbed her hand down her sore face. What they were agreeing to was a far departure from hiding in taverns. It was a colossal risk, and it could all be a lie. She wondered if Heather wanted to pawn her off on someone else. No, that wasn't like the brown witch. Still, Remy had been nothing but a liability to them all these years. This deal could make their lives better.

Biting her lip, Remy looked between Heather and Hale. The prince was still looking at her, waiting for her reply.

Remy made him wait, holding his stare, until she spoke.

"So you want us to help you find the *Shil-de* ring *and* the amulet of Aelusien *and* help you find a long-missing prince? That is a big ask of us."

"I am only asking you," Hale said, his smoky eyes piercing her. "If your companions wish to come, then I only ask that they do not slow us down, though I think it would be far better to send them back to that tavern."

"No," Heather said at the same time as Fenrin said, "Absolutely not."

"We stay with Remy." Heather gave Remy a warning look that told the red witch not to disagree with her guardian. The prince was right —it would be safer for the brown witches to stay behind. The brown witches only had healing magic, not the power to animate objects like the red witches. But Remy owed Heather her life. The brown witch had saved her more times than she could count, and so she could not deny Heather anything.

Remy assessed the Eastern Prince one more time. The things he spoke of were foolish at best and catastrophic at worst. She refused to trust him, but a tentative alliance with them seemed like a good move. She could help him until he revealed where the red witches gathered, and then she would flee before getting roped into a harebrained chase after a ghost prince.

It felt like their lives were frozen all these many years, and suddenly the name of Baba Morganna had thrown them back in the fires.

Decision made.

Remy watched as the firelight flickered over the prince's sharp features. "The brown witches are coming with us, and you will leave them be."

"Agreed." Hale smiled, knowing he had convinced her.

"Well then, *prince*, we have a deal," Remy said, sealing her fate.

The forests of the Western Court were endless. The terrain was rough and undulating, with large slabs of granite rock protruding through the soil. Aspens, firs, and maples dominated the forest's canopy. Light rays speared through the crowns of the trees, allowing for lush underbrush to spring forth from the crunchy layer of leaves on the forest floor.

The Autumnal Equinox grew closer. Some trees still flourished in shades of summer green, while others had already yielded their greenery to the chilly nights. Red, golden, and orange leaves danced to the forest floor, floating like feathers.

"Look—onion weed!" Fenrin said with delight, popping up from behind a yellowing shrub. He held up a handful of green shoots. "You can eat the leaves and the stalks, great for bulking out stews, and . . . you don't care."

"No, I care, I . . ." Remy began as she took the pungent green stalks and put them in the front pouch of the apron she'd borrowed from

Heather. She smeared the onion stench off her hand and down her crumpled maroon tunic.

"Remy, you don't care about onion weed, it's okay." Fenrin laughed.

"You're right, I really don't care." Remy grinned at him.

They had broken off from the rest of the camp to forage. The second their packs hit the ground, Remy shucked her too-tight boots. She was sure she would have blisters in the coming days.

Fenrin and Heather were both accomplished foragers, as most brown witches were. One walk through the forest could procure enough medicinal plants to line their pockets with *druni*.

Though the witch covens shared some magic in common, each possessed their own unique powers too. The blue witches had the gift of Sight, the green witches made delicious food and gardens grow, the red witches could animate objects, and the brown witches were healers and expert foragers.

Remy, however, was useless at identifying plants. She could not tell the difference between a medicinal mushroom and a poisonous one. She would still join Fenrin while he foraged, though.

In the past, they had a lucrative business going for themselves. They could have moved to bigger taverns closer to the Western Court cities, but their goal was to stick to the backcountry, where the living was rough and the money was bad . . . and it was all because Remy was a red witch.

"I wish I had my bow." Remy pouted, sinking her toes into the cool moss beneath her bare feet. She rolled her stone-gray trousers up to her calves. It felt good to have fresh air on her sore feet.

"Maybe if you ask really nicely, the prince will buy you one." Fenrin snickered, passing her two mushrooms as he carried on.

"I'd rather go hungry than ask him for a bow." Remy tucked the mushrooms into her pocket.

It felt so strange to fall into their easy routine. Here they were, on the road with a bunch of high-class fae, still breaking off into their little duo to forage.

"Do you trust him, the Eastern Prince?" Fenrin asked, his blue eyes scanning through the forest.

"Not even the slightest." Remy snorted.

"Good. Be careful with him," Fenrin said more to himself than to Remy. "The others I like well enough. They make good company. Carys told me she'd show me the East one day and . . ."

"You need to be careful with them too, Fen," Remy said. "They might act like your friends, but they're dangerous."

"I know." Fenrin passed back another handful of mushrooms. "Still, it's better than what we were doing, right? I'd rather travel with a bunch of fae warriors than scrub sheets at the Rusty Hatchet."

Remy smirked, rubbing her dirt-stained hands together. "Yeah, me too."

"Our mansion in Yexshire will have an armory." Fenrin laughed, ducking behind a tree. "Then you will have dozens of bows to choose from."

This was the game they played to pass the time. They would plan their dream home, a castle that they would erect in the rebuilt city of Yexshire. It was a daydream that began the day they met when they were twelve, and it still lasted even seven years later.

Remy looked up to the treetops at her left, as if she could see the High Mountains through the forest. On the other side of that crown of mountains sat her fallen court, her homeland. The High Mountain Court had the most beautiful seasons: hot, verdant summers and snowy, white winters. Even in the depths of winter the sun shone every day, if only for a few minutes. In the Western Court, weeks could stretch by on end without a single ray of sunlight breaking through the dismal gray clouds. Remy remembered her court as a magical place filled with sweeping alpine vistas. She wondered how much her memory had exaggerated the beauty of the High Mountain Court. The feeling of home still strummed through her body like a song only her soul knew.

"What was our plan?" Remy toed a fallen red leaf. "In this dream, did we just hope that the Northern King would fall and Yexshire would suddenly rise again, and we would stumble across a bounty of wealth and . . ."

"Hey—" Fenrin cut in. "This isn't part of the game."

"What was the plan, Fen?" Remy persisted. This daydream didn't seem to fit her anymore. "Was I meant to just hide forever or until the world fixed itself without me?"

Fenrin jutted his jaw to the side, considering. They didn't talk like this. They only worked their tavern jobs and planned their dream lives. It was different now that they had their lot thrown in with the fae. It felt like they were actually doing something about the state of the world.

"I don't know, Remy," he said. "I just know you are too important to go getting your head cut off trying to fix the world."

It was the same advice as Heather's. They both wanted Remy to stay hidden and insignificant. She was apparently so important that she had to make herself unimportant. She was sick of waiting for the world to be set right. Even if the quest for the talismans led to nothing, Remy felt the burning need to finally do something. The High Mountain Court deserved its vengeance.

CHAPTER FOUR

"Tell us a story of the red witches," Briata called to Remy from across the campfire.

They had stopped for the night ten minutes west of the trail, in case any other travelers happened to pass while they were sleeping. The night was crisp and whorls of icy breath appeared every time they spoke.

"I don't have any good stories." Remy looked at the starry night sky peeking through the trees. "I have lived with brown witches most of my life."

"Tell us the one about Baba Morganna pulling down the mountain," Bri said.

"Were you there? Did you see it?" Talhan crouched before a pot on the fire, stirring its contents. The Twin Eagles had caught a rabbit and two squirrels to add to the pot within a minute of their arrival at the camp. Fenrin had found greens and mushrooms. Remy's stomach rumbled at the aroma from the burbling pot. The three witches had all gaped when Talhan had produced a thick iron pot from his pack. No wonder he had legs as thick as tree trunks.

"She was six during the Siege of Yexshire. She can't remember anything," Heather said, wrapping her threadbare blanket more tightly around her shoulders. Remy jealously eyed the fae across the fire with their thick fur blankets.

Heather reached for Remy's hair, readying to braid it for the night. Cheeks flushing, Remy pulled away and gave her guardian a look. She didn't need her hair braided like she was a child anymore. Especially not in front of a bunch of fae warriors.

"Tell it to us anyway," Bri exclaimed from her bedroll. "These idiots can barely tell one good story between them."

Talhan and Carys laughed. Even Hale's cheek twitched into a faint smile.

"Fine. I can't promise it will be any good," Remy said, chucking the stick she had been fiddling with into the flames. "There once was a red witch named Morganna Stormfrost. She lived in the Temple of Yexshire with the rest of her coven. The night was like any other winter's night. The Castle of Yexshire sat across the valley between the mountains brimming with people as Hennen Vostemur, the Northern King, and his court visited their friends in the High Mountains."

Remy didn't look at anyone as she spoke, her eyes lost in the dancing flames of the campfire, thinking of the same flames that razed Yexshire.

"Nothing seemed amiss," she continued, "but Morganna had her first-ever gift of Sight that night. She saw the palace in flames before the first blade swung. With only minutes before the carnage broke out, she rushed the red witches to the road east, but Northern soldiers blocked the passage. Sure enough, they blockaded each of the four roads out of Yexshire. Morganna knew they had to flee over the saddle of the mountains if they were to escape. They climbed the mountainside, a near-vertical slope, but the Northern soldiers were right behind them, shooting arrows. One of them struck Morganna, right through the throat."

Carys gasped as Remy poked a finger into her neck.

"She was dying right there, trapped against the mountainside. But Baba Theodora, the High Priestess of the red witches at the time, was there. She invoked the *midon brik*, the most powerful magic any witch can cast, and she swapped her life with Morganna's. Baba Theodora knew Morganna was her successor. They say it was seeing her Baba's death that gave Morganna her own incredible power. She began catching arrows in the sky and turning them on their shooters. Morganna got the witches up and over the pass and then waited there for the Northern soldiers to reach her."

Remy saw Bri grinning across the licking flames.

"When the soldiers were all into the saddle, Morganna cleaved the mountain above them and crushed the Northern legion under the rocks of her homeland. She brought down a mountain to save her people and earned the title Baba, new High Priestess of the red witches."

A long silence stretched out between them until Hale spoke, looking at the fire.

"So the red witches didn't run to the aid of the High Mountain Court?" he said.

Remy glared at the Eastern Prince. How dare he insinuate that the red witches had not done enough to save the fae. It was all that mattered to the fae, it seemed: how much they would give of their lives.

"Many did—" Remy sneered. "And they all died."

Hale tilted his head, rubbing the stubble down his jaw. "How did you escape?"

"With others. I can't remember."

"You fled with your parents?" Hale asked as a log crackled and sparks danced up toward the starry sky.

Talhan pinched his nose now, Carys cringed, and Briata rolled her eyes.

"No. They're dead." Remy looked at Hale, daring him to say another word.

"You say you can't remember. How do you know? Have you tried to look for them?" Hale prodded, his sharp eyes watching Remy from across the flickering flames.

"Back off," Carys said in a quiet growl.

"I was just curious." Hale shrugged.

33

"Of course you were, because our lives mean nothing to you, we just exist for your entertainment. Witches are just curiosities to the fae." Remy's tether to her patience had snapped.

"That's not what I said." Hale narrowed his eyes at her. He had the audacity to act offended after all he had insinuated.

"Is our pain exciting to you, *prince?*" Remy jibed. Heather leaned her shoulder into Remy's, a silent request to cool down, but she could not. This attitude of fae superiority was everything that was wrong in the world. The High Mountain fae treated the red witches as their equals and the other fae didn't like that . . . especially Hennen Vostemur.

"You're twisting my words, *witch*," Hale gritted out through a clenched jaw.

"You haven't ever had a single struggle, have you? You need to employ others to share theirs with you." Remy knew little about hand-to-hand combat, but she knew how to crush her enemies with her words.

"You're being ridiculous." Hale threw her words straight back.

"You really are a spoiled, rich bastard," Remy snarled. Hale's eyes widened, his eyebrows shooting up for a split second before he pulled his face back into a scowl.

There. She struck a bullseye.

"Better a bastard than a hiding coward," Hale said. The unexpected blow hit her straight in the gut. That's what she was: a hiding coward. Worse, they all could see it.

Remy eyed her glowing red hands. She had lost control again. She stood up and turned to the forest, throwing an excuse over her shoulder.

"Nice, Hale." She heard Briata's snarl as she stormed away.

Remy heard Fenrin standing up, and she grumbled without breaking her stride, "Don't follow me, Fen."

Fenrin listened this time.

It was a short walk to the stream. The glow of Remy's hands was even clearer as she moved away from the fire. The soft red light let her see the forest floor beneath her, and she was careful to avoid the rocks poking above the fallen leaves. The dirt blackened her feet, but at least the pain of the day's walk had subsided.

Remy neared the narrow stream where they had refilled their skins and gathered water for their stew. She stood, looking at the slow, rambling water and took a deep breath. *Hiding coward*, Hale had called her. The shame of those words hit her anew. Her hands flared. She was sure if she had a mirror she would see her eyes glowing too. She sensed it now without looking, feeling the trembling buzz behind her eyes.

Remy took another slow, steadying breath. The buzzing faded. Darkness pulled in as her red magic dulled.

She heard soft footsteps behind her and knew without turning it was Carys. Remy had walked enough with these fae warriors to know their unique gaits. Talhan walked like a rumbling bear. Briata had a heavy gait, too, but less harsh. Hale walked with a confident, quiet stride like a mountain lion. Carys was the lightest on her feet, elegant and balletic.

The female fae stopped beside Remy, unwinding her long blonde braid and combing her fingers through it. They watched the stream in silence for a while. Remy decided to braid her long curls for sleep after all as Carys brushed out her own braid beside her. Remy's hands were clumsy. Heather had made it look easy. She couldn't believe she let the brown witch do it for her for so long.

Carys swiped a few more fingers through her hair, shaking it out so it landed right above her hips.

"I have never seen anyone get under his skin like you do," Carys said into the darkness. "It's impressive."

"Are you with him?" Remy bit out. She pinched her lips together after the words flew out of her mouth.

"I was wondering when you were going to ask me that." Carys even made her chuckle sound delicate.

Remy didn't respond, but simply kept braiding and waited for Carys to answer her question.

"No, I am not with him, nor do I want to be," the fae said.

"Why not? He's . . ." Remy didn't know how to finish that thought.

He was the most attractive person she had ever seen. Just looking at him made her feel unsteady.

"Handsome?" Carys laughed. "I mean, I have eyes, of course he is, and he's a good person too . . . ," Remy tutted, but Carys persisted. "He is. Truly. He's just a bit rough around the edges."

"So why don't you want to be with him?" Remy had seen them together. The two of them always broke off into a duo. Hale listened to Carys more than anyone else.

Carys opened her mouth to say something twice before her shoulders drooped.

"There was someone . . ."

Remy bobbed her head. It was all she needed to say. Remy had heard that story so many times. It was the story of broken hearts being left in shredded pieces.

"Hale was once Fated too," Carys added. Remy's eyes darted to the female's shadowed figure.

Fated love was another fae magic, the rarest magic of all. Some fae souls intertwined long before their lives even began. Their Fated magic was so strong that the bond was sometimes detectable even while they were still in the womb. Many of the richest fae families paid blue witch oracles to predict their children's Fated. Others were superstitious and believed it was bad luck to know, but Fated love was undeniable.

Remy's thoughts snagged on the words Carys spoke.

"Was?"

"She died before they ever met," Carys said. "His Fated was a princess of the High Mountain fae. She died in the Siege of Yexshire."

The darkness pulled in tighter. Remy's chest constricted.

"Some say it is a fate worse than death," Carys continued. "To live without that Fated bond can break people. Even worse, Hale knows he will never find it." Remy swallowed the hard lump in her throat. "I won't tell you to be gentle to him. He is a smug asshole sometimes." Carys laughed. "But he has been through more than he shows."

Remy gnawed her lip. An owl hooted through the forest, crickets quieting in response.

Carys turned back toward the firelight, the smell of the stew making Remy's stomach rumble. She heard the faint laughter of the Twin Eagles and Fenrin. The Eagles seemed to have taken to teasing the young witch, and he delighted in being included. It was clear Fenrin looked up to them.

"You coming?" Carys asked, heading back to the campsite without waiting for Remy's response.

Remy stared into the darkness, praying to all the Gods to tolerate the insufferable prince one more night.

It was another hard day of traveling before they set up camp. Remy dumped the apron next to the growing fire. Foraged food spilled onto the ground. Her feet ached after another tedious walk.

Carys added kindling to the flames while Talhan unpacked his pans. Heather unwrapped the linen around her delicate bottles, inspecting each one for cracks or loosened corks. Hale was nowhere to be seen.

But it was Briata that Remy wanted to speak with. The female warrior sat on her pack, sharpening a wicked-looking dagger on a stone.

"Do you have a knife I could borrow?" Remy asked her.

The fae's slender ears perked up.

"Absolutely." She grinned at Remy and produced a smaller blade from her belt.

"Wait, why do you need a knife?" Carys called over to them. She gave Briata a look as the warrior offered Remy her weapon.

"I want to go hunting for something to eat." Remy shrugged.

"Is what we provide not enough?" Carys asked as she snapped another stick in half.

"No, it's plenty, I just want to add something." Remy shifted, feeling useless even for asking.

"You don't need a knife, Remy." Heather chastised her. Remy hated that tone. Her guardian was so demeaning to her sometimes. She made sure that Remy remained as useless as she felt.

"I don't think you'll have much luck with a knife," Briata said, glancing between Heather and Remy. She flipped the blade over in her hand to pass Remy the hilt. "But it'll be fun to see you try."

"I hunt better alone," Remy said, taking the weapon. She bobbed her head in thanks.

"You're terrible at making friends, Bri." Talhan chuckled to his twin.

Remy looked between them. Was this them being nice? She turned away from their campsite and toward the woods.

"Do you want me to come?" Fenrin called to her. He was crouched, unpacking the apron of foraged food. Remy shook her head. She missed the time she used to have to venture out on her own, having only her thoughts and silence as companions. Being constantly under the watchful eye of the fae was grating on her nerves.

Remy stepped back into the forest. Her bare feet were even more sore after another day of hiking. She wasn't sure how much longer she'd be able to use those bloody boots before they chewed up her feet, but barefoot in the forest was where Remy felt the best. It was the witch blood in her, she presumed. She could move across the stones and scatter leaves without making a sound. She felt lithe and predatory when she was alone, like her magic rose to the surface of her skin when no one was watching.

The cool air pooled around her, her breathing slowed, and an invisible weight lifted off her shoulders as she sighed.

She heard far-off leaves scuffling and birds' soft tut-tutting. It sounded like some kind of fowl. She scanned the forest, her eyes resting on a grouping of pheasant digging through the leaf litter far ahead. Her eyes widened. She would be a hero if she brought one of those back to camp.

She tiptoed toward them before a voice halted her.

"Now this I would like to see."

Remy looked over her shoulder to see Hale, arms crossed, leaning against a tree. His pewter eyes twinkled as he saw the scowl on her face. Remy might have moved quietly through the forest, but Hale was as silent as death to sneak up on her like that.

"You really think you can catch a pheasant with a knife?" Hale's brows rose into his hairline as he grinned at her.

"I do." Remy sneered. Great, now she would have to prove him wrong.

"I will take that bet." Hale's cheeks dimpled.

"Good," Remy spat. "If I win, you will buy me a new bow and arrows in the next town we stop in."

Hale's grin widened.

"Agreed," he said, his voice a deep rumble, "and when I win, you have to give me a compliment."

"You're so deprived of friendly words that you have to place bets for them?" Remy laughed.

"Not from everyone, just from you." Hale's smoky gaze brightened. "I know how much you'd hate it."

It was the worst punishment he could think of for her, saying one agreeable thing to him.

"Fine." Remy squinted at him. "But no scaring them off."

Hale lifted and dropped his shoulders, his only form of acknowledgment.

Remy eyed the pheasants still digging in the forest floor. She crept from rock to rock, stealthily edging closer. She couldn't hear Hale behind her, but she sensed the prince was there.

If she had a bow, she would be within striking distance. She knew there was no point throwing the knife. It was sure to miss. She sensed Hale's smugness. But the prince had forgotten one very important thing: she had red witch magic.

Remy felt the rising buzz of magic flow out to her hands. Her splayed fingers glowed red, as she cast her thread of magic, looping it around the three fat pheasants.

The rest of the flock fled over the hillside, but her magic snared the three birds, now suspended in the air. Remy made quick work with her knife, slicing their necks. She held her catch by their feet so that the blood wouldn't drip on her. She smiled at the prince.

"Well, that was unexpected," Hale huffed. "Let it serve me right for underestimating you, witch."

"I'm looking forward to my new bow, Your Highness."

Hale's pupils dilated as he stared, seemingly mesmerized by Remy's glowing eyes. It was a strange sensation to have someone look at her with appreciation instead of fear. The only people who didn't run from her magic were Heather and Fenrin. But Hale looked at her with awe, not terror.

Remy dropped her eyes to her feet.

"Don't," Hale said, his voice dropping an octave. Remy looked back at him, but the intensity of his attention made her shift on her feet. "You don't need to hide your magic from me."

"Yes, you've already made it clear that I'm a hiding coward." Remy jabbed.

"I shouldn't have said that." Now Hale was the one to shift, his posture tightening.

"It's true though." Remy kept her eyes down, willing away her magic. She felt it ebbing, the glow fading.

Hale took another step and was right before her, a hair's breadth away. He lifted her chin so she would look at him. Her magic flared again, and she saw the red glow reflected in his eyes.

"You did what you needed to survive." His voice softened. His breath warmed her cheek. "But your magic . . . it's as powerful as it is beautiful."

Remy's heart leapt into her throat. No one had ever complimented her magic before. It had always been something to be ashamed of. But beautiful? He thought she looked beautiful with glowing red eyes and hands? It couldn't be true. But if the prince lied, she wondered why he said it at all.

"Thank you," Remy whispered, trapped in those gleaming eyes and the faintest connection of his finger pressed against her chin. Hale's gravity tugged at her, as if she would plummet into his arms if she released her control.

Remy scolded herself. It was not only a ridiculous thought, but also a dangerous one.

She cleared her throat.

"Shall we go bring back some dinner, then?" she asked, halfheartedly stepping out of his touch. She didn't know what else to say to him. Hale had only been rigid and callous before this, and she did not know what to do with this version of him . . . but at least she had won herself a new bow.

CHAPTER FIVE

They moved on foot through the woods, traversing a wide, dirt path. The back trail through the Western Wood was quiet, travelers preferring to take horses through the high roads. Only one other caravan had passed them, headed in the opposite direction.

The witches seemed to be the only ones in their convoy making a sound: sticks snapping under their boots and their ragged breaths echoing through the air.

"How much further?" Fenrin panted, breaking their long silence. Remy bet he was regretting carrying both his pack and the brown witch wares now. The sun was high, the promise of cooler weather ceding to the strong sun.

Hale had been walking far ahead, lost in his thoughts, but his fae ears had picked up on Fenrin's question. Carys hiked not far behind the prince. The struggling witches walked in the middle, with the Twin Eagles taking up the rear.

Hale looked at the witches, and the group shuffled to a stop. Remy's feet ached. Her muscles weren't yet tiring, but her feet were on fire. She was eager to stop, but she wasn't sure if she would ever start again.

"Only a few more hours," Hale said. He spoke like it was nothing at all.

"Hours?" Fenrin whined. Heather said nothing, but she leaned forward and rested her hands on her knees, gulping air. Her corn-flower blue dress was wet with sweat.

"Your legs are taller than me, witch. You should be fine," Briata called from behind them. Her brother snickered.

"We could stop here," Carys offered, "but then we won't reach the next town by tomorrow."

"Aw come on!" Talhan was the one to whine now. "I want to sleep in a bed tomorrow."

Remy found the nearest rock and collapsed with a groan. She couldn't wait another few hours. She needed to get her bloody boots off right away. Gods curse this fae prince. She should make him carry her.

"Let's break for some water," Carys said, eyeing Remy. "Ten minutes. Then we can decide how to proceed."

Remy noted how Carys had taken the lead. It seemed the rest of the fae warriors did not care that the witches were struggling. Fae had body magic, and so it was easy for them. That was the selfishness of the fae; they could never put themselves in someone else's shoes. And right now, Remy's boots were filling with blood.

Each of the fae dropped their packs and sat on them, except for Carys, who leaned against a tree trunk. She and Hale rested far ahead while everyone else sat in a circle. They maneuvered their packs in a practiced way that told Remy this was their normal life. How strange these nomadic fae warriors were.

"You must do this a lot," Fenrin said, voicing Remy's thoughts. Briata shrugged at him. "Where's the rest of your comrades?"

"Falhampton," Briata said, as if everyone would know where that was.

"It's on the border with the Northern Court," Talhan explained. His tan cheeks were flushed red, but that was the only sign of exer-tion. "The Northern fae like to cross the Eastern border and cause trouble there. They've been doing it for years. The King sent Hale last year to finally rid the town of them."

"And I'm guessing he succeeded?" Fenrin asked.

"It's not as easy as running out a few Northerners," Briata said.

"Bri's right," Talhan added. "You've got to build walls, train the locals, ensure that when the Northerners come back—"

"Which they always do," Briata cut in.

"—we will have trained the townspeople how to keep them out," Talhan finished. "Hale's soldiers are still there defending the town until the King gives the order to pull them back."

Fenrin took a long swig of his water and then passed the skin to Remy. She accepted it gratefully, the cool liquid soothing her scratchy throat. Passing it to Heather, she turned her attention to her feet.

Remy removed her boots with a hiss.

"You should leave those on." Briata nodded to Remy.

"Your feet will swell and you won't be able to get them back in," Talhan added, passing his sister a stick of dried meat.

"I'd rather walk barefoot than wear these one more second." Remy stifled a cry as she peeled her thick wool socks off her feet. The damage was visible now. Two egg-sized blisters covered the backs of her heels. The boots had rubbed the first layers of skin right off, opening red, weeping wounds. Her big toenail, too, was already turning blue. Remy was sure it would fall off within a day.

Heather gasped. "Gods, I thought those boots fit you?"

Remy shrugged. She thought her feet had stopped growing, but she was wrong. The boots had always been tight and uncomfortable but it had been fine working all day on her feet at the Rusty Hatchet, so she assumed it would be fine hiking too.

"Oof," Talhan said, looking at her feet.

"That's nasty," Briata said. Her sarcastic smile was at odds with the blunt words she spoke.

The Twin Eagles were a strange mixture of odd, beautiful features and muscular bodies. Talhan reminded Remy of every merry drunk who passed the taverns. Briata reminded her of the gruff old men who spat at everyone except for those with a crude sense of humor.

"Here." Heather was already pilfering through one of Fenrin's packs. She pulled out two brown bottles and a thin strip of clean white linen.

Remy realized Hale had disappeared.

"Where's he gone?" she asked, nodding toward his abandoned pack.

"Probably to have a shit," Talhan said, biting into a piece of hard cheese.

Briata elbowed her chuckling twin. "He's going to brief the King."

Remy arched an eyebrow at them.

Fenrin whispered, "Fae fires."

Ah, yes.

Remy had forgotten about that magic. Most of the fae's powers were powers of the body: incredible vision, hearing, smell, healing, and strength. But they also had other powers, like their power to glamour themselves into human form and communicate through fires. Through the flames, they had a direct line of communication with whomever they wanted to reach on the other side. Many royal fae kept a magical fire continuously burning in their palaces, attended by servants who could fetch them if ever they were contacted.

Red witches had stolen that magic from the fae, creating spelled candles to call upon each other. But the candles required vast amounts of magic and only worked for a single use. Remy looked to her pack, where one such red candle remained hidden. Most witches resorted to the same means of communication as the humans, though: sending messenger pigeons or letters through the traveling post.

"I don't know why he bothers going off like that," Talhan said, looking in the direction Hale went, "it's not like you witches can hear the whispers through the fire like the fae can."

"He's trying to be mysterious." Bri snorted.

Remy wondered what Hale was telling his father. Did King Norwood know his son had found a red witch? Did the King know where the *Shil-de* ring was?

A sharp stinging on the back of her heel pulled Remy from her thoughts. She hissed through clenched teeth as Heather dabbed a healing potion onto Remy's wounds.

"Damn," Briata said, shaking her short, brown hair out of her eyes.

"Sorry," Heather muttered as she yanked the cork out of the second bottle with her teeth. She poured a drop of thick, yellow ointment on her finger and patted it over the wound. At least the ointment didn't sting.

"You must be a powerful brown witch," Talhan said, his amber eyes moving from Heather's skilled hands to Remy's forehead. "That bruise on her head is gone already."

Heather's hands stilled for a moment, but then she carried on.

"My complexion hides the bruising better than some," Remy said, looking at the twins. "But yes, she is the most skilled brown witch I've ever met."

Heather smiled as she continued her ministrations on Remy's injured feet.

The brown witch sat back on her heels and said, "I'll bandage them to prevent any dirt getting into the wounds, but it won't do much to protect your feet on this terrain."

"I am not putting my feet back in those things." Remy tilted her head toward her discarded boots.

Heather made quick work of the bandaging. Remy regretted using up some of her remedies and linens. Heather would be a rich witch were it not for Remy's constant self-injuries. She silently promised that she would restock the used goods in the next town.

Hale reappeared through the trees. He and Carys exchanged glances and nodded. Hale drew a knife from his belt and cut the brown leather pocket off his pack.

The witches stared at him in confusion.

Without a word, Hale walked to Remy, cutting the leather in half as he moved. He knelt before her.

"What are you doing?" Remy looked at him bewildered as he took her freshly bandaged foot and placed it on his knee. He rolled back her gray trouser leg, the same shade of stone gray as his stormy eyes.

"We will not make it to the campsite if you are barefoot. The path turns to gravel up ahead," he said, as if that were reason enough for his pack's destruction.

Wrapping the leather around the sole of Remy's foot, Hale reached for her boots, unlacing them and holding her foot tightly. Goosebumps rose along her leg as his thumb swept over the top of her foot.

The prince poked the bootlace through the leather as if it were paper. It was such a minor act of fae strength, and yet it was still impressive. He laced up the leather as if he had done it a million times before, wrapping the extra laces around Remy's ankle and tying a bow. He was careful to avoid the wounds that he had not seen but sensed.

He put Remy's foot down and moved to her other. Remy didn't know what to say. Seeing him knelt before her, lacing up her makeshift shoes, felt incredibly intimate. Everyone else had fallen back into simple conversation, eating and drinking water. But Remy only stared as the prince's deft hands moved over her foot.

When he finished, their gazes locked. What was it about his eyes? She hated how they seemed to say so much more than his voice ever did. She hated how her eyes might tell him something in return.

"Good?" he asked in that low, rumbling voice.

Remy gave a tiny nod, pulling her foot away, and stood. Her raw skin still burned, but Heather's ointment was already helping.

Hale moved back to his pack and hauled it up over his shoulder.

"No more breaks. Let's go," Hale said and took off again.

Remy rolled her eyes. Hale was equal parts general and prince . . . and far too good at giving orders.

In a single breath, the fae seemed ready to go.

Fenrin moved to grab the pack nearest him, thinking it was his. He almost yanked his arm off.

"Gods," he said, looking to Briata. "Is it filled with rocks?"

The fae easily lifted her pack and put it on her back, her muscles flexing at the movement. Remy watched Briata through narrowed eyes. Fenrin was not weak. The pack must have weighed a ton, especially considering several weapons already weighted down each of the fae.

"Just the normal gear." Briata winked at Fenrin. "And a couple lucky stones."

It took the witches longer to pack their belongings. Talhan helped Heather, lifting her pack up to put on her shoulders.

They carried on, crunching through the leaves, the world quiet once more. Remy moved her feet with such relief, not having that grinding, burning pain every time she shifted her weight. She was grateful to Heather and her healing remedies for saving her feet from an arduous walk. She was grateful to the inconveniently handsome prince too.

The cool morning breeze whipped through Hale's hair as he stood at the clearing ahead. Carys had taken off her pack the moment they stopped and now leaned against a tree, looking in the same direction.

As Remy neared them, a village emerged. Downhill from the trail, rooftops and chimneys poked above the tree line. A signpost on the trail pointed eastward: Newpond 10 miles. Someone had nailed a smaller, scraggly sign below it: Guilford 1 mile. So the tiny village they saw was Guilford, then, and if they stayed on the trail, they would reach a bigger town called Newpond. Remy tucked that information into the back of her mind. She hoped to stumble upon a map in Guilford to get her bearings.

She suspected they were heading to the border between the Western Court and Southern Court, but she couldn't confirm it without a map. Remy, Heather, and Fenrin had worked their way only through the rural towns in the middle of the Western Court.

These quiet villages arose all along the Western trails. They serviced back-road travelers and proffered all the usual merchants and traders. Whatever they needed for their journey, they would find in the town below.

Fenrin, who had been trailing farther behind Remy all day, caught up. The grueling past two days were wearing him out.

Heather approached the lookout with Fenrin. The Twin Eagles

were right behind them. Talhan broke into a smile when he saw the village of Guilford. He had been talking incessantly about sleeping in a bed all morning. They offloaded their packs and plopped down on them straight away, seizing any opportunity for a break.

"What supplies do we need?" Hale asked without looking back to them.

"Just the usual restock." Carys folded her arms.

"Flint and twine for me." Briata grinned like a fox. "And maybe something to refill my flask."

"I wouldn't mind having a look at the pocketknives," Talhan said. He looked to the three witches and remembered. "Oh, and three more bowls and spoons."

Talhan carried light wood receptacles and utensils for his comrades. But he only carried four, one for each of the fae. The three witches shared Talhan's bowl while he shared with his twin, but three more bowls would help.

"I need some supplies as well," Heather piped up. She had used up a few of her healing remedies on Remy's feet.

"And I need new shoes," Remy added. Hale looked over his shoulder to Remy's makeshift shoes. They had gotten her this far, but the gravel trail wore away at the thin leather. They wouldn't last another day.

"The rest of us should get the supplies—one of us should take the witch to the inn," Briata said, waving her block of cheese toward Remy. "She shouldn't come."

"Good idea." Talhan was already producing a piece of dried meat from his pocket and fishing out his waterskin.

"Why?" Fenrin asked. He and Heather kept their packs on but leaned their heavy weight against a wide trunk of a conifer. It was too much effort to get the packs back on otherwise.

"Fae use the back road to Newpond," Briata said. "One might stop for supplies in Guilford. It's not a good idea for a red witch to be walking from store to store."

"Agreed." Hale lifted the hem of his tunic to mop his sweaty brow. Remy's eyes dropped to the peek of golden skin revealed at his waist.

It wasn't until his tunic dropped again that she remembered what she was going to say.

"How am I meant to get shoes if I can't come?" Remy waved her arms in exasperation.

"Bri has an eye for people's sizes," Carys said, folding her arms as she leaned against the tree trunk. "She will be able to pick you something suitable."

Heather leaned over to Fenrin and whispered, "I need your help getting supplies."

Remy pursed her lips at their exchange. Something more was being said there that she didn't understand. But Fenrin simply dipped his chin to their guardian.

"I'll head to the inn with the witch," Hale said, surveying the village below.

Remy opened her mouth to protest, but Heather gave her a look. The lines around her guardian's mouth deepened into a frown. She knew Heather didn't want her walking through a town filled with fae. Heaving a sigh, Remy knew the decision was made: she would go with Hale.

"Glamours," Hale said, turning into his human form even as he spoke. The shine of his wavy, brown hair dulled. The chestnut red streaks disappeared. His ears had rounded and his gray eyes no longer shone like steel.

Remy looked to each fae as, one by one, they turned into humans. They looked the same . . . mostly. They seemed shorter, less muscular. Their skin did not glow with health. The Twin Eagles still seemed otherworldly in the way they moved, but their golden eyes were now an amber brown. They wouldn't stand out as readily.

"You two are traveling companions," Briata said, eyeing Remy and Hale. "Make up whatever story you like but make it believable. Don't draw suspicion."

"Oh, and Bri?" Hale said to the golden eyed warrior. "I owe the witch a new bow."

He had remembered. Remy's lips tugged up at their corners, delighting in the thought of a brand-new bow.

Fenrin's eyes darted back and forth between Remy and Hale. "Do we have to stop?"

"Yes." All four fae responded in unison.

"My wife and I are traveling to Newpond," Hale said more regally than the human he was posing as. "We are in a caravan with four others from the East. We'll be needing three rooms."

The innkeeper standing before them at the inn's front door impatiently tapped her foot. She was a small, cantankerous woman, wearing a threadbare brown dress and a greasy apron.

"Newpond, you say?" she asked, glancing between the two of them. She did not step back to grant them entry.

"Yes, I've heard it's a fine place to raise a family." Hale smiled. Remy grimaced as he rested a gentle hand on her stomach. Great, not only would she have to pretend to be his wife, but his pregnant wife at that.

The innkeeper arched a thin brow at Hale. He was terrible at this game, and the woman saw through his act in one look. Her eyes darted to Remy and Remy knew she could see right through her plastered-on smile too. Something shifted in her expression as she assessed Remy, a flicker of recognition seeming to light up the innkeeper's face.

"How wonderful," she drawled sarcastically. "Welcome." The innkeeper stepped back, allowing them to enter.

Her eyes roved over them both, and Remy realized she saw it all: his shined boots and new fawn-colored riding coat, Remy's tattered cape and moth-eaten maroon tunic. Even with the Prince's glamour, it was obvious that he was more than an average human man and that Remy was not his wife.

The inside of the inn was inviting, albeit run down. Hardwood beams supported the upper floor, lanterns hanging from them and rows of candles dotted everywhere to boost the low light from the tall windows. Dusty paintings filled the walls.

The innkeeper guided Remy to a table in the center of the empty room. Hale leaned their packs against the wall in one of the few places without cobwebs and took a seat opposite Remy.

"I'm supposing you and your wife are hungry? I shall have the cook bring something out," the innkeeper said, walking halfway to the kitchens and then pausing.

She caught Remy's eye from over Hale's shoulder. The innkeeper lifted her hand and touched the center of her chest. Remy noted the move. It was a signal to other witches, tapping to where their totem bags used to hang around their necks. It was a simple, innocuous move that was only noticeable to those who were looking out for it.

The fae and humans often called them hex bags, but that was a misnomer. The bag was not for hexes at all. It carried special objects personal to each witch. They used to wear them around their necks before the Siege of Yexshire. Many witches still kept the totem bags anyway, sewn into secret pockets in their cloaks and dresses, just as Remy's own totem bag was tucked into the lining of her tunic now. The tradition lived on in secret.

The innkeeper was a witch then. Remy only moved her head in the briefest of nods to acknowledge that yes, she was a witch too. The innkeeper gave a half-smile. Good. She might have seen right through their husband-and-wife ruse, but if she was also a witch, she would keep quiet about them.

When she had exited the room, Remy snapped her gaze back to Hale.

"Why would you say I'm your wife?!" Remy hissed across the table in a hushed voice. "Is that really the only thing you could think of?"

"I thought if you were with child it would be a good excuse for you to not be venturing into the town with the others." Hale's brows dropped over his eyes. "Stop biting my head off about it."

Remy huffed a laugh.

"What?" The muscle in Hale's jaw popped out.

"Nothing," Remy said. "At least we bicker like a married couple convincingly enough."

Hale leaned back in his chair, the anger in his eyes cooling. "You play the role of a pregnant woman well."

"Do backhanded compliments just roll off your tongue so naturally?" Remy said.

A subtle smirk crossed Hale's face as he asked, "Do you wish to concern yourself with my tongue?"

Even with his glamour, Hale was gorgeous. Her gaze roved along his sharp jawline and full lips before settling back on those eyes.

Remy's heart leapt into her throat. Gods, those gray eyes were the smoke before the flame. They scorched her skin.

Remy wished Heather and Fenrin were still here. Maybe their constant meddling could be beneficial sometimes. Right now, Remy needed a buffer before she crawled across the table and showed the prince just how concerned she could be with his tongue.

"Three rooms?" Remy asked instead.

"What?" Hale arched a thick, brown brow.

"You told the innkeeper we needed three rooms," Remy noted.

"One for the Eagles, one for you and your . . . friends," he said, careful not to mention witches, "and Carys and I will share one."

"Oh," Remy said, then added, "Good. I mean, it will look strange if you were sharing a room with someone other than the woman you said was your wife . . ."

"Good point." Hale grinned. "I'm sure your friends will have feelings about that, though. Do you want to spend the night in a room with me?"

The sound of his voice made Remy want to chew on her lip, but she refused. A small thrill ran through her that he might have lied about them being married so they could share a bed.

Remy warred with herself. What did an offer like that mean? What would happen if she said yes? She bounced one leg under the table.

She remembered what Carys had said in the forest, but something about the fae warrior and Hale sharing a bed still rubbed Remy the wrong way.

Hale put an elbow on the table and rested his chin in his hand. He was watching her, and from the smug look on his face he knew what she was debating.

A blush crept up Remy's face. She instantly felt more aware of her appearance. Her beauty had only ever been a problem for her. She tried to hide it behind her tied-back hair and unwashed face. She had been receiving advances from drunken men in taverns for years. But so rarely had she wanted to encourage a male's attention. Only one time in fact . . . well, two now.

Remy's goal in life was to not draw attention to herself. Yet here she was, thinking about how she wanted to look and dress to draw Hale's gaze. She wanted the prince to think she was beautiful, and she hated herself for it. These fae royals were not good males. She shouldn't care about anything other than how quickly she could escape.

The innkeeper returning with two glasses of water saved Remy from the prince's penetrating stare. Another small, mousy woman behind her carried two plates of food to the table.

"That smells delicious," Remy said, smiling at the cook. The woman's thin pink lips pulled up at the sides before she turned and walked away. Remy sensed the cook's magic stirring behind that smile. She was a witch too. Thank the Gods. The more witches around, the better.

Remy considered Hale as he devoured the meal before him. He did not know he had entered a tavern with at least two more witches.

Remy took a bite of the roasted potatoes and approvingly hummed as she chewed. The perfectly crisped vegetables had just the right amount of rosemary. Remy had eaten her fair share of roasted potatoes over the years, along with all the usual tavern fare. Judging by the deliciousness of the meal, Remy assumed the cook was a green witch. Green witches were native to the Southern Court, their magic making mouth-watering food and growing beautiful gardens.

Remy ate, keeping pace with the prince. It surprised her how fast Hale ate, considering he was a royal. She gobbled her food because she rarely got time off to eat her meals and so she had to shovel them down during kitchen dashes. Remy supposed it was Hale's warrior side in practice. The stories of The Bastard Prince of the East took place everywhere but the Eastern capital city of Wynreach. He and his soldiers were nomadic, moving from town to town on the orders of King Norwood.

"Newpond . . ." Remy mused as she looked about the room. There, mounted on the wall, was a dusty map of the continent of Okrith. "We're nearing Silver Sands Harbor at the Western Court's border. Are we crossing into the South?"

The Silver Sands Harbor was a deep inlet separating the Western and Southern Courts. Only one road crossed the border. It wended through the dense forest at the base of the southwestern most reaches of the High Mountains. Remy stuck out her lip as she traced the map with her eyes. They would come so close to the harbor. It seemed a pity to be so close and still not view the ocean.

The prince frowned at the map. "You know I cannot tell you where we are going. Not yet."

"What could I possibly do with that information?" Remy said, batting her eyelashes.

"You can keep playing this game, little witch," Hale spoke in a softly menacing voice. "But I will not underestimate your power. Most of your kind were killed off in the slaughter thirteen years ago for their allegiance to the fallen crown. You are a rarity. And when we stumbled across you in that tavern, I knew we had struck gold. You are our ticket out of this war. So no, you are not some meek, little tavern witch. You can stop pretending."

Remy snarled at Hale.

"There she is." He grinned.

"What can you tell me, then?" Remy folded her arms across her chest.

"Nothing." Hale lifted another spoonful of peas to his mouth.

"Can you tell me your full name or is that not allowed either?" Remy asked.

That threw him off guard.

"My name is Hale." He pursed his lips to contain his mouthful of food.

"Oh please, all you princes have ten names. Go on, what's yours?"

Hale chuffed out a laugh as he sipped his water.

"Fine, my name is Hale Bastion Haast Ashby Norwood. And that is only five names, not ten."

Remy cackled. There was nothing delicate or demure about the way witches laughed. They laughed with their entire bodies, and Hale couldn't help but laugh along with her.

"I wish I could say that it was a pleasure to make your acquaintance, prince." Remy laughed again, throwing his title at him like a playful punch. She took a long sip of her water and looked at him through her long lashes. "Perhaps if the circumstances were different."

She didn't know why she said it, merely wanted to. But she delighted in the way Hale's eyes widened. That wanting smile stretched back across his face. He may have been fae, but when it came to women, it didn't matter: fae males were as simple as human men, it seemed.

"And what is your name, little witch?" Hale's voice dropped an octave as he spoke. It did wonderfully terrible things to Remy's insides.

"Remy Singer," she answered.

"Liar." The prince smirked.

Maybe he wasn't a complete fool, then, and he was formidable. His other soldiers were skilled to be sure, but Hale's power was like a living thing. Remy sensed it, power radiating off him in pulsing waves, her ears ringing with the low hum. She feared for anyone who ended up on the wrong end of his blade.

"How about some wine?" Remy looked forlornly at her empty plate. She had been half-tempted to lick it clean. Too many days she had been eating rabbit and squirrel stew.

"You are with child, *wife*," the prince reminded her.

"Ugh, fine. Cake, then." Remy grinned. Cake was what she wanted anyway, and compared to wine, it was inexpensive too. "I'm sure you can afford it."

The prince barked out a laugh as he grabbed a gold coin from his pocket. He may have been glamoured as a human but carrying around pieces of gold was a dead giveaway that he was fae. Remy snatched the coin off the table regardless and waved it to the green witch cook, who was talking to the barman in the corner.

"Three slices of cake please," she called to the witch, waving the prince's coin.

"Three?" The prince raised his eyebrows.

"Oh, did you want a piece?" Remy asked. Turning back to the green witch, she shouted, "Sorry, four pieces, please."

The green witch nodded to her with a knowing grin. Whatever kind of cake it was, it would be delicious if a green witch had baked it.

"Well, it is worth the coin to see you eat four whole slices of cake," Hale chuckled more and more at the thought. Something in Remy loved that he laughed like a witch. It was deep and hearty, making his whole body shake. Entirely different from the begrudging sounds he usually made, this sound was genuine.

"Like you said, *husband*, I am with child." Remy rubbed her stomach.

CHAPTER SIX

R emy's stomach was so full she looked pregnant. Hale had given in and ordered an ale for himself too. The dimple of his right cheek twitched as Remy moved the fourth and final slice of cake in front of herself, determined to finish it.

The cake of the day was apple spice with maple buttercream frosting, perfect for the autumn weather. The green witch superbly flavored it with aromatic cinnamon, ginger, and cloves. The frosting melted on her tongue.

"You sure you don't want some?" Remy said through a mouthful of moist cake. "Last chance."

Hale pressed his lips to the rim of his glass as he shook his head.

"I want to see if you can do it." He winked.

"Don't bet against me," Remy said, narrowing her eyes at him as she scooped another heaping mouthful.

"I wouldn't dare." Hale's eyes twinkled.

His posture had loosened over the hour. She liked this version of Hale. He normally seemed so in control. He unbuttoned the top button of his tunic and rolled up its olive-green sleeves. He looked more like who Remy imagined he was under his princely mask. She wondered if this is how he was with his friends.

The bell on the front door jangled again. They both turned to look, but it was not their comrades. Among the locals drifting in, a traveling couple took a seat in the far corner, and two scruffy men with leathery faces and brawny muscles dropped their packs against the wall before heading to the bar. At the threshold, a father with his adult son stepped in, sniffing appreciatively at the kitchen's aromas, and they dropped their packs with everyone else's before seating themselves at a table behind Remy and Hale.

Hale sighed as he watched the other traveling couple settle in, rubbing the back of his neck.

"What's wrong?" Remy asked, noting his frustration.

"I'm just ready for the others to be back." Hale gripped his glass tighter.

"They had a lot to get. They probably won't be back for at least another hour."

Hale frowned. "Will you just finish that cake so we can go upstairs?"

Remy arched a brow at his mood shift. His leg bounced under the table with impatience, and then Remy knew what was bothering him.

"Do you need to use the lavatory?" She snorted. The muscle in Hale's jaw flickered as he stared at her.

"Yes, I do," Hale growled. "So hurry up."

"Just go. I'll be fine." Remy laughed.

"I don't want to leave you here alone."

"Gods, how long does it take you to piss?" Remy cackled, the sugary cake going to her head.

Hale's lip curled into a sneer. "Fine." He threw the cloth napkin in his lap on the table and stood. "I'll be back in a minute."

Remy bit her lips to keep from laughing as he walked to the back of the inn. She dug into the cake with her fork.

Cutlery clanged as the father and son behind her stood from their table.

All at once, Remy's chair tipped back. She threw out her hands reflexively to catch her fall.

"Oops, sorry, miss," the older man behind her said.

He tilted her chair back forward until all four chair legs were steady on the ground again.

"No problem," Remy said, flustered.

She looked to the bar and met the sharp eyes of the two burly men. Remy's magic buzzed under her skin. Had her eyes glowed as she was falling? She didn't think so, but they might have when she was startled.

Looking away, she let her gaze fall to the cake on her plate as the father and son left the inn. She realized the magic she felt buzzing at her fingertips was not hers, it was coming from the men at the bar. They were not humans: they were glamoured fae. There was only one reason Remy could think of for them to be glamoured . . . they were witch hunters. The barman disappeared behind the kitchen door as the two fae males stood up. Remy fixed her eyes on the table in front of her. Her breathing remained steady. Hale would return any moment now.

Don't run. Don't run.

She folded her hands into the napkin in her lap in case they glowed with fear. She kept her gaze lowered.

The door to the kitchen burst open, and the innkeeper called to her, "I found it, love."

The two fae males paused, watching as the innkeeper bustled over to Remy. The woman had a bizarre, merry smile plastered on her face as she urged Remy to stand.

"Here, come," she said to Remy. "I found that gift for your baby I was telling you about." They walked past the two fae who exchanged looks between them. "Sam can help you at the bar, boys," the innkeeper said, dismissing the two males.

Remy smiled to herself. This is what she loved about witches. They could cut down a man twice their size with one withering stare.

The innkeeper kept her hand on Remy's back as she carried on.

"I'm not as good with the knitting needles as I once was, but I found the sweetest blanket pattern . . ." They passed through the doors to the back kitchen. Most taverns and inns in the Western Court had a similar layout, and this one looked the same as the Rusty Hatchet. The innkeeper placed a bag into Remy's hands and said, "Go. Mother Moon bless you, sister."

The green witch cook stood holding open the back door and said, "Take this road straight to Bleecher Street and take a left. At the end of the street is the forest. There's a deer path that leads into the hills— stay on it. In two hours, you will be in Westdale. Ask for Magda at the local tavern, and she'll find you passage South."

Remy went over her words in her head. She could do it.

"Should we tell the Bastard Prince or are you fleeing him too?" the innkeeper asked.

"You knew it was him?" Remy said.

"Of course I knew! I wasn't born yesterday," the innkeeper said with a shrewd grin.

"Tell him where I'm going," Remy answered without hesitation, surprising herself. The innkeeper frowned but merely shrugged and pushed Remy toward the door.

"We'll stall them for as long as we can," she added.

"Moon blessings to you both," Remy thanked them in the only way she knew how.

"Go!" The cook hurried her to the door. "But don't run, blend in."

"That was the best cake I've ever had, by the way," Remy said over her shoulder as she vanished around the corner. She could hear the cook's laugh following her.

Hale would catch up to her any minute now. She needed to put some distance between herself and the witch hunters until he did. If she had stayed in that tavern one more second, her head might not have stayed attached to her body.

Remy had to remind herself to slow down again as she turned left onto Bleecher Street. She kicked up dirt from the dusty road as her eyes scanned over the town. It was the same rural and cheerless village as every other in the Western backcountry. It was the kind of town for people who didn't want to be noticed. Those without secrets would pass through to a bigger township rather than stop off in a place such as this.

She scanned for any sign of Heather, Fenrin, or her other fae companions. But the main road with all the shops was behind her, past the inn, and Remy couldn't risk doubling back and running into the witch hunters. Hale had to be on the way. As she rushed past cobwebbed windows and paint-chipped doors, she told herself once more that she would be okay. She needed to keep walking past the thinning rows of shops and increasingly neglected houses until he found her.

The sun was hanging low in the sky and the shadows were growing longer. It would be getting dark by dinnertime as they headed into autumn.

The forest beckoned up ahead as she heard the scuffle of feet behind her. She glanced back, only to find a haggard old man shuffling back to his home for the evening. She released a heavy breath. Two more houses before she reached the woods.

When Remy turned back, two men stepped out from an alleyway and stared at her. One was tall and gaunt, and the other was a younger copy of him. Both wore tattered brown clothing. It was the father and son from the bar.

Remy flinched. They were witch hunters too, then.

It made sense now. The father had tipped Remy's chair back on purpose to sense if her power would flare up, while the other two at the bar watched for signs of her magic.

This was not good.

"I have no money and no time," Remy said with a bored voice, moving aside to walk past them, hoping that all her fears were not true and they would simply let her through.

"It's such a pity, isn't it?" the older man asked the younger.

The younger gave Remy an evil smile as he pulled a short sword from a sheath hidden down the spine of his shirt.

"I hate to cut off such a pretty head." He pointed his sword out at her. "Grab her," he ordered to his father next to him.

The older one reached out to Remy, and she retreated a step. She dodged the man's hand and kicked his knee. Normally, that move would at least topple an opponent, but these were not human men, she realized.

"Don't touch me!" Remy shouted, red glowing flames already licking up her arms.

More people popped their heads out of doorways and windows at the shouting and then quickly shut them, the sound of turning locks echoing down the street.

They weren't going to help a witch.

She spun around but saw the two other men from the bar turning the corner. Her eyes frantically searched for an escape, a door or alley, but she was trapped between the four witch hunters now.

Her gut clenched as the four witch hunters closed in. Her hands trembled.

Where was Hale?

She needed to use her magic, but how? She had pulled down a giant pine tree before. Why couldn't she think of what to do now? She looked to the slum houses on either side of her. People were inside them.

Think.

But there was no time to think as the men from the bar advanced on her. She did the first thing she thought of and threw out her magic toward the father and son now at her back. She heard them stumble. She would have laughed at the thought of two fae males tripping, but she was too focused on the other two in front of her.

Remy cast out her magic toward the larger male, unbuckling his boots and belt. He involuntarily dropped his hand to catch his falling trousers, not noticing the belt slipping free and hovering behind him.

"Seriously? That's the best you got?" He laughed. He was the ugliest fae Remy had ever seen with putrid teeth and yellowing, bloodshot eyes. His companion was equally foul. The life of witch hunting had ruined them.

Remy's glowing red hands still shook as she focused on the male's belt floating in the air behind him. She was clumsy with her magic, unpracticed. She had to hold her mind in many places at once. She couldn't forget the rest of the fae around her, but she couldn't drop the focus on the belt either.

She flung one scarlet hand toward the male holding up his pants, and the belt wrapped around his neck. Too late did he register what she was doing. His eyes bugged as he clawed at the leather garrote, face going a deep shade of crimson. More blood vessels burst in his eyes as his companion dug furrows in his flesh, trying to get a finger under the leather's chokehold. Remy pulled the belt tighter, tighter.

A punishing blow crashed into the back of Remy's head, and she stumbled down to her knees. She had lost focus on the other two fae.

"Hold her down," one male shouted.

Remy looked toward the one who had yelled, but someone slugged her in the mouth. She spat blood as the world spun. A heavy boot shoved her to the ground. The father from the duo body-slammed Remy, crushing her into the dirt with such weight she struggled to breathe.

A small thread of her magic held onto that belt even still. The choking male had fallen to the ground, unconscious, but Remy held that belt, pulling it tighter until she felt his thread of life snap.

"You bitch!" The male who had been scrambling to save his friend pulled two daggers from his belt.

"End this!" the man atop Remy snarled to his son.

The older male pinned her neck to the ground with his forearm, and another hard boot collided with Remy's ear. She saw spots, desperately clinging to consciousness as her heart slammed into her chest. Her mind was so jumbled she didn't even register the pain. She couldn't hear them anymore. Her ears rang. Her eyes strained upward to the young male as he brandished his sword.

This was it. The cake in her stomach rebelled, and Remy heaved up a stomachful of acrid-smelling food, spilling it onto the dirt. The three remaining witch hunters only paused to laugh at her.

Remy braced for the impact of the blade. She heard the whoosh of metal through the air and clenched her eyes shut.

Blood rained onto her, splattering across her face. The warm liquid poured through her hair. The male on top of her spasmed, rolling off her.

Remy peeked up. Standing above her was Hale.

The warrior prince wielded a sword in one hand and a dagger in the other, his eyes darting back and forth between the two remaining fae. Hair dragging through the muck, Remy glimpsed the body of the older fae. The spasms had stopped and unseeing eyes stared back at her. A gaping wound still spurted blood from the male's slashed neck.

Hale stole Remy a quick glance before blocking a blow from the young fae with the sword.

"Run," he mouthed. He stood stock still, muscles taut, a coiled spring ready to unleash himself on the two fae pointing weapons at him.

Pure white-hot fury was on his face. Death was in his eyes.

Remy scrambled to her feet and ran on wobbling legs. Swords clanged behind her, but she didn't stop to look. She raced for the forest.

As she hit the tree line, she realized she had left Hale to fight off two witch hunters by himself. She stole a quick look. The prince danced around his opponents, moving with dizzying speed. Remy wished she could stay and watch his graceful death dance.

But she plunged deeper and deeper into the forest. She needed to put as much distance between herself and those hunters in case one broke free. She willed a bit more magic into her legs, spurring her onward. But her limbs felt heavy and her lungs burned.

A scream behind her shredded her nerves, but it was not Hale. It was the sound of someone dying on Hale's blade.

Remy fell to her knees before a stream. The trembling in her legs was too great. Reeking of vomit and blood, she heard another dying scream. Hale had killed them.

She put her shaking hands into the cold water. Trying to take a deep breath, only shuddering bursts of air came out. The shock took over her body now. Tendrils of blood flowed down the stream. She cupped a handful of water up to her bruised face. Cool liquid pulling her more into her body, she splashed her face several more times until the water ran clear.

A twig snapped behind her, and Remy spun, eyes buzzing with red magic.

Hale stood panting, his hands held out.

"It's me," he said.

He looked like the God of War. Blood speckled his face, the ichor smudged across his clothes. His tangled and gore-clotted hair stuck to his forehead. Like a warrior ready to cut down a dozen more men, his chest still heaved and his muscles flexed.

That menace ebbed from his eyes as he looked at Remy.

"You okay?" he asked, his eyes darting to Remy's ear and mouth.

Remy swallowed a lump in her throat as she hung her head. She wouldn't let herself fall apart in front of him. A strange desire to be wrapped in his arms made her hands twitch. Somehow, she knew exactly what it would feel like.

She moved to stand on shaky feet. In the blink of an eye, Hale was over her, offering his bloodied hand. Remy took it, pride be damned, as he pulled her up with ease.

She swayed like a newborn baby deer. Hale gripped her hand.

"Take your time," he mumbled. That soft look in his eyes was so at odds with his bloodied warrior's clothes.

Tears welled in Remy's eyes at that gentleness. She couldn't handle it, that he saw her and allowed her to feel the trauma. That he would not reprimand or dismiss her. He was simply there, seeing it all without judgment. Remy bit the inside of her cheek so hard she thought she might draw blood. More blood. She already knew how horrified Heather would be. She could hear the brown witch lecturing her even now.

They stood in silence for a long time as the shaking lessened in Remy's legs. Her head ached and her lip throbbed, her body finally feeling the injuries as her heartbeat steadied. After the long days' walk and the tremendous amount of power used to fell that pine tree, only a wisp of magic still flowed through her. It surprised her she had any left for that belt. She thought back to that vacant male face. She had killed him. She had killed someone.

Hale seemed to sense the tension pulling back into her body and spoke.

"Why am I always chasing you into the bloody forest?" Hale laughed as he stared off into the shadowed woods.

Remy searched for a quick, smart retort, but she had none. She knew what he was doing, trying to snap her back to her senses and out of the numbing shock.

He lifted a hand and pulled a leaf out of her hair with a soft smile.

"You took on four male fae and survived, little witch." His voice was a whisper as his gray eyes bored into hers. The way he looked at Remy now . . . it made her quiver. He looked at her like she was beautiful, but, more than that, he looked at her like she was brave.

"We should go find the others." Remy looked away. Her voice was scratchy, like she had been screaming. Maybe she had been—she didn't know.

"Yes, we need to find the others," Hale said, his eyes still lingering on her face. "We can't stay in Guilford. We need to keep moving through the night in case those males had any others working with them."

Remy shuddered.

"Talhan's going to kill us for depriving him of a bed another night," Remy said, trying to break the tightness in her chest.

"Let me deal with Tal." Hale's voice was thunder over velvet.

That tension in Remy's chest eased at the prince's warm eyes and smoldering smile. She took a step on her left leg, steady. The prince released her hand as her shaking dissipated. It was a mistake. She shifted onto her right leg, which immediately gave way. Hale shot his arms out to catch her. With a gasp she fell forward onto him, pushing his foot back against a tree root. The two went down. Hale took the brunt of the fall, his brawny arms slowing Remy's fall onto his chest.

He chuckled.

"I knew I should've just carried you." He smirked up at her. Remy's midnight curls hung down around his shoulders.

"I had a cramp in my right leg," she shot back. "It just gave out from under me."

"Here?" Hale asked.

His hand snaked around the back of Remy's knee and up to the bottom of her right thigh. He pushed in, and Remy's thigh seized again. Hale dug his thumb into the muscle and slid it up the back of her leg. Hissing, Remy gritted her teeth. He did it again, and the muscle relented for a moment. Hale rubbed deep strokes up and down the back of her thigh.

At last, the muscle loosened and Remy sighed in relief. Hands still cupping the back of her leg, Hale smiled up at her. Remy was aware of how close those fingers drifted to the apex of her thighs.

Hale's eyes dropped to Remy's lips, chest rising and falling against hers. She felt all the places their bodies met—that claiming hand on the back of her thigh. It would not be far at all for that hand to drift up . . .

In the shadowed forest light, she stared at Hale. Scattered rays of evening sunlight highlighted the red streaks of his hair. His face glowed faintly red, and Remy knew it was from her glowing red eyes again. They were not glowing out of fear now. He stared and stared into them. He did not shrink away, mesmerized by their glow. It would take nothing for her to bend down a mere inch and press her lips to his.

She heard a barking call through the trees.

"That's Tal, they're following our scents," Hale said, his voice rough with a frustration that Remy was feeling all too well. What would she have done with one more minute with this prince warrior? It was easy to imagine what it would look like if she and this gorgeous male were in the same position, but with fewer clothes.

The prince cleared his throat. As Remy climbed off him, she wondered if his mind was wandering to similar places.

She shook the thoughts from her mind. It was pure adrenaline. She was in shock. She had a bashed-in face and the stink of vomit clung to her. Whatever fantasy swirled in her head was a delusion. The attraction came from relief alone: Hale had saved her. That was all it was. She would feel different in an hour.

CHAPTER SEVEN

R emy was the closest she had ever been to the ocean, yet she
still could not see it. She heard the rhythmic sound of soft
waves lapping on the shore. Silver Sands Harbor lay
through the thicket of trees to their right. Smaller foot trails led
toward the beach from the main path. She kept looking down them,
hoping to glimpse the harbor, but the shadows were too dark. She had
imagined so many times what the ocean looked like. She had seen it in
the far distance a few times during their travels through the Western
woods, but it had been a thin strip of blue in the far distance. But to be
standing on its shores . . . she wondered what it would feel like to over-
look an endless sea of blue. She had seen the Western lakes and a few
large rivers before, but that was different. Remy could swim . . . sort of
. . . if flailing to keep her head above water counted as swimming, but
there had been no waves. She had heard stories of waves taller than
houses, swallowing ships in stormy seas. It sounded unbelievable.

An ocean scent hung in the darkened forest air, taunting her. The
smell was strangely familiar. It reminded her of the fae prince several
paces ahead. He carried the ocean on him even when they were far
away.

They walked silently. The other fae had doubled back to fetch Hale and Remy's packs, and the group forged ahead on the trail south, skirting Newpond. They only stopped once at a river. Remy hadn't been able to scrub the smell of blood out of her hair. It still clung to her. She let Heather tend to her wounds and give her a tonic for the pain, but Remy insisted they kept moving despite her injuries. The sounds of Heather's shocked cries at seeing her bludgeoned face still rang in her ears. Shame still stained her skin from the looks in the brown witches' eyes. She pressed her lips together, swallowing the hard lump tightening her throat.

She had abandoned her bloodied clothes rather than trying to carry the wet ones. They were patchy and worn thin, anyway. Carys had bought herself new clothes and gave Remy her old fighting leathers. They were a bit too long, but they were supple and comfortable. Even secondhand, they were the nicest clothes she had ever owned. Wearing the leathers changed something in Remy's posture too. It made her feel more like a warrior. Flashbacks of the attack kept her muscles coiled and jumpy. With the leathers on, Remy pretended it was her muscles readying to fight an unseen enemy. Focusing her attention on the swaying trees and sounds of the waves, she was determined to ignore the feeling of her stomach dropping over and over again.

She moved easily through the trail, too, thanks to the new boots Briata had bought her. She thought the Eagle would find her something secondhand, but these were brand-new boots, still smelling of leather polish. They needed breaking in, but they fit like they were made for her. Briata truly had an eye for guessing sizes, it seemed.

They walked in a tighter unit along the trail now. Heather and Fenrin struggled behind Remy in the darkness. The moon lit the path barely enough for them to navigate it.

Remy looked to the sky peeking through the trees. It was a full moon. In times past, the witches would celebrate on the full moon. They would cook a bountiful meal, light candles, and swap stories into the night. They would spread totems from their bags in beams of light and say a prayer to Mother Moon, asking her guidance for another lunar cycle.

Even on the road they would light a candle and say a simple prayer. Remy carried a long white candle in her pack for her full moon ceremonies.

"Let's stop," she said to no one in particular.

"There is nowhere to camp here. We have to pass the harbor," Hale called from the front without breaking stride. "There is an abandoned mining town a few minutes off the trail. We will bunk down in a cabin there."

"I wasn't saying let's camp here. I was saying we should take a break," Remy said.

"Do we think these cabins will have beds?" Talhan grumbled from behind her.

"Doubtful," Briata said.

Talhan loosed a string of muttered curses. Everyone was in a foul mood. Even Talhan's normal joviality was wearing thin.

"It's the full moon," Remy pushed, looking at the sky. And not just any moon. Tonight the swollen blue harvest moon shone down on them. The witches believed that the candles they lit on the harvest moon could communicate with their ancestors.

"And?" Hale said.

Carys cast a glance over her shoulder at Remy, giving her an apologetic look.

"So we need to light a candle and say a prayer," Remy said, though she did not truly care about prayers and candles in that moment. If she could stand by the ocean maybe she could breathe, maybe the trembling in her hands would finally ebb and she'd feel steady again. "We could go down the path to the beach and—"

"No," Hale said in a clipped tone, dashing her hopes of seeing the ocean.

"We can light candles when we get to the cabin, Remy," Heather said from behind her. Heather had been silent since seeing Remy's bloodied clothes and bludgeoned face. The brown witch was more distraught than Remy was herself.

"It will only take five minutes," Remy said.

"You are *not* lighting a candle visible to the whole harbor. I do not care how much you want to talk to the moon," Hale growled.

"Hey," Fenrin snarled at the prince. He was either too tired or grumpy to check himself. "The attack was not Remy's fault. You were the ones who thought it would be a great idea to split up. *You* were meant to be protecting her."

Everything moved in a blur. Hale reached for the sword at his hip. In a flash, Carys was at Hale's side with her hand on his arm.

"Don't," she hissed to the prince.

Even through the shadows, Remy saw Fenrin's eyes widen at Hale. What was the prince planning on doing? Cutting down her friend because he said something that was true?

Remy was sick of this male posturing. Hale thought that because he was a prince that made him better than everyone else. She had agreed freely to this journey, but she was not a servant of the Eastern Prince. It was time he remembered that.

Remy veered down the foot trail to her right, away from the group. The dirt trail descended, and she felt the grit of sand beneath her boots.

"Enough. I'm going to the beach," she called over her shoulder. Only a few more steps and she'd be able to see the ocean. A breeze whooshed past her face and in the blink of an eye Hale was there, standing forebodingly in front of her, blocking her path forward.

"Keep moving," Hale ordered the others. His piercing gray eyes stayed fixed on Remy. She matched his authoritative gaze with one of her own.

The fae all turned and walked at the prince's orders, but Fenrin and Heather paused. Hale looked over Remy's shoulder, his voice lethal as he said, "Keep. Moving."

"They don't take orders from you," Remy snarled. Hale's eyes darted to hers.

She heard Heather call from behind her, "Why don't we carry on? You two can catch up."

Remy turned to look at her guardian, quirking her eyebrow. It was unlike Heather to leave her, but perhaps her guardian knew it was best to keep out of this battle. Dipping her chin, Remy gave Heather a silent acknowledgement. She was okay to stay behind. The brown witch looped her arm through Fenrin's, dragging him along the trail. Fenrin grumbled something as Heather pulled him.

Listening for their steady footsteps marching away, Remy turned back to Hale. The arching of her eyebrow made the muscle in his jaw pop out. Clearly, he did not like that the witches ignored his orders. But Remy was powerful, if only she would claim it, and she was getting precariously close to embracing what she was. When that day came, the prince would have to tread lightly.

"Get. Out. Of. My. Way." No one got between a witch and her magic. She heard the ocean waves beckoning her. The trail below her boots had turned to sand, but it was too dark to see if it shone silver.

"No," Hale said, crossing his arms, the sleeves of his jacket straining over his muscled shoulders.

"I won't light a candle." Remy relented through gritted teeth. "I just want to see the moon over the ocean."

She made to dodge around him, but the trail was too narrow and Hale blocked her with ease.

"This isn't about the ocean," Hale said. "This is about you trying to distract yourself from what happened today."

"No, it's about seeing the ocean and the full moon," Remy growled.

"This isn't a joke, witch." Hale matched her tone. They were two predators standing off, each readying to strike.

"I am not laughing, *faerie*," Remy hissed back.

"Get back on the trail. Now." His entire body was still as stone, but his eyes were raging and wild.

Remy grabbed her last bit of restraint.

"What is wrong with you?" her harsh growl rose as she said, "Why are you pushing me so hard?"

"Because you almost got your head cut off!" Hale exploded. "I should have been paying attention! I should have known that those hunters were fae, and I was too distracted to notice! When I saw that male with the sword, I . . ." He swallowed and ground his teeth so tightly she feared one might break. Even with all that effort, his voice cracked when he spoke again. "Gods, Remy, you almost died."

Remy. Not witch. Not Red. He had called her by her name.

A long silence stretched between them as Remy watched emotions flash through Hale's eyes in rapid succession: panic, fear, sorrow. He had thought he wouldn't reach her in time.

The prince cleared his throat and all those whirling emotions disappeared as fast as they came. It happened so quickly Remy wondered if she had really seen them at all.

"I mean," Hale said, looking to his shadowed feet. "It would take ages to find another red witch."

And there it was. That princely, careless mask fit him so well.

Remy knew the prince built walls around himself to keep everyone out, but he flipped from caring to cold with such speed that she didn't know what was real anymore. Her heart felt those words whether or not they were real: he only cared about her as much as he could gain. He was only scared of losing her because it would mean more work for himself.

Maybe that's who she was: someone fun to flirt with in taverns and entertain him on his quest for the High Mountain talismans. But she was a tool to him, not a person.

The moonlight danced through the trees. The sound of gentle waves and rustling branches betrayed the storm brewing between them.

Remy let Hale see that his indifference landed harder than any blow. It felt worse to be stomped by his words than a witch hunter's boot.

Remy glared at Hale.

"Yes, that would be a real tragedy for you," Remy said, meeting those eyes one more time before turning around and heading back to the trail.

"Remy, I—" Hale called from behind her, but she was already stomping away.

He had said her name again, the second time in a matter of seconds. She didn't know what that meant, that new familiarity. It cracked her open in a way that she despised. Why did he have to speak to her like a friend and treat her like an enemy?

One day she would see the ocean. One day she'd feel as mighty as those giant waves. The full moon followed her along the trail as she swallowed the tears threatening to destroy her.

Remy wasn't sure when she had fallen asleep. The dim firelight flickered and cast shadows about the cabin. Someone must have fed it while she slept. The night wasn't as cold now that they had skirted past the harbor into the Southern Court.

Groggily sitting up, Remy rubbed her eyes. She wiped away their blurriness and scanned the cabin that had become their campsite. Two lumps slept on either side of her, Heather and Fenrin. Fenrin's snores shook the floorboards under her. He had come down with some sort of cold during their travels, turning his normal soft snores into loud honks.

Three bodies slept lined against the far wall: the Twin Eagles and Carys. And one in front of the doorway, Hale. It was a strategic position to guard against any unwelcome guests. Remy wondered if the witch hunters had spooked him.

The light of the full moon illuminated the open doorway. The door had long been ripped off its hinges, leaving the cabin open to the elements.

Bright moonlight beamed into the room. The harvest moon. Curses, she forgot. Heather and Fenrin had invited her to light candles when they arrived at the cabin, but Remy had been so tired she had all but collapsed on her bedroll.

She crept on bare feet to the door, careful not to wake Hale lying across the threshold. Her injured feet had healed. Of course, now she had a swollen lip from the witch hunter's punch that stung every time she moved it. A bruise spread from her brow to her jawline where that boot had collided with her face. Her right ear still had a high-pitched ringing, and it popped every time she swallowed.

She reached into the outer pocket of her hiking pack and blindly found the longer of two candles. Her fingers skimmed over the stubbier red wax candle. Every time she touched it, she wondered if she would ever use it. She stealthily tiptoed over Hale's sleeping body. She paused, but he did not stir, his breathing slow and steady.

As she stepped out into the night, she braced for the chill, but it was still temperate in these parts. The South was indeed warmer than the West.

She stayed close and found a spot below the window where the moonlight kissed the ground. She knelt, pressing one finger into the earth. Remy dug a little hole to hold her candle straight.

With a rock and flint from her totem bag, she struck a spark to light the candle, whispering, "Mother Moon, bless me this night."

Remy took totems from her bag: a fledgling raven's feather, a piece of red string, a snail shell, a stick of cinnamon, and a pressed white flower. She laid them out in front of the candle. The moonlight bathed her totems in gleaming white light.

Remy looked into the blue base of the flame. She wondered if the souls of her ancestors listened through the witch candle of this harvest moon. What would she say to her parents if they could hear her? Pressing her lips together, tears filled her eyes.

"I almost died yesterday," she whispered to the flame. A tear slipped down her cheek and fell off her chin. "I thought of you. I wondered if I'd see you in the afterlife. I wondered what you'd say to me."

She took a ragged breath as more tears fell.

"I don't think you'd be very proud of me. I have amounted to little in this life. I've just been a hiding coward."

She spoke the words Hale had called her around the campfire those nights before. It was true. All she had ever done was hide.

"I'm going after the *Shil-de* ring and the amulet," she said, one side of her mouth pulling up. "A quest like the ones you used to tell me as I fell asleep at night. I've made some friends too. I think you'd like them." Remy imagined her father laughing along with the Twin Eagles, swapping battle stories, and her mother trading tales with

Carys. "A prince saved me yesterday. Just like in those stories. I think you might like him too," Remy added, afraid even in the darkness to invoke Hale's name. She wondered what her parents would tell her, what advice they would have, which direction they would steer her.

Her eyes welled with another bout of tears. "I miss you."

She moved the pressed flower from her totems and swapped it for a small red leaf nearby. The leaf would be her totem for the next moon cycle.

She waited for Mother Moon's wisdom, for something to whisper into her mind, an intention for the month ahead. The flame bobbed in the windless night.

Something murmured in her mind, but it was not the moon. She knew that warm, soulful voice. It was her mother. A flicker of memory spoke from the flame: "Never let anyone else tell you who you are, Remy, not even me. No one decides how bright you shine but you."

Remy's heart cracked open at that. She remembered the night her mother had spoken those words to her. Bundled in blankets, they had looked up at the night's sky in Yexshire. It had been a harvest moon, like this one. The light snow had dusted their eyelashes and head-scarves. She remembered looking out over the twinkling lights of the city, how they mirrored the stars above. Her mother had woken her simply to look at the moon. Her older brothers and younger sister still slept, but Remy and her mother had taken in that night's sky, just the two of them. She still felt her mother's warm arms around her, pulling her into the warmth of her embrace. What she wouldn't give to have her mother's arms around her again.

Remy relived that moment for a long time, savoring that memory. She took one last deep breath.

"Thank you," she whispered to the candle. Then she said the last words, rolling in a chant off her tongue, "This or something better now manifests for the highest good of all."

Blowing out the candle, she collected her totems and put them back in her bag with care. She wiped the last of her tears on her rough tunic sleeve.

As she walked up the steps, there was no lump sleeping across the threshold.

Scanning the room, Remy found Hale sitting in a far shadowed corner. It was too dark to see more than his outline, and yet she was sure his eyes watched her. Careful not to disturb her sleeping companions, she made her way over to him. Her bare feet made it easier to pad silently across the wood floor. Remy wondered if his fae ears had heard what she said to the candle. She prayed the crackling of the fire had covered the sound of her words.

"You should rest. We have another hour before we break camp for the day." His voice was gravelly with sleep.

"I can't rest anymore," Remy whispered. "I'm surprised I slept at all."

Memories of those witch hunters flashed in her mind. She still felt their phantom grip on her. It was only through sheer exhaustion after hiking into the night that sleep had claimed her.

Hale grumbled something under his breath and handed his skin of water to Remy.

Gingerly moving to avoid aggravating her injuries, she sat next to him.

"Where are we headed today?" Remy whispered, taking a cool sip of water.

"You know I can't tell you that," Hale muttered.

"What do you think I could possibly do with that information?"

"There are many things you could do. You could try to go after the ring yourself. Or warn your other witch friends of your location so they could ambush us, for example," Hale said. He kept rubbing his pointer finger as he stared at the wall. Something was still bothering him.

"Firstly, I have no other friends apart from Heather and Fenrin. They are the only other witches I know." Hale's cheek twitched. "And secondly," Remy whispered, "you think highly of our abilities to evade you when we are only three witches against four trained fae warriors. Look what happened the last time four fae ganged up on me."

She regretted the words as soon as she spoke them. She didn't miss Hale's jaw clenching as the words came out.

Gods, you almost died!

She was sure she had heard his voice crack. That moment when his mask fell, genuine fear peeked through. What happened on the road to Newpond had shaken him, but it wasn't until she was shouting at him that he revealed it. He felt responsible for her attack, Remy realized. That was why he slept at the threshold of the cabin.

"You were frightened," Hale said with a shrug. "You forgot to use your powers. With a little more training you could be a warrior."

"I know how to use a bow." Remy frowned. She looked over to the new beautiful carved bow sitting against the wall. Bri had picked the finest maplewood bow Remy had ever seen but in the aftermath of the witch hunter attack she could not test it yet. "But I don't think a bow or more training would have turned the tides of that fight if you hadn't shown up."

"Is that a thank you?" Hale looked to her. Even through the darkness, Remy sensed when his eyes were trained on her.

"No," Remy ground out. Hale let out a low chuckle. His breath skittered across the hairs of Remy's arm. She pressed her lips together. "I do not want a prince to save me. I want to save myself."

"Then you should train," Hale said. "Bri could teach you. She's more patient with beginners than me."

"Why does that not surprise me?" Remy smirked.

Hale's face hid in shadow, but she saw his lips tilting up at the sides.

"Ruttmore," he said.

"What?" Remy asked.

"We're headed south to Ruttmore, it's near Saxbridge."

"Oh." Remy nodded. "I've always wondered what the Southern Court looked like."

Of all the courts, the Southern Court was the one she had heard the most outlandish tales about. Stories had reached her of wild jungles, brightly-colored birds, and revels that lasted until sunrise.

A long silence passed between them before Hale spoke.

"Listen, what happened yesterday, I—"

"I think I am tired after all," Remy cut him off.

There was nothing good that could come of what he was about to say. She went back to her bedroll wedged between her two protectors and lay there, unsleeping, thinking about what would have come out if she had allowed him to finish his sentence.

CHAPTER EIGHT

The day was heavy with rain. The darkness of the early morning had yet to lift off the land. Remy felt the little clouds in her head. She always felt sleepy when there was no sun. She wasn't designed for this gray, humid climate. It burdened her soul. She knew more sunshine lay ahead as they traveled further South. They headed toward the capital city of Saxbridge, at the very bottom of the Southern Court where it was rumored to be warm all year round.

Remy preferred when they made camp in the woods. The cold stone ruins were uncomfortable to sleep on and haunting to look at in the night. The taverns were noisy, overcrowded, and full of prying eyes. She wished, however, that they had slept in a place with a roof last night. Even with the shelter of the overhanging trees, she had still felt pinpricks of rain. The wetness of the ground sank into her bedroll in the night too. The weather was warmer than in the West, but wetter too, it seemed. They laid their soggy hiking clothes on a makeshift frame over the fire.

Briata had bought a new maplewood bow and a quiver of arrows for Remy during their unfortunate stopover in Guilford. Remy had taken over hunting duties on their trek. It made her feel good that she could offer something to the group. She knew the others could catch a rabbit or squirrel just as quickly, but it still made her feel useful and they seemed happy to have someone else take over for a change.

Briata's boot in her back woke Remy.

"Get up," the golden-eyed female said, tossing Remy her traveling attire from the clothing frame. "Let's go."

Remy had dressed quickly and followed Briata away from the fire and the rest of their sleeping companions. The sun strained to peep through the heavy clouds on the horizon as Bri led her to a small clearing in the forest, freshly opened to the sky from a fallen redwood tree.

When they reached the center of the clearing, Briata turned to Remy and crossed her arms.

"Why do you want to train?" The Eagle's jaw jutted to the side as she looked at Remy. Chewing on her lip, Remy considered her answer.

She did not want to cast her mind back to the witch hunter attack, so she simply said, "I want to be able to defend myself. I don't want to be rescued again."

"Good." Briata nodded. She pulled the dagger from her left hip and gave it to Remy, adjusting her grip on the weapon. "This way," she said so that the knuckle of Remy's pointer finger aligned with the top of the blade.

Briata instructed Remy where to put her feet, how to hold her body, and how to move her arms. It felt awkward and strange, unlike how she thought it would feel. Her body didn't move the way the others did. Briata taught her three different foot positions: a strike, a block, and a series of hits. It was a simple combination, and yet Remy couldn't seem to get her feet to move at the same time as her arms. She felt all twisted up in her mind. She would freeze for several seconds after Briata called out a combination before her body would move. It felt ridiculous. Briata was going so easy on her, and yet she still wasn't moving right.

"You're still holding it wrong," Briata corrected Remy for the 200th time in ten minutes.

"Why does it matter how I hold it?" Remy dropped her arms in frustration.

Briata unsheathed the sword from her right hip and swung it before Remy could blink. The dagger went flying out of her hand.

"That's why," Briata said. "Now pick it up and hold it the way I showed you."

"Why can't I just use a sword like you?" Remy felt like a child holding the smaller weapon.

"Because your scrawny human arms won't be able to lift a fae sword," Briata said. Remy looked to the warrior's considerable biceps and frowned.

"I'm not a human, I'm a witch." Remy tucked a sweaty ringlet of hair that had escaped her bun behind her rounded ear. Her breathing was already so heavy, and she had barely moved.

"Well, you all look the same." Briata shrugged. "Were it not for the smell of magic on you, you'd be human to me."

"My arms aren't scrawny—I've been lifting trays of ale since I was seven." Remy frowned.

"Your arms are shaking just from holding up that dagger for the last ten minutes." Briata smirked.

Remy cursed. She didn't think the shaking was so noticeable. The fae missed nothing.

Briata darted a glance to Remy's feet and looked back at her, cocking her eyebrow. Remy rolled her eyes. Without saying a word, she swapped her feet back into the fighting stance that Briata had shown her. The whole thing was demoralizing. If anything, she felt less able to fight in this position.

"This is hopeless, Briata." Remy clenched her teeth.

"Call me Bri," the fae warrior said. Remy's lips pulled up a bit at that. She had earned the right to call the fae by her nickname. That was at least one victory.

"It's not that bad," Carys's voice came from the forest. The female appeared and perched herself on a thick branch of the fallen redwood. "You should have seen some of the people we trained in Falhampton and they were fae. You've got to remember fighting is like a dance . . ."

"It is not like a dance," Bri said, annoyed.

"Yes it is." Carys grinned at her.

"It is nothing like dancing," Bri growled. This was clearly something the fae had argued about before.

"I don't care what it's like—I just want to be good at it," Remy said. The two of them fought like sisters. It was the same way she and Fenrin bickered. Remy once had a little sister, but she had died at five years old during the Siege of Yexshire. She wondered if they would have squabbled the same way.

"No amount of talent will make up for time and perseverance, Rem," Bri said, pulling her focus back. There was not a single drop of sweat on the female Eagle. "Eventually, we'll add in your red witch magic to your fight training too. You need to be able to fight with your hands and magic at the same time. Now that we're in the Southern Court, it shouldn't be as big of a problem for you to be casting spells."

The Western Court was rife with red witch hunters. The Western Court queen did nothing to curtail their hunting. Even if Hale had declared himself the Eastern Prince, those hunters back in Guilford would have tried to snatch Remy anyway. But in the Southern Court there was more vigilante justice. The Southerners didn't like their green witches being mistakenly snatched or killed. They had already passed two towns with gruesome gnarled heads on spikes, a warning about what would happen if they caught a fae hunting witches. There was not much King Vostemur could do about it other than voice his discontent. To do anything more would be declaring war on the Southern Court. The threat of war loomed over Okrith. Vostemur had already slaughtered the High Mountain Court—would he do it again?

They fell into a steady rhythm once more. Bri would call out a combination, and Remy would fumble to execute it. Carys watched in serene silence. Over the next half hour, the movements became easier. Remy didn't have to pause as often to think about where to step. Her body moved without so much conscious direction. Breathing ragged, she was covered in sweat. Her right arm was so sore she could barely lift it, but she felt good. Fantastic. It felt like she was reclaiming something, taking back control. She had always been passive. Life had happened to her. She was ready for that to change.

"That's good for today. We've got to break camp," Bri said. She was still immaculate. Not a single strand of her short, brown hair was out of place.

"It's been less than an hour—let's keep going." Remy held up the dagger again even as her arm barked to be lowered.

"So eager for punishment." Carys laughed.

"You'll be plenty sore already, even though you're a fast healer," Bri said, her eyes darting down to Remy's new boots. The blisters from her old pair had already disappeared. The mottled bruising on her face was beginning to yellow and fade. "We can pick this up tomorrow."

"No, let's keep going," Remy pushed.

"Why?" Bri cocked her head at Remy.

Swallowing a lump in her throat, the thoughts of that day in Guilford bubbled up again. Fear still gripped her chest, making her breathless. She didn't want to be that afraid ever again.

"They almost killed me," she whispered. The pain of that admission opened the wound afresh. Remy thought to the limp, lifeless face of the witch hunter whose life she had taken. "I killed someone."

"I know." In a split second, Bri was a single step in front of her, peering at Remy with the full intensity of those golden eyes. "Those ghosts will always be there—that part will never change—but at some point you'll stop resisting their presence, and that will help. The choice gets easier too."

"What choice?" Remy asked.

"The one you make every time you pick up a blade: that if it comes to your life or theirs, you'll take theirs every time, no question." Bri's deep, warm voice swirled around her.

Remy hung her head. It should be a simple choice, but it wasn't . . . not yet, anyway.

"We will do this every morning before we break camp," Bri said, sheathing her sword and taking the dagger from Remy. There would be blisters on Remy's hands by nightfall. "You're already strong and impressive with the bow—we just need that same skill with a dagger and you'll be sorted."

Carys hopped off the tree branch and passed Remy a skin of water.

"That simple," Remy said.

"Simple, yes. Easy, no." Bri gave Remy a strong clap on the shoulder, toppling her to the side. "We'll make a warrior of you yet."

They trekked through the heady perfume of garnet wildflowers, a trail of pollen strewn down the track, sparkling like gold dust. The air was so thick it felt hard to breathe. However grueling the trek through the Western Court had been, this was worse.

The leather straps dug into Remy's shoulders, her wet tunic chaffing against the pack with each step. Heather's face was tomato red, a thick sheen of sweat covering her skin. A sweat mark stamped Fenrin's chest.

When Remy saw Carys and Hale's packs on the ground up ahead, she thanked the Gods. They were getting a break at long last.

Her eyes followed the trail branching out from the main path up ahead, and she gasped. The path led to a clearing and, towering in the middle, was a gnarly ancient tree. Its twisting bare branches reached up in supplication. But it was not its size or its haunted bare limbs that made Remy gasp: it was the red ribbons tied to it. From each branch flowed long, waving scarlet ribbons, some of them bleached pink by the sun. They waved on the light breeze like strands of hair.

"What is this place?" Remy whispered, dropping her pack and stepping slowly forward. Her body felt lighter and lighter the closer she moved into the clearing.

"It's a prayer tree," Heather said from behind her. "A ribbon is hung with a prayer for the fallen."

"I have never seen anything like it," Remy said in awe.

"It is a practice of the Southern Court," Heather said, releasing a heavy sigh as her pack hit the ground.

Remy's gaze tore away from the towering tree at the sight of Hale kneeling in front of the trunk. His hand skimmed over something before him, and Remy stepped closer to see a small fountain. The copper basin had greened over time, water spilling over its sides only to be sucked up again into five arcing jets of water. The five jets, Remy mused, symbolized the five witch covens or perhaps the five Kingdoms of Okrith.

Hale's fingers traced symbols carved into a stone beside the fountain.

"What does this say?" he asked.

"It's Mhenbic," Fenrin said, panting as he walked over. "It says: 'In memory of our fallen family.'"

Remy stared at the fountain. It was the red witch magic that kept those streams of water moving. Red witches created this memorial. Only red witches and the High Mountain royal fae could cast the red magic that animated objects.

Remy felt the emotional punch to her chest as she looked back at those ribbons. There were hundreds of them, each one a memory. Someone had hung each ribbon as a prayer to a fallen loved one . . . and there were hundreds.

It reminded Remy of the Temple of Yexshire. The Temple had a flagpole on its highest spire, and every season the witches would add a red ribbon as a symbol of the city's prayers. The ribbons blowing in the wind were once a symbol of hope for the future; now they were symbols of mourning. Remy was certain whoever made this memorial was giving a nod to their homeland's landmark, the Temple of Yexshire.

Seeing those red ribbons flapping made Remy's throat constrict. The numbers of fallen were unfathomable, but seeing these ribbons waving along the branches made her clench her hands by her sides. This was the impact of the Siege of Yexshire. King Vostemur's shadow was seen even in the Southern Court.

Carys walked over to Remy, holding a long bundle of ribbon. The ball of red fabric was leaching of color. The heavy rains of the warm region aged the fabric. How long was this bundle of ribbon here? How many times had it needed to be replaced?

The fae warrior unwound a length of ribbon, pulling her dagger from her hip. She sliced through the fabric, passing the first stretch of ribbon to Remy. Carys passed out ribbons until each of their group held one.

Remy felt no weight to her body as she moved, like her soul was trying to flee the haunted setting. The group fanned out around the wide, knobby tree, each finding a branch.

Remy stood there, rubbing the fraying ribbon between her fingers. Heather and Fenrin muttered Mhenbic prayers to the witches' mother goddess in the moon. The witches prayed only to the goddess, but the fae were praying to their many gods as they hung ribbons. It seemed that they called upon every god to mourn the fallen witches and whispered promises to avenge them.

Remy had spoken those Mhenbic prayers so many times over the years with Heather and Fenrin. So many red witches had died to keep Remy and her secrets safe. At least Baba Morganna lived. Remy felt the pull behind her navel, tugging her back toward the High Mountains. She needed to find the High Priestess, needed to beg her forgiveness for all the witches who had sacrificed themselves for her.

Remy thought to their faces, to the handful of red witches who protected her for a year following the Siege of Yexshire. It had been the bloodiest year of her life. The horror of it all imprinted on her mind, never to be forgotten. And when the last witch fell, Heather was there, and she took Remy in. Remy was a terrified seven-year-old then. Heather had been strict but doting, pulling back together the parts of Remy that frayed like the ribbon between her fingers. There would not be enough red fabric to hang one for each of the witches she lost.

Remy opened her mouth to speak the Mhenbic words, but a different prayer came out. It was an ancient Yexshiri prayer, spoken only in the capital city of the High Mountain Court. Remy did not know how she remembered it, but the muscles in her throat seemed to recall.

"Immortal creators, guardians of the afterlife, wombs of this world, hear my prayer," she whispered. She could not roll the Yexshiri Rs as well as she once could, the chanted prayer in her head not matching with the sounds that escaped her mouth. "Guide these spirits into the afterlife. May they know your grace. May they feel your peace. Fill them with your eternal light."

Remy's fingers trembled as she knotted the ribbon to the tree. Invoking those ancient words felt like a hot poker to the chest, and it made her ache for her fallen family. She stared for a long time at that knotted ribbon, waving as though the spirits of her people blew them on an unfelt wind.

How many more ribbons would they add if Vostemur was not stopped? Would time forget the High Mountain Court? Would all the courts fall to the poisonous North?

A cool hand on the nape of Remy's neck made the tingling in her hands ebb. She looked over into Heather's hazel eyes, brimming with tears. Remy crumpled at that, throwing her arms around her guardian. She knew the same horrific memories flooded the brown witch at that moment. Heather's arms wrapped her tightly in a warm embrace. Remy clung to her guardian, burying her head into the brown witch's copper hair, breathing her soft lavender scent. Heather stroked a gentle hand up and down Remy's back. Even as the tiny insects of the humid jungle buzzed around her ears, Remy did not let go.

Fenrin approached in long strides. The young brown witch wrapped them both in his long arms, pulling them into his lean torso. He rested his chin on Heather's head. Remy wondered if Fenrin had hung a ribbon in honor of his parents. Fae slew his father in the witch hunts, the bloodlust of Northern soldiers driving them to murder more than only the red witches. Remy suspected she knew how his mother went, too, by her own hand, though they never spoke of it. They were both casualties of war in their own ways. Remy had never seen Fenrin mourn his parents, but she knew that broken heart of an orphan all too well.

The fae said nothing as the witches held each other. No one hastened them along. This moment was thirteen years in the making.

Remy clasped her trembling hands together behind Heather's back. It was not enough to hang ribbons anymore. Something had to be done. She felt the anger rising in her chest, the warm pull of her magic following. She knew then that she would do whatever it takes to find the High Mountain talismans, to use them to hack away at the Northern power, until she was certain that not another single ribbon was added to this tree.

"The Heir of Saxbridge is holding a game in Ruttmore in six nights' time," Hale said, tossing another stick onto the evening's fire. "The prize, it is rumored, is a very special ring."

Fenrin rolled his eyes at the title. Remy leaned her shoulder into him in a silent reprimand.

"The heir is in possession of the ring?" Heather narrowed her eyes at Hale from across the campfire. How had the heir to the Southern throne come into ownership of the long-lost High Mountain ring?

"What kind of game are we talking about? I can't imagine it being a gentleman's game if it is happening in the South." Talhan snorted.

The Southern Queen had buried her sorrows over the past thirteen years in bottles of wine and lavish parties. Her child was neither male nor female and preferred the title Heir of Saxbridge, rather than prince or princess.

"It's a poker game," Hale said.

"Of course it is," Carys sighed, swiping her braid over her shoulder.

The South ran rampant with drinking halls and pleasure houses. Something already predisposed the Southern fae to merriment. Their green witches, too, were renowned for enhancing pleasures: love potions, magic ales, and the most decadent and delicious of foods. Remy looked forward to heading into the heart of it. Only half a day's ride from the Queen's castle in Saxbridge, Ruttmore was equal parts decadent and seedy. It was where the rich fae went for their debauchery.

Fenrin turned to Hale. "Are you any good at the game?"

"Not particularly," Hale replied with a grin.

"Wonderful," Bri ground out.

"But I do not plan on obtaining the *Shil-de* ring through a betting game," Hale said, poking at the fire with a stick.

"Then what's the plan?" Bri asked, bringing the prince back to task. Remy grinned at Bri. Every word she spoke got right to the point.

"First, I want to authenticate that it is truly the *Shil-de* ring." Hale's gaze slid to Remy, shadows dancing across his face. "That's where you come in. Do you need to touch the ring to know of its power or will getting close enough do?"

"I don't know. I haven't been around many magical talismans." Remy didn't meet Hale's gaze. She hadn't looked him in the eyes since the night of the full moon.

"You are rubbing off on her," Talhan mumbled to his twin.

Remy had spent her entire life being discouraged from using her magic, and now she was being asked the nuances of its power.

"I will know for certain if I touch it, but I can usually feel power from a distance . . . I don't think I will be able to do it without revealing I am a witch, though."

If Remy reached out with her power, others could feel it, sense it too. If she used enough of it, she would glow red and then the game would be up.

She swatted at another bug that landed on her skin. The night was unpleasantly hot with the addition of the fire, but they needed it to cook their meal.

"That is why we reveal who you are up front," Hale said. Everyone's eyes turned to him.

"Are you insane?" Fenrin sputtered. "You want to waltz in there and reveal she is a red witch?"

"Not just any red witch," Hale said with a knowing smile. "*My* red witch."

Remy's heart skipped a beat as Hale reached into his pack and produced a thick leather cord. On it was a stone pendant engraved with the Eastern Court's crest: a lion's head over two waves.

"Absolutely not," Fenrin hissed, staring at the object: a witch's collar. It was a symbol of ownership that they forced upon witches in the Northern Court. Witches in service to rich and royal fae in other courts wore them too.

"It's okay, Fen," Remy murmured to her friend.

"It's not okay," Fenrin snapped at her, glaring at the prince. "Remy will never be your slave."

"It is not real," Hale said, grabbing two more collars out of his bag. "I had Tal carve these last night . . . they don't look that good under close inspection, but they will be enough to prove to any naysayers that you are mine."

"We belong to no one," Fenrin spat.

"Gods, you are a simple-minded one, aren't you?" Hale laughed.

"Watch it," Remy hissed. She could tolerate the prince's jibes, but no one insulted Fenrin except her.

Fenrin made to stand, but Heather put a hand on his shoulder and nudged him back down. Fighting with a fae prince was a bad idea. Remy wouldn't have stopped him, though. If he wanted to take a shot at the prince, she would have backed him. She bet it would be very satisfying to punch the prince in that gorgeous face.

"You'd rather swagger into Ruttmore with a bunch of drunk, rich, entitled fae and *not* have the protection of any court?" Carys asked pointedly to Fenrin.

Narrowing his gaze, Fenrin said nothing more.

Remy stood then on her sore legs. The fight training each morning was taking its toll on her overworked body. Still, she was far better now than she was on the first day.

She moved to Hale, grabbing the witch's collar out of the prince's hand. It was a simple leather cord with a metal clasp, nothing notable about it apart from the stone tag. How many witches wore these collars? How many felt safer for it? She bet no one.

"So I'm just meant to openly be a red witch?" The lines on Remy's brow creased as she looked at the collar in her hands. It was the exact opposite of what she'd been trying to do her whole life. Not having to hide her powers, to cast her magic with impunity . . . the idea was thrilling.

"King Vostemur, I am certain, has many more red witches alive in his dungeons than he will admit," Hale said, his voice on edge.

The prince took the collar out of Remy's hands and stood. He held it up to her with raised brows and waited for her to agree.

"But he extended his *grace* to the three remaining courts: he entitled each royal to one red witch," he said. Remy knew Vostemur didn't have the authority to be telling the other Courts of Okrith what to do . . . he also didn't have the authority to raze her homeland either. The Western, Southern, and Eastern Courts would only push back so much against the threat to the North. Following his rules about red witches seemed to be not worth the battle.

Lifting her hair, Remy dipped her head so that he could fasten the necklace to her.

"And you will be mine." His voice was a low rumble across the shell of her ear. His calloused fingers brushed her neck as he fastened the collar. Remy prayed Hale couldn't hear her heart pounding in her chest.

As she toyed with the stone pendant, Heather groaned. Her guardian's tight grip on self-control waned as she looked at the witch's collar encircling Remy's neck.

"It is only for a few days, Heather," Remy reassured her. "How else do you plan on getting us close enough to the ring? Think of what it could do in High Mountain fae hands?"

Heather's lips remained puckered, but she said no more.

"The brown witches shouldn't be coming with us," Bri cut in.

"We—" Fenrin scowled.

"Fae travel with witch servants all the time," Carys interjected.

"We are not your servants." Fenrin clenched his fists.

"Though much less mouthy ones," Talhan laughed. "A few balms and potions on the road are a welcome service. I've seen brown witches in fae entourages before."

"I still think we should cut them loose," Bri said, flipping her knife mindlessly in her hands.

"No!" Heather panicked at that, leaning closer to Remy. "We can act the part." Heather glanced at the prince. "We can do it. It will be fine."

"And what about him?" Bri waved her knife at Fenrin. "I'm sorry Fen, but you're clearly unwell."

The past few days, Fenrin's face had grown more flushed, his voice congested. His cough grew progressively worse. Heather grabbed a vial from her pocket and passed it to Fenrin. Remy noted the move and wondered how long Heather had been secretly caring for Fenrin. She chewed on the inside of her cheek. She hadn't been paying close enough attention to them.

"There are only so many potions," Bri said.

Surprise crossed Remy's face at the apologetic look Bri gave Fenrin. It was rare to see the fae warrior showing that kind of emotion.

"He needs rest," Bri continued, "not magic. You should stay here and we can double back for you."

"I'm fine." Fenrin coughed. "It's just a cold. It will be gone by tomorrow."

Remy knew Heather would never willingly leave her side, but she wondered if Bri was right. The Twin Eagles had taken a liking to Fenrin's company, but the warrior spoke the truth.

Hale bobbed his chin, "Fine. You can come." He passed the two witch's collars to Heather and Fenrin and reached back into his pack. "Tal, Bri," Hale said, throwing Bri a bag of coins.

Remy gaped. How much money did the prince travel with? No wonder his pack sounded like a boulder when it landed on the ground.

"Find horses and ride ahead," Hale said. "Secure lodgings at an inn outside Ruttmore. I don't want us staying in town in case we must make a hasty retreat. We'll arrive the day before the game to not arouse suspicion. We are on a quick holiday of drinking and debauchery, understood?" Carys's lips pulled up, a wicked gleam in her eye. "We leave as soon as the game's over. Oh," The prince added as the Twin Eagles stood. He tipped his head toward Remy. "And get some appropriate clothes."

Remy crinkled her nose at Hale.

Bri looked at the heavy bag in her hands and then looked to Remy. The warrior's golden eyes scanned Remy up and down, taking her measurements by sight alone. The fae female's face held a glimmer of twisted delight. Remy shook her head to Bri in silent protest.

Don't buy me anything stupid, she demanded with a stabbing look.

"Keep up your training with Carys," Bri said with a nefarious grin, winking.

Hauling up his pack, Talhan turned with no other parting, as though he had not been walking all day to get there, only to be sent off again. The Eagles would ride through the night, no questions asked.

CHAPTER NINE

The inn outside Ruttmore was nicer than any tavern Remy had ever seen. Swept floors, washed windows, no leaks fell from the roof, no tables tilted at odd angles. Even the courtesans by the bar dressed ornately in expensive jewelry and immaculate makeup. It was clear they entertained a well-off clientele.

The matron bustled into the main room of the inn to receive them. She was a short, round woman with smooth umber skin. She wore a low-cut, floral yellow dress and a corset that heaved up her ample bosom. A long, white feather adorned her brilliantly dyed red hair.

"Your Highness." She bowed with a flourish of her hand, her golden bangles jingling on her wrist. "It is an honor to have you stay with us."

"Thank you, your establishment is very pleasing indeed," Hale said, with all the practiced splendor of a royal.

The matron blushed and bowed again.

"The stable boy said you arrived on a wagon?" She asked. Remy watched the matron, worried that she'd uncover something about their ruse.

"We did," Hale laughed nonchalantly. He didn't seem troubled at all.

"Where are your horses?" The matron nosed.

"I'm in the market for some new ones, if you know any good places . . ." The matron lit up at that. Hale made it look easy.

"I have a cousin who can sort you out, Your Highness. The finest horses you've ever seen," she said. Remy was certain the innkeeper would be cut in on this deal if it were to take place. This was the woman who knew a person for every such need.

"Would you care for some food or drink, Your Highness? The chef is just starting a roast but we could set out a platter while it cooks . . ."

"No, that is quite all right," Hale said, surveying the room with casual indifference.

The four courtesans at the bar tittered to each other as they eyed Hale. Remy imagined they were wagering which one of them would successfully take him to bed. Without a thought, Remy stepped closer to Hale's side. If she was to be his witch, then these other women had better fear her. She gritted her teeth, staring daggers at them. She decided then and there if she was to pretend to belong to him, then he would equally belong to her. The courtesans' giggles turned to whispers.

"We have had a long day's ride, and we wish to rest before we begin our holiday." Hale slung his arm over Remy's shoulders, startling her. He must have noticed that small step closer.

She knew what being a royal prince's red witch implied. She knew magic wasn't the only service red witches often provided their lords. Remy stood taller, regardless, leaning into Hale with a nonchalant familiarity. It was an act, Remy told herself, but that didn't mean she couldn't enjoy it.

Remy heard shuffling behind her as Carys shifted in front of Heather and Fenrin. She knew the fae warrior was hiding the witches' looks of distaste at Hale's arm around her. Heather and Fenrin looked to the entire world like the traveling servants they were cast to be, laden with heavy packs.

Talhan thundered down the stairs, followed by Bri, a glass of ale already sloshing in his hands. His shirt was half unbuttoned showing off his huge, muscled chest. He swayed on drunken legs at the landing but as he neared them, Remy saw his eyes were sharp and clear. Talhan was acting too. This ruse perfectly cast him in the part of a fae male on holiday: that easy smile, that air of recklessness.

Talhan fit perfectly into line with the Ruttmore plans. Hale was, after all, the Bastard Prince of the East. Rumors of his drunken philandering had spread throughout the realm. Drinking and bedding his way through the South was what the world thought he would do. It was an excellent cover for obtaining the *Shil-de* ring . . . if only the brown witches and Remy played their part.

"Come on," Talhan called merrily to his comrades. His drink splashed as he pointed his glass toward the stairs. "I've got us rooms overlooking the river."

"I can arrange a romantic trip down the river for you and your witch, Your Highness, should you wish it." The matron offered with a plastered-on smile. No doubt the punter of the boat would be an employee of hers too. The matron was what Remy imagined she would find in the South: overly embellished clothes, dripping in jewelry, a caked-on face of makeup, and a penchant for revelry. She was equal parts innkeeper, actress, and pleasure house madam. So this was how the people of the Southern Court lived . . .

Hale dropped the arm from Remy's shoulders, wrapping his muscular hand around her stomach. He tugged her back against his broad chest, his hand splayed wide and possessive. Remy schooled her surprise. Letting out a tittering laugh, she rested her head against Hale's muscled shoulder. She prayed her act was as convincing as Talhan's. She needed everyone in this town convinced that she was the toy of a powerful and careless prince. No more witch hunters could think she was up for grabs.

"Perhaps another night," the prince said, smirking at Remy. "Tonight we go into Saxbridge to have a bit of fun." He winked at the innkeeper and she returned it with a knowing smile.

"If you would care for any recommended establishments," she said with a flourish of her hand. The way she said *establishments* told Remy exactly what she meant. "Or any bookings, please let me know how I can be of service, Your Highness. Enjoy your stay."

She bowed one more time and tottered off to the bar. The courtesans all leaned into the matron to whisper about what had just passed.

They climbed the stairs and out of sight into a narrow and dimly lit hallway. Carys grabbed the pack off Heather. The brown witch sighed as the fae warrior lightened her load. Bri took Hale's pack from Fenrin. He shook out his sore arms and gave her a begrudging nod of thanks.

Talhan handed Heather a key.

"Your room," he said, nodding to the first door down the hall. Fenrin frowned. All witches knew the first door on the first floor of a tavern was a cursed door. It was the smallest room cut off by the stairs. It was the loudest door of any inn, too, and it would be sure to be a challenging time sleeping in it.

"Be grateful I didn't throw you in the servant's lodgings by the stables," Talhan said, reading the look on Fenrin's face. "I figured the witches of the prince should have at least some comfort."

"How generous," Fenrin groused.

Talhan looked to Carys. "The three of us are at the end of the hall on the left." The female fae shouldered her bag and took off in that direction with no more prompting. Talhan passed a key to Hale. "And you two are up two more flights in the corner room, naturally."

"You two?" Remy asked, darting looks between Talhan and Hale.

Talhan scrunched his face at her, waiting for her to catch on. His brows lifted as if to say: *you are his red witch, what were you expecting?* Remy's cheeks reddened. She should have assumed as much.

Heather moved to interject as another patron's footsteps sounded on the stairs. Remy quickly grabbed the key from Talhan and shouted, her voice an octave too high, "Come, Your Highness, let us go see our view."

"With pleasure." Hale guffawed, hurrying Remy along as she pretended to shriek in delight.

Remy had seen this flirtatious act play out so many times in so many taverns. She never thought she would be one of those women, yet here she was, pretending to be the lover of a prince.

She glanced over her shoulder, seeing Fenrin stare her down, his cheeks flushed red and something between anger and amusement playing across his face. Fenrin had never thought he would pretend this way either. Remy couldn't deny the twinge of guilt that hit her as she realized she was the reason they had dragged him into this. Perhaps Bri was right after all. Perhaps it would be kinder to Heather and Fenrin if she cut them loose.

Bri caught Remy's arm before Remy could move past to the stairwell.

"I left an outfit on the bed for you to wear today. Your other apparel and shoes are in the wardrobe," she said with a smile.

"How much did you buy?" Remy asked.

Bri shrugged. "Not too much."

"Did you spend all my money?" Hale laughed.

"You didn't want us to spend it all?" Bri smirked, passing them and stalking off down the hall.

The corner suite of the inn was the finest room in the place. The large windows looked over both the turquoise river and the verdant gardens. A giant four-poster bed sat against the far wall, billowing white curtains flowing from each post. A sitting area with a blue velvet couch and two matching armchairs were arranged in one corner. Bookcases framed either side of a fireplace with a fire already burning away. Another door led into a bathing chamber holding a giant marble tub.

Remy gawked, looking around the room. It was fit for a queen. She glanced at Hale as he watched her with a smug expression. She supposed they designed it to fit royalty, since he was, in fact, a prince. His status hadn't confronted her so much as it had in this moment. They had travelled through the woods and backcountry. There had been no praise or fawning over Hale as they journeyed this far. But now, in fae society, he held himself differently. He acted like he was aware of the deferential stares of the surrounding people. He stood straighter, his chin tilted higher. It made Remy wonder if she knew which face was the mask and which one was real.

A new traveling pack for the prince already sat on a low table next to a grand armoire, open and overflowing with clothes. A red, floor-length gown hung prominently on the hook behind the door.

"You did well," Hale said, sitting in one of the velvet armchairs. He removed his boots and set them by the fire.

"Thanks . . ." Remy said, still staring at the enormous bed.

"It probably is as comfortable as you're guessing," Hale followed her gaze, "but we will be out for most of the night tonight. Tomorrow when we return from the game, successful or not, we will make a hasty exit."

"Such a waste." Remy pouted at the luxurious white linen.

"Indeed." Hale laughed.

Remy sensed him watching her. He held her eyes for a moment too long before she broke their stare. It was the first time she had looked into those gray eyes since the night of the full moon. She doubled her efforts to avoid that magnetizing face.

Hale moved to his old pack against the wall. Fishing something out of the bottom pocket, he handed it to Remy.

"Here," Hale said, "put this on your necklace."

Necklace. He said it as if the collar were a piece of jewelry and not a symbol of ownership. Still, Remy held out her hand and accepted the golden ring the prince passed her. She turned it over in her fingers. HN, his initials, engraved the golden surface. Remy untied her collar and threaded the ring through.

"But I am wearing your family's crest already?" Remy questioned, pursing her lips at the ring on the collar.

"Yes, but that ring says you do not belong to my family . . . you belong to me." His words dropped into a low rumble. An unknown heat deep in Remy rumbled along with it. *You belong to me.* "It also says I treat you well and that I trust you not to run off with my gold."

Remy finished clasping the collar back on her neck. She reached under her tunic and into the hidden pocket sewn into the lining, pulling out her totem bag.

As Remy opened the small pouch, the sound of the ring on her stone tag clinked along her collar. Remy produced a long length of red string from the bag, then closed it and tucked the bag back in her pocket.

"What is that?" Hale asked, looking at the string.

"Give me your wrist," Remy instructed. The prince narrowed his eyes at her but did as she said. Remy wrapped the string around the prince's wrist, once, twice, three times and then tied it in a neat knot.

"There," she said. Still holding the prince's wrist, she refused to look into his smoky gray eyes as she said, "Now you belong to me too."

Hale's pulse hammered against her fingertips.

Hale shook his head and said, "Good thinking, Red," winking.

"My name is Remy."

"Remy." He nodded softly, turning to the armoire. The prince took his time scanning her figure and then a wicked smile appeared on his handsome face as he said, "Ready for your acting debut . . . Remy?"

Remy stood at the first-floor landing and rapped on the door in front of her. Heather opened it on the first knock. Seeing it was Remy, she stepped out into the hallway, shutting the door behind her.

"What's going on? Are you ready?" Remy asked, shifting back and forth. They were heading into Saxbridge for lunch with the Heir to the Southern Court. Remy could hardly contain her excitement. She had always wanted to see the Southern Court's capital city, half an hour's carriage ride from Ruttmore.

Heather's hazel eyes skimmed over Remy, and she smiled. Remy wore the duck-egg-blue dress that Bri had left laid out on the giant bed. The lightweight fabric had a high boatneck that hid most of her witch's collar. She wanted to keep it that way, but the point was for it to be seen, so she forced herself to pull it from under her dress and lay it on top in prominent display. Her dress clung around the bust and top ribs, spreading out from her waist into a bell-shaped skirt that landed at her ankles. The dress had short, sheer sleeves slitted so her shoulders peeked through. Remy wore her hair tied in a low ponytail, her hair extra voluminous in the Southern humidity. A few escaping curls framed her face. She wore round, silver stud earrings that matched her flat silver slippers. It was a modest outfit compared to the opulence she had seen others wearing, but it was perfect for a member of a royal's entourage.

"You look so beautiful," Heather said. She reached out her hand and tenderly stroked a sheer sleeve between her fingers. "This is a fine dress. You look like a queen. You look like your mother."

Heather gave Remy a sad smile. Remy had forgotten that Heather had lived in Yexshire for a time. She had known her mother, though they never spoke about her. This is the closest they ever came to speaking of secrets they kept locked tightly away.

"Are you not coming?" Remy asked, looking to the door shut behind Heather.

"Fenrin is still a little under the weather today," Heather said with an unconcerned shrug. "I will stay back and make some more medicine for him. It will be no problem."

"But . . . Saxbridge." Remy's eyebrows lifted. "Don't you want to see it?"

"I have been there before, actually." Heather's smile was soft. It was then Remy realized how little she knew of who Heather was before the brown witch had taken her in. "Once in my youth. It was beautiful. I'm excited for you to see it."

Remy clasped her hands in front of her. She didn't know much about Heather at all. She blamed Heather for their boring, backcountry lives but Heather could have had a much more exciting one were it not for Remy. The brown witch sacrificed her own life to hide Remy's secrets.

"You don't mind me going without you?" Remy asked, squinting at her guardian.

"You have told me time and time again that you are not a child." Heather's cheeks dimpled. A strand of her copper hair fell free of her bun and she tucked it behind her ear. "These past weeks have shown it to me more clearly. I'm sorry it took me so long to listen."

Remy swallowed. She never expected Heather to acknowledge her as an adult. She thought if it were up to the brown witch she would go on doting and fussing over Remy forever.

"You don't need to worry," Remy said, even though she knew Heather would, because worrying about Remy was what she did best. "I will have four fae warriors around to protect me."

"I wish there were more, but I'll accept it." She chuckled, cupping Remy's cheek. "You are priceless, Remini." Remy stilled at her full name. "Do not forget your purpose. Do not forget who you truly are."

Remy's heart beat faster as she nodded to Heather. Her purpose had only ever been to stay alive and keep hidden. There had never been a plan beyond that. She wanted to ask Heather what came next. What happened beyond the hiding? But they never talked like this. Now, as she was showing herself in the world, it seemed she needed reminding.

"I won't forget," Remy said, looking at her hands.

"Let's go, Rem!" Talhan called from the floor below. The rest of their fae companions waited at the bar.

"I should go," Remy said sheepishly. It felt strange to leave Heather behind.

"Have fun," Heather said. It might have been the first time Heather had said that to her in her entire life. "But be careful with that prince."

There it was. Remy couldn't help but chortle at her guardian's warning.

"Always warning me away from the boys, Heather." Remy laughed.

"I'm not talking about blushing at some fiddle player, Remy." Heather pressed her thin lips together. So she had noticed the fiddler player's looks then. "I see the way you look at that prince. It is something more than flirtation."

Pulse drumming in her ears, Remy looked away. She hated that Heather could see all that. Her guardian was willing to say the things that Remy wouldn't, even in her own mind.

Remy opened her mouth to deny it, but Talhan called out again, "Come on! I'm hungry!"

Heather's lips pulled up at his proclamation, but she kept her eyes fixed on Remy. "Just . . . be careful with him. Remember who you are," she reminded her ward again.

Remy chewed on her bottom lip and bobbed her chin.

Remember who you are.

It was the one thing she wished she could forget.

CHAPTER TEN

W hite flagstones baked below their feet, the air warm and humid. It felt as hot as the peak of the Western summer, even though Remy knew the Autumnal Equinox was mere days away. She was grateful for the billowy light dress that Bri had picked for her.

The rest of the fae wore similar light fabric trousers and short-sleeved tunics. But they remained covered in leather belts and back-straps, armed to the teeth with weapons. They looked less rough in Saxbridge; even as menacing warriors they looked like refined fae out on the town. The Twin Eagles and Carys all wore straight-legged, moon-gray trousers. The Eagles favored tunics the shade of golden-rod that made their eyes seem to glow, while Carys picked violet, the color of the Eastern Court.

Everywhere around them, fae walked informally through the shopping precinct, wearing every color of the rainbow. The brilliant colors matched the tropical flowers bursting from planters placed around large, white marble columns. In the Western Court everyone wore muted earth tones. It was a celebration for the eyes to see so many colors and fabrics. The shopping fae around them slowed or paused as Hale's crew walked past. They were sure to be the talk of the town soon. Gossip would fly about the Bastard Prince being in Saxbridge.

Hale looked ever the swaggering prince in his lightweight pewter tunic. Covered in intricate embroidery of silver, gold, and light blue, it matched his fitted trousers, the same duck-egg blue as Remy's dress. Bri had dressed Remy to match the prince she was pretending to serve.

Pointedly looking from her dress, Remy gave Bri a sideways glance and Bri shrugged, "It's the fashionable color here—what can I do?"

"Likely story," Remy jeered. Hale's golden ring clinked against the stone tag of the witch's collar with her every step. "I see you and Talhan *and* Carys all found different colors."

"They didn't have any in your size," Bri shot back with a grin. The Eagle knew what she was doing.

They continued along the grand outdoor mall. Domed white and tiled roofs peeked up beyond its high walls. In the farthest distance was a giant, golden geodesic dome, sitting like a crown in the skyline. A forest-green pennant waved in the wind from its peak. Emblazoned on it in gold was the flowering tree of the Southern Court crest. That must be the castle of Saxbridge.

Remy felt another crowd of fae eyes upon her. The scrutiny in them was relentless as they looked her up and down. Snickering, they noted her rounded ears and her witch's collar. Remy ground her teeth together. She bowed her head, shoulders deflating a bit into the stance she had assumed for most of her life.

Carys's light touch on her elbow pulled her out of her spiraling thoughts.

"Chin up," Carys said through smiling lips.

Remy straightened and looked to the female fae. Her white-blonde hair was not in its traditional braid but unbound, flowing down her back. She looked elegant and showy, like a princess. She would look perfect draped on Hale's arm. Remy's gut tightened. She needed to stop thinking that way. Carys said that they were not together. She needed to let go of this story she was telling herself about them. Carys had only ever been kind to her. But even now, when she saw Carys's beauty and thought about her and Hale sharing a bed in the past . . . it made her want to punch her fist through one of these marble columns.

They neared a pavilion crowded with seating areas of white tables and chairs. Remy's stomach rumbled as the warm aromas of coffee, ginger, turmeric, and cloves wafted to her. She had heard the food in the Southern Court surpassed anything else in the realm.

As they neared the seating area, an opening at the very edge came into view. A ring of empty tables surrounded a person sitting by the balcony. The figure's shoulders hunched over a book. Beyond that lone person lay beautiful, manicured gardens. A long, rectangular reflection pool bisected the lush foliage. A thin white gravel promenade wrapped around its crystal-clear water. Small groups of fae sashayed around it, taking in the gardens.

"Neelo!" Hale called.

The person sitting in the untouched corner of the café lifted their head.

"Thank you for agreeing to lunch." Hale reached out and shook their hand as they begrudgingly put a bookmark into their tome and laid it on the table in front of them.

As Remy neared, she took in the sight of the withdrawn bookworm. They were nothing like Remy had imagined they would be.

The Heir of Saxbridge had strong cheekbones, thick lashes, and a rounded jaw. As most natives to the Southern Court, they had dark red-brown skin. Their slender fae ears poked out through their thick, straight black hair, which was tied in a knot at the nape of their neck.

This was the face of Neelo Emberspear, Heir to the Southern Court. They sat small and stooped, despite their muscled frame and hefty weight. Their unusual aesthetic was an androgynous mixture of fae beauty and strength.

Hooded brown eyes watched Remy approach as the rest of the fae took their seats around the table.

"Neelo, this is my new red witch, Remy," Hale said, waving a hand at her.

Neelo gave Remy a prompt, grim look and said, "Pleasure" before looking back out over the gardens.

They wore an oversized, long-sleeved, black jacket, the black a stark contrast to the light colors worn by everyone around them. A thick, golden rope, tied in an intricate knot, held the jacket together. The rope belt was purely decorative, a sign of the Southern Court's wealth. Neelo's charcoal gray pants were simple and narrow, showing off strong, muscular legs. It was far too much clothing for the Southern Court's muggy climate, but not a single spot of sweat dripped down Neelo's face. They must dress like this all of the time if they were so acclimated to the hot weather.

Remy sat in a chair between Hale and Carys, looking over the grounds. Green witches were the caretakers of the botanical gardens before them. Not a single weed grew. Okrith's best gardeners perfectly positioned every flower and shrub like a living painting. Brilliant green parrots flew from tall palm trees, squawking in a strange sing-song Remy had never heard before. The Southern Court was enchanting. Remy felt Hale's eyes watching as she drank in its beauty. She still refused to meet his gaze.

"Where did you find a red witch?" Neelo said, their attention fixed on the reflection pool.

"In the Western Court," Hale boasted. He spoke as if Remy were a treasure that he had stumbled upon.

"Are there any more red witches in the West who would like a patron?" Neelo's brown eyes slid to Remy.

"Not that I know of," Remy hedged. Neelo pursed their lips at her. She wasn't sure how to speak to the Heir of Saxbridge. They didn't seem particularly welcoming.

Remy had only ever known fae as males or females. The fae were not men and women like the witches and humans—they were different creatures. But the heir was neither male nor female, neither prince nor princess, and it left Remy feeling on the back foot at what she should say to Neelo, fearful that she would offend them.

Everyone else seemed so at ease with what to say and do. Remy felt a rising tide of shame that she had never considered a person like

Neelo before. She had met feminine men and masculine women, like Bri . . . but she had met no one who existed outside of that dynamic entirely, like Neelo. Remy grimaced. Maybe she had and didn't even realize.

"Thank you for meeting with us. You know how I love the food here," Hale said. He looked over his shoulder to a waiter and mimed a drink. That seemed to be enough information as the waiter scurried away.

"I was required to conduct another outing this week," Neelo said, tracing the gold embossing of a serpent on the cover of their book. "My mother will be pleased."

"Still making you show yourself about town?" Hale asked with a chuckle.

"It's getting worse now that I'm of eligible age." Neelo pushed their jaw to the side. Remy looked over the Heir of Saxbridge. They must be eighteen. Something about them seemed much older and much younger at the same time.

The Queen of the Southern Court and her heir subverted the traditional parent-child relationship. The Queen was a wild reveler, and Neelo seemed levelheaded and quiet. She had heard so many wild stories about the Southern Court Queen. Remy wondered what it must be like to be the child of an oversexed Queen who bragged about her parties and orgies around a dinner table. What expectations did that put on an introverted child?

"What other debauchery has your mother scheduled for you this season?" Hale asked, like he did not care, but everyone around the table listened more intently.

"Ugh, everything is a game to her. She's arranged duels where the winner gets to promenade with me around the gardens, an archery tournament I must attend, and, oh, there's this card game tomorrow night." Neelo frowned. "Mother has long been in possession of a High Mountain ring."

"The *Shil-de* ring?" Hale mused.

Neelo leveled him with a look and said, "Yes."

"Why would Queen Emberspear not wear it herself?" Remy asked.

All eyes turned to her, and she instantly regretted speaking. It was not their goal to convince the queen to keep the ring.

"Because it would take all the fun out of her revels if she knew the games of fire spinning and poison drinking could not harm her," Carys cut in with an annoyed tone.

"I've missed you Carys." Neelo laughed morosely. Carys winked at Neelo. So the two of them knew each other too. Carys didn't look like a Southern Court fae, but, now that Remy thought about it, the fae warrior had a hint of a Southern lilt. Her words always seemed to go up at the end of her sentences. Remy spoke all the three languages of Okrith: Ific, the common tongue, Mhenbic, the witch's language, and Yexshiri, the native tongue of the High Mountain Court. "So she's gambling away a priceless talisman for fun?" Remy furrowed her brow. All the eyes looked at her again. She should really stop talking. It was their goal to get this ring after all.

"You mean rather than give it to her only child?" Neelo's voice dripped with sarcasm. "Yes. The Queen doesn't think to the future or to whoever might possess the ring if it leaves the Southern Court." Neelo looked to Hale again. "I know you're terrible with cards, but you're welcome to come."

Yes. An invitation.

"You know I'm always up for a bit of fun." Hale gave Neelo that charming smile of his. It did nothing to Neelo's gloomy facial expression. Remy liked that. The prince's charms did not work on the Heir of Saxbridge. It was nice to see him knocked down a peg.

"It's at nine o'clock at the Crownwood Parlor in Ruttmore," Neelo said. "Come if you like."

The edge of the promenade led right under the café balcony. People lingered along it to gawk at them. The two heirs to the different thrones were far more fascinating than the gardens. Neelo looked to the group with a stony, tight face but bowed their head. The flustered group responded with flourished, deep bows to the heir. This was part of the royal world: bowing, simpering onlookers.

A server arrived with a tray of steaming hot coffees in painted ceramic teacups. They placed a miniature mug before Remy. She looked at the thick black liquid inside. It smelled nutty and spicy, unlike anything she had smelled before. She looked around the table as the fae all picked up their delicate cups and began sipping. No one added cream or sugar like they did with tea, Remy noted. What was this strange elixir they called coffee?

She lifted her cup and took the smallest sip. Her eyebrows shot up into her hairline. The strong, bold flavor blasted over her tongue and down her throat. Bri chuckled at her as she took another sip. Remy wished they drank their coffee with cream and sugar to cover the bitterness. A pleasant warmth spread through her body though, along with an electrical current of sudden energy. She took another sip of the bold, revitalizing drink, its flavor more pleasant on the second try.

Another server arrived and laid out a huge tray that ran the length of their table. A selection of breads and crackers ringed the edges of the tray while the middle held an assortment of dented copper bowls.

Talhan pointed to the bright red sauce in the center. "Careful with that one," he said to Remy with a wink.

The Twin Eagles descended on the tray, grabbing crispy round crackers to scoop up food from the bowl of yellow potato and beans.

Remy grabbed a triangle of soft, buttery bread and dipped it in a warm, thick mixture. She took a tentative bite. A spicy explosion of ginger, cumin, and chilies burst into her mouth. Remy had to force down the indecent noises she wanted to make. It tasted that good. These green witches may seem passive, but their magic was as powerful as any other. Remy felt like she was floating outside her body—the flavors dancing on her tongue pulled her into the clouds better than any alcohol she had ever drunk.

"Good, right?" Talhan said through a greedy mouthful of food.

Remy hummed happily as she bobbed her head and reached for another cracker.

They sat eating and sipping coffee, delighting in the sunny splendor of the Southern Court for several hours. Plenty of time to get them noticed by all the highborn fae in the capital city. By the time a tray of little powdered cakes appeared in front of them, the sun was setting behind the garden's distant palm trees. The sky was pink and orange, as if even the sun painted with more colors in the Southern Court.

A string quartet had set up on the grass near the café, ready to entertain the evening crowds. The lively music mixed with the decadent food and balmy evening air. Remy felt even more overcome by the melodies as the coffee switched to honeyed wine. Her entire body felt like it was vibrating, every sense in her stretched to its fullest. She would never forget this moment in the Southern Court.

Carys reached out and grabbed Remy's hand, pulling her to stand. "Come on," she said, her bright blue eyes twinkling at Remy. "Let's go dance."

"I don't know how to dance." Remy yanked back on Carys's arm, but the fae warrior merely tugged harder.

"I will show you, it's easy." She laughed, swaying to the sounds. She was bubbly and loose from all that wine.

Carys guided Remy down the marble steps of the café and onto the grass past the white gravel promenade. A few other fae had gathered here in front of the orchestra and were dancing in spirited couples. Carys wrapped her hand around Remy's back and pulled Remy to stand in front of her.

"I'll lead." Carys giggled. Her cheeks were rosy as she moved. The Southern Court was working its magic on her too. "Put your hand on my shoulder."

Remy did. Carys took her other hand and guided her into a simple box step.

"I thought you didn't know how to dance?" Carys asked as Remy followed her lead.

"I don't . . . not really," Remy said, falling into a simple rhythm along to the slow tune. "I learned a little when I was a young child. I think it's just muscle memory."

A few of the other couples circled closer for a better look. Carys simply offered them an effortless, if not slightly patronizing, smile.

"Do you know them?" Remy whispered.

"Some of them, yes," Carys said through her smile. She twirled Remy further away from the onlookers, dipping Remy low with a laugh. "This will give them something to talk about."

"You used to live here?" Remy asked, clinging to Carys as she hoisted her onto her feet.

"I grew up here," Carys said. Remy squinted at her. "My parents were Northerners by blood but they both grew up here too . . . it's a long story."

Remy pursed her bottom lip over her teeth. It probably wasn't a long story, only one that Carys didn't want to tell. The song slowed, and Carys spun Remy one more time before they both dropped into a bow to each other.

Polite clapping sounded from around and above them. Remy looked up to see Bri, Talhan, and Hale leaning over the balustrade, watching the two of them. Hale's white teeth gleamed as he smiled at them, but Remy could tell from her periphery that his eyes bored into her with an intensity that did not match that charming smile.

The music picked up into a faster tune, and Carys swept Remy away from that intense look. She moved her in wide, arcing circles until Remy's head was spinning. Her feet stumbled a few times at the quick, side-skipping steps. She kept pace, though, moving in time with the female fae, but Remy breathed a sigh of relief when the song slowed to its final notes. Panting from the exertion, she bowed to Carys again. Another round of polite clapping. She sensed Hale's eyes upon her still, but she didn't dare look his way.

Talhan's voice pulled them from beginning the next dance.

"Off to do some shopping. See you later," he called to the two of them with a wink. They knew what he was off to buy: an item needed for the game tomorrow night. He turned to Neelo and said, "Care to join me?"

"That would be a no, Tal," Neelo said, their eyes glued back on the pages of their book. Talhan shrugged and kept walking.

"Enough with this dancing," Bri said, leaning on one elbow, effortlessly swinging her legs over the ledge and landing on her feet before them. "It's time to train."

"What, here? Now?" Remy balked as Bri handed Remy a dagger and unsheathed her sword. It had been nearly a week since she had seen Bri. The training with Carys had been much less grueling.

"Yes, here. Now." Bri smirked. Her golden eyes also gleamed with too much honey wine. "Time to burn off all that coffee."

"I'm too full," Remy groaned. The tight waistline to her dress felt like it was cutting into her. She should have stopped eating when it tightened, but the food was too good.

Bri leaned in and said quietly, "We're here to be noticed. Think of all the tales of the Eastern Prince's ruffians sparring in the gardens."

Bri didn't give Remy enough time to respond as she swung her sword. Remy lifted the dagger in her hand to block. The surrounding crowd gasped. The dancing couples around them moved out of the line of attack.

Bri shoved Remy playfully. She hooted and ran down the promenade. Remy laughed, chasing after her. Carys was only a step behind, taking out her own sword as she ran. Bri leapt onto the lip of the reflection pool as Remy swung for her legs. Bri easily jumped the sword and swiped back at Remy. Carys entered the fray, and they took turns trading strikes and blocks. This wasn't like their real training. Bri pulled every strike and Carys moved at half her usual speed. This was all for show. Remy couldn't contain the laughter that erupted from her as they moved. She felt like a child chasing Fenrin around with a stick again.

Carys leapt onto the edge of the reflection pool to attack Bri. The two parlayed, balancing along the thin stone. Remy couldn't help the thought that crossed her mind. A little voice inside her nudged her to do it. She rushed forward, throwing out her red magic, causing the two fae to plummet into the reflection pool.

Carys floundered when she hit the water and then popped back up, laughing so hard she didn't make a sound. She dipped her hair into the water again to slick it back off her face.

"You witch!" Bri shouted, though her wet face was still grinning. She turned to Remy. "What are you laughing at?" She yanked the red witch in with them.

The cool water was welcome from the sultry evening air. Remy wiped back the hair stuck on her face. Her body shook with unstoppable laughter.

The three of them sat there in shoulder-deep water on the smooth tiles of the pool. A whole crowd had gathered around the edge. Bri turned her golden amber eyes on them and they all scattered.

"Ah, that was fun." Carys smiled as her hands swirled idly through the water.

Remy's cheeks hurt from smiling. Her core felt like she had just done a hundred sit-ups. She had used her magic. In public. And no one had run away or screamed.

She heard crunching gravel and looked over to see Hale standing with his arms crossed over his chest, smirking at the three of them.

"Ladies," he said as one cheek dimpled. "You put on quite a show."

"Care to join us?" Carys taunted, flicking water at him.

"I think perhaps we should take a turn around the promenade to dry off a bit before calling a carriage back to Ruttmore." Remy kept her eyes on the whorls of water as he spoke. "I don't want to spend a bag of gold on compensating the carriage owner for ruining their upholstery."

Bri snorted but stood. Carys and Remy followed. As Remy moved to climb out of the pool, Hale's hand appeared. He offered it out to her expectantly, and she reluctantly took it. After she climbed out of the pool, she moved to let go of his hand but he said, "Walk with me."

She wasn't sure if it was a request or command as he released her hand and offered his elbow. Remy felt the eyes of people on her and knew she shouldn't refuse. She took his arm and let him guide her down the long walk, leaving a trail of dripping water in her wake.

CHAPTER ELEVEN

I f they had been in the West, Remy would be freezing. Her wet
dress clinging to her curves would have made her shiver. The
slightest breeze would have made her teeth chatter.

But in the Southern Court . . .

The warm air twined around her legs. The evening breeze danced
with the floral scent of night-blooming flowers. And the Prince of the
Eastern Court radiated heat all along her right-hand side.

The fabric of her dress was light and quick-drying. Remy
welcomed the darkening night as she feared her dress might be
sheer when wet. The trail of dripping water behind her had long
stopped as they crunched their way down the white gravel
promenade.

They walked in tense silence for many paces. Remy pretended she
was looking at all the unusual tropical plants, but she was aware of
those gray eyes upon her. They entered a smaller path that snaked its
way through large bushes with waxy leaves and maroon flowers. It
was darker on this trail. The umbrella-shaped trees obscured the last
light of the setting sun. Tea light lanterns were lit at regular intervals
along the path. Remy wondered if there was a servant lighting candles
up ahead, even still. How many tiny candles did they have to light

every night? These were questions the fae probably never asked themselves.

The parrots nesting in the palm trees were quiet now, only the softest tittering as they settled to sleep. In the silence she heard Hale's slow, steady breaths. She could hear her own heart beating through her ears. She knew keenly that no other eyes could see them now. They were alone.

"You've been avoiding me," Hale said to the night air. Remy thought it would be a relief for one of them to speak, but now she wished for that awkward silence again.

"That's ridiculous. I am right here, holding your arm," she replied, giving too much of her attention to the yellow-leafed shrub illuminated by a lantern.

"You haven't looked me in the eye since the night of the full moon," Hale said.

Ah yes. That night.

Four witch hunters had nearly killed Remy. The past weeks of training with Bri and Carys had helped her nerves some. Though she wasn't planning on dueling with four fae males anytime soon, she felt like at least she knew how to hold a weapon now. Remy knew the attack wasn't what Hale was talking about. It was what happened after on the trail around Silver Sands Harbor and in that cabin after the full moon had whispered her mother's words to her. Something had shifted between them, something intangible that the harder Remy tried to grasp, the more it evaded her. She wasn't sure what that feeling was, but it frightened her to know that Hale felt it too.

"I think we should head back," Remy said, peeling her arm off Hale's. She was doing precisely what he had accused her of: avoiding him. But she didn't care. She made one quick step down the path and Hale caught her hand.

"Remy." The weight of him wielding that word felt like a boulder on her chest. "Look at me."

Remy relented, looking up into those smoky gray eyes. She felt her emotions pull in every direction. It was new, thrilling, terrifying and yet also . . . familiar, comforting. Her chest tightened. She wasn't sure how many disparate feelings she could hold at once. She wondered if anyone else ever felt that way, like they were free falling every time they looked into a person's eyes.

Not any person. Just this one person.

Remy didn't know how to look at him. She wasn't sure how much he saw. She wondered if Hale felt that same pull looking into her brown eyes, if he'd get trapped falling into the flecks of green. She tried to keep her expression determinedly neutral, if not slightly perturbed.

The dimples flashed on Hale's cheeks, but his voice filled with gravel as he simply said, "Hi."

How could she feel that one syllable word echoing through her entire body? The things that sound did to her.

"Hi," she replied breathlessly.

It had to be the Southern Court and the honey wine. The food and drink, the sweet smells, the warm air: it had made her drunk on revelry. She had danced in the twilight, dueled in a fountain, and now she wanted to kiss a prince in a hidden garden. But it was not her doing, it was all the magic of the Southern Court, she reassured herself.

Hale looked down to where their fingers still interlocked.

"I'm sorry," he said. "For that night and for what I said. I've wanted to apologize every day since, but you've been keeping away from me."

"I . . . ," Remy said, struggling to find the words she wanted to say.

"That day really frightened me," Hale said. "More than I was willing to admit. And I felt responsible—*feel* responsible, for your safety."

"Right." A long-held breath escaped Remy's lips. He was feeling guilty about the attack. That's what he had meant.

"I pulled you into this," Hale said. "I asked you to come with us. I made you put yourself in danger and I promised I would protect you."

"You have protected me. You did protect me," Remy said. Hale shook his head like he wouldn't believe it was true. "And Bri and Carys are helping me to take care of myself."

"You don't give yourself enough credit," Hale said. "You were brave and powerful before their training too. You fought off those fae. If there had been even one fewer, you would have dispatched them all."

She noted the way he said dispatched. He did not want to say kill. But she had killed one of them, and he had killed the rest. It still bothered her, the fact that she had killed that fae. Training with Bri had not lessened that feeling, but it had taught her that the feeling was okay. All warriors carried the ghosts of those they killed with them. Bri made it okay to feel powerful, to know that she would kill again if it came to it.

"You better watch out." Remy tried to lighten the tone. "I won't need much protecting after another few sessions with them."

Hale gave her a half-grin. "I don't doubt it. They are some of the most skilled fighters I know. Although . . ." He looked at the trees over her shoulder. "Seeing you tackle them into a pool is something I won't be soon forgetting."

A flush blanketed Remy's skin. She had tackled them into a pool with her magic. Her hair was almost dry now and coiled tighter from the water of the reflection pool. A few perfect ringlets framed her face.

"So you accept my apology?" Hale said.

"There's nothing to apologize for . . ." Remy said. Hale opened his mouth but Remy continued, "You saved me that day and if another day like that happens, though I hope it won't, you have my permission to save me again." She tried to add a lighthearted laugh, but it felt strained. "I'm sure you protect all your assets well."

Hale recoiled, his mouth tightening, forehead crinkling.

"I shouldn't have said that." He fiddled with the red string around his wrist. "Yes, I am grateful that we have found a red witch to help us. It would be impossible to acquire those talismans without you, but . . . your life means more to me than that."

Remy turned those words around in her mind, picking them apart in different ways. Her life meant more to him than what? Than only being a useful tool in their quest for the High Mountain talismans? What did "more" mean? Remy did not know. *Ugh*, she thought, *these bloody fae and their half-truth words.*

She looked up at him. His hair fell across his forehead as he bent to look at her. Remy's fingers twitched with the urge to brush it off his face. Nibbling her lip, she knew she wanted to find an excuse to touch him. When she was pretending to be his red witch, it was the closest to an honest feeling she had. He had caught her in this spider's web. She did not know how to untangle herself from what was real and what was pretend.

Remy was sick of these cycling thoughts. She wanted to give herself over to the heady music and sweet fragrances and reckless abandon. Enough of wishing to do things and never doing them. She smoothed Hale's hair off his forehead. That wavy, brown hair was as silky as she had hoped it would be. His ocean air scent mixed with jasmine and evening primrose.

"Your life means more to me too, Hale," she said, her voice huskier than she intended.

Those dark pupils dilated. It was the first time she had ever called him by his name. The look on his face sent a quiver through her. She moved to take her hand out of his hair, but he reached up and held her hand on the side of his face.

Remy took a shallow breath. Hale's eyes wandered to her large lips. He unthreaded their other hands and slowly traced his fingers up her arm, leaving bolts of lightning in the echoes of his touch. His hand smoothed up her shoulder and down her neck. His thumb braced her cheek right before her ear as his fingers curled around to the nape of her neck.

She wasn't sure she was breathing. It only took the slightest pressure on those fingertips to pull her in. The scent of honey wine wafted off his breath. She was so ready for . . .

"Hale!" Bri's shout came from behind the trees. "We're heading to the bar. You coming?"

Hale growled, but he released Remy.

"Hale?" Carys shouted in a whining sing-song. "Come on. More wine. Let's go."

Remy laughed quietly.

"We should go," she whispered.

Hale hung his head, resigned. When he lifted it again, that charming princely mask was back on his face. He extended his elbow to Remy again, and she took it. Walking back onto the main promenade, Remy's whole body still tingled with that one soft touch. Hundreds of glowing lanterns illuminated the promenade, their flickering light dancing across the smooth surface of the reflection pool.

Bri and Carys sat perched on the ledge of the pool. They looked at them with knowing, wicked smiles. Carys winked at Remy. Remy narrowed her eyes back at her, but that only made the female fae smile wider. She wasn't sure what they had thought had happened between them. Remy blamed it all on the magic of the night. She thought of Heather's warning. The brown witch would go on a lecturing rampage if she had known what happened this night.

Remy sighed.

She was in so much trouble.

They had walked most of the way home over the course of the night, stopping in crowded pubs and music halls, drawing as many eyes to them as possible. It was strange being so openly watched. Remy had shied from it at first, but by the end of the night she welcomed the looks. The rush reminded her of when she and Fenrin would go sledding as children: the high speed, the blurring of her periphery, the absolute surrender to the sensations through her body. She had never felt so alive. She didn't know why such revelry felt like an accomplishment, but as the evening wound down, she thought back on their escapades with a strange sort of pride.

The hours bled together until fires dwindled to nothing but embers. They stumbled back to the inn, the sky perking with fresh morning light. Sounds of the night still echoed through her body as they stepped into their quiet corner suite. A high-pitched ringing filled her ears at the sudden quiet. Happy, satisfied tiredness filled her body. A sore ring of red had worn its way onto the tops of her feet as they swelled from all the drinking and walking, chafed by the ribbons of her silver slippers. But Remy didn't care. It was a soreness that felt like a victory, like after a hard morning's training with Bri.

Hale kicked his soft leather boots off by the door and collapsed into a heap on the blue velvet sofa.

"You can use the bathing chamber first if you like," he said, slinging his arm over his eyes. "I think I could fall asleep right this second."

Remy looked between Hale and the gigantic bed. Maids had turned down the bed, the sheer, white gauzy curtains pulled around its edges. Four giant, plump white pillows rested against the wooden headboard. It looked more enticing than chocolate cake.

Remy looked back at Hale.

"You're not sleeping on the bed?" She asked.

"No," he said resolutely, his voice tinged with sleep. "This couch is perfectly comfortable."

"But *that* bed is . . . ," Remy said, looking over the bed again. Somehow she knew it would feel amazing to slip her tired body beneath those smooth sheets and rest on the soft pillows. Surely Hale would want the same.

"Do you want me to join you in bed?" He peeked out from under his arm at her.

"Oh, um . . ." Remy stumbled, and Hale laughed.

"You take the bed, Remy," he said, chuckling. "I get to sleep on beds like that all of the time."

She had forgotten that. This wasn't a big deal to him. She frowned at her feet. For a moment it slipped her mind that he was a prince and used to all the creature comforts of the world. When hiking through the woods, he had simply been Hale to her. Even tonight in the capital, even with a princely mask, she had forgotten who he was and the weight of his title. She couldn't forget who she was too.

Remy made her way over to the armoire and pulled out a basket of clothing Bri had left in the bottom. In it were three chemises, satin scarves, and a week's worth of undergarments. Remy couldn't believe how much clothing Bri had purchased for her. It was going to be hell to carry it all when they left the following night. But she refused to complain when Bri had outfitted her with a decadent new wardrobe.

She selected the black satin garment with short sleeves and a hem that dropped below the knee. It was lighter weight than the other two, but she hoped with the black color it would be less revealing than the white ones. Her eyes snagged on a matching black satin robe hanging over the armoire. Gods, Bri had thought of everything.

She grabbed the chemise, a black-and-purple satin scarf, and the robe. As she tiptoed to the bathing chamber, she heard Hale's loud, slow breaths. If he wasn't asleep already, he would be soon.

Remy was too tired to enjoy the giant bathtub. That would be her mission for tomorrow. She hastily readied for bed: tying up her hair, washing her face, and brushing her teeth. Tying the robe around her, she took a quick, appraising glance at herself in the mirror. She looked . . . happy. Remy and her reflection exchanged conspiratorial smirks at the night they had. It was the most they had ever lived.

She sneaked back into the bedroom, blowing out all the candles except for the one on the bedside as she went. In the darkness, she removed her robe and slid into the giant bed. The feeling made a pleasurable hum escape her lips. The bed was so soft it made her feel like she was floating, cocooned in fluffy pillows and eiderdown blankets. She blew out the bedside candle and lay back down. The sensation was just as overwhelming the second time.

A chuckle sounded from the couch. She only saw Hale's outline in the darkness. He had removed his arm from over his eyes, and even though Remy couldn't see them, she sensed him watching her. She wondered if his fae eyes could see her face.

"It's that good, is it?" His laugh was gravelly with sleep.

"It is . . ." Remy didn't have any words to describe how it felt. The warm way it cradled her body made her drowsy. She was sure they would all sleep through most of the day, only waking for dinner before heading to the parlor that night. "Tonight was fun," she said to the darkness.

"Yes, you put on quite the show today." Remy beamed at that amused voice. It had been a crazy, exciting act . . . but it had been an act and that part still stung. What she would give for this to be their lives. For the fae to want to be her friend. For the prince to want to kiss her in the moonlit gardens.

"Yes, we certainly did." *We*. She threw it out there like a shield. *We had been putting on a show. It wasn't real.*

Hale didn't respond. What else was there to say? It had been fun . . . fake, but fun. And tomorrow they'd have to act some more. Tomorrow they would go after the *Shil-de* ring, and they'd be one step further to finishing this quest.

"Goodnight, Remy," Hale said. The sound of her name on his lips still made her tingle from the crown of her head to her toes. She wondered if it would always feel that way.

"Goodnight, Hale," she replied, wondering if his pulse increased too when she spoke his name.

This was a game, she reminded herself. It was a game with no happy ending. But she wanted to keep playing it anyway, consequences be damned, because to be in his orbit felt so good. She needed to wise up if she was going to survive this.

CHAPTER TWELVE

Carys came to collect the prince while Remy bathed in the enormous marble tub. Hale had called to her, "See you at the game," through the bathing chamber door and left. Carys had mumbled something to him, and Remy had heard Hale's growling, "Shut up," in reply. They had a strange dynamic, Hale and his warriors—they seemed like his fatal weapons one moment and his bickering siblings the next. Remy had seen nothing like it, that familial bond. It made her ache for the siblings she had lost.

Remy took her time getting dressed. The scarlet, floor-length gown was made of light flowing fabric that billowed at her feet. She couldn't help the tightening in her chest as she adjusted it. The top of the gown was little more than a V shape of fabric. It had sleeveless straps over her shoulders and a plunging neckline that ended right above her belly button. Remy gulped. People wore more clothing to go swimming.

Bri had left a bag of jewelry for her and another bag of makeup in the bottom of the wardrobe. Remy donned two long gold chains that hung down her chest. They were more beautiful than the thin leather collar she wore and accented the prince's gold ring. She was grateful for the extra coverage on her skin that the chains provided too. She put on the three gold rings, bangles, and matching gold cuffs for the top of her rounded ears. Then she put on the shimmering red teardrop earrings, the gems inside shining like rubies. A sudden thought seized her: they probably *were* rubies. The prince had left her in this room with enough wealth to feed an entire village . . . an intrusive voice told her she could grab them and run. She pushed the thought away.

She was sick of rural taverns and keeping quiet, hiding her powers, and living in fear. Hale offered her protection, and she didn't have to hide who she was to accept it. It felt superb to be allowed to exist for once. Remy wondered how much better her life would be the longer she stayed with him.

She looked at herself in the large mirror next to the armoire and didn't recognize the woman staring back at her. She looked so much like her mother . . . though her mother would have never worn something so revealing . . . but she carried herself with that same easy, regal air. It was there in her, buried in her soul somewhere. Her mother's voice whispered in her memories, "Never let anyone else tell you who you are, Remy, even me. No one decides how bright you shine but you."

Remy realized that the reflection in the mirror had tears in her eyes. She sniffed.

Not now, she scolded herself.

She grabbed the makeup bag, powdering her red nose, rouging her tear-stained cheeks. She lined her eyes in kohl and painted her lips the same red as her dress. It took her a few tries to get it right. She was not very skilled at face painting, but the courtesans had indulged her occasionally, showing her the art of makeup during lulls in business. Heather had always told her to take it off straight away. The brown witch said she didn't want it to give patrons the wrong impression . . . well, that was the exact impression Remy was trying to make right now.

Remy slipped on the red high heels left in the bottom of the armoire. They already hurt her feet as she bobbled around like a newborn calf for a minute before she got the hang of it. She adjusted her neckline one more time in the mirror, terrified one of her breasts might fall out of the thin fabric. She huffed a frustrated sigh and decided it would have to be good enough. Remy put on her new black cloak, clasping it at the neckline. Luckily, it covered most of her body except for the tiniest peek of red.

She went to the door to find Briata and Talhan leaning against either side of the hallway chatting. They straightened when they saw her. Talhan's mouth dropped open as he looked at her face, his eyes drifting down that peek of body behind the cloak. Bri pushed off the wall and smacked her twin hard on the shoulder. Talhan coughed and averted his eyes.

"You look good," Bri said with an approving grin. "Let's go."

They held the game on the upper floor of an exclusive inner city parlor. The establishment arranged the bottom floor in several small seating areas. Large leather armchairs clustered around low wooden tables. Two card tables sat at either end of the space. A crystal chandelier hung from the center of the room. Wisps of cigar smoke circled the dimly lit space. Only a few sconces dotted the forest green walls. This was where high-society fae came to drink and gamble.

Talhan set three glasses of ale on the small side table that Bri and Remy sat around. They had picked a place in the corner where they could survey the room. In a room filled mostly with fae, they were some of the biggest and most brutish looking ones Remy had ever seen. All armed to the teeth, they dressed as if they were about to enter a battlefield and not a gambling hall. She spotted a few witch's collars in the crowd too. One witch caught her stare and gave her the briefest nod, as though they were sisters and she, too, knew what it was to be owned by a powerful fae.

"What did you learn?" Bri asked Talhan, adjusting the dagger at her hip. Bri and Talhan had come dressed for war too.

"There's five players and the Heir of Saxbridge, though Neelo isn't playing," Talhan said, taking a long drag on the foam of his drink.

Remy guessed that he had talked the bartender into sharing some details of this secret game. Talhan looked cautiously to his twin. "Renwick is here."

"Shit," Bri cursed.

Remy froze. Renwick Vostemur, the Witchslayer, was the only son of the Northern King, Hennen Vostemur. Renwick had earned the name for all the red witch heads he brought his father over the years. Ruthless, he was equally cunning and cruel. Remy prayed they would not need her for this plan. If Hale could simply win the ring outright, she wouldn't need to be called up. Remy did not know if she could look into the eyes of the Witchslayer. What if he threatened to take her head once he learned of her red witch powers? Her throat tightened.

Bri's hand on her arm snapped her out of her panic. "Hey. We won't let him harm you. You are safe under Hale's protection."

Remy swallowed, giving the briefest of nods to Bri.

Talhan pushed the glass of ale to her. "Drink this," he said, as if it were a magical elixir to fix all her problems. Remy frowned at the ale. She had spent her life in taverns, permanently branding the smell of old spilled ale on her skin. That stench still took hold of her stomach.

"I do not drink ale," she said with a frown. Talhan shrugged and grabbed Remy's drink for himself.

"Here," Bri said, passing Remy a flask. "You need some liquid courage."

Remy took the flask. The liquid burned hot down her throat and she screwed up her face, trying not to gag on it. The hairs on her arm stood up.

"What *is* that?" Remy sputtered.

Bri threw a devious smile back at her, "Moonshine."

"Ugh, it's awful." Remy gagged, coughing out the taste on her tongue.

"It grows on you." Bri winked. She turned to her brother, "Who else is playing?"

"The Western Princess, Abalina. And her cousin, Delta. Both have seats at the table," Talhan said, averting his eyes from his twin.

"Delta is here?" Bri's low voice rose an octave as her golden eyes widened. Remy looked at the Eagles and the unspoken conversation between them.

"Easy Bri," Talhan warned. "We're not here for fun."

Bri rolled her eyes. "Right."

"The last player is Bern," Talhan said.

"Bern . . . how do I know that name?" Remy looked to the ceiling, pondering its origin. She was certain she had heard it before.

"He's the one who told Hale about the witches," Bri said. Remy remembered—Hale had said Bern was tied to the High Mountain Court, though he had never said how. "I remember his name," Bri continued, looking to her twin, "but I keep forgetting which one he is."

"He's that silver-haired courtier, you know, the one with the scar." Talhan moved his finger down his neck, indicating the line of the scar.

"Oh, that smug bastard from the summer revels?"

"One and the same." Talhan chuckled.

"What court does he even serve?" Bri took another long sip of her drink.

"I'm not certain. He seems to always be on the move, but judging by his character I would say the South." An uproar of laughter cut above Talhan's voice. Someone must have won a big hand gambling in the corner.

"Wonderful," Bri growled. She looked to Remy. "He's a harmless party boy, but he fancies the males, so at least you can avoid one male's shameless flirting."

"Great," Remy said tightly. She did not want any male's shameless flirting . . . well, apart from one. She took another long drink from Bri's flask, fire scorching her throat.

"Whoa," Bri snatched her flask out of Remy's hands. "You keep going like that and you will be unable to stand when you get called upon."

Talhan guffawed. He looked longingly to the card table where a group of fae males had gathered.

"No," Bri scolded her twin as if he were an overexcited puppy and then added in a lower tone, "This is not a pleasure visit."

"Heads up," Tallhan said, his eyes flicking to a door at the back of the room where Carys stood. The female fae dressed in fighting leathers, her hair back in its usual long braid, but she wore a metal chest piece with the Eastern crest etched into it too. She was an official Eastern Court guard tonight. She tilted her head to the doorway. Talhan chortled, "Bet Hale's nearly lost already. Looks like you're up, Rem."

Remy's heart pounded in her ears as she stood. She swayed for a moment on her feet, the liquor coursing stronger through her body at the movement. Bri snorted. Remy's limbs felt loose and warm. Her brain felt pleasantly fogged over. It was enough that, while she still felt fear, it existed in a place further away from her.

"Leave the cloak," Bri murmured. Remy looked down to realize she was still wearing it.

She took a deep breath and unclasped the neck, letting the cloak part and fall onto the chair behind her. The room stilled. Many male eyes turned to her and she felt every inch of her exposed skin.

"Remember who you are meant to be," Bri said, her voice barely above a whisper. Remy straightened, shifting her shoulders back, trying to ignore how it made her chest stick out even more. Her long black curls cascaded down her back and hugged her exposed sides. She lifted her chin and let her emotions fade into the background. Let those wanting males look. She let their gazes slide over her with an air of indifference. She pretended like she knew exactly how beautiful she was, that she was better than all of them.

"Good," Bri said as Remy stepped confidently through the throng.

Low whistles and whispers erupted around her: "Who is that?" "I haven't seen *her* in the South before" "Does she belong to the East or West?" "Gods, what I would give for a taste . . ."

She let them all wash over her, steeling herself. She thought of her mother's words flickering in that candle on the harvest moon and decided that she would shine as brightly as she could.

As she neared Carys, the female fae smiled mischievously at her.

Delight twinkled in her eyes. She said nothing until they exited the back door and moved into the quiet stairwell. Halfway up the stairs, Carys paused and turned to Remy.

She said with a laugh, "I knew you were beautiful but this is . . ." her hands swept over the air in front of Remy with approval, "I think our prince's heart may stop with one look at you."

"I . . ." Remy didn't know what to say to that. Carys's long, elegant finger lifted Remy's chin up.

"I may have a sword on my belt, Rem, but you are wielding a weapon too. Do not forget that," Carys said. Her ocean blue eyes pierced into Remy, and her cheeks dimpled. "Now, let's go have some fun."

~

Remy followed Carys up the stairs and down the long hallway to where two large fae males stood, guarding the door. Carved Mhenbic witch symbols covered the door: a warding spell. No one could cast magic on the other side of this door.

Remy noted one guard wore the crest of the Northern court: a sword crossed with three arrows and a snake coiled around the point where the weaponry intersected. The other guard wore the crest of the Western court: a horizontal battle axe with a ram's skull over it. They must be the personal guards of the players inside, just as Carys dressed as Hale's soldier. Technically, the Twin Eagles and Carys *were* his personal warriors, but Remy had never considered them as such.

As if noticing her thoughts, Carys whispered to Remy, "Guards and weapons have to stay outside."

"The prince's witch," Carys said to the other guards, tilting her head at Remy. Without missing a stride, she pushed open the door for Remy between the two enormous males.

Remy said a silent prayer to Mother Moon as she lifted her chin and strode into the room like a queen holding court. The room was smaller and cruder than she expected. Wallpaper peeled off the walls. The floorboards were uneven. The heavy scent of cigar smoke and heady floral perfume hung in the air. One single, golden lantern hung high above a large card table that took up the entire room.

Seven sets of eyes stared back at Remy. The action of the room skidded to a halt to assess her. The widest eyes were those of Hale. His mouth opened as he scanned her from head to toe. That look made Remy feel like she was the moon in the sky. A tiny flicker inside her hoped that his yearning expression was more than just an act. Remy held his eyes like it was common to glory in those looks from him.

"You called for me?" she said in that sultry bedroom voice she had heard used through the taverns. A madam had never trained her in the art of seduction, but she had watched many a courtesan hone their craft. It was her turn to try her hand at it.

She sauntered over to Hale, making sure her hips swayed. The prince gave her a pleased, predatory grin. Remy perched herself on his lap, placing her arm around his neck. Hale's warm hand wrapped around her as she surveyed the table for the first time.

Coins, papers, and even a few precious gems littered the table: bets. And in the very center, beyond the reach of any player, was a simple golden ring with a small ruby embedded into the band. There was nothing special looking about the ring, but even with the wardings, Remy felt the ring's power shuddering out of it in a low hum only Remy seemed to hear.

The *Shil-de* ring. It was real. It was here.

"You've only begun playing and you've already lost this much." Remy laughed in a light, teasing way at Hale. His thumb circled her bare skin in carefree touches. "Looks like you need a witch's luck."

"This room is warded against your witch's luck."

Remy's attention snapped to her left. A female fae sat beside them. She had obsidian skin and glowing mahogany eyes. She wore a high-necked gown in a cornflower blue and yellow geometric patterns that showed off her generous curves, ample bosom, and plump belly. She braided her hair up on top of her head, held in place by a golden, diamond-encrusted clip. She dripped in jewelry, every part of her shining with golden light. She must be Abalina Thorne, Princess of the Western Court.

To her left sat a broad-shouldered female with copper brown skin and dark brown eyes. She styled her hair in short corkscrew curls adorned with golden rings, modest but matching Princess Abalina. The female held her cards like a weapon. This was the Princess' cousin, Delta. The one Bri had been so excited about. Remy understood why. Delta was equally beautiful and handsome. Her strong muscled body could not be hidden under her long-sleeved blue tunic.

Upon a wooden stool wedged into the darkened back corner sat the Heir of Saxbridge. Neelo hunched over a thick book, a different one from the day before. This one had a dragon breathing orange flames on the cover. This was how the Heir of Saxbridge hosted an event. Queen Emberspear was renowned for her lavish parties and revels that lasted days on end. What huge shoes to fill for a quiet, reclusive person. But here Neelo sat, upholding the traditions of the Southern Court, albeit begrudgingly, with a bunch of their royal peers. The Heir looked sideways at Remy, giving her a quick once-over, the only acknowledgement Remy got before Neelo once again pored over the book in their hands.

Remy's lips twitched at the heir's response. She looked back at the Western Princess and forced an air of indifference, as though being the Eastern Prince's witch was equal to being the Princess herself. Remy carefully constructed her mask so they would think her an arrogant, lustful fool: the type of woman who was given the least credit for any sort of crime.

"I am not here for magic," Remy said, turning her gaze from the princess and back to Hale.

She caressed his neck, threading her fingers through his wavy, brown hair. Pulling his head to hers, she placed a kiss on his neck below his ear. She got a deep whiff of his heady scent that smelled like the salty sea air. It was intoxicating. As she pulled herself away, she found the prince staring at her with a burning, breathless look. His eyes told her he intended to finish what she had started. But he loosed his grip with the hand that had drifted to her hip, allowing her to turn to the princess and say, "I'm only here for moral support."

A snort came from across the table, "Is that what they're calling it these days?" Remy looked to a smirking fae male across the table. He took a long swig from his glass, smiling at her over the rim. His hair was white-blond, glinted with streaks of silver, such a stark juxtaposition to his golden sand skin. His eyes were so light blue they almost disappeared into the whites of his eyes. He looked eerily beautiful. She had never seen anyone look like him. An angry scar snaked from under his jaw to beneath his forest green tunic. This must be Bern. For all his strangeness, he had no menace in him, seeming more like a jolly drunk. "I should really get myself a witch if they all look like you, my dear," he said with a wink.

"Only royals are permitted witches, Bern." The sharp voice of the fifth player pulled Remy's gaze to him at last. She had been avoiding his looks.

Renwick Vostemur, Prince of the Northern Court. The Witchslayer.

He had long, ash-blond hair and pale white skin, his face ruddy from drink. A silver circlet haloed his head, matching the silver rings covering his fingers. There was no kindness in those green eyes as he shifted from Bern to Remy. This was the son of the man who had slaughtered her entire family, her entire Court. The smoke still burned her nose even now; the screams still ringing in her ear.

She wanted to hold her breath, but that light squeeze of a hand on her hip reminded her who she was meant to be. As if sensing her fear, Hale shifted his head, brushing his lips up her neck and planting a kiss on the shell of her ear. Remy shuddered, her eyes fluttering closed for a second. All the fear and those haunted memories pushed into the background as every cell in her body tuned into those lips on her ear. Hale's fiery breath skimmed across her face. When the prince pulled his head away, Remy felt heavy with desire. She wished every player would get out of this room so that she could finish that kiss.

The Northern Prince's voice brought her back to her body.

"What kind of witch are you?" He asked in a cold, even timbre.

Remy leveled the Witchslayer with a look even as her heart pounded. "You know what kind of witch I am." She did not know that warm, sultry voice that came out of her. Her eyes would glow red if not for the wardings on the room.

The cold prince's lips tilted up at her, though the smile did not meet his eyes.

He looked to Hale, "She's a good one, well-picked."

Remy didn't know what to do with that kind of praise. What did it mean to have the approval of an evil man?

"Can we please get back to this game?" Delta said in a raspy, caustic brogue from across the table. "Are you in or out Bern?"

"Err, out," Bern said, throwing down his cards. A stack of coins tumbled over as he moved.

The last person sitting at the table was a small human man, dressed in a black, button-down shirt and white bowtie. He collected the cards from the table with exceptional speed. Remy had almost missed him entirely. With the richest and most powerful fae at the table, he seemed to fade into the background. Remy knew his silent, timid posturing was as calculated as her dress was.

The dealer gestured an open hand to the Witchslayer. His turn.

"Call," Renwick said, throwing three more gold coins into the mountain of treasures on the table.

They all looked at Hale. He skimmed his nose across Remy's temple and bent to nibble the top of her shoulder. They were both enjoying this game too much, it seemed. His rough, calloused hand slowly slid across Remy's bare side. She bit her lip in response. Heat pooled below her belly button.

"Do you want to play, or do you want to go back to your lodgings and see to your desires?" Delta's Western accent grew stronger with her anger.

Hale laughed casually. "Sorry, Delta," he said with a smile that let her know he was not, in fact, sorry in the slightest. He threw three coins into the pot from the dwindling pile by his left hand and said, "Call."

"By all means," Bern said to them with a sparkle in his eye, "don't stop on our account. I do not mind watching."

"I bet you don't," Remy crooned, proud of how easily she volleyed back to these highborn fae.

Bern chuckled into his drink, "Well-picked indeed, Hale." He turned to her and said with a wink, "But don't worry darling, it's not you I'd be watching."

"I've told you, it's never going to happen between us, Bern." Hale chuckled, though his eyes remained fixed on Remy.

Bern laughed. "Every boy dreams of finding his prince." He turned to the Witchslayer to continue his antics, but Renwick shut him down quick with a sharp, "Don't."

The way they spoke to each other with such casualness indicated to Remy that these fae knew each other well, probably for all of their lives. They had attended balls and banquets, important weddings and funerals. They all ran in the same important social circles. She wondered what the life of a courtier was like. To her, it had always sounded exceedingly dull. But playing this game, with a prince's hand drifting down the thin fabric on her thigh . . . this was a game she enjoyed playing.

"Call," Abalina said, tossing her coins onto the table.

"I'm out." Delta chucked her cards to the dealer.

"Let's see them then," Abalina said to the Witchslayer.

Renwick laid down his cards: a flush. Hale threw down his cards then.

"You had nothing," Remy said, scrutinizing Hale's hand.

"I was calling his bluff." Hale shrugged.

She pressed her lips together to hide her smile, shaking her head at him. "You are truly terrible at this game."

"And you have a truly terrible mouth, witch," he taunted. He pulled her closer against him. She felt the word *witch* rumble through his chest.

"Let me show you how truly terrible I can be," Remy said, and before she could second-guess herself, she grabbed the prince's face and pulled it to hers. She enveloped his lips in a light, sensuous kiss. He growled as his arms wrapped around her tighter. Remy smiled against his mouth.

Delta let out a loud, pointed cough.

"Ignore them," Abalina ordered her cousin.

Remy pulled back lazily from the kiss to meet the prince's blazing eyes. It was the first time she had looked into those hypnotizing gray eyes since yesterday. He knew the weight of that move. His lips remained parted as he stared back into her eyes.

Abalina laid down her cards: a straight, not enough to beat the Witchslayer. The Northern Prince permitted himself the briefest stony grin as the dealer began moving the winnings toward him, careful to sweep around the *Shil-de* ring at the center of the table. The ultimate prize.

Renwick's hoard was three times the size of the others. He was a skilled card player, it seemed. It would only be a few more rounds before he surely won. And then he would have the *Shil-de* ring, a talisman so powerful it could protect the wearer from any harm. If that ring passed into the hands of Renwick's father, King Vostemur, he would become unstoppable in any coming war, especially if he figured out how to wield the Immortal Blade too.

Hale's mind must have been thinking the same.

"If I don't win this next one, let it be the last hand," his deep voice murmured.

The last hand: it was their agreed upon code word. Remy prepared herself for what was to come next.

"Thank the Gods," Delta rolled her eyes.

The prince wasn't finished though as his lips swept up Remy's neck again, "and then we can finally go see what else that terrible mouth can do."

As he spoke, his hand dipped under the fabric of Remy's dress, across her belly. His thumb skimmed the exposed skin as he pulled her more tightly into him. Remy moaned softly.

Bern choked on his drink.

"Damn. Maybe you should throw your witch in the pot." He chortled. "She'd be worth a few more hands."

"The ring is a good prize, but if the choice was between her and immortality, I'd choose her every time." Hale's voice shook from his chest, making every hair on Remy's arm stand on end.

"Wow, she must be some—" Delta started and Abalina shot her a look. ". . . witch," she finished.

He'd choose her. Every time. Even if it was all a ruse, the thought made Remy's whole body shudder.

Hale's hands idly slid up and down Remy's thigh. Her skin tingled, radiating heat. Her entire body felt like it was shimmering. Remy shifted on Hale's lap again. His arousal hardened against her thigh. He wanted her. At least some of this act was real. Warmth pooled between her thighs as Hale's nostrils flared, smelling her excitement. Remy kept her eyes lowered from Hale's gaze, knowing that one more look promised to set her aflame.

The human had already dealt out the next hand, but Remy had barely noticed. She swam in thick desire for the Eastern Prince. She shifted herself further against Hale, moving against his hard length. He groaned, his hand splaying further across her abdomen to hold her still. Remy couldn't help but smile as she bent her head back and trailed kisses along the prince's collarbone. This is what she had lain awake at night longing for. She had wanted it for longer than she would admit, and this ruse permitted her to do whatever she pleased. She let her arms casually rove his body, feeling the hard muscles of his arms, shoulders, chest in slow sweeps.

The rest of the fae darted uncomfortable glances at them as they touched each other, distracted by their wanton affections. Good. They each passed in cards to the dealer, getting new cards to finish their hand. Remy watched over hooded eyes as Delta and Bern smiled at their new cards. An easy giveaway. The only one too distracted to change cards was Hale as he continued his ministrations against Remy's ear. She was breathing so heavily now it was indecent. The prince's hand roamed dangerously close to the underside of her breast again as his other hand squeezed her hip once, twice: the signal. It was time.

Remy refused to overthink it as she turned to Hale. Eyes flaming with desire, she leaned up to his ear and whispered in a voice loud enough for all fae to hear, "I need you inside me now."

Her words snapped the leash on Hale's restraint. He lifted Remy by her backside and splayed her across the table. Coins and papers went flying. He pounced on top of her. His mouth collided with her own as he consumed her in a scalding kiss.

She moaned louder as their hands moved in a frenzy across each other's bodies. Remy scrambled for the prince's belt buckle before a razor-sharp voice shouted, "ENOUGH!"

Renwick yanked Hale by the neck of his tunic with enough force that his feet left the ground. The sizable evidence of Hale's desire strained at the seam of his trousers as he gave the room a boyish, cocky grin. Remy giggled drunkenly as she adjusted her neckline.

"Seriously, Hale? I expected this sort of shit when we were boys, but I thought you had grown up at least an infinitesimal amount," the Witchslayer hissed at him. "Now get out of here."

Everyone stared at the two of them except for Neelo. They kept their eyes fixed on the words of their book, but an amused smirk pulled up one side of their lips.

"Keep the coins." Hale laughed. "Just pittance anyway, right?" he said as if the mountain of gold coins he had lost was nothing.

Remy sauntered over to him, still laughing uncontrollably as if she had finally lost her senses to the drinks. Hale slung his arm over her shoulder and they stumbled to the door.

"Have fun you two." Bern called out to them from the table.

"Shut up, Bern," Renwick growled, returning to the table that the dealer was frantically tidying.

CHAPTER THIRTEEN

They did not speak a word to each other as they left the parlor, their three guards in tow. It wasn't until the five of them piled into a carriage that Hale nodded to Bri and she nodded back. It was the only indication he would give.

He had the ring.

A fake from the jewelers Talhan had visited the day before now lay on the card table. The power of the *Shil-de* ring thundered around them now that they were out of that warded room. Remy clutched her black cloak tighter as the aftermath of their escapade played over in her mind. She couldn't believe what she did, what she *said*.

No one spoke for the rest of the ride.

They pretended to drunkenly stumble through the bottom floor of the inn, giving drunken kisses on the cheek to the matron who herself seemed halfway lost in drink. It wasn't until they hit the stairs that Hale said quietly, "Prepare to leave. Twenty minutes."

The fae warriors nodded and entered their room as Remy and Hale headed to their corner suite. When they closed the door of their room behind them, Hale looked at Remy for a moment before dropping that arrogant mask and smiling at her.

"You were magnificent." He grinned, producing the ring from his pocket. "Remind me never to double-cross you."

"You better heed your own warning," Remy said, her eyes twinkling.

Hale held out the *Shil-de* ring in an open palm to Remy. "Here," he said, as Remy took a step away from the ring like it would burn her. "Put it in your totem bag. It's better you hang onto it than me."

Remy took the ring with tentative fingers. Its power radiated from her fingertips, hammering through her bones. As soon as the ring touched her skin, the ruby embedded in the gold started to glow red.

Hale looked to the eerie red light, the muscle in his jaw popping out. "Why is it glowing?"

"Probably because I'm a red witch," Remy said, quickly twisting toward the armoire. She had left her totem bag in her blue dress from the day before. The red dress she wore was so revealing, it had no space to hide the bag.

Pulling out her totem bag from the hidden pocket, she put the ring inside, grateful to not be holding that enormous power in her hand anymore. She took out the jewelry bag and began unfastening the golden chains around her neck and then the bangles, rings, and earrings. She unhooked the leather witch's collar at last. She held it in her hand, sliding the prince's golden-initialed ring off the end.

"Here," Remy said as she turned to give it to him.

She froze. Hale stood half-undressed in his black, fitted under-shorts. The collar of his tunic was unbuttoned, revealing his smooth, tanned skin.

"Get your mind out of the gutter." He smirked as he grabbed the back of his tunic and hauled it over his head. All the thoughts faded out of Remy's head as she took in his sculpted chest and arms. He was stunning.

"I'm getting changed. Leaving in twenty minutes, remember?"

"Right," Remy said, spinning around as he chuckled. She heard the bathing chamber door close. She cursed herself for gawking at him but cursed him equally. He knew what he was doing changing in there instead of the bathing chamber. He had wanted Remy to see him.

It might have been the moonshine or the thrill of the heist but

Remy thought: *The game continues, I see. Fine, then.*

She untied the back of her dress, letting its red fabric flow to the floor as she stepped out of it. She stood in only her red lace panties and red high heels. Bri had chosen her lingerie. Remy tried not to think about how the fae warrior had selected something that would fit her so perfectly.

Remy grabbed a hanger and hung the dress back up in the armoire. She would not be bringing it with her. It was not a dress for hiking or hunting the amulet of Aelusien. She put one heeled foot up on the armoire and bent over to undo the tiny buckle at her ankle. How did they unclasp these things? It had been a miracle she had buckled it in the first place. Remy fumbled with it, desperate to get these torture devices off her feet. At last, she got it. The heel dropped to the floor. Remy placed her foot down, relieved to have it flat on the floor again.

As she swapped to the other foot and began her fiddling with the second buckle, she heard the bathing chamber door reopen.

Silence. Not a single footstep sounded.

She tossed her loose, onyx hair over her shoulder as she looked back at the prince in the doorway. He wore his riding leathers. His mouth hung wide open in stunned stillness. Remy freed her foot at last and kicked off her second heel.

"What?" she asked with a knowing smile. She stood and turned to Hale, revealing the entire front of her body to him. "I'm just getting changed—get your mind out of the gutter."

Hale barely bit out the words, "Touché."

The prince stalked toward her. Remy thought for a second he'd grab her, but he halted right before they collided. He held up an open palm to her.

"My ring?" he said with an arched brow. His warm breath skittered over her bare skin, her chest, and her belly. She was well aware her nipples peaked against the brisk air.

Remy loosed a breath she hadn't known she was holding. Without breaking eye contact with the prince, she reached down blindly to the armoire and grabbed the prince's ring. She put it in his hand, still ensnared in his gaze, and he slid it back onto his finger.

He moved to take the red string off his wrist. Remy placed a gentle hand on his arm, "Don't," she said. "It will protect you."

She had whispered a simple protection spell over it. The string wouldn't do much to ward against larger dangers, but it was still lucky.

"Your eyes are glowing red," Hale said, mesmerized. She saw the red flames reflected in his own.

Remy lowered her gaze out of habit. A flush crept up her cheeks.

"What did I tell you?" Hale murmured. He held out a long finger, lifting her chin so that she would meet his eyes again, just as he had that day in the forest. He paused, his eyes searching her face, clenching and unclenching his jaw. After a long pause, he spoke, "You are the most beautiful creature I have ever beheld."

He said it through gritted teeth.

"You say that like it's a problem," Remy breathed.

"It is," Hale said, shaking with restraint.

"It doesn't have to be," Remy said, her voice only a whisper.

Hale's nostrils flared like he could not believe what she had just said. He shook his head even as he leaned in closer to her, drawing himself slowly to her lips.

His soft mouth brushed lightly over hers.

"Remy," he whispered her name like a prayer.

The sound made goosebumps ripple over her arms.

With a dizzying fervor, she kissed him back. Moving her body in tighter against him, she kissed him harder. Hale groaned as his hands moved over her body, skimming over the lace and settling on her backside.

"Seeing you tonight . . . in that fucking red dress." His voice was no more than a predatory growl.

His mouth moved faster across hers. Remy opened for him, welcoming in his hot exploring tongue licking into hers with deft skill.

He pulled away only long enough to whip his fresh shirt off over his head and then his mouth was back on hers. Hale lifted Remy, pinning her to the door of the armoire as she wrapped her legs around him. He pressed his hips harder into her and she moaned. Reveling in the sensation of her skin pressed against his, Remy ground herself into him. She absorbed his hiss with her mouth.

A loud knock at the door halted their frenzy.

The continued knocking on the door hastily sobered them both. Hale thrust his arms back through his riding shirt, stalking to the door as he pulled it over his head once more.

"What?" he barked as he yanked the door open only a crack.

"Sorry to . . . interrupt." Remy heard a laughing male voice through the door. She recognized it as belonging to the silver-haired male from the card game.

"What do you want, Bern?" Hale said with an air of annoyance rather than anger, like he had interrupted them in the middle of love-making and not thievery.

"You always were the trickster, Hale," Bern said. "That little heist of yours was well played."

Remy went rigid from behind the door. He knew.

"I have no idea what you're talking about." Hale sighed, feigning a yawn.

Remy put her drunken swagger into her step as she moved to the door, grabbing a fur blanket off the bed and wrapping it around her shoulders. "Come back to bed . . . ," she slurred, revealing herself in the cracked doorway in nothing but the blanket and her underwear. She slid herself under the prince's arm, molding her body against his warm torso.

Bern held her eyes. He did not dare look over her body, but she could tell by the flare of his nostrils that he was scenting her. Whatever he smelled made those icy blue pupils widen.

"I'm not here to take it back from you," Bern said, shifting his gaze back to Hale. "My . . . friend only wanted me to ensure it did not end up in Renwick's hands."

"Yes, this elusive employer of yours—would you care to tell us more about who is bankrolling you these days, Bern?" Hale wrapped his arm around Remy's waist.

"He is someone that I suspect has similar goals to your own," Bern said.

"And what goals do I have beyond drinking and fucking?" Hale cocked his head. His searing palm swept down Remy's side like a brand, resting on her hip. His rough fingers squeezed into her skin.

Bern narrowed his eyes at Hale, unamused.

"To stamp out the rising power in the Northern Court," Bern said as he shifted his gaze and spoke to Remy directly. "I think my employer would rather you have it, anyway."

Remy's throat tightened. What did he mean by that? What did he know?

"Then why are you here?" Hale asked with a chilling slowness.

"I may have been the first one to notice," Bern said, shifting glances between the two of them, "but the others will soon figure out what you have done. I think Abalina is on to you. You must make haste."

Talhan, Briata, and Carys were ready to move when Remy and Hale reached their door. The Twin Eagles sat on their packs on the floor, talking as though they sat around a campfire. Carys lounged on the bed by the window. Each had their weapons out, cleaning and sharpening them, as though an army lay on the other side of the door. The life of a warrior, Remy thought. They were always ready to fight or run.

Hale lifted his chin at them and all three were up on their feet, slewing their heavy packs over their shoulders.

The harbinger of bad news had disappeared as swiftly as he came. There was no sign of Bern as they moved down the hallway to Heather and Fenrin's room. Hale gave a light knock. It took Heather a moment to open the door and when she did her face looked strained, nearly panicked.

"What's wrong?" Remy asked, pushing in front of Hale.

"Fenrin, he's . . . not well." Heather replied, wringing her hands.

"I can come . . . ," a weak, croaking voice called from inside the room. Remy brushed past Heather into the space. Hale was telling the Twin Eagles to ready the horses. Their heavy boots rumbled down the stairs. Carys remained in the hall, keeping watch.

When Remy got into the room, she inhaled sharply. Fenrin lay on the bed, ghost white and sweating. Dark half-moons bulged out from under his eyes. He was still in his riding clothes from the day's travel the morning before. A green balm was spread across his chest, his shirt unbuttoned to the navel.

"It has gotten this much worse over the last few hours?" Remy whispered. She had seen Heather at dinner, and she still seemed to think Fenrin would be fine. But this . . . he looked on the brink of death.

Fenrin struggled to sit up, wheezing as though his lungs were filled with cotton wool. Remy rushed over to him and pushed him back down with more strength than she intended.

"Lie down," she ordered. Fenrin had no fight in him to deny her. He smelled of mint and astringent leaves, one of Heather's healing concoctions.

"Will he be all right?" Hale's voice came from where he leaned, arms crossed, against the closed doorway.

"His fever is breaking," Heather said with a tinge of relief. She held a glass bottle to the light to see how much was still inside. "He will be all right in a few more days, but it will be a long recovery."

Remy did not fear becoming infected with whatever malady had befallen Fenrin. Hale, too, would likely be immune because he was fae, but Heather was looking gaunt and green as well. Remy knew Heather would also soon run the gambit of this infection. At least Heather would heal Fenrin enough to take care of herself by then.

"Do you have enough?" Remy asked, waving to the assortment of brown glass bottles on the table. "Enough for you too?"

"Yes," Heather said, grimacing at how Remy knew she had taken ill as well. Fenrin's eyes fluttered shut, as though sleep might claim him at any moment.

"He cannot travel in that condition. Neither should you, if you don't want to end up like him." Hale tilted his chin at Fenrin. "But Remy and I must go."

"No." Fenrin's eyes opened at that. "We are coming with you."

Remy put a cool, gentle hand to her friend's burning forehead. "You cannot come. You need to rest." She turned back to Hale. His eyes tracked her every movement. "We cannot leave them here either, in case people come looking. The innkeeper knows that they are *your* servants. We cannot risk them staying here."

Hale nodded, uncrossing his arms and pushing off the doorframe.

"We will secure private lodgings across the river for you both to recover in. You shouldn't be around people, anyway," he said, opening the door behind him. He said something to Carys in the hall. Remy heard the warrior's boots thudding down the stairs as Hale ducked back into the room.

"Carys is on it." His eyes darted back and forth between the three of them. "She'll leave you with enough provisions that you won't need to leave the lodgings. The people who will come searching for us will have cleared out by then."

"Who is coming to look for you?" Heather stared at Hale. Even with her calm expression, Remy knew that was her angry face.

"It is fine, Heather," Remy said carefully, "we have it under control . . ."

"We?" Heather asked, narrowing her eyes as she looked between Remy and Hale. This was the exact thing Remy didn't want to happen. Not after Heather had warned Remy against any growing affections for the Eastern Prince. Remy's cheeks flamed. If only Heather knew how much of a "we" there almost was if Bern had not interrupted them.

Remy turned to Hale and said, "Can I have a minute alone to say goodbye?"

"We have to go," Hale said in a demanding tone.

"One minute," Remy insisted, ignoring his command. Hale opened his mouth to say something more, but Remy cut him off. "*You* are the one wasting our time right now."

Hale scowled at her but relented.

"One minute," he reminded her bitterly as he stepped out into the hall. Remy wasn't sure if it was far enough for his fae hearing to not eavesdrop. She hoped the bustle of the late-night tavern below would cover their voices.

"You handle him well, at least," Heather said, eyeing the door. Remy hated the hint of disappointment in that statement, like Heather had resigned herself to Remy not heeding her warnings.

"You see? I'll be fine." Remy feigned a smile. Heather shook her head, but Remy carried on. "You can't travel like this. It will get you both killed. I must go on alone."

"I don't like this." Heather rubbed her hands over her tired face.

"Neither do I, but you must admit that I can move at the pace of the fae and you two cannot," Remy said with regret.

"Remy . . ." Heather grabbed for Remy's hands and squeezed them in her own. "I know these fae seem . . ."

"Heather—" Remy chided.

"I just need you to promise me you will be careful. I've known you since you were a girl," Heather said. Her voice cracked and her eyes began welling up. "I've sworn my life to hide you and protect you."

"And you have, Heather, you have." Remy pulled the woman into a tight hug. How familiar it felt to be wrapped in this woman's arms. "Thank you. You have saved my life more times than I can count." It was Remy's turn to get choked up. "You are just as much my mother as the one who bore me, Heather." She felt Heather's muscles clench at that.

This woman had been a mother to her. Heather had been so hard on Remy, working her to the bone, strict with keeping a low profile, always moving them from town to town . . . but she loved Remy. She loved her like a mother loves her daughter. That much was clear.

"I will get to the Temple of Yexshire, and I will find the other red witches," Remy said, wiping her eyes to keep any tears from spilling. She said it more to convince herself than her guardian. "You will find me there. This isn't goodbye forever. It is just a short parting."

Heather bowed her head in acceptance. Pulling away from the hug, she wiped her cheeks. They both knew it was not a short parting.

They may very well never see each other again. Remy still had to seek out the amulet of Aelusien and navigate her way to the Temple of Yexshire undetected. Both felt like impossible feats. But if there was any hope of success they needed to move with haste, and that would not happen with two sick brown witches holding them back.

"Be safe, my darling," Heather said, lifting a hand to Remy's cheek in an act of tenderness she so rarely showed. "And do not trust anyone but yourself," she warned her again.

Remy looked away, moving to the bed. Fenrin puffed heavily through his mouth, but his eyes fluttered open as Remy sat beside him.

"Remy," he said with a weak smile.

Remy grabbed a cloth from the bedside table and swept it across his sweaty brow.

Fenrin pointed a crooked finger to the bedside drawer. "Open it," he said.

Pulling open the drawer, Remy lifted out a thimble-sized glass vial. Inside, it looked like shimmering silver glitter.

"What is this?" She inspected the vial.

"It's for you," Fenrin rasped. Remy looked to him, confused as he continued. "I traded for it two towns back. That is a vial of sand from Silver Sands Harbor. I know you wanted to see it, but I thought this might . . ."

He stopped to cough, doubling over as he hacked. That hard lump seized Remy's throat again.

"It's beautiful," she said, her voice strained with sorrow. She reached into her new riding tunic. Someone had already sewn a hidden pocket into it for her totem bag. Bri did not forget a single detail when she had outfitted Remy with a new wardrobe. Opening the small, black bag, Remy put the vial of sand inside.

"I will carry it with me always," she whispered.

Fenrin gave her a weak, woeful grin.

"It's always been you and me against the world, Fen," Remy said, her voice wobbling. "You are my best friend, and I will miss you while I'm gone."

"I'm sorry, Remy," Fenrin said through pale, bloodless lips.

"Sorry for what?" Remy asked, adjusting the pillow behind his head.

Fenrin looked up to the ceiling with half-glazed eyes, "I'm sorry I wasn't enough for you."

"Fen . . ." Remy couldn't hide the torture in her voice.

Part of her had always known he loved her as more than friends. He never pushed or cajoled her into anything, but she knew he had hoped. It was no wonder he got worked up into a rage any time a man paid her any attention. It was no wonder he ran off to tell Heather every time Remy had flirted with someone. They talked so often about their future lives, about the grand adventures they would one day go on in a world where red witches weren't hunted and she didn't have to hide. They had always been in that daydream of a future together. A sad and nasty feeling twisted itself in Remy's gut at that admission, that her best friend thought he was not enough for her. He probably thought that she needed a life and a partner grander than he could ever be, someone like a prince. She felt the bitter taste of Fenrin's disappointment.

He knew how his words pained her, but he waved them off, his hand sitting on Remy's arm.

"Go have an adventure for me." His laugh came out more as a wheeze and sent him into a coughing fit. Remy patted his back in hard blows to help dislodge whatever was rattling around inside his chest.

Hale returned with Carys behind him. "Your minute is up. Let's move."

Carys grabbed the bags scattered around the room, while Heather grabbed her bottles off the bedside. Hale moved to lift Fenrin from the bed.

"I can walk." Protesting with all his energy, Fenrin sat up.

"No, you can't." Hale scooped Fenrin into his arms.

Even though Fenrin was well over six feet tall, Hale dwarfed him in muscle. Hale picked Fenrin up as if he were a feather, and they hastened out of the room. Now that they had the High Mountain talisman, they needed to flee Ruttmore.

CHAPTER FOURTEEN

They moved Heather and Fenrin across the river with haste, setting them up in a third-floor apartment overlooking the other side of the river. It was a full apartment, with a kitchen, bathing room, sitting room, and bedroom. It was far better than any lodgings they had ever stayed in before. They left bags of food on the kitchen table, rapidly acquired by the Eagles on orders from Carys. Before they departed, the prince set a bag of gold on the table. Heather protested, but Hale waved her off.

Their hugs were brief and their goodbyes fleeting. They had already said their true goodbyes at the inn.

By the time they reached the landing, Remy was clenching her jaw so hard she thought she might break it. It kept the tears from falling, at least. She hated this goodbye. Even more upsetting was the inevitability. She felt like she knew from the moment Hale grabbed her wrist in the Rusty Hatchet. An electric shock still coursed through her as she thought about it. Deep in her bones, she knew he was the start of a new adventure. She only wished she knew how it would all end.

"You okay?" Hale said in a deep, soft voice. He stood so close to her she felt the heat from his arm.

"I'm fine," Remy gritted out. She did not want to indulge her sadness. There was no time to cry. They had to get out of this town before Abalina came looking for them, or, worse, Renwick's blue witches discovered he had won a fake ring.

"Liar." Hale smirked, causing Remy to stifle a laugh. It was that obvious, then.

She took a deep breath. "That bag of gold will take care of them for years. There's no way I can thank you enough . . ."

"Try," Hale teased.

Remy met his gaze finally, and he was grinning at her, his gentle taunting an attempt to cheer her up.

"Let's move," Bri interrupted as she and Carys descended the tight stairwell behind them.

Talhan stood outside, holding the reins of the first of five horses, the others hitched to a post. The male fae had unbuckled their packs along the midline strap, bisecting them into two messenger bags that sat on either side of the horses' flanks. Remy stared at the new pack loaded with clothes that Bri had bought for her. She had not realized they could break them down into two parts so they were weighted for riding. Her old pack had been one big leather sack with shoulder straps attached.

Remy's new pack sat on a caramel brown mare.

She stared at the horse for a beat before Hale said, "You don't know how to ride do you?"

Remy shook her head. They had walked most of the way from the Western Court, occasionally hitching rides in carriages and wagons.

Talhan cursed himself. "Sorry, I just assumed. I should have known." He moved the two packs off the front black horse and onto Remy's mare.

"What are you doing?" Remy asked as the warrior loaded up the caramel horse.

"You'll ride with me," Hale said.

Remy opened her mouth to protest, but Bri let out a low whistle. Everyone froze. It was a warning sound. They followed Bri's gaze across the river. At first Remy didn't see it, but then she spotted the inn, so far upstream that it was a mere speck.

"What is it?" Remy whispered, as if whoever they were watching could hear them from all that way.

"Northern guards," Carys whispered back. "Six of them. They don't look like they've come for drinking."

"We've got to move. Now," Talhan said.

In the same moment, Hale grabbed Remy around her waist and lifted her onto his horse. She clung to the horn of the saddle as the horse shifted. Remy was certain it leaned so far to the side that she would topple off, but then the horse shifted back to an even weight. Hale mounted the horse with ease and settled in the saddle behind her. Every part of his front pressed into her back. Her thighs pushed into the solid muscles of his, her back felt the steady rise and fall of his chest, and her bottom pressed right back into his pelvis . . . Remy gulped. She couldn't think about it.

"Hang on," Hale whispered into her ear. That fluttering breath sent tingles through her entire body. But those warm tingling thoughts flew out of her mind as the horses moved.

The hard toe of a boot poked into Remy's back.

"What, here? Seriously?" Remy hissed at the owner of the boot interrupting her first rest in several days.

They had spent three days traveling nonstop through the humid Southern jungles. The surrounding nature was so different from the Western Court. The jungle thrived with stinging, thorny plants, spiders the size of dinner plates, and swarms of biting insects. The trails were so overgrown with thick vines that they had to take turns slicing through the trail to make way for the horses. Remy had volunteered her magic for clearing the path ahead because her hips and thighs ached from riding in the saddle. Walking was easier, even with the constant casting of magic to push back the foliage. Walking also provided some distance from Hale. They hadn't seen another soul for several days; if they were lucky anyone trailing them had gotten lost or gone the other way.

Remy had heard Bri rise from her bedroll behind her and had prayed that the fae warrior only needed to relieve herself, but no, here she was, fully dressed and ready to train.

"Yes, training doesn't only happen when it's convenient." Bri kept her voice both quiet and threatening.

"We didn't train in Ruttmore," Remy grumbled into her arm.

"And I'm sure you're already weaker for it." That insufferable boot poked at her back again.

Remy reached for her bow on her pack above her. Careful to avoid Carys's sleeping body in front of her, Remy swung it back, colliding with Bri's leg.

The warrior above her chuckled, "You see? If you were training, you might actually be able to knock me over. Let's go."

"It is too hot, Bri, please." Remy felt like a child when Heather would try to drag her out of bed.

"That's why we're training before the sun rises," Bri said.

Remy peeked her eyes open at that. It was still dark. The faintest glimmer of light was lifting through the dense foliage. Remy pulled the thin piece of fabric up tighter to her chin. She would have forgone the blanket, but there were too many bugs in this place and she was getting eaten alive in her sleep.

Remy sat up on one elbow and looked over their stack of packs to the Eastern Prince sleeping on his side. His hair had fallen into his eyes, his breathing slow and heavy. He looked so different without that constant tension in his body. His jaw muscles weren't tight, his shoulders relaxed. Remy liked this version of him. She had peeked at him in his sleep often these past three days.

They hadn't spoken more than two words to each other since leaving Ruttmore. She could only assume it meant that Hale regretted the way they acted the night of the card game. They had gotten carried away in the Southern Court. They fell too hard into their act. The pendulum of Remy's emotions regarding the Eastern Prince swung violently between needing to get far away from him and needing to be as close to him as possible.

"C'mon." Bri nudged Remy again. "We won't be able to train as much once we reach the Eastern Court tomorrow. We need to get at least one session in before you lose all the muscle I have worked so hard to build."

Remy snorted at the word "I". Bri took credit for Remy's muscles now too.

They had three more days of trekking through the jungles before they would reach the port town of Westdale on the banks of the Crushwold River. It would have taken them less time if they had gone on the main road, but Hale had insisted they stay hidden in case Northern soldiers came looking for them. Once they crossed the Crushwold River, they'd be in the Eastern Court, and Renwick wouldn't be able to confront them there.

The snapping of branches came from up ahead. Remy looked over to Talhan's empty bedroll and then to the sound of the jungle shifting. He muttered soft curses as he moved back toward the campsite.

"Hear anything?" Bri called to her twin.

Talhan burst through the thick jungle, looking like he had battled a monster to get to them.

"Yeah," he panted. "They're okay."

Remy sat up then, tiredness leaching from her body at those words.

"You spoke to Heather and Fenrin?" she asked, hopefully. Remy had been nagging at them every day to contact someone by fae fire to check on her friends. It seemed Talhan had finally relented.

She thought about using the red witch's candle in the outer pocket of her new saddlebag. She could use it to contact Heather, but then that would be it. The witch's candle worked only once. Remy had thought about using that candle so many times over the years. She thought about lighting it and calling for her parents or for her siblings in some lost hope that one of them had survived the Siege of Yexshire. But that sad, mourning voice in her head had always told her that no one would answer and it would waste her candle.

"I spoke to Neelo," Talhan said. Remy's eyebrows shot up. Talhan communicated with the Heir of Saxbridge? "They sent some of their guards to check in on Heather and Fenrin."

"And?" Remy asked, trying to mask the eagerness in her voice.

"Fenrin has nearly healed. Resting for three days has done him a lot of good." A knot loosened in Remy's chest. Fenrin was okay.

The bottle of silver sand from Fenrin was tucked away in Remy's totem bag along with the *Shil-de* ring. The further the distance between them, the more Remy missed her companions.

"And Heather?" Remy sat up and pulled on her boots. She had slept in her riding clothes because they were thicker and protected her legs from biting insects.

"Heather has taken ill," Talhan said but added, "but she is doing well, not nearly as sick as Fenrin was. She told the guards she would be healed within the next few days."

"Good." Remy began to smile but paused at the expression on Talhan's face. "What else?"

Talhan kicked at the jagged vine in front of him, reluctant to speak.

"Heather told the guards that they would head back to the West when she was recovered." Talhan's usually cheerful disposition seemed withdrawn at those words, like he was waiting to see how Remy would respond.

Carys spoke, head buried in her bedroll.

"You know I care for both of them," she grumbled. "But we can talk about it in another three hours. If you all don't shut up right now, I'm going to grab one of those yellow snakes and impale you on its fangs."

Talhan chuckled, kicking off his boots and lying on his bedroll. It surprised Remy he woke so early to check in on her friends. *Their* friends, she supposed now. It was clear the fae had taken a liking to the brown witches too. And now they knew they would probably never see them again.

Remy waited to move until she was sure she would not reveal the pain in her eyes. Heather and Fenrin were returning to the Western Court, not following them east. It made sense. In her logical brain,

Remy knew it would be safer for them in the West. It was their home-land, after all. And perhaps one day they would make it to Yexshire and find her again. But Remy and the Eastern fae warriors still needed to get the amulet of Aelusien. Climbing Mount Aelusien, the Rotted Peak, would be dangerous. Part of Remy was glad her friends did not want to come. She would be more worried about them on those magical slopes than finding the High Mountain talisman. Remy wondered, too, if they didn't follow because of what Fenrin had told her. That tinge of regret struck her again. She had messed it all up. Hiding her had taken over their entire lives, and she had never repaid them for it. Indeed, she had led Fenrin on and dismissed Heather's warnings. She had let them both down.

As if sensing some of that sorrow, Bri grabbed Remy by the forearm and pulled her to a stand.

"Training," she said as if it were the answer to everything, pulling Remy down the trail to practice.

CHAPTER FIFTEEN

Remy had never been on a boat before. She held onto the banister with a white-knuckled grip as the creaky wooden barge crossed the Crushwold River. Behind her sat the Southern Court, and so far in front of her that it was a dot on the horizon were the shores of the Eastern Court. The stench of the humid Southern jungles still clung to her skin. The last week had been a grueling slog. The cool river breeze should have been a relief . . . but not while on a wildly rocking boat.

Red witch magic could animate objects and, if the magic was strong enough, it could keep them moving, like the fountain at the prayer tree. Whatever spell was cast on this barge, the magic was ancient. It must have taken a hundred red witches to spell the barge to carry on crossing back and forth without sails or oars for all these many years. Only red witches possessed the level of magic to spell inanimate objects. It surprised Remy that their magic lived on, even though so many were killed. She wondered how many more years this barge would last before it broke, never to be repaired. There were so few red witches left. One day there would be no more magical objects such as this.

Carys and Hale had gone to the other side of the boat to discuss something while Remy perched against the railing between the Twin Eagles.

"Seasick?" Talhan asked, noting her peaky, pale face. The boat swayed wildly up and over the choppy waves. At least the wind on her face calmed her churning stomach.

"This feels really unsafe," Remy said through clenched teeth. She was sure the banister would splinter if she gripped it any tighter.

"Only if you can't swim." Bri glanced sideways at Remy. "Can you swim?"

"What?!" Remy asked, sucking in quick breaths. The unpredictability of the rocking had her legs wobbling.

"She's kidding," Talhan said, chuckling. "The barge is perfectly safe. We make this crossing regularly to come to the South."

His words did not soothe Remy. She had learned to swim as a child whenever she and Heather stopped into towns that had rivers or ponds, but she never swam out of her depth and not in water with heavy waves or rushing currents.

"Are you excited to be heading back to your court?" Remy asked, trying to take her mind off the swaying boat.

"None of us have particularly good relationships with the Eastern Court," Bri huffed.

"Do you have any family in . . ."

"No," Bri cut her off. No, they did not have any family in the East and that was that. No more explanation.

"I am looking forward to some chimney cakes from that bakery in the garden district," Talhan said with a wink. "Maybe His Highness will give us a couple of days to enjoy the city before we head back into the mountains."

"I doubt it," Bri said. "He's on a mission from the King, a mission he still hasn't completed, and so we're just passing through." She chewed off a bit of her fingernail and spat it overboard. "With any luck we will not have to see the royals at all."

Carys's voice called from behind them. "Hale needs to speak with you at the back of the boat."

"As long as it's not below deck . . . ," Remy groused.

Looking at Remy's green face, Carys snorted.

"Keep an eye on the horizon," Bri said, giving a patronizing tap on Remy's hand still grasping the railing for dear life.

Remy walked shakily to the stern of the boat, where the Southern shoreline was pulling farther and farther into the distance. No other passengers gathered there, most looking forward toward the East. Hale leaned his forearms on the balustrade, confident on his feet.

Remy wobbled like a newborn fawn toward him. Turning her way, Hale was about to make some teasing comment when Remy cut him off.

"Don't," she snarled.

Hale remained silent, but that insufferable smirk crossed his face.

Remy grabbed on to the railing, holding it tight to keep her from moving. Hale stared out at Westdale. He twirled a purple flower in his hands. He must have picked it before they boarded.

"What is that?" Remy raised her eyebrows at the delicate flower.

Hale handed it to her, his expression sombre. Remy gave the flower a deep sniff.

"The fragrance is lovely," Remy said. It had a beautiful sweet and fruity aroma. "It reminds me of something . . . though I'm not sure what."

"Veliaris rudica, commonly known as blooming amethyst. It's a wildflower native only to the banks of the Crushwold River. The violet witches of old highly praised it." Hale's thoughts seemed far away as he spoke. "You may well have smelled it before. They used it in many perfumes. It was once a favorite of the High Mountain royals . . . perhaps you were around them enough as a child you may remember it?"

That made Remy's heart clench. Yes, she knew where the smell was from. The scent took her back in a way that no word or sound could. The pinprick of tears welled in her eyes as the wind whipped her hair against her cheeks. Swallowing the lump in her throat, she sniffed the flower again.

"It's lovely," Remy whispered to keep her voice even.

"It was my mother's favorite flower," Hale said, watching the purple petals spin in Remy's hand.

"Was? I'm sorry—"

"She is not dead," Hale corrected, "though for all we see each other she might as well be."

"She doesn't live in the capital?" Remy twirled the flower again, realizing she released her grip on the bannister to hold it. Her legs felt steadier when she stood beside Hale.

"I see the stories and gossip of the Eastern Court have not made it to your little tavern in the West?" Hale gave her a half-hearted laugh. Remy shook her head. "My mother lives on the Eastern coast in a remote fishing village called Haastmouth Beach. My father banished her there when he married the current queen."

Remy stifled a gasp. Banished? How could the King be so cruel to the woman who bore him his first child?

"Why?" It was all she could think to ask.

"I think he really loved her. But she was below his station, and he had ambitions that she got in the way of. It is not the way of the Eastern royals to marry for love." Hale exhaled as Remy passed him back the amethyst flower. "When he announced he was to marry the current queen, it broke something in my mother. They say she went mad. They said it would be kinder to send her away than to lock her up."

Remy clenched her jaw to keep her mouth from falling open. "They would have locked her up?"

"They kept me away from her for many years . . . I was six when she left. It was another six years before I ran away to find her." He had been the same age as Remy when she lost her parents. "Of course, I found a perfectly sane woman. Sad, yes, but she was still in her wits completely. I think my father loved her and just wanted her gone."

"That's awful." Remy chewed on her bottom lip.

"I visited her every few months after that for many years. I spent every summer of my teen years there too. My father would allow it during the weeks my tutors were away on holiday. I made friends with the locals. I learned to fish and swim in the big ocean waves. I'd always bring her a gigantic bouquet of these flowers that I had picked along the eastern banks of the Crushwold. They don't grow by the seaside."

"Those sound like very happy memories . . ." Remy couldn't quite finish her thought: *And yet when you speak of her you sound so sad . . . what happened?*

"It has been a decade since I've seen her. Though my soldiers tell me she still lives," Hale said so quietly Remy had to strain to hear over the wind cupping her ears.

"Wh—why?" she asked.

"When I was eighteen, my father assigned me my first job. I was to assemble a group of soldiers and we were to take back the Eastern village of Falhampton from Northern control. Drive them out. Oversee the building of better walls and guard towers. Train the villagers to defend from future attacks. It was a task for a general, and yet he gave it to me, despite my partying and childish behavior." Hale huffed. "Only recently, though, did I realize he thought I would never succeed. He wanted to make a show of effort."

"But you did succeed?" Remy smiled knowingly to the river. Hale's shoulders lifted a bit at that smile.

"Indeed I did—it took nearly a year. And when I returned, you should have seen his face. It was the first time he had ever really acknowledged me. He made me a general, the youngest in the kingdom." Remy felt the pride radiating from him as his chest puffed up again briefly before deflating. "I had planned to go visit my mother upon my return, but my father thought that would be unwise. I needed to show the people I was a true Prince of the East and that I had chosen him and the crown over her."

"That is nonsense," Remy dismissed with a wave of her hand.

As if broken from a spell, Hale looked at her and laughed. "Where were you to tell me that then?" He threw the flower into the river and watched as the choppy currents carried it away. "I wrote her a letter apologizing for not visiting and telling her I needed to focus on my job as a newly appointed general. She wrote me a letter back."

"I'm guessing she understood." Remy already knew the answer.

"She did." Hale's eyes crinkled as he gave her a sad smile. "She told me she was proud of me and that I knew where to find her when I was ready and to remember to bring her a bouquet of flowers." He sighed. "And as the years went on, the shame felt greater. It felt harder and harder to make that trip. It felt less and less likely that she would forgive me."

"She will," Remy said confidently, leaning her shoulder into his.

"You seem very certain of that." Hale chuckled.

"I am." Remy pressed her shoulder into him again. "She loves you. A mother's love . . . it does not fade with years. It burns brightly forever."

"Where did you hear that?" His cheeks dimpled as he looked at her.

"From my own mother," Remy said.

In that moment, standing there on the bow of that boat, they both seemed like two small children, missing their mothers. It was something deep and vulnerable that they rarely showed others. Remy saw her own pain mirrored in Hale. It made him seem less like a prince and more like a normal person, a son, with a family he loved and missed like she did her own.

"After you find the High Prince and restore him to the throne, you will go to her with a big bouquet of fragrant flowers, and she will smile and hug you like no time has passed." Remy smiled. Staring off into the distance, she imagined it was her going to see her own mother.

Hale's mother was still alive, and Remy couldn't let his shame keep him from seeing her ever again. It left a deep hole in her heart to think someone had the opportunity to hug their mother again and didn't.

"You seem awfully confident that all this will happen," Hale said. He had shuffled closer to her so that the whole sides of their bodies touched. It felt incredibly intimate after days of barely looking at each other.

"It will happen." Remy nodded.

"And how would you know?"

"I'll make sure of it," Remy said confidently.

"You plan on sticking around after all this?" Hale said, turning his gaze back to the river. "You are a red witch—you will want to stay in Yexshire."

"Red witches used to serve the courts of every kingdom, you know, not just the High Mountain Court." Remy couldn't believe what she was offering by saying it, but she forced herself to continue. "And you, Your Highness, and your rag-tag bunch could surely use the guidance of a red witch."

Hale chortled. "Yes, I suppose you are right." He bent his head down to look at Remy. His face pulled so close to hers that she felt his hot breath on her cheek. "I think you are the first witch I've ever met who feels free to speak so boldly. There is no point to people who tell me what I want to hear. It is the very thing I looked for in each of my soldiers: warriors who would be honest with me, tell me when I was out of line, be loyal to me only if I remained loyal to them."

"They sound like good people." If the rest of his crew was anything like Carys, Talhan, and Bri, then they must be.

"They are." His eyes softened, scanning her face. "So you want a job then? You'd be willing to follow me?"

Remy shrugged, and he grinned. Her voice was softer than she intended when she spoke. "I will pledge to you the same thing that your crew has: I will be loyal to you as long as you are loyal to me."

Hale smiled then, a true genuine smile, and sighed. His breath tickled her lips. Each hair on her body rose as though trying to reach out and touch him.

Remy had been hiding all her life and it still hadn't protected her. Maybe living openly as a red witch with the protection of a royal fae would be the safer option for her. She knew the mission they were on would eventually fail, and she needed protection for when they realized they would never succeed. But there was something else too. Something inside her that said, despite everything, she wished to stay by Hale's side.

Hale's grin widened as he looked at her. "And as my new head witch, do you have any advice you would like to give me?"

"My first guidance I would bestow on you is to go see your mother." Remy's smile was so wide her cheeks pinched her eyes half closed.

Hale leaned over and tucked her flapping hair behind her ear. Puzzled by the gentleness of the gesture, Remy looked at him. She felt ensnared in the long stare they shared, lost in those gray eyes.

The boat rocked, and they pitched forward. Remy clawed at the railing as the boat evened out again. Hale pressed his lips together to keep from laughing at her.

"I take it you are not looking forward to heading home?" Remy said, changing the subject.

"No." Hale sighed. "The East is a beautiful and pleasant court, so I am told, though I've never seen it much that way."

"I'm sorry for that."

"That's what I wanted to talk to you about," Hale added. "When we dock on the other side of the Crushwold . . . I will have to be a different sort of person."

"More princely?" She jested.

"No, I . . ." Hale struggled for the words, and Remy regretted being so lighthearted. "The world sees me as . . . they call me the Bastard Prince."

"I know," Remy said. She had called him that before, and she hated that she had wielded those words like a weapon. "I will forever regret calling you that."

Hale looked to her, one side of his face pulling up as he said, "Thank you."

Remy knew how much those names dug their claws into a person. She knew how being called a witch had evolved into an insult over the years, as if she were something evil or lesser than others. And she knew how—despite how hard a person tried to not let those words sink into them—they would linger. Then a person would start to believe them to be true. It stung to know she had ever called him a bastard; she had added to that belief.

"So you become the person they fear you to be?" Remy guessed.

"It's nice, this." Hale's eyes crinkled at the corners.

"What?"

"Talking to someone who actually understands what it is like to pretend to be something they're not."

Remy looked out to the river and cleared her throat. "Yes, hiding my red witch powers felt like my only purpose in life."

She could no longer make out the shores of the Southern banks of the river. The enchanted boat neared the other side already. They moved with incredible speed.

"I have arranged for you to go with Carys when we enter the city. You will stay with her until it is time to depart for the Rotted Peak." Hale's eyes dropped to his hands. Remy turned to him, an unasked question on her face. "I'm sorry you will have to hide your magic once more."

"Why?" she said. "Shouldn't I be coming with you? They know you have found a red witch and possess the ring, I assume?"

"I don't want you or that ring getting anywhere near my father," Hale ground out, that muscle in his jaw popping out again. "The knowledge of who you are and where that ring is gives him a power I am unwilling to put in his hands."

"You think he will take it?" Remy wondered. "But wasn't it his idea to find the High Prince and reunite him with the lost talismans?"

"It was," Hale said, his attention pulled back to Remy's face, "and yet, I still do not trust him or any of his advisors."

"Why not?" Remy regretted asking. Hale's body language said everything. The prince didn't trust his father for many reasons. There was a history there she did not know.

"You don't have to tell me," Remy added, "I trust in your judgment."

Hale held her eyes again, another long look. She saw her reflection in them. It was like a mirror to her own soul, her own fear, her own wounds. There was something there, some magic that existed only between them.

"Won't your father know who I am if I go with Carys?" Remy asked.

"Carys joined our ranks from the Southern Court a year back during one of the skirmishes on the border with the North," Hale said. "My father knows Bri and Talhan, but not her. Still, it won't be long until they identify who this red witch is that we brought with us, but hopefully by then we will be on the move into the mountains again."

"Will you be all right?" Remy asked. Her question seemed to surprise Hale, though he hid it well.

"I'm used to walking into the lion's den." Hale faked a laugh, but Remy knew well enough by now that the sound wasn't genuine. "But I'm glad that you won't be dragged into that place too."

"I don't know . . ." Remy bit her lip. "I'm pretty good at playing the doting red witch."

"That you are." Hale laughed again, his smile broadening into something more real. He toyed with the red string still around his wrist, as though contemplating the moments that they had shared in the South. "But I don't want to put on an act like in Ruttmore."

"Oh." Remy tried to hide her disappointment. He didn't want a repeat of what happened in Ruttmore.

"My father is a cunning man—he sees more than most. He'd take one look at me with you and he'd know," Hale said.

"Know what?" Remy breathed.

"That I'm not acting."

Remy froze at his admission. He said it so nonchalantly, and yet she knew what a tremendous thing it was to say those words out loud. Hale pushed off the railing and walked away, leaving her with that confession. He wanted her to stay away from the King because he cared about her and didn't want the King to hurt her to get to him. She opened and shut her mouth. What could she say to him? That she returned those feelings? Remy did not know what that would mean for them.

The distant shouts from land sounded. They had made it to the Eastern Court.

CHAPTER SIXTEEN

Acrowd of onlookers and royal guards met Hale, Bri, and
Talhan. Remy watched from the boat as that crafted mask
fell over the Eastern Prince's expression. He seemed cocky,
with a lazy royal air as he waved and winked at the crowd. He
thumbed a few gold coins at children and laughed like he basked in
their cheers. That laugh grated against Remy's ears. Remy hated
seeing the performance but didn't have to watch for long. The landing
party had brought horses for Hale and the Eagles. They rode off into
the city before Carys and Remy departed the barge along with the rest
of the crowd.

Beautiful seafaring ships filled the port of Wynreach. One was
hoisting its sails, readying to head down the Crushwold and out to
sea. The Eastern Court was known for its merchant vessels. They
traded all manner of Eastern goods from wool to perfumes
throughout Okrith.

The Eastern Court had built the city of Wynreach between dense
pine forests and rolling pastoral hills, leading out as far as the eye
could see. Remy knew beyond that was the ocean. The majority of the
buildings were crafted with intricate wood detailing, mirroring the
history of logging and woodwork throughout the city. The capital had

a mix of smells from chicory smoke fires to freshly baked bread and the crisp air that promised winter was nearing.

Towering in the center of the city was the castle of Wynreach. The castle's twelve narrow towers connected with giant walls of gray stone, dominating the skyline. The outer walls had small windows for archers, while the inner walls had towering windows of stained glass. All the way from the river, the windows glowed. The castle was a combination of lovely and lethal, its delicate towers and glass windows in strange juxtaposition with the dark gray stone ramparts and battle armaments.

Hale and the Twin Eagles had disappeared toward that castle on the hilltop, lost among the crowds and winding roads. That castle was the prince's home. How fitting, Remy thought, that the prince seemed a strange combination of lovely and lethal too. She looked at her hands, thinking about what he had told her moments before. He did not want her coming to the castle because his father would know Hale's affections for Remy were real.

His affections for her were real. He cared for her.

Remy shook her head. She could not imagine any happy path forward, even if they stamped out the war with King Vostemur. There was no peace. They would never live happily ever after in that castle before her. That wasn't who she was. She knew the consequences of the path she was taking and didn't care, not nearly enough. Wanting to be in Hale's life was going to get her killed. That was what Heather had warned her about.

Carys's arm on Remy's elbow pulled her out of her worried, cycling thoughts. The blonde fae steered Remy into the throng.

Carys navigated the city with ease. Remy couldn't believe how densely packed it all was. Even as they turned away from the major thoroughfare, people filled the roads. Carts, boxes, tents filled with various trade goods sat stacked along the narrow roads. The smell of too many bodies pushed in on Remy, the same smell the taverns would get by the wee hours of the morning when too many revelers had danced for too many hours.

"This way," Carys said, tugging on Remy's arm again.

Remy readjusted her pack on her back. Carys led them down a quieter back street filled with densely packed three-story dwellings. It was a residential part of the city, one step up from a slum. Clotheslines hung high above their heads, drying servants' attire and children's clothing. This is where the humans who served the fae lived.

"You live with the humans?" Remy asked, eyeing the clothing above them.

"I don't really dwell in the city, but my sister does, so we'll stay with her while we're here," Carys said, ducking down another unnamed alley.

Even in this part of town, the houses had intricately carved doors and windowsills, detailed patterns shaped and painted into each of them. They were beautiful, even here. The entire city seemed to carry with it a sense of artistry, of vibrancy and color, that belied the image of King Norwood that Hale and his warriors had painted.

"Your sister lives with the humans?" Remy asked. The fae kept to themselves. They ruled every kingdom in the land and had done so with the help of the witches, but the humans were always treated as the servant class. Now the witches existed even below them, with very few allowed to exist freely without a fae master. Remy knew what it felt like to be treated like she was beneath everyone else. She would never forget it. She couldn't imagine the humans enjoyed living with a fae.

"She's not my full sister," Carys said. Her long blonde braid swished across her back as she walked. "She's my half-sister, and she's half-fae."

That statement made Remy pull up short. She stood there blinking for a moment before she carried on after Carys.

"I have never heard of a half-fae before," Remy said, bewildered. She hadn't even realized it was possible. Why had she never considered it before? She knew the High Mountain fae had witch blood, but . . . she'd never heard of fae mixing with humans.

"They exist," Carys said. "Though many of the fae wish they did not. They get rid of most halflings."

Her words bit into Remy. She said them so casually—too casually

—for what it meant. The fae didn't want any halflings because it complicated their vigilantly constructed hierarchy of the world, a world where the fae sat on the top.

"Do you share the same father or mother?" Remy asked, though she already suspected she knew.

"Father," Carys confirmed bitterly. "When Morgan's mother found out she was with child, she fled the Southern Court, afraid of what my father might do."

"How did you find her?" Remy asked. She gripped her bow tighter in her left hand. She had left it strapped to her pack during their travels, but walking through a foreign city she felt safer holding it.

"My father confessed it on his deathbed," Carys said, still with that cool detachment, that steely warrior exterior that Remy knew was merely a well-built facade. "My father knew of Morgan. He would arrange for good patronage for her mother, made sure that they were housed and cared for, all without Morgan's mother knowing . . . but he kept Morgan a secret from everyone in my life until his dying breath . . . everyone except Ersan, that is."

Remy had never heard the name Ersan before, but she suspected she knew who it was. Carys had admitted to her before that she left the Southern Court because she got her heart broken. Her not explaining who Ersan was any further told Remy enough.

"I'm sorry," Remy said, trying and failing to be delicate with her words. "It sounds like he tried to do the right thing."

"No. He didn't." Carys bit out. Remy wasn't sure whether she was referring to her father or Ersan now. "She is my only sibling, and I didn't know about her until a year ago. My mother died when I was a child, and my father was absent most of the time." Carys ducked under a low-hanging blanket. "I didn't know I had a family."

Remy knew the pain of those words all too well. All her family was gone too. But she had Heather and Fenrin. She had been with Heather since she was seven, a year after the Siege of Yexshire, and Fenrin had come along when she was twelve, and they had swiftly become best friends. The thought of them made Remy ache. She regretted the way they parted, how easily she dismissed Heather's concerns as she discarded them like a loaf of too-stale bread. They were her family, and she hadn't appreciated them enough. Memories of the Southern Court flitted through her mind on the wind. The lush gardens, the rich foods, the beautiful clothing . . . she wondered how Fenrin was faring, if he was much better this day. She wondered if they would head west again and then carry on northward to meet her in Yexshire, or if they would remain in the South with their bag of gold. She knew it was a hopeful thought that they would come to Yexshire. Traveling into the North was dangerous enough, let alone traveling in the North as a witch. She hoped they wouldn't follow her.

"Here we are," Carys said, more to herself than to Remy. She had stopped in front of a small wooden door in an alley. Whorls of turquoise, violet, and gold were carved into the wood, though the paint was chipping away. The swept stoop had a few modest pots of flowering herbs dotted around the doorway. Carys stepped up off the street and knocked.

A human man opened the door. "Carys!" he said, grabbing the warrior and wrapping her into a tight hug. "It's been months since we last saw you. How are you?"

"I'm good." Carys laughed as the human put her back down. "I'm only in town for a couple nights, but I was hoping I could stay over. I brought a friend."

The human man peered around Carys to size up Remy. He was middle-aged and lean but looked strong. His shaggy brown hair was beginning to gray at the temples along with his thick brown beard. He smiled at Remy, and it made her fidget with the bow in her hand.

"Remy, this is my brother-in-law, Magnus. Magnus, this is Remy." Carys introduced them.

Magnus put out his hand and Remy shook it. His hands were rough with calluses from his unknown profession. "Pleasure to meet you, Remy."

"Likewise," Remy said. She felt wary. No stranger was kind to her. Magnus probably thought she was a human and not a witch.

"Come on in, Morgan's just put the kettle on," Magnus said, ushering them inside.

THE HIGH MOUNTAIN COURT

The townhouse was modest, with plain wood floorboards and peeling wallpaper, but it felt warm and welcoming. Magnus led them down the hallway through the home, ending in a sizable kitchen.

"Carys!" Small, delighted voices shouted as three small children bombarded Carys. She dropped to one knee to scoop them all into a giggling hug.

The woman at the stove turned, brushing her hands on her apron. She was a striking middle-aged blonde woman, the same color hair and blue eyes as her sister, though her cheeks and jaw line were softer. Her ears were longer at the top but didn't taper into the fae peaks at the end. It was so strange to see ears looking somewhere between human and fae. She was much shorter than Carys, too, her figure was more filled out with motherly curves rather than Carys's muscular soldier's physique. But the familial link was clear—they were sisters.

"Hi," the woman said, turning to Remy and shaking her hand. "I'm Morgan."

"Remy," she replied.

"Nice to meet you, Remy," Morgan said. She had a tender counte-nance, very different from her sister in that regard as well. Morgan looked to the heap of children clamoring over Carys. "My eldest is Matthew," she said, nodding to the boy with flaxen blond hair and warm brown eyes. He stood in the middle of his siblings. "Then Maxwell and little Molly."

Remy smiled. They all had names beginning with the letter M. Her own siblings all had names beginning with the same letter. Some rolled their eyes at the tradition, but she had loved it. It had made them feel like one solid family unit.

"Have you brought us anything?" Maxwell asked. He would have looked the twin of his sibling were it not for him being an entire head shorter. Matthew nudged him. He had that well-mannered confidence of the eldest child.

Carys laughed. "I'd never forget to bring you something." She raised a conspiratorial eyebrow as she pilfered through her pack. The boys lit up with excitement. The youngest, Molly, couldn't have been over three. She played with her golden hair braided over her shoulders as she looked to her brothers, more interested in their reactions than the presents brought for them.

Something in Remy ached at that look Molly gave the older boys. She remembered that feeling so well, like her older brothers hung the sun in the sky, with her following their lead like a duckling, to their great frustration.

"Gifts from the West," Carys said as she produced a bundle of cloth from her pack. Unwrapping it, she produced three small clay disks, a string loop attached to the top of each one. A different detailed little painting covered the face of each ornament. She handed the painting of a falcon with a fish in its talons to Matthew, a moon and constellations to Maxwell, and an oak tree brilliant with autumn colors to Molly. Remy wasn't sure why she had chosen each painting for each child, but they seemed to be delighted with her selections.

Carys had brought these gifts all the way from the Western Court. They had been in her pack for weeks, undamaged during the endless hiking and riding. Remy thought back to how mindful she was not to sit on her pack round the fires like the rest of them. It now made sense. Carys had brought those clay ornaments all this way. She had been thinking of them this whole time.

"All right you three, go wash up for dinner." Morgan's voice cut above the din of her squealing children.

Morgan and Carys hugged each other at last, a long, beautiful hug that Remy yearned for. The children did as they were told, rumbling down the hallway and up the stairs to prepare for dinner.

The tightness in Remy's muscles loosened. She felt that loving warmth as if it hung in the air. It was the feeling of being in a family.

After the children washed, they all crushed in to eat dinner around the kitchen table. A fae, a witch, a halfling, and a human sat at the table. It sounded like the beginning of a joke. Two chairs had magically appeared from somewhere in the house. Although the house was a bit run down, there was a sense that they loved the home. A patchwork of paintings hung on the walls. Baskets filled with grains and fresh produce were tucked into the corners. A mishmash of painted teacups hung on hooks on the wall. Evidence of three young children was everywhere: toys, drawings, and shoes strewn about the floor. It was happily chaotic and brimming with love.

Morgan prepared a delicious meal for them. The stew was hearty and spiced to perfection, the bread fresh and spongy. They carried on pleasant conversations, Carys telling the children exaggerated stories of all the places she had traveled. Morgan and Magnus seemed to understand that Remy didn't want to answer questions about her life, so they chatted about their own. Magnus was a carpenter. He owned a shop on the high street selling ornate dining sets to his Eastern fae patrons. Morgan was a seamstress and repaired other humans' clothing at night when the children were sleeping. They talked about their lives in such simple terms. Magnus would ruffle Maxwell's hair, and Morgan would rub a hand down her husband's back. Such mild, affectionate touches. It was a family.

The shadows grew long, and the bowls of stew disappeared. Remy lost herself to the fantasy of what a family would be like—to sit around a large dining table with loved ones and friends. Heather and Fenrin would be there, her children chasing each other around the table. She would sit with a swollen belly, her third child, and her husband would rest a warm hand on it and beam at her with happiness. She knew that husband's face, though she dare not admit it to herself. They would laugh and eat until the candles burned out.

And as they did, that daydream twisted into one of smoke and screams. Northern guards running in as she ran to cover her children . . .

"Remy?" Carys's voice snapped her out of her waking nightmare. "You want any more bread before I finish it?"

Carys held out the breadbasket to her. Remy shook the visions from her mind. It was a fantasy to think she could ever have something like that. Until the Northern King was dead, she would know no peace.

"No thanks," Remy said, forcing a smile. "I'm stuffed." She turned to Morgan and Magnus, "It was delici— "

A knock came at the door. Carys stood, "I'll get it," she said, wiping her face with a napkin.

When Carys returned, she was frowning. She grabbed Remy by the forearm, pulling her to stand.

"We've had a long day—we're going to bed," Carys instructed. She clenched a piece of cream-colored paper in her fist as she nodded to Remy's large traveling pack in the hallway.

"Thanks for the dinner, Morgs, you know how I adore your cooking." Carys winked at her sister.

Remy followed Carys down the hall to a sitting room. Carys dropped her pack with a heavy thump onto the floor and pushed the two tiny couches together on either side of a worn wooden chest. Carys opened the chest and started pulling out cushions and blankets, transforming the lounge furniture into a bed. She did it in a silent, practiced way, without acknowledging or releasing the paper clenched in her hand.

"What's going on?" Remy cut in, watching the female fae manically make the bed.

Carys collapsed, sitting onto the bed, her head in her hands.

"I knew this would happen," she said, dropping her shoulders.

"What's wrong?" Remy sat beside her.

"The last time Hale communicated with King Norwood by fae fire, the King told him to stop in the city to meet with him before continuing on his quest." Carys passed Remy the wrinkled piece of paper in her hand. "The King is curious to meet you, it seems."

Remy unfolded the crinkled piece of paper. A watermark of the Eastern crest marked the back. On the front in flourished writing was an invitation.

"A ball to celebrate the Autumnal Equinox," Remy read.

"The herald who brought it made very clear that they expect both of us to attend." Malice touched her voice. "It took them a handful of hours to find us, faster than Hale or I predicted. The King doesn't like his son keeping secrets."

"Is he really as bad as he seems?" Remy muttered to the invitation.

"Worse." Carys frowned. It was an invitation to a royal ball, and yet it felt like a punishment. The heavy hand of the Eastern King's control was felt all the way in this townhouse at the edge of the city.

"At least we don't have to meet with him alone," Remy said, grasping for a positive.

"At least there will be excellent food and drinks." Carys leaned into Remy, her voice brightening. "And we can go to the high road tomorrow and buy too-expensive dresses and charge it to Hale's account."

"Am I to wear a dress like the one in Ruttmore again?" Remy grimaced. The idea of parading around not only in front of the Eastern Court but the King himself in nothing but a slip of fabric made her queasy.

"Gods, no." Carys laughed. "If anything, we'll try to cover you up as much as possible." Remy narrowed her eyes at Carys, forcing her to continue. "Oh, don't give me that look. I don't need to tell you that you are the most beautiful witch I have ever seen and that red dress nearly lit every male in the room on fire."

Remy smirked. She did need to hear it.

"But tomorrow will be a different game entirely," Carys said, cocking her head.

"How so?"

"Ruttmore was about drawing every eye to you. Now, we want them to not see you for what you really are."

Remy looked to Carys, rubbing her hands nervously down her legs. "And what am I?"

"You are a weapon," Carys said. "And many of those greedy fae will want to possess you for themselves. We don't want them seeing you as a powerful red witch, and we definitely don't want the King to see how important you are to Hale. I wouldn't be surprised if Hale avoided you entirely the whole night."

There it was again. Even Carys could tell that Remy was important to Hale, though she didn't say how. Remy wished they could lay it all bare, these words and half-spoken truths. She wished she could be who she really was and not hide her powers anymore.

"Right," Remy said, shucking off her shoes. "Let's get some sleep. We have a big day of shopping tomorrow."

Carys's face split into a wide, white-toothed grin.

CHAPTER SEVENTEEN

The palace was beautiful in the twilight. Magical shadows danced along the walls of Wynreach castle. Strings of golden-tipped leaves covered the stairs up to the palace's giant wooden doors. Two pumpkin lanterns framed each step. Carved in intricate details, the pumpkins drew lingering views by courtiers, who stopped to examine them at each step.

Witches celebrated the Autumnal Equinox, too, but nothing like this. They lit candles, feasted on the last of the summer crops, and cast spells of resiliency for the coming winter months. Winding down into the winter, it was a time when they prepared to hibernate along with the rest of the forest creatures. But the fae celebrated differently. Everything was big, loud, and decadent in the fae world.

The Eastern Court preferred to wear deep jewel tones, nothing like the riot of colors in the Southern Court or the neutral earthy colors of the West. Carys looked resplendent in a sleeveless, emerald-green gown. It hugged her body like a glove down to the knee, then fanned out into a mermaid tail. Wearing her hair up in intricate braids, she had taken hours of the afternoon to perfect them. She had to raise her hem at every step so as not to trip herself from her tight dress, but she looked stunning. Standing next to her, Remy was sure she would be invisible.

Remy wore a plum purple gown that matched many of the shades of purple worn by other courtiers. Purple was the patron color of the Eastern Court in honor of their violet witches, though that coven of witches was all gone now. Her dress had a modest scoop neck and three-quarter length sleeves. She wore small hoops under her dress to create a bell-shaped skirt. Wearing all that scaffolding, Remy had no sense how close she could get to things before her skirts would bump into them. She much preferred riding leathers. Her hair cascaded down her left side, pulled back with an elegant silver clip on the right. She had let Carys re-do her makeup, and the female fae did a much better job of making her look elegant rather than garish.

As they took another step, a pair of fine leather boots came into view.

"You look good." An amused voice came from above them.

They looked into the face of Bri. Bri wore a teal tunic detailed with delicate golden lace and merlot-colored trousers. The golden cuffs at the tips of her fae ears brought out the molten gold in her kohl-lined eyes. She looked incredible and eccentric. Remy smirked. She could never imagine Bri in a dress.

"Thank you." Carys demurred with a mocking bow. "I am sure I will capture the eye of every male in there."

"And many of the females too." Bri winked with a cocky grin. She turned her golden eyes to Remy. "You look good as well," she said. "Except you need one more thing."

From behind Bri's back, she produced a black leather belt. Suspended from it was a steel scabbard and the hilt of a small dagger.

"A gift for you," she said, handing it to Remy. Painted red lips parting, Remy ran her fingers over the hilt. Swirling constellations and bursting golden stars etched every inch of its silver. On the other side was a shining sun, radiating beams of gold down into the sheath.

Remy grasped the hilt in the way Bri had taught her. It fit the size of her hand perfectly. The blade was the perfect weight and sharpened so finely that even the lightest touch would draw blood. It was lovely and lethal—like this castle, like Hale.

"This is mine?" Remy whispered, running her eyes over the blade again.

"You've been training hard," Bri said. "You deserve your own weapon. Careful with that, though." She warned. "People will think it's decorative, but it's as deadly as anything."

Remy beamed at the female warrior, her friend. She would treasure this gift forever.

"Thank you." Remy bit her cheek to keep the emotions from overwhelming her. Bri simply shrugged as if it were nothing.

"Put it on!" Carys urged with an excited squeal.

Remy sheathed the dagger and grabbed the belt. She buckled it to her waist, the scabbard sitting off her body from the hoops of the skirt. It sat at the perfect height, her forearm skimming the hilt at her hip. She felt a lot less exposed wearing the dagger.

"Ready to enter the lion's den?" Bri asked, crossing her arms as she looked to the belt around Remy's waist.

Remy looked at the two giant stone lions sitting guard on either side of the massive doorway into the grand hall. The lion was the prominent feature of the Eastern Court crest. She noted more hints of the lion motif: lions' heads, wild manes, and paw prints carved into the doors in the same style as the carvings on the doors throughout Wynreach.

Remy shifted back and forth, wanting to pace at the sight of the sentinels ahead of her. A steady flow of courtiers kept passing them on the stairs, most of them not even stopping to look at the three of them. It was a good sign that they weren't interesting enough to be noticed.

"No, not really," Remy responded. She took a deep breath.

"Me neither," Carys said, wrapping her arm around Remy's and pulling her forward. "Let's go find the wine."

~

Dazzling splashes of burgundy, ginger, and gold decorated the grand hall. Food tables ran the entire right-hand length of the enormous room. A feast lay across it, with cornucopia centerpieces dotted along them. The grand space smelled of spiced meats and warm cider, and a twelve-piece orchestra played on a balcony above the feasting tables. The rest of the space opened out to the horde of guests. Dancers carved out a wide circle in the crowd with dozens of couples twirling to the light music. At the far end of the hall sat the dais where King Norwood presided.

The ruler's dark mahogany armrests curled into lion's claws with the giant head of a roaring lion cresting the top. King Gedwin Norwood sat rigidly on his throne. Looking nothing like what Remy had imagined, he had silvery white hair and black, sunken eyes under large bushy eyebrows. He was so lean, he looked sickly. His cheeks hollowed out, his frame drowning in a giant black velvet coat. His long, knobby fingers grasped the arms of his throne. He was the opposite of Hale, wholly grim and devoid of life.

Beside the throne sat a wooden chair with purple upholstered cushions. A plump, blonde-haired woman perched on it, frowning. Remy assumed that was the queen. She looked much younger than Hale's father, wearing a jaded, morose expression.

She did not smile from her thin-lipped mouth like the two blond-haired young men standing to her left. They had short, blunt noses, plump cheeks, and rounded jaws. Their blond hair was in stark contrast to their black eyes. Those must have been Hale's younger brothers, Belenus and Augustus. The younger one twirled a purple flower in his hand. Crushing a petal with his thumbnail, he sniffed it in a sinister way that made the hairs on Remy's arms stand up. Hale did not stand beside his father's throne. He must have been mingling through the crowded hall.

Remy searched the room, her eyes landing on Hale. His eyes darted away from her gaze as soon as it landed on him. He looked magnificent. He wore a high-necked, cinnamon brown jacket that matched the highlights of his hair. A hint of a white shirt peeked through the intricate wooden clasps of his jacket. The tailored clothes suited him, but it was the way he stood, the pompous way he rested his fist on his hip and waved his glass of wine about as he spoke that made him look like a handsome stranger. His larger-than-life persona was befitting of a crown prince in his home court.

Talhan stood to his right. His laughter boomed over the music as Hale regaled a gaggle of gray-haired females with a story. Hale cut a quick glance to her and then looked away again. That was all the recognition he would give her.

"Drinks," Carys said, steering Remy with ease through the shifting assembly.

Remy distracted herself with food and drink. The sight of so many fae faces made her pulse quicken. What would they do if they knew who she was? Most of them ignored her. She caught a few curious glimpses, but they were fleeting. She released a scant breath as she popped a grape into her cheek.

Bri grabbed a whole turkey leg, eating it with little decorum. Carys drank a whole glass of wine in one gulp and grabbed another. She'd be fine as long as she stayed wedged between these two and avoided any notice from the King.

A flaxen-haired female walked in front of the hungry trio, her eyes snagging on Bri. The golden-eyed warrior smirked at the beautiful courtier and gave her a wink. The female blushed furiously and stormed away. Carys pulled her mouth away from her goblet just long enough to chuckle.

"Hello." A grating, nasal voice came from behind her.

Remy turned from the table and looked up into the mocking smirk of one of Hale's brothers. The taller one, he couldn't have been more than twenty. She tried to recall which one he was. The elder was Belenus, she believed. The thin gold circlet he wore had blurred into his blond hair when he stood on the dais. Remy stared at him as he gave her a look of dissatisfaction. She felt Carys's foot dip under her large skirts and stomp on her toe and understood.

She was supposed to bow. Remy had only bowed to Hale once, before slamming a door into him. The thought of doing so now seemed laughable.

Remy dropped into a low, awkward bow and mumbled, "Your Highness."

"Witches never did have many manners," he said to her with a frown. He looked over to where Hale stood and smirked. Hale was trying and failing not to watch them.

"Apologies, Your Highness," Remy murmured looking down at her hands. A crowd had gathered around them, flocking to the young prince. This was exactly what she feared happening. She did not want the attentions of Hale's little brother. It could only lead to bad things.

"Do you know how to dance, witch?" Belenus asked, extending his long, slender hand.

"No," Remy said, but Belenus flashed her a malevolent grin.

"I will show you," he said like a command. Dozens of eyes drilled into her skin as she looked to that outstretched hand. She knew she had to take it.

She swallowed and took Belenus's cold, soft hand. He led her to the center of the circle of dancers. Everyone gave them a wide berth. Some stopped dancing to watch them. The entire Eastern Court was staring at her now. She didn't dare seek out Hale in the crowd. She knew the exact look he would have on his face.

Belenus placed his free hand lightly on her waist. Remy was grateful for her hoop skirt in that moment and the buffer of distance it would keep from the young prince. He led her into a slow waltz. Those black eyes bored into her as if he could see every thought swirling in her head.

"I see you favor the same shade as I," he said, his eyes skirting unabashedly across her bosom and down her plum dress. He wore a jacket the exact matching shade. "Excellent taste."

She wanted to tell him she had looked at twenty other dresses, but that Carys had forced her to wear this one because it was a less flattering shade on her. It would have been helpful to know that it was the prince's favorite color. Remy said nothing but inclined her head in thanks.

Belenus looked at her bare neck. "I'm surprised my brother hasn't offered to make you his personal witch. I'm sure my father wouldn't allow it, but I'm surprised Hale still didn't at least try."

Remy bit the inside of her cheek. Little did Belenus know she had offered her services to Hale only yesterday. Hale had not said that his father would forbid it. Hale didn't seem inclined to mention her at all to the King. What would Gedwin Norwood do if the crown prince wanted to take a red witch? Surely he wouldn't punish the heir to his own throne that severely?

Her hair flew off her shoulders as Belenus whipped her around in a twirl. As she spun, Remy saw the King was watching her too. He tracked her with a stillness that made her want to shudder. She knew she would not win his favor anytime soon, and she prayed the King would not call on her for a closer inspection. He had probably ordered his son to invite her to dance, designing this trap to draw a reaction from Hale. She was sure of it.

Remy saw Hale's cinnamon brown hair and matching jacket in the crowd, but his back was turned to them. She was glad for it. She could not think of a single appropriate reaction from him—each would break her in a different way. Hale spoke to Talhan, who was laughing away, the picture of a merry courtier. It was good Hale was with Talhan too. His easygoing cheer offset Hale's rigidness.

As they moved, Belenus followed Remy's line of sight and saw that it snagged on the back of his brother's head. He smirked.

Damn. She knew she shouldn't have looked for him in the crowd.

"Are you fucking him?"

Remy's eyes flew to Belenus. She stared at him as his mouth twisted, pulling up to one side. She shook her head, trying not to gape at the smug expression on his face.

"Ah, so you want to be fucking him." He smiled.

"You have a foul mouth for a child." Remy's voice filled with venom, though she kept her face neutral. Too many people were watching for her to show her true disgust.

"I am not a child. I am nineteen," he said, sneering. The same age as Remy. "And you will watch your tone when speaking to me."

"Why did you ask me to dance, *Your Highness*?" Remy said in a sickly-sweet voice. Belenus scowled at her as the music swelled to its finale.

"I wanted to see why my brother tried to hide you from us," he said, giving her one more sweeping look. "I was expecting a rare treasure."

"I'm sorry to disappoint," Remy said flatly. The music played its last long note.

"Everything Hale touches ends in disappointment," Belenus said, bowing to her and walking off before she could rise from her curtsy.

What an awful, hateful man. No wonder Hale avoided Wynreach like the plague. Imagine growing up with *that* as your little brother.

Remy pushed her way back to the food tables but couldn't find Carys or Bri. She grabbed a goblet of wine and kept searching. Hale and Talhan weren't where they stood either.

"Dancing with a prince, lucky girl," a middle-aged female said to her. She wore a short-sleeved lapis gown, her neck dripping with diamonds. She had a pleasant if not bored look on her face. "Many eligible young ladies will be quite jealous of you tonight, my dear."

Remy tried to laugh, but it came out more like a snort. She could imagine no one fawning after Belenus.

"The prince is an accomplished dancer," Remy said, throwing out the first thing she thought to say.

"For a foreigner to court life, you dance like a princess." The female clasped her hands as she smiled, swept up in the romance of the dance. "It is a shame you are not fae."

She took Remy by the hand and pulled her into conversations with four other middle-aged males. She showed Remy off like she was a new oddity for them all to examine. Remy nodded to each one when introduced, forgetting their names the second they left the older female's mouth. Not saying a word, Remy continued to scan the room for her friends.

She found herself jostled into another conversation, squished between two bantering old males. They droned on about trade, the changing of seasons, and redecorating their houses. The group seemed to ignore her. She wasn't fae, so she wasn't worth noticing.

"What a waste it was for Gedwin to claim that bastard." Remy's attention snapped back to the male at her right. She considered unsheathing her new dagger as she scowled at him.

"Well, if his Fated had lived, it would have been worth it," the female who had found Remy chided. Sounds of the room pressed in on Remy more. The heat and the noise made her feel queasy.

"No one saw the Northern Rebellion coming." A gruff laugh came from another male across the circle.

"Still, he shouldn't have hung the succession of the Eastern Court on a Fated love match," the male to her right said incredulously.

"What was that princess' name again? There was Raffiel, Rivitus . . . Ruafora was it?" the female recounted, swirling her hand through the air. Remy held her breath as they spoke.

"No, that was the last one," the gruff one said.

"Risabella?" the female mused.

"I think not, but it was just as strange." The male chuckled.

"It doesn't matter anymore, regardless." She waved off the thought.

"King Norwood should bend to the Northern Court if he knows what's good for him," the fourth person said in a scratchy, thick voice.

"That's blasphemy," the female balked.

"You're telling me if Vostemur walked in here you wouldn't bend the knee to him?" the male's eyebrows rose as he replied.

Remy's magic stirred at the name of the Northern King. The conversation faded under her ragged breathing and her heart pounding in her ears. She needed to get out of there before she started glowing red. She pushed her way through the crowd, making her way toward the opened archway and the empty balcony beyond.

She was halfway through the crowd when she felt the air shift. Her whole body froze a second before the screams started.

The room filled with shrieks as the crowd pushed back against her, away from the center of the grand hall. All eyes held fast on the scene before them. Remy craned her neck to see past the tall male pushing in front of her.

She saw the flash of metal armor first. Three males stood in the center of the room. Clad in full suits of armor, they faced the dais. The one in the center held an empty burlap sack, the contents of which were strewn about his feet. Remy's stomach roiled. They were severed heads.

"What is the meaning of this!" thundered King Norwood from his throne. A line of Eastern guards formed a step below the dais, protecting the King.

"Presents from King Vostemur," the tallest guard boomed. The three of them were impossibly tall, seeming like giants in the fae crowd.

How could Remy have missed spotting them amongst the courtiers?

"King Vostemur would like to remind you—" the one holding the burlap sack had a heavy, grating voice, "—that this is what happens when you try to claim back disputed territory. These heads are from Valtene."

Gasps echoed around the room. The throng of fae pressed in closer together like a flock of scared sheep. Remy tasted the fear, thicker in the air than muggy days in Saxbridge.

Valtene? Remy knew that name, but how?

In a split second she remembered it was a Western Court town that bordered the Northern Court. Was the North moving its borders into the Western Court?

"The same will happen with Falhampton if you do not heed his warning," the tallest one said.

"Falhampton is an Eastern town. It has been for centuries!" King Norwood stood at last. He was tall, nearly the height of Fenrin, his lean build hidden by his heavy black coat and furs. The king glared at the armored soldiers.

"It is a Northern town now," the tall soldier said. "You have one week to withdraw your troops, or you will be gifted more presents from King Vostemur."

The Northern soldier spoke the words so lightly for the weight of his threat. It was tantamount to a declaration of war. Remy's eyes kept darting back to the graying, twisted faces on the floor. She thought of how close she nearly came to the same fate when she was in the Western Court. Her heartbeat punched into her ribcage.

With his beady black eyes, King Norwood stared down at the soldiers for a long time. Remy waited for the orders for the Northern soldiers to be seized, but that order never came.

"Get out of my palace. Now," Norwood finally said in a low, biting tone.

The soldiers sketched mocking bows. "Enjoy your presents, Your Majesty."

The crowd parted, giving them a wide berth, and the soldiers stalked out of the hall. Their eyes were shadowed by the helmets that covered half of their faces, but she saw their smirking lips. No one touched them as the fae granted them free passage out of the castle.

The crowd began to murmur as the soldiers left, but King Norwood's voice could still be heard, cutting above the rising din.

"You!" he shouted, pointing into the crowd. Remy followed the point of his finger and saw Hale. His face was hard, his brows furrowed as he stared up at his father. Talhan stood close to the prince's side. "Get your soldiers, I need to speak with you. Now."

The noise of the room rose into frantic chatter. Remy continued her push out to the balcony, skirting past the five rotting heads without looking at them again. The cool autumn air hit her, pulling her back to her senses.

Breathe, she instructed herself.

She should not have come here. The second she saw that invitation, she should have gotten back on that boat and left for the Southern Court. She had lost all sense of self-preservation not only to find the talismans but to be near Hale. That magnetism would be the death of her.

Shadows shrouded the sweeping palace gardens as Remy gazed out over them. Wandering further along, she moved away from the bright windows and into the quieter dimness of the balcony. With each step, she felt her pulse slow.

She needed to get out of the Eastern Court at once. They were wasting their time here. They needed to get the amulet of Aelusien and find Baba Morganna. If Vostemur had grown so bold that he did not question sending severed heads to a neighboring kingdom, then war was at their doorstep. Norwood, fearing repercussions, only proved Vostemur's power by not killing the Northern soldiers. Vostemur must be close to cracking the blood bond on the Immortal Blade then, if he was becoming so bold. Remy had to get to it before he did.

The thought stabbed into her side like a blade. There was no time to question her path anymore. The world would not wait for her to be ready.

Remy made her way to the very edge of the balcony, where a small stained glass lantern perched. She stared into a flickering candle, watching the colors dance across the stone railing.

She stared for a long, silent stretch into the candlelight, trying to imagine any successful outcome to the Northern threat, but she could not. Every twist and turn favored Vostemur. Every time she thought she had a plan, another snag would unravel it. She needed the High Priestess of the red witches to tell her what to do.

"I'm not interrupting, am I?" She knew that rough voice without even turning.

"It's not a witch's candle," Remy replied, staring into the flame.

Whatever Hale's father had told him, it had been quick. She did not know if that was a good or bad thing.

"I know." Hale moved to her side, his eyes dropping to the dagger belted at her hip.

"I see Carys isn't the only one who has been spending my money," he laughed, guessing correctly who had obtained the dagger for Remy. "It's an extravagant blade—I should take it out of Bri's wages."

"No, I . . ."

"I won't. It suits you too well, anyway," Hale cut in before Remy could protest anymore. She would offer to pay for it herself, but she had no money. Hale took another slow sidestep toward her. "You look beautiful."

Remy kept her eyes averted. She didn't know how to respond to that. She should have simply thanked him, but she couldn't, not after what Hale had admitted on that boat.

"What did the King say?" Remy changed the subject.

"I will wait until we are elsewhere to tell you the finer details, but it is not good." Hale rubbed his hand down his face. Remy wanted him to continue but knew he wouldn't. It seemed like the walls were listening in this castle. "Of course he did still find the time to scold me for my general behavior, drinking and partying too much, the usual." Remy had seen little of that side of Hale at all. Only for one night in Saxbridge, and that had all been a strategic show. It wasn't the first time she had heard of his bachelor lifestyle, though.

"Renwick seemed to think that sort of behavior is normal for you too," Remy mused. "I presume you have slept with many women?" Remy couldn't believe she had asked that out loud. She had wondered it, but perhaps that quick chug of wine had loosened her tongue.

"There have been some dalliances over the years, though not as many as everyone seems to think." Hale chuckled.

"Have you ever slept with Carys?" Remy felt like she had leapt off a cliff. She had wanted to ask that question so many times, but she never had the courage.

"No." Hale regarded her for a moment before he continued. "You should have seen Carys when I invited her to join my crew. She was so . . . brokenhearted. She found a purpose again during the battles at Falhampton, but . . ." He rubbed his thumb across his pointer finger. "I may have been partial to a bit of philandering once upon a time, but I would never toy with someone like that, and definitely not someone whose heart is already broken. Besides," he said, turning those gray eyes to her, "she was never the one for me, anyway."

Those dangerous eyes made Remy a fool. She wanted to bare her soul to them. She wanted to spill every secret to those eyes, not caring if it consumed her.

"I don't think you should be out here with me," Remy breathed, breaking that spell. "You don't want the King to see us together."

Hale looked at his hands, let down. That hint of sadness shredded her. She couldn't do it anymore. She couldn't shove him away.

Remy remembered what Belenus had said to her. *Everything Hale touches ends in disappointment.* Remy didn't want to be another disappointment. She knew in that moment it was no longer a choice. Consequences be damned, she would follow him anywhere, even into hell itself. She rose onto her tiptoes and planted a soft kiss on Hale's cheek. He turned to her with surprise.

"Remy!" Carys called from the doorway. "I'm here to save you from an evening of royal boredom. The King's councillors want to speak with you, Hale."

Hale's shoulders slumped by Remy's side as Carys hooked a thumb toward the staircase at the other end of the gardens. "Let's get out of here."

Remy turned to look at Hale.

"Go." He chuckled. "Save yourself."

"I'll see you tomorrow, Your Highness," Remy said in a teasing tone.

"Hale," he said in a vacant voice. "Only ever Hale to you."

"Hale," Remy said in a soft, breathless voice.

She watched the way his name on her mouth made him go still as she stepped away from him.

CHAPTER EIGHTEEN

C arys and Remy neared the townhouse in the human part of the city. Remy's fingers twitched with a sudden urge for magic. Her senses prickled at the silence. It was too quiet. They had walked through streets filled with equinox celebrations, but when they turned down this alley, it was dead. Every door was closed and every window on the street had shut their curtains. It was early in the evening still, the following day would be a day of rest, and yet the street seemed frozen.

Remy followed Carys warily back to the door of her sister's house. Morgan opened it before Carys could knock. The halfling looked agitated but otherwise fine.

"All well?" Carys asked, adjusting her chest in her emerald dress for the hundredth time to keep anything from spilling out.

"Yep. Just as you said." Morgan opened the door further and allowed Carys and Remy to enter. "Three of them came, nothing I couldn't handle."

They turned to their right, into the sitting room where they had slept. The room looked ransacked. Their packs lay emptied on the wooden chest, clothing and trekking gear strewn about the floor.

"What happened?" Remy gasped, looking to Morgan. The halfling stood with her arms crossed, leaning against the doorframe.

"Eastern soldiers said they needed to search the house for an unknown reason," Morgan said with a long-suffering sigh.

They had come for the *Shil-de* ring. They wanted it that badly.

"I'm so sorry." Remy set her jaw to the side. This was her fault. She brought this chaos into Morgan's life. Her eyes whizzed up to the ceiling. What about her children?

"It's fine," Morgan waved her hand, following Remy's silent thoughts. "Carys warned me. I've been dealing with fae assholes my whole life. I sent Magnus and the kids to his parents' house for the night." No one would blink an eye at a halfling's home being raided. They would all blame her for it, anyway. Morgan slid her blue eyes to Remy. "They found nothing."

Remy felt the talisman's magical pulse against her chest. She had brought her totem bag with her, tucked between her breasts and her corset. She thought about Belenus's wandering black eyes. He had kept looking at her chest. Remy realized far too late that he was not admiring her figure but sensing the magic of the ring.

"I'm sure they'll come back once they notice you're not at the ball," Morgan said, eyes boring into Remy's chest. Remy wondered if the halfling sensed the ring's magic, too, or was simply perceptive.

"That's why we're not staying," Carys said, shimmying out of her dress. The fabric pooled around her ankles as she unabashedly stepped out of the circle of emerald. Picking up the dress, she laid it over the armrest of the couch. "Sell these dresses, Morgs, it'll be a good bit of coin. Sorry about all this."

"Anything for you, little sister," the halfling said, that motherly warmth edging back into her voice. "Especially if you leave me with dresses that cost more than Magnus makes in a year."

Carys looked at Remy. "Get changed—we're going to Lavender Hall."

~

Remy had assumed Lavender Hall was the name of a bar or restaurant, but as Carys led her further into the shadows, she realized they were heading into an abandoned part of town. The surrounding buildings had fallen into complete disrepair: shingles missing off the roofs, doors bashed open, windows smashed. In the center of this derelict part of town was a looming dark temple.

Not a single brazier was lit, but in the moonlight Remy could barely make out the giant edifice. Built like a five-tiered cake, it poked above the line of houses. Black stone columns held up the raised entryway of the structure. The two giant wooden doors displayed elaborate flower carvings that were painted in violet and gold.

It was an old violet witch temple, Remy concluded upon seeing the door. The violet witches, natives of the Eastern Court, had made astonishing perfumes and exquisite scents that did all sorts of magic: ensnare a person's mind, bring money or fame, and even cure ill health. Like all the covens of witches, the magic often passed through the female bloodline. Female witches were the ones who had more magic, and the violet witches lost sight of that balance of things. They created magical scents that encouraged the womb to produce female heirs, thus creating more magic for their order, but within a generation there were so few male witches that their numbers dwindled even with polygamous pairings becoming common. It was rumored that the High Priestess of the violet witches cast a spell on her coven in an effort to control them, though Remy knew of no such spell. The younger generation of violet witches resented the mandate from their forebears to produce more witchlings and bucked against their overbearing predecessors by refusing to reproduce. And so the violet witch numbers shriveled into near nothing. They abandoned their temples and scattered like the wind across the east.

That was over eighty years ago. This temple was an old relic now.

Remy climbed the stone steps and followed as Carys pushed her way inside those enormous violet doors.

Moonlight beamed in through the high arched windows. The illustrations of flowers and Mhenbic symbols on the vaulted ceilings seemed to dance in the glowing light. Marble icons of the long-gone witches looked down upon the stone floor. An amethyst-colored rug split the room in half from the doors to the pulpit at the far end. Rotting, rectangular banners draped from either side of the raised, carpeted platform. A shrine covered in dusty candles and smooth stones sat in the center.

The temple remained untouched, unlike the surrounding area. Remy wondered if the humans misinterpreted the runes painted on the doors for curses. Humans feared witch magic and didn't know how to read their Mhenbic symbols.

Remy followed Carys down the long aisle between the wooden pews and past the pulpit into a small back stairwell. Carys moved like she had done this many times before. They climbed five flights of creaky, steep stairs. Remy groaned, adjusting her pack, wondering again why she had to bring her heavy load when Carys had left hers behind.

"If you think this is challenging, you'll never make it up the Rotted Peak," Carys jeered.

Remy frowned but didn't reply. They reached a small landing where a ladder rose into the ceiling hatch, already open to the night sky.

Remy said nothing as she followed Carys onto a circular roof. Waist-high stonewalls surrounded the rooftop, and beyond them . . . the sight of the city took Remy's breath away. The view was even more spectacular than from the palace. Remy went to the edge of the wall, leaning over as she looked down all five stories of open air to the ground. Her legs felt wobbly again when she realized how high up they were. But her racing heart calmed once she looked at the glowing lights of Wynreach. The celebrations of the equinox ball seemed to still be going strong at the castle far on the hill. It was lit from every side by giant fires, and the colors of the glass windows seemed to glow with the firelight from within the castle itself.

"It's beautiful, isn't it?" a male voice rumbled next to her.

She hadn't realized that Hale was beside her. So entranced by the flickering lights of the capital, she had not noticed that the Twin Eagles and Hale were already on the roof.

"Hi," Remy said. In her mind, she rolled her eyes at herself. It was all she could think to say after that moment on the balcony, otherwise she would spill all her words and feelings to him.

"Hi," Hale said back with the smirk that sent shivers dancing around Remy's body.

Hale leaned beside Remy, watching her rather than the view. She looked over his face: those thick dark eyebrows, those full soft lips, that hard sculpted jawline. Remy had only been away a handful of hours and yet . . . she had missed him. She had missed looking at that gorgeous familiar face, hearing the deep timbre of his voice, smelling his ocean air scent.

The position they took next to each other was so similar to the day before on the Crushwold river boat. It felt like a lifetime ago. His parting words from that morning seemed to stretch between them, just as the feel of the stubble on his cheek still tingled across her lips from that fleeting kiss on the balcony. His affections were real. Her affections were real. She prayed Hale's fae ears could not hear the pounding of her heart.

"What?!" Carys's shout snapped them out of their silence.

Remy looked over to the three fae soldiers. They had a scattering of blankets laid out against the opposite curving wall. Candles flickered beside plates of food and bottles of wine that they passed between them. It was a picnic under the stars.

The prince turned to Carys, his fae ears probably hearing their whole conversation. "It's the King's orders, Carys. There's nothing we can do."

"What's going on?" Remy wondered.

She went over to the blankets and sat beside Carys. Hale followed, and Remy did not miss it that he chose to sit beside her.

"The King is a dick, that's what's going on," Bri said, shoving a slice of cheese into her mouth.

Talhan snorted. "She's not wrong."

"I take it your meeting with the King went well?" Remy grimaced.

"He has ordered Bri, Carys, and I to go back to Falhampton." Talhan cursed, setting the plate of fruit down roughly. "He says we are to pull back Hale's soldiers and help in the evacuation of the town."

Remy blinked at them. He could not be serious. King Norwood was ceding his borders to the Northern Court? Did he really think giving them his border town would do anything other than encourage a bigger push into his lands?

"It's bullshit," Bri snarled. "The soldiers there could handle an evacuation fine without us. He just wants to keep us from Hale."

"Why would he do that?" Remy pursed her lips.

The four of them exchanged looks, unspoken conversations seeming to happen between them.

A quiet anger threaded through Carys's voice. "He wants him to fail."

"Why?" Remy couldn't understand why the King would send his eldest son on such an important mission and then plot for his failure.

"He wants you to get the amulet of Aelusien, doesn't he?" she said. "Surely we would have better success if we all went together."

"Exactly," Talhan said, jutting his jaw to the side as he chewed.

"Then why?" Remy pushed.

"He asked for the *Shil-de* ring," Hale said, craning his neck down to her from where he sat at her side. "His advisors are just as scheming as he is, and they have convinced him he should be its guardian until Prince Raffiel is found. He wanted you to stay in Wynreach with him too."

Remy recoiled.

"Hale didn't tell him where it was," Bri said to Remy, as if reading her mind. "He didn't give you up either."

Remy looked at Hale, his eyes shadowed in darkness. *He didn't give you up either.*

"Yeah, and get this." Talhan rolled his eyes. "He said that a future king should have more than enough power to conquer the Rotted Peak alone."

"I don't understand." Remy was so confused. Why would the King separate them? Just because his son had refused to give him the ring?

Hale had gone still at her side. She knew the answers to her questions were bringing him pain.

Carys answered for him, "The King does not want Hale as his heir." Remy's head whirled to her as she continued. "The King had claimed Hale as his son because of the blue witch's prophecy on his birth that Hale was Fated to a High Mountain fae. That union would have brought the king incredible power to be so closely tied to them . . . and it would mean that Hale would marry into the High Mountain Court and his next child, Belenus, would become heir to the Eastern throne."

Cary's words speared through Remy even though she had heard them before. She remembered what Hale had confessed to her about how King Norwood had treated his mother.

"After the Siege of Yexshire, Hale was . . ." Carys couldn't find the words to continue.

"An inconvenience," Bri said, angry for her friend. "An obstacle standing in the way of Belenus's ascension to the throne."

"He's sent you on so many fool's errands over the years," Talhan said to Hale, "and you've proved him wrong every single time. But this . . . going up the Rotted Peak just the two of you . . ."

"He hopes I will never come back down," Hale finished.

Anger rose in Remy's veins at the sad, deflated look Hale tried to hide. He had thought if he completed all his father's impossible missions that he would earn his love. But the pride his father showed after each accomplishment was short lived. How convenient for the King to have his eldest son die a hero and, in doing so, both bring him glory and pave the way for the son he wanted as his heir. Remy hurt for him in a way deeper than she ever hurt for herself.

She threaded her fingers through Hale's, giving his large warm hand a squeeze. He looked at their hands and gripped hers in return. As he removed a piece of the wall he'd built around himself, Remy glimpsed the pain that thrummed below the surface.

"Well, the King was right about one thing," Remy said. The four of them all turned to her. "I am a red witch, and I am more powerful than he knows. I do not fear Mt. Aelusien." Carys pressed her lips together as she gave Remy a grateful nod. She knew how Remy spoke the words directly to the prince's broken spirits. Remy believed the truth in her words too. The red witches placed the amulet in Mt. Aelusien, but only the fae had ever sought it out. Remy would be the first with red witch magic to try. If anyone could succeed, it would be her. Her only regret was that they could not come with her. "I will miss all of you."

They were her friends, Remy realized all at once. These fae warriors she had once only admired were now her friends. She couldn't bring herself to make another tearful goodbye.

Talhan gave her a small smile. "We'll sort out Falhampton in no time and get those people to safety," he assured her. "And then we'll come find you on your way to Yexshire." He said it like it was a simple, straightforward thing.

But they all knew that they may not see each other for a long time, perhaps never again. Bri uncorked the bottle of wine by her side and poured it into the jumble of random mugs before her. She passed them around to everyone, keeping the bottle to drink from herself. The prince held tight to Remy's hand, reaching with his far arm for the mug being passed his way.

"To the red witch and our prince," Bri said, raising the bottle, "May the Gods bless your journey."

"Hear, hear," her twin said as they clinked mugs.

They fell into relaxed conversation, telling jokes and stories, eating from the tray of fruits and cheeses. The stars sparkled over their heads, the constellations shining bright in this darkened part of town. Every time they drained a bottle of wine dry, another seemed to appear out of Talhan's bag as if by magic.

Hale pulled a fur blanket over himself and Remy, holding onto her hand through the night.

The promise of morning sun lay pink and golden in the far clouds as Remy stirred awake. She felt Hale shifting beside her. She had fallen asleep sitting against that stone wall after laughing and drinking long into the night. A blanket covered her up to the shoulders. She rested her head against the prince's shoulder, feeling his heat radiating into her cheek. Winter would be here within a couple of months, and the mornings were turning icy.

Remy didn't want to open her eyes. She didn't want to move at all. The bottles of wine last night had done her no favors. Her head squeezed under an invisible force. Her brain was spinning and scattered. She could not grab on to any line of thought, and she wanted nothing more than a few hours of sleep, hoping it would bring her more coherence.

The prince shifted his head down to hers. His lips swept across Remy's temple and hovered at her ear.

"Time to go," he whispered. His warm breath in Remy's ear made her finally open her eyes.

He was smiling at her like he was trying to hold in a laugh.

"What?" Remy narrowed her eyes at him.

"Your eyes are glowing red." Hale smirked.

"Oh," Remy said, "Oh!" she said again realizing what he meant. Her eyes were glowing red because of that whisper in her ear. That whisper made her want to pull his lips to hers, headache or no.

Remy's cheeks heated, but the prince was already moving. Last night had felt somehow even more intimate than that night at the card game in Ruttmore. There was no blaming it on getting caught up in the act today. It was honest and slow.

The prince packed the blankets with stealth. They made to move to their packs by the hatch door, and as they did Carys reached an arm up and gently squeezed Remy's ankle.

It was the only acknowledgement the tired fae gave her before she dropped back into sleep, but Remy knew what it meant: goodbye and good luck.

Bri didn't open her eyes either as she mumbled into her blanket, "Don't die, Rem."

Remy touched the hilt of her new dagger she had belted onto her waist and smiled as she descended the ladder.

Small city stables sat at the back of Lavender Hall, fallen into near disarray. Two horses waited in the stalls. Remy watched as Hale made quick work of saddling them. He set them in the same configuration as they had on their ride through the Southern Court: one carrying their two packs and one for both of them to ride.

The smells of the barn made Remy's stomach roil. She was sure her face had gone green.

"How are you acting so normal?" Remy groaned as Hale tightened the saddle's buckles. He had drunk an entire bottle of wine by himself last night, and yet he seemed clear-eyed and light-spirited.

"Not too partial to the wine, are you?" Hale laughed while keeping his eyes on his task.

Remy was not much of a drinker, and when she did she made a point of never imbibing too much. She had spent too many tavern shifts kicking out hungover patrons to think getting drunk was a good idea. But she had newfound empathy for what they must have been feeling. She tried not to think too hard on it. The thought of the wine alone would turn her stomach to acid and it would all come spilling back up. How in the Gods' names was she going to ride a horse?

Remy went to the packhorse, pilfering through the outer pocket of her bag as the horse shifted. She knew each of the glass vials in her pack from feel alone, each one wrapped in thin strips of scrap linen, no two vials identical in size or shape. Her fingers encircled the one she wanted. She lifted it out, unraveling the linen to reveal a thumb-sized vial of light-brown glass. The paint of a five-point star and a mint leaf had rubbed off long ago, but Remy knew this was the right elixir. Heather had made most of her *druni* from bottles of this very magic: a hangover tonic. In backcountry taverns, this stuff was gold. Remy had never needed it herself before, but she kept one vial in her potions bag just in case. It sat along with two dozen other vials that were also for "just in cases" she hoped she would never need to use.

Remy uncorked it and gulped the contents in one foul swig. It made her want to retch, but she forced it down. If she could keep it in her stomach for any amount of time, it would be helpful. She scrunched her face, her nostrils flaring with the effort to not gag. She took another breath and her stomach settled, the pounding in her head already lightening a bit.

Thank the Gods for brown witches, she whispered a silent prayer to Heather. Her guardian was protecting her even still.

By the time they mounted their horse and headed north through the city, the sun was cresting above the pine trees ahead. More and more people emerged from their homes for the day.

The smell of freshly baked bread swirled around them as a baker pushed his cart loaded with loaves and cakes down the cobbled road. He must have awoken in the middle of the night for them all to be baked and ready to sell this early.

Hale flagged him down with a hand. Some sort of silent request flowed between them. The baker stopped, lifting the fine netting over his baking, and produced two round loaves of bread the size of dinner plates. The prince passed him a gold coin and the baker's eyes widened at it. It was far too much payment for two loaves of bread, but the baker simply bowed and mumbled, "Your Highness" and kept on his way. It was neither adoring nor fearful, merely appreciative.

Hale passed Remy a brown loaf of warm bread dotted with dried fruits and swirls of cinnamon. The buttery fruit and spice scent eddied in currents of steam emanating from cracks in the crispy crust. The aroma made her stomach gurgle.

Hale laughed at the sound. Her back pressed so tightly into his front that it wouldn't surprise her if he felt the rumbling.

Remy tore off a piece of bread with her fingers, a whorl of steam lifting into the brisk morning air. With the entire piece in her mouth, the spiced, rich flavors lit up her tongue. An indecent sound groaned out of her. Hale straightened behind her, coughing.

Remy bit her lip to keep from laughing. She was grateful he couldn't see her face. She delighted in what that little sound had done to him. It was hard to turn her mind away from wondering about all the other sounds he might elicit from her.

"I take it you like the bread," Hale said, as Remy devoured the first half of her loaf.

"It's delicious," she replied, cheeks so stuffed with bread her words were barely intelligible. "I've never had anything like it."

"It is my favorite too." She sensed Hale smiling without turning to look at him. "The Northside Baker is famous in Wynreach. I had to make a detour on our way out of the city for you to try it."

That made Remy pause before she continued chewing. Hale had wanted to share this with her. It was something small and simple, yet special enough to him that he had thought to include her in it.

"Thank you," Remy said, ripping into the bread again. "I think as your red witch I should advise you to hire that man as your personal baker and make him ride out into battlefields after you with this raisin bread."

Hale laughed, not a princely laugh but an honest witch's laugh. It would be a sight to behold: a baker riding into battle to deliver his prince his bread. Remy chuckled too. They rode and ate in companionable silence to the far reaches of the city.

Most on the street were humans, heading in the opposite direction, toward the heart of the city to work for the day. Most fae and witches would have the day off after their equinox celebrations, but there were some jobs that were always needed. They were the most under-appreciated ones too. Some humans stole quick glances at Remy and the Eastern Prince. A few others stopped and bowed, but most carried on ignoring them. It wasn't the reception Remy expected for their crown prince.

Ahead of them, three human men stumbled out of a doorway and into the early morning light. They swayed and laughed with the same joviality Remy saw in her taverns. She knew this type: the ones who wanted the festivities to never end, who would drink and dance and sing and laugh until the sun rose. The sun was well into the sky now, climbing above the tree line of the forest slopes ahead. The stumbling men looked barely of age. They still hadn't grown into their height or bodies yet. The prince slowed their horses in case one of the drunk men stumbled forward.

They looked at Remy and then Hale, recognition lighting their faces as they scowled. Remy was used to this too. The sun worked its powerful magic, turning the nightlong merriment into vicious spite come morning.

"Ignore them," Hale said, bracing for them to say something. Remy hated it, that he knew how these men were about to treat him because he had experienced it so many times throughout his life.

Humans had called Remy all sorts of brutal things in her life, some clever and cutting, others predictable, and she had learned to let the drunken jibes roll over her like water off a duck's back. But for some reason, directed to the male whose warmth bled into her back and whose breath was hot on her hair . . . this felt different.

The tallest and boldest of the humans waited until their horse reached them and spat onto the ground.

"Bastard," he cursed.

Bastard.

It was the simplest yet most cutting word of all. Remy knew deep down Hale felt everything that word meant was true. Not only that his mother had borne him out of wedlock, but also that he was unworthy of everything he had, that he somehow deserved these barbs and razor-sharp words. Remy had done it to him too, called him bastard more than once. She was as much to blame as these drunken fools.

The two men behind the tall human laughed. That cruel, taunting laughter snapped something in Remy. Before she knew what she was doing, her foot was flying, swinging over the horse's black mane and dropping to the ground. She couldn't feel the impact or the heaviness of a whole loaf in her stomach. She couldn't feel her feet running or her hand grabbing the dagger on her belt.

She was just there, as if she had blinked and it had happened, bowling the tall man over onto his backside and pinning him to the wall. Her dagger pressed across his throat.

The man's blue eyes were wide in their sockets, his breathing shallow and rapid. His companions stood frozen above them on either side of her.

"Apologize," Remy snarled, crouching in front of him.

"Remy," Hale called, but she would not acknowledge him. She

knew from the reflection in the human's glassy eyes that her irises were glowing red. Her hands and eyes vibrated, filled with her power.

The man went ghost white. Remy grimaced as his bladder released. She was truly not a meek hiding creature anymore, but someone to be feared. She smiled icily at the man as she ordered again, "Apologize to your prince."

"I'm sorry," the human whispered, his voice shaking so violently his words could not be discerned.

Remy loosened the pressure of her dagger, but her magic kept it floating an inch away from the man's neck.

"Louder," she demanded.

"I am sorry, Prince Norwood," he whimpered. Remy was sure tears were building in his eyes. "I beg your forgiveness, Your Highness."

"You are forgiven." Hale spoke in a powerful and stoic voice.

Remy stood then, snatching her dagger from midair and sheathing it. She gave one last look to each of the other human men. They flinched from her glowing red gaze, as if looking in her eyes alone would curse them. Remy didn't take the prince's outstretched arm as she grabbed the horn of the saddle and moved into a perfect reverse of how she had dismounted the saddle, her leg sweeping over the horse's mane. Her leg muscles barked at her, but she did it anyway, just to let them see how strong she was.

Hale huffed an impressed laugh at her acrobatics and then turned to the cowering men.

"Let this be a warning to you," Hale said, his voice deadly as he looked down on them. "I may tolerate your disrespect, but my red witch will not."

My red witch.

The red glow of her magic flared anew from her eyes in response to those words. He said it like they were an unstoppable pair. Lifting her chin a bit higher, Remy straightened her posture.

They rode on in silence until they had turned out of sight. The buzzing behind her eyes abated, the red glow clearing from her vision. The prince's heart thundered against her back.

"That stunt was impressive . . . stupid, but impressive," he murmured into her hair.

"What, you mean you can't jump off a horse mid-stride while pulling out a dagger?" Remy asked with a mischievous grin.

Hale's laugh echoed through her. "Well played. If I didn't know any better, I would say you were part fae."

"Another piece of advice from your red witch," Remy steered the conversation back to those men. *Your.* She loved saying it, indulging in the fantasy that she was his. "Any person who treats you with such disrespect deserves a dagger at their throat."

"It's a good thing I have you to do that for me then." Hale's arms tightened around her as he passed the reins from one hand to the other.

She would do it. She would cut down any man who called him a bastard. It was true, and it spoke from a part of her that existed beyond logic. It was wild and base. She could not deny that instinct.

They passed the last of the houses, through stretches of empty open land before they reached the city's far wall of huge tree trunks rammed deeply into the ground and spiked into sharp points at the top. The iron gates lay open to the forest beyond. No enemies here to defend against.

As they ventured past the wall and into the forest, Remy knew that today their enemy was not one wielding a sword— it was a steep, foul mountain that lay on the other side of this forest.

CHAPTER NINETEEN

They rode through the day, only breaking along streams to refill their water supply. The paths through the pine forest ended after an hour of riding uphill, and then they were freely navigating through the cool forest, trees towering above them. But the Easterners clearly planted the pine forest for logging, so it was easy to navigate with the trees separated at regular intervals. Plenty of room for the horses. It was another story when they reached the top of the hill.

The pine plantation gave way to undulating woodland, growing steeper and wilder until it reached the Eastern summits of the High Mountains far in the distance. In the middle of those snowy-capped mountains rose a black jagged monolith: Mt. Aelusien, the Rotted Peak.

The peak was like a guiding star, drawing them closer, demanding to be noticed in the skyline. Far to the east through the forest, smoke swirled from smokestacks toward the sky, towns and villages dotted along the main highway. But no towns were between them and those haunted slopes. The promised stench of rotten death wafted toward them even from a considerable distance, and Remy knew in a few more hours she'd be gagging on the reeking odor.

"That smell is . . ." Remy wrinkled her nose, pulling her tunic up over her face.

"You can smell it already?" Hale mused. Remy didn't reply. "We'll break camp for the day at that clearing up ahead. We need to get a fire going before sunset," he said with an edge of urgency.

"It gets that cold so quickly?" Remy asked. The snowline of the mountains was still high above them and the air still clung to summer's warmth. But autumn evenings were deceptive, plummeting into a frost.

"The fire is not for the cold—it is for the beasts who roam these woods," Hale said.

"Beasts?" Remy looked out over the woods: aside from a few song-birds and rabbits she had seen no other creature on their ride. She had heard no tale of these Eastern beasts either.

"The one to worry about is the Eastern mountain lion, *tigris galanthicus*," Hale said.

Remy snorted. "We have mountain lions in the West too. They catch livestock sometimes, but they fear magic. We shall be fine."

"We are not in the West," Hale said with a hint of annoyance. "Are your mountain lions the size of horses in the West?"

Remy chewed on her lip. It couldn't be the truth.

"They're really that big?" she asked.

Hale's guffaw pushed her forward.

"They say the lions lived on deer and smaller game for centuries, but when the ancient High Mountain fae hid their precious amulet in the mountains here, it drew magic out of the mountain itself. Towns sprang up along the Eastern slope. And the lion's food became food for the townspeople, and so the lions hunted people too. There are no towns this far inland in our Court now, but the lions still remember what the humans did to their forest . . . and how tasty they were."

"Great," Remy grumbled.

"They are nocturnal hunters, using the element of surprise. They don't like the firelight," Hale said. Remy looked to the sky, the sun lowering into the tree line. Long shadows were being cast through the forest already.

A mountain lion the size of a horse? She shivered.

"Nearly there." Hale laughed.

When they reached the clearing, Remy frantically collected firewood while Hale coaxed a spark to life from his piece of flint. They were both practiced in the art of making quick fires. It wasn't until the flames were blazing high in the sky that they brushed down the horses and set up camp.

Remy had gotten used to this nomadic way of living by now. She knew precisely where each piece of gear was, which pocket carried her rations, and that her bedroll and blanket always sat at the top of the bag and her clothes below to prevent getting wet. Remy had brought some of the clothing that Bri had purchased for her in Ruttmore but most of it she left behind at Morgan's house in Wynreach. They were fine clothes, and Morgan deserved them more than her. Plus, it was impractical to wear such attire in the middle of the forest, let alone if she had to fight off a horse-sized mountain lion.

Remy pulled out her change of clothes. She turned her back to Hale as she undressed. She had gotten used to changing in front of the others too. Bri had no problem getting buck naked in front of everyone, but Carys had a method of changing that Remy copied. She used her tunic to cover her lower half as she changed her trousers, then turned her back to swap her tunics. Even though Hale turned in an act of modesty, she still sensed his awareness tingling across her naked back.

Remy took her dirty, sweat-crusted clothes and hung them on a branch above them, careful not to step beyond the fire's light. The horses seemed to know instinctively to keep to the light as they grazed.

Hale unpacked for the night as she changed. She assumed he was taking out provisions for dinner, but when she turned, he had unpacked an array of weapons: daggers, throwing knives, an extra quiver of arrows, and a hand scythe.

"Seriously?" Remy balked. "You think you will need all that?"

The prince still wore his two swords on his hips as well. Remy had only brought her one dagger from Bri and her bow.

"I wanted to be prepared." Hale shrugged. "Most will be too heavy to haul to the peak, but once we get the amulet, we will head into the Northern Court . . . and we will find no friends there."

Remy frowned at the display of weapons. Climbing a rancid-smelling mountain was going to be the easy part of this journey, it seemed.

The Eastern Prince had enough food for a few days in his pack, but they ate lean just in case, always preparing for stretching their rations beyond their intended length. The journey had taken its toll on Remy. She was tired and sore from riding and had to climb a mountain in the morning.

Hale moved to his sleep roll across the fire. They had added enough logs for a few hours' worth of sleep before they would need to add more.

Remy was about to move to her bedroll when a shrieking snarl tore through the forest. She spun so fast for her bow she nearly toppled over. She nocked an arrow and froze, staring into the darkness. The sound was like that of a house cat, but deeper, louder. The trees shook with the reverberations of the far-off growl. Remy ground her teeth together. She would not be getting much sleep.

She hefted her pack and bedroll. Walking around the fire, she dropped them directly in front of Hale. Setting her bow and arrow in precise grabbing distance, she lay back down.

Hale smothered a laugh behind her.

"Shut up." She scowled, but he did not make fun of her for wanting to sleep closer to him. With her bow at her front and Hale at her back, she would be safe.

"You ready for tomorrow?" he whispered.

"No," Remy rolled over to meet Hale's stare. His eyes had disappeared into the shadows, but she saw his faint grin in the firelight. "You?"

"Probably not." Hale chuckled. That smile made her stomach muscles tighten. His chestnut hair tossed across his forehead. Remy remembered how she had brushed it back in the gardens of Saxbridge. She knew exactly how it would feel, how silky soft it would be, how her hand would smell like the waves rolling off the ocean.

"Remind me why we're doing this again?" Remy asked instead.

"Vostemur has the Immortal Blade," Hale said like she didn't already know. "And in order for the last High Mountain fae, Prince Raffiel, to stand a chance in reclaiming it, he will need his ancestor's talismans."

"The *Shil-de* ring and the amulet of Aelusien," Remy whispered.

A vision of the prayer tree in the Southern Court flashed through Remy's mind, all those ribbons flapping in the breeze. How many more people would have to mourn their dead if they did not succeed? She thought to the severed heads on the Eastern palace's floor. Vostemur grew bolder by the day. He was pushing into the Western Court. Hale's soldiers, Remy's friends, were helping aide in the Eastern Court's retreat as well. They needed this ancient magic if they had any hopes of defeating the northern threat.

Remy sensed the ring's red magic, the power of the High Mountain fae and the red witches. Her hand skimmed over the lump where her totem bag rested. "You should wear the ring tomorrow, Hale."

He smiled as she said his name. She did it so rarely, she realized. He seemed to cherish the sound.

"That would defeat the purpose of obtaining the ring," Hale said. He couldn't put the ring on and then give it to another.

Anyone could use the *Shil-de* ring, unlike the Immortal Blade, which was tethered to the High Mountain fae by red witch blood magic. But once the ring was on its wearer's finger, it was there forever or until they took it off, and then . . . all the deaths the ring had saved them from would reclaim them. The ring only protected from violent deaths, though. Age and time would reclaim the ring bearer, eventually.

"Besides," Hale said softly, and she felt his eyes searching her own in the darkness, "if anything, you should be the one wearing it."

"Why?" she asked. Her heart began pounding louder, and she hoped he could not hear it.

Another hissing growl shook the earth. The horses whinnied.

Remy flipped over, trying to search in the sound's direction, but the wild noises were still far away in the night. How long until the lions caught their scent and came prowling this way?

Remy flopped back down in frustration, feeling like lion bait. She reached out for Hale's muscled arm and pulled it around her. He chuckled, wrapping her in his warmth, one arm snaking around her side and splaying across the rough fabric of her tunic.

"Quiet," Remy growled again. She pulled the fur blanket over both of them. Yanking her bag to her front, she wedged herself between her pack and the prince.

Yeah, that would protect her from a horse-sized mountain lion with a taste for human flesh.

She still felt Hale smiling into her hair.

"Go to sleep," she ordered.

He pulled her back until she was flat against his warm front. The rise and fall of his chest was a comforting rhythm to her now, after days of riding with him. She knew the sound of his steady heartbeat as easily as she knew her own.

Remy woke in the night. Had she imagined the snarl of a lion? She didn't know if it was a dream. She looked at the fire. It still blazed strongly. She wasn't sure how long she had been asleep. Both horses were still there, calm. She scanned the night for any large reflective cat eyes, but there were none. She had rolled more onto her stomach in her sleep, lying halfway across her pack. In doing so, she had trapped Hale's arm under her and where his hand rested . . .

She had pinned his hand between her pack and the apex of her thighs.

Going rigid, all at once Remy was not sleepy at all. *That hand.* That Gods' damned hand was right there. She felt the heat emanating into her, that perfect spot. Hale's deep sleeping breaths rolled like waves from behind her. His perfect ocean air scent wrapped around her entire body, making the sensations coursing through her even sharper. She wasn't sure where her scent ended and his began.

And that hand.

Remy shifted her hips to unpin him but stopped the second she moved. *Gods.* That delicious split second of friction was enough to set her on fire. The prince's hand twitched in his sleep. With a shuddering breath, Remy bit her lip.

"Do you like that?" A rough, sleepy voice sounded from behind her.

"You're awake." Remy could feel her cheeks heating. She made to move, but Hale rolled so his front was half on top of her back, holding her in place.

His lips slid up Remy's neck to her ear. "Your scent could wake a male from the dead."

Remy trembled as thousands of tingling lightning bolts shot through her body. She tilted her hips forward again as his breath whispered into her ear. His hand moved, pressing in, and Remy gasped.

She had never felt this aroused before. Never. She had a few encounters with a boy in the one of the tavern towns they were in. They were fun and quick, but anticlimactic. This was something entirely different. Hale's hand alone through the fabric of her trousers had liquid heat pooling between her legs.

"Do you want me to keep going?" he whispered into her ear again. His voice alone almost had her coming undone.

Remy breathed without thinking, "Yes." She was lost to the sensation of his body pressed against hers.

Hale pushed his hand against her as she ground her hips forward, stifling a moan. Shifting her onto her side, Hale slid his hand up to the waistband of her trousers and inside. His calloused fingers dipped down until he found that hot, wet button between her legs. Remy turned her face into her arm as his fingers slid against her, moaning into her sleeve.

"That sound," Hale said as he moved his fingers again, "is my undoing."

Remy felt him harden against her backside. She reached her hand back to palm him, and he growled.

"Not tonight," he ground out. "There are beasts in these woods, and there will be nothing quiet about the first time I have you."

As those promised words skated across the shell of her ear, he dipped one finger into her wet core. Remy bit into her shirt to keep from crying out. Hale snarled, skimming his teeth across her neck.

It felt so good. Too good.

Hale groaned as he added a second finger, making Remy writhe.

"Are you always this wet when you think of me?" His fingers paused, waiting for an answer.

"Yes." Remy's voice sounded nothing like her own, filled with a feral pleading for those fingers to move faster.

Hale obliged, pumping them in and out of her as the heel of his hand pressed down on that tight bundle of nerves. His other hand drifted up, languidly circling her nipple. She arched into his hands, her panting breaths the only sound. His heady scent enveloped her, bringing her higher to that edge. Remy ground herself harder into his fingers. Harder, faster. It was all she could think to do. Moving. Demanding more.

Hale nibbled her ear as she cried out again.

"Remy," he whispered.

At the sound of his voice, she shattered. Biting down on her arm, rolling waves of ecstasy overcame her. Hale massaged her until the last of her moans turned into heavy breaths.

Remy had never in her entire life felt that way before. Echoes of that ecstasy shot across her body as her breathing slowed. Hale slid his hand out of her trousers, pulling her back across his broad chest with satisfaction.

His lips brushed across her temple.

"Dream of me," he whispered smugly, and she did.

CHAPTER TWENTY

H er labored breaths stabbed into her lungs like blades of ice. Remy had long lost count of the steps as they climbed. Hewn into the jagged mountainside were hundreds and hundreds of stone stairs. They had climbed above the tree line. Her bottom teeth felt numb from dragging cold air over them as whirls of snowflakes blew around them. A powdery white covered surrounding peaks, but even the snow feared the Rotted Peak.

Remy had given up keeping her mouth closed to the stench. Her body was too tired to roil against the foul rot. She did not dare look back down. The climb alone would make this trek only possible for the fittest soldiers. They could have carried no fancy weaponry or tools up such a long, steep ascension. No animal could traverse the narrow, vertical climb to carry a heavy arsenal either.

Remy considered dropping her dagger several times. Hale left his swords with the horses, favoring only a dagger and a hand scythe. Still, they felt every ounce of the extra weight now. The summit was not far, yet the climb felt endless. The memories of pleasure from the night before had long left her body, surrendered to the steep climb. She knew they would have to talk about it eventually . . . if they survived. Perhaps it would be better to die on these slopes than to lie to him again . . . perhaps it would be better to die than to tell him the truth.

Remy's chest burned. Her legs felt weighted with lead. She willed enough of her magic into her body to keep her moving. Their water skins were empty and ditched along the trail. Her only goal was to get to the top.

Get to the top, get to the top. She chanted it to herself.

For at the summit of this mountain was the only opening into what lay inside Mt. Aelusien: a magical lake. The ancestors of the High Mountain fae had imbued the lake with their magic, a safeguard to protect their talisman. King Vostemur thought he possessed the entirety of the High Mountain power, but he was wrong.

The ancient red witches had created the amulet of Aelusien and gifted it to the High Mountain Court during a time of pestilence. Disease had swept through the continent. The red witches had worried what would happen to Okrith if they were all wiped out, worried their magic would go extinct. They created the amulet of Aelusien, a necklace that when worn gave the wearer the power of red witch magic, more heightened and undiluted than any one witch had themselves, even Baba Morganna. Anyone could harness the power of the amulet if they learned how: witches, fae, even humans. The amulet was the red witches' insurance that their magic would survive the plague. The High Mountain fae hid it in their mountain range, where it remained to this day.

The ancients knew whoever held possession of this precious talisman would gain incredible power. So they made it almost impossible to obtain. Only the bravest, strongest, shrewdest warrior could reach it: a person worthy of it.

Every step Remy considered stopping. She knew even one long pause would be the end of her climb.

She had told Hale death was more likely than victory, and every time Hale insisted that with a red witch by his side, he would be successful. Remy heard the prince's labored breaths far behind her. He had grumbled something about how it was easier for her because she was half his weight, but now he had no breath for complaining.

They began climbing with hands and feet up the sheer rock side. Time had worn away the path. It was no longer hard rock underneath them. They now traversed loose shale. With every step forward, they dropped almost the same distance back. It was grueling punishment, each step more disheartening than the last, but they continued to make their way ever so slowly higher.

At long last, Remy climbed high enough to see it: a black hole carved into the stone.

It was not some grand entrance or archway like she had expected, nothing regal or befitting of the High Mountain Court. No, this was a small, dark tunnel looming before them, too small to even crawl on hands and knees. They would have to inch their way on their bellies like crocodiles in this pitch darkness. It looked like a terrible, terrible idea. Someone probably designed it to look that way.

Remy rested on the narrow platform next to the tunnel, her back leaning against the mountain, surveying the distance they had come. Forest stretched out long into the distance, and beyond that she saw a distant town's small circle of smokestacks. If she squinted hard enough, she could just make out the ocean on the horizon. She blinked several times, trying to discern where the sea met the sky but could not. It might be the last time she ever saw the ocean. Even if they survived, they would head inland to Yexshire.

Hale clambered onto the ledge, sitting beside Remy. As he took huge drags of air, she wished she had some water to pass him, but there was nothing. Perhaps the lake water inside was drinkable? But, knowing the red witches, she dared not risk it.

She made to move toward the tunnel, but Hale put a hand on her shoulder.

"Wait for me," he panted. "We go in together."

They sat for several long minutes of contemplative silence before Hale's breathing slowed enough. Even as a fae male in peak condition, the climb had been relentless. She wondered how many had failed to even get this far. How many had turned back when they saw the never-ending stairs before them? Abandoned swords and armor had littered the mountain where the vertical climb turned to shale. The ones who turned back were probably the wisest of them all.

Hale made to move around Remy toward the tunnel. She put her hand on his shoulder to stop him.

"I should go first," Hale insisted. He leaned so close to her that his hair touched her face. Even with the exhaustion of the climb, it was a thrill to be so close to those lips again. A flash of the night before shuddered through Remy as she dropped her eyes.

"No, I will go first," Remy said. Before Hale could argue, she added, "This may not even be the true entrance. We do not know if the tunnel leads to anywhere or how narrow it becomes once inside. I am the smaller of the two of us, I should go first."

"Fine." Hale narrowed his eyes at her. "But if it becomes too narrow for only you to pass, you will tell me. We will both turn back and find another way in."

Remy didn't respond at first.

"What is going on in that mind of yours?" he asked, his breath skimming across her cheek. She saw the stone gray flecks in his silver eyes.

She didn't say what she wanted to say: that she had no use or desire to possess the amulet of Aelusien. She didn't tell him all the secrets clawing up the back of her throat.

Instead she said, "I pledged my magic to you, and we did not discuss compensation. I want ten pieces of gold per month that I am in your service."

Hale laughed. "You bargain with me now?" He looked out at the drop below them. "Fine, agreed. I will give you your first coins when we return to the horses. Now promise me you won't go on without me."

"Fine. I promise I won't leave you behind," she said with an eye roll. But she knew it already, knew it deep in her bones, that she couldn't leave him behind even if she wanted to, even if it would save her life.

She rolled onto her belly and began her crawl into the tunnel. It was tall enough for her to get on her hands and knees before her back pressed against the rocky top of the tunnel. Remy was sure Hale was belly crawling. The tunnel slanted downward, making their movements easier. Remy's face broke through more than one spider web as she inched forward. She tried not to itch at the thought of spiders in her hair. She had just climbed an indomitable mountain, and yet one spider on her body had her wanting to flail and scream. Pushing the thought from her mind, she kept moving. Remy could not run; Hale blocked the way back. She could not think of how trapped she was in that tight space or it would make her panic. Remy released a slow breath out her nose and kept going.

Within a minute they were crawling through pitch blackness, and the tunnel declined more steeply. Remy's forearms strained to slow her descent. She worried that the prince behind her would lose purchase and collide with her.

A faint, eerie green glow began to form in front of her. As she moved, she could make out the tunnel more clearly as the green light amplified. The tunnel moved into a straight drop into open air. Peering down the hole, she saw the ground beyond.

"Wait here while I descend or you will crush me," Remy warned.

She prayed the drop would not be big and that she would not fall face-first into stone. She pressed her hands and legs hard into the rock as she crawled. Already-tired muscles screamed at her. She saw that the ground was close, the drop only an arm's length.

Her hand slipped, and with a grunt she slid the rest of the way to the ground below. She twisted enough that her shoulder and not her face took the hit. She made a pathetic thwack as she crumpled onto the ground.

"Are you all right?" Hale called.

"I'm fine," Remy grumbled, dusting herself off. She would be covered in scrapes, but nothing more. "Let's see if you can be a bit more graceful, Your Highness."

She heard Hale's echoing laugh as he slid forward. One hand appeared and then the other, reaching to the ground. The muscles on his arms and shoulders bulged as he lowered himself from a hand-stand into a push-up and down onto his stomach. Remy gave a begrudging huff as he sat up, trying to not acknowledge how impressive or attractive that was. But Hale was looking toward the green glow to his right.

Stretched far out before them was a bioluminescent lake. Its glow lit up the giant cavernous walls that stretched high into the darkness of the mountain. In the center of the lake was a small island holding a large rectangular slab of stone, and on top of that stone was a goblet and a shining red necklace: the amulet of Aelusien.

Hale coughed, pulling his tunic up over his nose, and that's when the rotten smell hit Remy. She thought she had overcome the stench outside, but this was far worse. Yanking her shirt up over her nose, too, Remy looked and saw them around the shoreline: bodies. Dozens of bodies in various stages of decay dotted the craggy rock floor. Many of them were already skeletons from hundreds of years ago. She looked at her boot, standing on a piece of cloth—it looked like a coat of some sort but no corpse was inside it. She shuddered. Many more articles of torn and shredded clothing lay strewn about. She wondered if the people had disrobed before attempting to swim across the lake so they could cross faster. There was far more clothing than bodies.

Hale nudged Remy with his elbow, "Can you read this?"

He was looking at the cave wall above them. Mhenbic, the witch's ancient language, was etched into the stone. Remy spoke Mhenbic with Heather and Fenrin occasionally, but Heather preferred they used Ific, the common tongue. Remy had never read it before but the lettering was close enough to Ific that she tried to speak a translation.

"If the Amulet you seek, then go for a swim. But beware the poison waters. Reach the antidote before the poison claims you. There is enough to save one life. Only the worthy will reach the goblet. Only the worthy will claim the amulet. May the red magic bless you."

Remy shuddered. A poison lake. They designed the waters to kill. It seemed many a seeker of the amulet had panicked and retreated to the shores only for the poisons to claim them.

Hale stripped off his tunic.

"Wh—what are you doing?" Remy stuttered even as her eyes

moved to his sculpted, muscular torso. If the poison lake would not kill her, that body surely would.

"I'm going in," Hale said as if she were the crazy one.

"Are you a fast swimmer?" she asked. She knew he must be a powerful swimmer. He had told her of his teen years at his mother's fishing village, learning to battle mighty waves. But surviving giant waves was not the same as moving quickly, and it was speed he needed now.

"Are you worried about me?" Hale grinned. He was being awfully cavalier about his own life. Meanwhile, Remy was having a hard time keeping her eyes off his bare chest.

"Of course I am!" she barked and his grin widened.

"If I don't make it, then the coin and the horses are yours." Hale winked. "You can bribe your way back into the South and buy yourself your very own little witch tavern."

"Great," Remy said bitterly as Hale removed his shoes. She looked toward the wall and the ancient warning carved into it.

May the red magic bless you.

"Wait!" she said.

Hale turned toward her. She reached out and grabbed his arm, placing her palm on his bare chest above his heart.

"What are you—"

"Sh," she reprimanded.

She summoned her well of red witch magic. She pulled up as much as she could and pushed it out into her palm. Muttering ancient Mhenbic words, she pressed onto Hale's chest and let her magic flow through him.

She looked into his eyes. They were wide with shock. Remy wasn't sure what it must feel like for him to have her magic coursing through him.

"This is a protection spell, stronger than that red string," Remy said, holding his gaze and repeating the words sliced into the mountain: "May the red magic bless you."

Before she knew what was happening, Hale reached out for her. Cupping her face in both his hands, he pulled her mouth to his.

Remy clung to him as he worshipped her with that slow, reverent kiss.

Hale pulled away just enough to rest his forehead on her own. Holding her eyes with that deep silver stare he whispered, "Thank you, Remy."

Mouth opening and shutting, she knew what that kiss was. It was a potential goodbye.

She pushed against the urge to grab him and kiss again, to convince him to leave this foolish quest now before it separated them forever, before they never got the chance to see what a thousand more kisses could turn into.

Her heart leapt out of her ribcage, screaming for her to tell him everything. Say all the words locked tightly in her chest.

But she let him go.

With a heavy breath she steadied herself and said, "Good luck," as he stepped one foot into the glowing, poisonous lake.

She should have told him everything. She should have poured out the contents of her heart into him, not her stores of red magic. The second he entered the water, she regretted it.

As soon as his foot entered the glowing green water, he dove head-first in. He wasted no time with quick, powerful strokes and rapid fluttering kicks. He was fast. Good. Maybe he would make it to the other side.

Remy watched with bated breath, stroke after stroke. Each time his arm raised above the water, the color in it had faded, the tone of his muscles withered. Hale paused, lifting his head, and wailed.

Remy gasped. His hair was falling out, face sinking in. The poison was sucking the life out of him, withering him into a corpse.

"Don't stop!" she screamed to him. The sight of Hale paralyzed her whole body in horror save for her drumming heart.

Hale kept moving, his muscles weaker, his pace slower, but he kept moving. He was more than halfway now. He could make it.

It was then Remy saw it in the water: a shadow. The large black form moved under the water toward the struggling prince. Fear gripped her tight as she grabbed a discarded knife by her feet. The creature emerged, only eyes and tail popping above the surface. It was a black scaly creature unlike anything she had ever seen.

"On your right!" she shouted, throwing the blade.

It flew wide. Damn.

"Look out!" Her echoes bounced around the cavernous lake.

The creature was only a body's length away from him now. Remy scanned her feet, grabbing a spear from the trove of discarded weapons. She wished she had brought her bow now as she hurled the spear. This one struck the beast in the back, but the point glanced off its thick scales.

The creature's gaping maw opened, displaying several rows of sharp white teeth. The flailing swimmer who turned to face the beast was no longer the prince she knew. His skin sucked to his bones, he looked like a week-old cadaver. He was so close to the island. He needed to get out of the water and get to the antidote. But the beast at his side trapped him.

Remy rained down weaponry, knives, axes, rocks toward the beast as it launched itself forward. Hale held up his dagger and swiped the beast's muzzle. The creature screeched and drew back, only to lash out again. Its whip-like tale swept out in a punishing blow that Hale managed to duck. The tail whooshed in the other direction, knocking the dagger out of Hale's hand. Remy threw another blade, and finally it stabbed right in the creature's yellow eye. It shrieked again, eye oozing an amber goo, rotten teeth gnashing, as it turned its one remaining eye to the skeletal figure struggling before it.

Hale feinted to his left, and the beast followed. Bringing up the scythe in his right hand, Hale slammed it into the beast's scaly snout. The creature jolted as the scythe hooked its jaws together, dropping in a splash below the surface.

Remy breathed for the first time in over a minute.

Hale moved in small, floundering kicks. His hand reached out and grasped the edge of the island. He hoisted his emaciated torso onto the rock just as two more pairs of yellow eyes appeared above the green surface of the water.

"Hale!" Remy screeched, shredding her voice, as the black water snakes launched toward his legs.

One of the scaly beasts reared its lean body out of the water like an asp readying to strike. Hale held up a bony arm, trying to dodge out of the way, but he had no strength or weapons left. The beast snapped down on his raised forearm, crunching it as it yanked him below the surface.

"No!" Remy screamed so loudly that rocks crumbled from the ceiling.

Without a second thought, she was shucking off her shirt and shoes. As she ran to the shores of the lake, she unsheathed her dagger.

Leaping into the water, Remy wished she had saved some of her red witch magic for herself. She begged the Gods that there was enough magic still left in her to keep her protected. Hale and the two beasts had not breached the surface, though the green waters by the island still stirred.

She had to hurry.

She prayed that those years being tossed in gigantic waves had taught Hale how to hold his breath. Remy was a weak swimmer, but she pushed with a supernatural force toward that swirling water. Gods, she hoped that no more beasts called this lake home.

Maybe it was her red magic, maybe it was her blood, but something within her spooked the beasts. As though sensing her imminent approach under the water, they released Hale. His unconscious body floated to the surface.

He was dead.

CHAPTER TWENTY-ONE

A deep guttural scream burst out of her throat.

No, no, no.

She swam faster as one of the creatures emerged again. Its wary eyes pierced into her as the other snake made its way back to Hale's body. Remy threw out the last sputtering bursts of her magic, and the yellow-eyed serpent dove below the surface. The other, so focused on reaching Hale, had turned its back to Remy. She grabbed the monster by its formidable black tail and yanked it backwards before it could snap its jaws into Hale again.

The brute turned wildly toward her, but she was flush with its side, and those snapping teeth could not twist far enough to reach her. She held tight to its back as it thrashed. The sharp scales sliced into the parts of her stomach and arms left bare by her leather until they were bloody. Still, she did not let go.

Remy wrapped one arm around the beast's throat as she slammed the blade of the dagger through that yellow eye and into the creature's skull. She leapt off its thrashing body as she pulled back the blade, glistening with glowing amber. It might not have been a killing blow, but it should buy her enough time.

Time.

She feared they'd already run out of it as she scanned the waters, finding Hale's lifeless body bobbing face up. The waves from her battle with the lake beast had pushed him against the rocky island. The stone table with his cure loomed above him.

Moving frantically, Remy reached him in only one stroke. She slung her arm around his pale, limp body and heaved him out of the water. His chest did not rise.

She snatched the goblet from the stone and dropped hard on her knees beside Hale. Prying open his withered purple lips, she poured the inky red liquid into his mouth. She shut his mouth, trying to force the antidote down.

"Come on, come on," she willed to herself, to the world around her, to the magic she had poured into him.

As if hearing her command, Hale swallowed. His chest heaved, taking a long heavy drag of air. Another and then another.

"Thank the Gods," Remy whispered. It was only then that she realized her body was shaking.

She watched Hale's features returning as his body reanimated before her eyes. A magical force straightened his crushed arm. His eyes flew open, searching until they landed on her.

"You're okay, it's okay," Remy reassured him, but his eyes filled with horror. He scanned her face, her bloody torso, and the empty cup in her hand.

"What have you done?" His voice was one of terror. He reached for the goblet beside him in shock, peering at its empty contents. "You gave it all to me?"

His hands shook as he swept the last red droplet with his finger and pressed it to her lips.

"How are you still alive?" he whispered, wide-eyed.

"I was hoping my magic would hold out long enough to reach you." At those words, Remy doubled over. A shooting pain seared through her stomach. The adrenaline was wearing off, giving way to the poison. "Grab the amulet quick. We need to get down the mountain and find more of the antidote."

"More of the antidote?" Hale rasped, watching terrified as Remy clutched her stomach. He snatched the red amulet that lay across the stone slab. As he lifted it, stuffing its golden chain into his pocket, a loud rumbling sounded. To their left a stone rose from the lake, creating a bridge across it.

Remy gritted her teeth and keened. Fire was filling her veins.

"Gods, Remy, you stupid, brave fool," Hale said, slinging her arm around his neck. He wrapped his hand around her waist, half carrying her across the bridge.

"That's the thanks I get for saving your life." She gritted her teeth.

"You should have let me die," Hale snarled.

"Never," she groaned again as they reached the tunnel they had emerged from. When Hale released her, she dropped to the ground. He grabbed their tunics, yanking hers over her head in a near frenzy.

"I told you I wouldn't leave you behind," Remy said. Hale paused as he threaded her arm through her shirt and looked into her eyes. She saw the pain radiating out of him, the fear that moments ago was her own.

"We will find an antidote," he assured her. "We are getting you out of here."

He pulled her to her feet, guiding her to the rocky opening of the tunnel. Wrapping his hands around her waist, he lifted her into the vertical space until she had reached the ledge of the jagged incline. She wriggled herself in, Hale right behind her. Pushing herself faster, she could not feel the bloody scrapes on her arms or torso. Her lips and toes tingled. She would have felt compelled to comment on Hale's firm hand on her ass pushing her upwards, but her innards burned and locking her jaw was all she could do not to scream.

She rolled out onto the ledge above them, looking down at their perilous descent. Her eyes closed for a moment in defeat.

She knew then. She would not make it.

Hale emerged behind her and leapt to his feet.

"We can't rest—we have to move," he said.

Remy suppressed another painful cry. She was panting quick breaths, trying not to let the poison take over her body, trying and failing.

"The poison is taking hold too fast," she panted. "I'm not—"

"Remy," Hale warned her. "We *will* get down this mountain."

She nodded, gasping between words as she said, "When we get to the horses, there's a red candle in my satchel. Light it and call for Baba Morganna. She will tell you what to do."

Her eyes fluttered, and Hale grabbed her face hard.

"Open your eyes, Remy," he commanded. She hollowly did as she was told. "Now move."

Remy's eyes remained half closed as she positioned herself to slide down the shale. Hale gripped onto her belt to keep her from sliding too far. Scuttling backwards on her belly, the prince guided her in a controlled fall. She collapsed in a heap on the first stone step, her face smacking hard into the stone, but she could not feel it.

"Open your eyes, Remy." Hale meant it as another command, but she heard the pleading in his voice.

"Red candle," she gasped. "Morganna."

Hale tried to pull her to her feet, but she collapsed. She could no longer feel her limbs, only the pain swirling in her gut. She would not make it. But Morganna needed to know of her passing either way. The High Priestess needed to let go of all the hopes that had rested on Remy's shoulders. She feared for the chain of events her death would set off, yet she still regretted nothing. She would have jumped into that lake every single time. She was glad she had saved him.

"Hale?" Remy gasped wet breaths into the stone. Hale's face crumpled as he watched her. "Take those flowers to your mother for me."

Remy's eyes guttered closed. She gave in to the poison burning through her body.

"Remy, open your eyes." Hale's voice cracked. "Open your eyes, damn you!"

She felt only a faint sting at the slap across her cheek. The poison had taken control of her muscles. She could not open her eyes.

Her body drooped.

Hale bellowed an agonized scream. "I will not bury you!"

She heard him leaping to his feet, faintly felt him yanking her arm up and slinging her over his shoulder. Her diaphragm slammed hard against him as he pounded down the stone steps two at a time.

Even through his labored breathing he said, "Stay with me, Remy."

Her body jostled around like a limp rag doll.

"You will come with me to bring those flowers to my mother. My mother will love you. You will see the ocean." His voice broke more with every word.

She smelled the pine trees, the wet moss, and the lushness of the forest again. Had they descended so quickly? Hale ran like the Goddess of Death was chasing him. She heard the whinny of horses as Hale unceremoniously dropped her body to the forest floor, thick with leaves.

She heard as Hale scrambled for the candle and in her mind she was grateful that Baba Morganna would be there for her passing, just as she had been there for her the night her family had died.

Flint striking sounded. Hale was lighting the candle.

"Baba Morganna." His trembling voice sounded distant, like he was underwater. "I call on you, High Priestess of the red witches."

"I am here, Your Highness." A voice as old as the stone mountains echoed through the woods. The voice of the red witch shimmered in Remy's mind.

Baba Morganna was here.

Remy exhaled her last breath and faded away.

Remy no longer had a body. She existed somewhere else, somewhere far below in the earth, in the soul of the land.

She lay there in the womb of life, looking up at the body above her. The vision was blurry, as though she lay at the bottom of a lake, watching the scene: her limp body lay in the leaf litter. Knelt beside her, holding her so tightly the veins in his arms were popping out, was Hale. Beyond him, a transparent form flickered: Baba Morganna.

The old witch had projected her spirit to the site of Remy's death.

It was powerful magic that would likely drain the High Priestess for a long time once she let go.

Baba Morganna had a light brown face that was deeply lined. Her white, wavy hair hung loosely past her shoulders. Her eyes shone like polished bronze, even in her spirit form. Red magic sparked from her hands. She did not hunch but stood rod straight as though she wore an invisible crown, chin held high, her red flowing cloak covering the rest of her body.

It appeared as though she were speaking to Hale, but Remy could not hear. Hale shouted at the ghostly image, teeth bared, his soul seeming to tear apart as he gripped Remy's lifeless body.

Baba Morganna's voice rang out from the blackness. It was all around Remy, echoing into the earth.

"It has been a long time since I've seen your face, Little Sparrow." The red witch's form was still speaking to the prince above Remy, but she spoke through the earth at the same time.

"Don't call me that." Remy protested in her mind. She spoke no words. She did not have a mouth, but she communicated with the old witch as if the words flowed from her lips.

"You deny who you are even in death?" The witch's voice was scratchy, higher than the tone Remy had remembered.

"So I am dead then?" Remy knew it and couldn't believe it at the same time. She could not absorb the truth that this was the end of her.

"That depends on you," Baba Morganna said. "You have a choice before you now. Go forward: claim back your body, claim your rightful place in this world, or go, leave all the pain and destruction, yes, but leave any future too."

"How do I know my future will be worth the suffering?" She doubted it could be. If she lived, it would lead to war.

"How does anyone? The things that bring us the most joy are the things hardest won. However hard you fight you will be equally thus rewarded," Baba Morganna prophesied.

"And if I don't want to fight anymore?" If Remy had a body she would cry, but her voice only echoed desolately through the darkness.

"Then I will tell you this," Baba Morganna said. "You may think that you are untethered to this world, but your choice is not yours alone. It will ripple out into the realm in ways you cannot yet fathom, and you, Little Sparrow, will exist in the afterlife, watching it all unfold, unable to lift a finger to change it."

"That is cruel." Remy ached in the darkness.

"It is the burden of those who pass: to watch, to bear witness to all that comes from the lives they led, to watch the ripples of all that they have done. With time it will fade. You will become an earth spirit, watching from the soil and the rivers and the trees, whispering and nudging as much as the earth will allow." The old witch's voice was calm, yet tinged with sorrow. "I have seen so many of your family fall."

"They're all gone." Remy had never felt more truly alone. Even her body abandoned her now.

"Not all." Morganna's voice cut through the emptiness. "Ruadora lives."

"Rua?" Remy had mourned her little sister's death long ago.

"A red witch rescued her that night. The witch hid with her in the forest, slowly finding her sisters and pulling the coven back together. We have been circling through the deep forests around Yexshire but do not venture into the valley, though the Northern eyes that once watched the valley of Yexshire are starting to turn away. Rua is with the red witches. Come to Yexshire. Follow the path behind the temple. You will find our camp there . . . that is, if you choose to come back," Baba Morganna said more slowly. "I hate to lose another one of your family, but if you choose to go, I will find a way to bear it."

"Why do I have a choice at all?" Remy whispered. She could feel herself fading into the ether. "Surely most do not get to choose between staying or going."

"Because someone still tethers you to this world." Baba Morganna's voice warmed.

"Who?"

Remy heard the smile in the old witch's voice. "You know who. You know what he is to you."

Remy looked at her body. Hale cradled her head in his lap. His forehead pressed to hers as he wept. He clenched fistfuls of her black hair in his hands as his tears fell onto her face.

Remy knew then that she never had a choice. She would hold on to life just to wipe his tears away. That is how much she loved him.

"Good luck to you, Little Sparrow," Baba Morganna said, knowing Remy had made her decision. "Make sure you cast as many stones into that water before you go, so you may watch those ripples for centuries to come."

Remy looked to Hale's broken face and something in her felt again. She felt those thumbs stroking her wet cheeks. She heard the soft tremble of his cries. The sound anchored her to this world. Turning toward her destiny, she decided to make as many damn ripples as she could before time took her again.

"May the Gods help me," she thought to herself.

Eyes flying open, Remy gasped.

"Remy."

He whispered her name through the night, like a chanted prayer.

A fever had gripped her through the long, dark hours. She remained half conscious, shivering through the blackness, unable to speak.

It had been too late in the day to flee the forest and in Remy's delicate state, she couldn't move. Hale had set up their camp again in the same spot they had camped the night before.

He had held her through it all, breaking his hold of her only to add more logs to the roaring fire. By the time her fever broke, sweat soaked through her clothes. She felt Hale's arms finally loosening, like he had been holding her from dropping off a cliff all those many hours. Sleep claimed him then as the adrenaline ebbed and he knew she would survive this night.

The promise of another day lightened the skies when Remy's body purged the last of the poisons burning through her veins. Her body had survived the toxic waters without an antidote. The blood in her body fought it off better than any other could. There was so much she needed to tell Hale. So much she had regretted not saying sooner, but for now they would sleep.

She would worry about all the truths in the morning.

CHAPTER TWENTY-TWO

W hen Remy woke, Hale was not there. Her sweaty clothes had dried. Her body felt mostly healed. She drank half a skin of water, her throat so dry. Sitting up, she combed a finger through her hair.

She needed to talk to Hale.

Remy grabbed her bow and arrows, in case the lions still prowled, and followed Hale's scent into the forest. Finding him downhill in a little grotto, he knelt before a fae fire. He had pulled up the hood of his charcoal gray cloak, obscuring his face. The base of the flames glowed green with fae magic instead of their normal blue. Remy winced at the green flickering light, the same shade as the lake that had nearly killed them both.

Hale crouched over a small fire, speaking to someone. A guttural male voice spoke out of the flames.

Remy waited at the edge of the clearing, camouflaged behind a tree. This was not a conversation to be interrupted. She willed enough of her magic into action to hear Hale's soft voice from the distance ahead.

"Yes, Father." She heard him say.

He communicated through the fire to the Eastern King as he had on their treks through the Western and Southern Courts.

A distorted voice spoke out from the flames, "My patience is growing thin. Every day Vostemur's power grows stronger and closer to unlocking the Immortal Blade. We need that blade in Eastern control and to do that we need the High Mountain Prince dead."

It took all her strength not to gasp.

Dead?

Remy was certain the Eastern King would say they needed the High Mountain Prince to wield the Immortal Blade and restore balance to the turbulent kingdoms. Wasn't that the goal they had been working toward all this time? The Eastern Court had been allies for centuries with the High Mountain Court.

The truth smashed into Remy all at once. They had never wanted to help the High Mountain Court. Norwood wanted to find the last High Mountain fae and kill him. With the last living prince dead, it would release the Immortal Blade from the magic tied to that bloodline. Whoever then possessed the blade would have unworldly power over the other kingdoms.

King Norwood was making a play for the blade. And Hale knew. He knew all this time, and he didn't tell her.

"We are getting closer every day," Hale said in a dark voice. Remy didn't know that voice. It was like he was speaking a different language.

"You are being too soft to that little bitch witch." The voice from the flames spoke again. "Make her bring you to the prince. Now. If you are not up to this task, I will send one of your brothers to do it for you."

"That won't be necessary," Hale snarled. Who was this man before her?

"Good," the voice crackled as the flames shrank. "Don't disappoint me. Kill the prince and bring me that blade. And son, the moment you find the prince, you put a knife in that bloody witch, no loose ends."

"Yes, Father," the Eastern Prince said, and the flames flickered out.

Her spine snapped straight at those last words. He was planning to kill her. She couldn't wrap her brain around that thought. Had it all been a lie? Had she come back to life for Hale only to die by his hand? How had she not seen it? Had she been so blind? She knew giving in to Hale's gravitational pull might lead to her death, but she never thought it would be by the prince's own hands.

Her blood was boiling. She was ready to nock one of her arrows and put it through Hale's back. She needed to get away.

Remy ached. The witches who died for her to live would be so deeply disappointed in her now, trusting their enemy. Each breath felt like a punch to her chest. She had fallen in love with a man who wanted to kill her.

She started to run, but a twig snapped under her foot.

Dammit. She was not paying attention.

Hale stood, spinning around.

"Remy?" he said, scanning the trees. "Is that you? How are you feeling?"

He was going to lie to her even now. He did not know she could hear him from that far.

She heard his feet crunching through the leaves with that fae speed. He moved toward her until he was standing downhill, only a few paces away. One glance at her face and he knew she had heard everything.

They stared and stared at each other, neither one ready to call the other's bluff.

"You really are a bastard," she hissed, trying not to cry. She saw her words pierce him like an arrow before he steeled his expression again. "If you were planning on killing me, why didn't you just let me die?"

"So you did hear that conversation," he said, almost amused, confirming what he suspected.

Why was he not angry? Why was he not upset? She felt her heart being shredded, and he seemed so damned calm.

"Yes, I heard you conspiring with your father against me and the

High Mountain Court." She sneered, feeling a bottomless pit of sorrow opening beneath her, ready to swallow her whole.

"Interesting," he said, lips twisting. The gray of his cloak made his eyes even darker from beneath his hood.

"What?" Remy's fingers twitched, readying to grab her bow.

"Only the fae can communicate through fire," Hale said. "You shouldn't have been able to hear that."

Shit.

"It was witch magic," Remy said, even as she retreated from him again. She knew she gave even more away by retreating, but she needed to create distance in case he rushed her.

"It was not witch magic," Hale said, his gray eyes darkening as he took a few slow steps forward. She thought she still might be able to outrun him if she summoned all of her powers. "I know who you are, Remy . . . or should I say, Your Majesty?"

Without a second thought, Remy grabbed her bow and nocked an arrow, pointing it at him. She did it in less than a blink of an eye. If he knew who she was, there was no point in hiding her speed anymore either.

He knew.

Hale stared at her in shock, watching her unleash her full speed.

"You are incredible." He grinned.

Why did he seem so pleased, even awed, by her? He looked at her the same way he always had, and yet seconds ago he had promised to kill her. Why was he still pretending?

"Why are you smiling?" Remy's voice filled with rage, even as she blinked away the tears filling her eyes. She would not wipe them away. She would not move her hands from her weapon. Let him see all the ways he had broken her trust.

She didn't let Hale answer. Her anger consumed her as she released her arrow.

It flew straight for the middle of Hale's head, which she knew he would dodge. She knew how he would move, like a part of her lived inside his body. The arrow landed precisely as she planned, pinning the hood of Hale's cloak to the tree behind him.

He looked up in surprise. He reached to release his hood, and she unleashed another two arrows in rapid succession. Remy knew Hale's movements that well. She skewered his sleeves, one above his head and one by his side. He would break free any moment, but it would give her a head start. She turned and took another step uphill.

"Remy, wait." She hated that Hale's voice made her feet halt.

"Why should I?" The knot in her throat tightened again as she looked at him, and she saw that his calm, amused mask was crumpling too. "You have sworn to your father that you will kill the last High Mountain fae and the *bitch witch,* and now you realize I am both. My elder brother Raffiel is a ghost, I'm sure of it. I am the reason Vostemur can't wield the Immortal Blade . . . you will kill me the second you are free."

"I will not," Hale said, his jaw hardening. "I was only lying to my father until I could get you close enough to the Immortal Blade. I will never hurt you."

"You liar." Remy laughed coldly at him, even as more tears welled. "Why not?"

"Because you are my Fated mate." Hale's voice was thick with gravel as emotion overcame him too.

The breath stole out of Remy. She had known it, too, for so much longer than she was willing to admit to herself. The night Carys told her that Hale's Fated was from the High Mountain Court, she had wondered. The thought was a glimmer of light in Remy, a whisper of "I wish it were me," a wish she could never acknowledge even in her own mind. But she had hoped she was his Fated all this time.

She had hoped because she knew there was this undeniable thread tying them together. She loved him irrationally from the moment she first looked into those smoky gray eyes.

"Why should I believe you?" Remy gritted out even as another treacherous tear slid down her cheek.

"Because you know it's true." Hale's body remained taut as he stared at her, a hint of desperation on his face.

"Why didn't you tell me?" Remy bit her lip between her teeth to keep it from wobbling.

"Because I thought you would either run or shoot an arrow through me . . ." Hale looked up at the arrow lodged mere inches from his head, "I suppose I was right. Your name is Remini, isn't it? Remini Dammacus, third child of the King and Queen of the High Mountain Court?"

Remy floundered, staring at the prince trapped against the tree. When was the last time she had heard her full name? She could not remember.

The morning sun rose in the sky as the birds sang.

"It's you though, isn't it?" Hale's throat bobbed, overcome by the same emotions that were roiling through her. "You are my Fated mate."

The tears came slipping heavily down her cheeks as she heard him call her that. That's why she couldn't deny him anything, why she stepped toward him when her brain told her to pull away. Fate had pulled them together.

"When did you know?" Remy still stood there, frozen, as tears poured down her cheeks.

"You run through the woods too easily, too fast. You can hunt in the dark. But I truly suspected when the *Shil-de* ring glowed in your hands. That ring was meant for you, for your family." Hale's cheeks dimpled even as he swallowed again. "But there is only one reason I know for certain that you are my Fated."

"What?" Remy could barely breathe.

"I am so desperately in love with you," Hale said as tears welled in his eyes.

A sob racked Remy.

Hale slid his arms out of his still-pinned sleeves, leaving his cloak like a ghost against the tree. He ran to her. Colliding into her, he pressed Remy against a tree trunk as his lips covered hers. He kissed her with a desperation she matched with her own.

It was real. Her Fated mate.

She wasn't sure whose tears covered her cheeks. Remy wrapped her arms around Hale's back, pulling him in tighter until every part of them touched. She needed this, needed him for so long. He was the other half of her soul. Their love had existed before they were even born.

"You almost died," Hale cried, his lips still on hers. The impact of that past night was hitting him at last. She thought of his grief-stricken face holding her lifeless body and kissed him harder.

"I'm here," she promised, sliding a hand up to his cheek.

Hale's hands gripped her hips tighter. Remy opened her mouth to him, letting his tongue explore into her. Hale groaned hungrily. Remy grabbed him around the neck and hoisted her legs up around his hips. He pinned her against the tree, and she moaned as his hands moved along her body. She would not feel whole until their souls melded into one.

An ear-splitting growl rent the air. They froze. She heard their horses' restless whinnies from far away. It did not sound like the mountain lions from the night before, but some other beast that called this forest home.

They both looked at each other, resigned and deflated that this joining would have to wait until later. They needed to get out of the forest. Hale gave Remy one last gentle kiss and put her down. His fingers threaded through hers as he led her back to camp, unwilling to let go of her.

As they began their long trek out of the forest, there was nothing else, nothing but their certainty and the silence in the morning forest between them. They were Fated mates.

Having sold their horses at the Northern Court border, they now trudged on foot. They planned to buy Northern horses, bred for the cold weather and thick snow, once they reached their lodgings in Andover. Remy knew Rua was alive, and so they could not delay. They had come so close to death. The quiet now pulled those horrors into stark relief. The adrenaline had worked out of her system, and she faced the terrible truth of who she was: the next in line to the High Mountain throne.

How could she claim that? How could she put an entire court's hopes onto her shoulders? She and her sister may be the last of the fae, but there were the red witches too. Yexshire was home to others as well: many humans, witches, and fae who had called Yexshire home, all displaced by war. She would need to rebuild the city . . . and that's if she took back the Immortal Blade from her family's murderer, King Vostemur. It was too much, far too much to even fathom.

"Are you okay?" Hale's voice sounded so far away from where Remy sat resting. He appeared through the midday fog like a phantom. He knelt down to her and placed a warm hand on her cheek. She hadn't realized how cold she was until that warm hand was there. Snowflakes dotted the air and snow would soon cover the land. Hale took off his jacket and wrapped it around her, that salt air smell enveloping her as he sat.

"I thought you were dead too," Remy whispered, exhaling a curl of steam.

The vision of his gaunt, skeletal face flashed in her mind. She still felt gripped by that fear, thinking of the scaly beasts emerging through the murky water. An unwelcome tear slipped down her cheek. Now that she had started crying, she wasn't sure if she would ever stop.

"Hey," Hale said, wiping her tear with his thumb. "I'm okay. We're okay, we're safe now."

The word *safe* was her undoing, and the tears spilled down her face once more.

"Remy," he murmured, as he gathered her into his arms, holding her with a gentle firmness.

Safe.

She had never felt safe in the past thirteen years. She knew she wasn't safe from the world, even now. But being in Hale's arms, feeling that warmth and love radiating into her from every angle, it was the closest she had ever felt to safe.

"I had to jump into that lake. I had to," she said into his chest, the tears heavy again. "I couldn't watch another person I love die."

Hale's arms tightened around her in silent acknowledgement.

She heard his voice through the rumbling in his chest, "I love you too."

He stroked a hand softly across her tousled, black hair, circling her back. With gentle, caring strokes, he moved as though massaging the pain out of her body.

He loved her.

She pulled back again to look at him. Her Fated mate was so handsome. The moment she met him, she had thought he was the most gorgeous male she had ever seen. Looking into those shining gray eyes made it hard to breathe.

She knew they were Fated mates, but to hear him say it, the last little barrier surrounding her heart crumbled. She loved him. She loved him, and it was terrifying. The Northern King had taken everything she ever loved from her.

Remy looked out over the mist-covered hills. Frost covered the grass. She heard the faint bleating of sheep as the sun warred with the clouds, its strong rays banishing the mist.

"I wasn't in the castle that night," Remy said into the fog. She felt Hale's eyes shift to her. "I was meant to be at that banquet. I was meant to put on a pretty dress and parade around to the courtiers and have the Northern King and his soldiers compliment my clothes and my features and make some inane comment about how I make an excellent princess, perhaps one day I would even make a good queen, and try to bargain my hand to Renwick."

Hale growled at her side.

"The council had been gossiping about it for weeks before the Northern Court's arrival. My father knew Vostemur was ambitious—he thought that meant he'd try to secure a High Mountain bride for his son, not . . ."

She couldn't bring herself to say it. *Not slaughter all their people.*

"I was six," Remy continued, sniffing, "and so stubborn."

"I see some things never change." Hale laughed. Remy elbowed him.

"I knew all the secret ways to sneak out of the castle, all the low windows I could climb out of. The servants indulged me. I remember their laughs and how they rolled their eyes at me. I thought I was so sneaky, but they all knew what I was doing and let me do it, anyway." She laughed.

"I was on my way to the red witch temple—it was a short walk through the valley, sitting on the foothills of Mount Lyconides."

"I remember it well," Hale said. Remy stole a glance at him, lost in his own memories.

"I forget you had been to the Castle of Yexshire yourself. Of course you had." She sighed.

They had probably met each other before, though she had no memory of it. King Norwood would have seized every opportunity to get Hale before the High Mountain Court, presenting him as their future son-in-law.

"You were at the temple when it happened?" Hale asked, leaning forward and resting his forearms on his legs.

"No, I had just left the castle. I dressed as a human child to fool the guards. I had thought nothing of all the extra soldiers outside. I thought that the Northern King was just overly cautious . . . I did not know they were there for battle. I just thought it was strange." Remy took a deep, slow breath. "I was nearing the tree-lined path to the temple when Baba Morganna . . . well, she was just Morganna then, she came running through the forest. A few breaths later, the screaming began."

"Her first Sight?" Hale recounted from the story Remy had told them around the fire weeks ago in the Western Court.

"Yes," Remy said. "She had Seen the doors locking, the fires starting—heard the screaming before it happened and ran to warn the guards. Instead she ran into me. She stopped to save me—if she had kept going . . ."

"Don't," Hale warned, his voice the only thing holding her to this moment and keeping her from being sucked into the depths of that horrible memory. "Don't play that losing game. She would not have been able to save them. It was all she could do to save you."

Remy bobbed her head. Guilt still twisted a knot in her gut. She had thought she was the only one spared that night. Now she knew Rua had made it out of there too.

"She bade me to run. She practically dragged me into the woods through the snow. I tried to turn back: I saw the fires blazing and heard the screams. The smoke was so thick, even from that far. The smell . . ." Remy swallowed a hard lump in her throat. "I could hear the skirmish of our guards with theirs. I heard the swords clashing. I heard so many people die."

Hale put a steadying hand on Remy's back as she willed the tears welling in her eyes not to spill over again. She wanted to curse those tears. She had never shed so many in her life.

"So many people fled into the woods . . . but they had expected that. Soldiers were stationed at the other side, waiting to cut down whoever ran forth. A few more red witches had found us, and we all ran together. Our only option was to go up and over the saddle of the northern mountain, Eulotrogus. It was a straight climb."

"You were six." Hale shook his head.

"The witches' magic helped me," Remy replied. "They practically levitated my body up and over. But the soldiers chased us—they knew we would go that way. They were torturing blue witches for their visions even then." Remy let the anger wash out of her in a heavy breath. "There were so many of those soldiers chasing us. Baba Morganna turned back. I watched as her magic crushed the top of that peak: she brought down the summit of Eulotrogus with magic alone, and I watched as the rocks tumbled into the saddle and blocked the pass."

"They say her magic felled a hundred soldiers, the rocks falling perfectly all around her so that only she survived," Hale whispered. "No one knew a High Mountain Princess was with those fleeing witches."

"I did not know Baba Morganna lived for many years. I thought it was her *midon brik*", the last stand of a witch, used to swap her fate with another, "I thought she was swapping her life for my own. All five of the other witches went that way: one by one, we were chased down, and each one sacrificed their life for my own. Heather was there when the last red witch fell, and she took me in. They sacrificed their lives for me." Remy seethed against that pain. "They sacrificed their lives for a hope that even after thirteen years amounted to nothing."

"No," Hale said in an adamant voice. "Not for nothing. They pledged their lives to protect your family, and they died with honor, fulfilling that promise. That sacrifice is meaningful, powerful."

"It is only powerful if I make it count for something," Remy said with quiet wrath. "And I have done nothing but hide. I have not once dropped this glamour since I was six." Hale's eyes widened at her. "What?"

"I forgot that this is not your true form," he said, shaking his head. She would not have been able to convince many that she was a human, since she could not glamour her witch magic the way she could her fae form. But with her red witch magic, it was easy enough for people to assume she was just that: a witch.

"I don't feel fae. I don't know that I want to feel fae," Remy said more to herself.

"Can you do it? Can you drop your glamour?" Hale asked. "Are you ready to?"

Remy half grinned. "I don't know if I'll ever be ready."

Dropping her glamour meant facing who she really was, something she had been hiding and denying for the past thirteen years.

Hale put his hand on her knee and squeezed it. He didn't need to say anything. She knew he didn't care what form she possessed, that he saw her true essence through any glamour. He, of all people, knew what it meant to face the truth of who you are.

Remy reached for that flicker of fae magic, straining as if lifting with a phantom muscle, but she was pulling against nothing. The memory of her fae form was as fogged and distant as the images of her fallen family. She was a ghost even to herself. Her eyes searched desolately, scanning for that feeling inside her.

"It takes time to face it," Hale said, as if reading her mind. "Permit yourself that kindness." He idly stroked her back again. "And when you are ready, I will be there."

Her heart clenched again at that. He would be there. He wanted to be there. She felt the tears welling again. Every time she thought she had cried herself dry, a fresh wave would rise.

"It's too much," Remy said, choking on her words. "I am the only person between the Northern King and the Immortal Blade." She thought of her elder brothers, Raffiel and Rivitus, and of her little sister, Ruadora, and the weight her sister must also feel on top of her. Remy would do anything to keep her sister from feeling that same way.

"I had held out hope for so long of finding Raffiel," Hale said. A tear slid down Remy's cheek as she heard his name. He was twelve during the Siege. The memory of his face had faded, like looking through a fogged mirror. "Raffiel was a good person," Hale said. "So unlike the other firstborns in the courts. He was the only one who treated me as an equal."

More tears slid down Remy's cheeks as she asked, "Do you remember my mother?"

Hale put his arm around her. "She could command an entire room with just one look, yet she was kind, gracious. She was the sort of leader any kingdom would want. She was hard but fair. She took up every space when she walked into it . . . just like her daughter."

Remy allowed the sobs to come. She cried until there was nothing left in her to give to it. And then the voice of Baba Morganna came back into her mind, "Make enough ripples to last centuries."

That was what she must do. If she wanted to protect her Fated, if she wanted to protect this love that now existed in her life, she would have to fight for it. And if she lost, at least it would be at the tip of her dagger and not hiding in some broken tavern. The world would keep coming for her, keep taking from her, either way. So she would take from the world, she would fight for her right to this happiness.

The sky was already darkening even though it was before dinnertime. They were almost there. Remy looked forward to the warmth of the inn Hale promised was up ahead. She wanted a greasy meal, a warm bath, and a soft bed with Hale in it.

Horse hooves clopping on the thin blanket of snow sounded from up ahead. Remy turned to the noise. It revealed itself to be four armored soldiers wearing the Northern Court crest.

"Curse the Gods," Remy whispered, ducking her head so her black cloak fell further across her face.

Hale put a gentle hand on her back.

"Just keep moving," he murmured.

Another horse and rider appeared in forest-green finery. Remy could tell who it was from a mile away based on that arrogant riding posture alone. Ash-blond hair and green eyes, tall and lithe, sitting stiffly upright on his sorrel steed was Renwick, Crown Prince of the Northern Court.

"Damn," Hale echoed, clenching his hand in a fist. "Just play along."

Remy adjusted the neckline of her cloak, making sure that her missing witch's collar was not visible. Hale was the first to acknowledge the Northern Prince as though it were a pleasant surprise to run into him.

"Renwick!" he called with a wave.

The Northern Prince halted his horse in front of them. A cruel smile spread across his face. His eyes seemed to bore into Hale and then settled on Remy. Without the drinks and that red dress, she thought she may buckle under the weight of his stare.

"Hello again," Renwick said unhurriedly. His eyes scanned Remy's cloak as though he could see the missing witch's collar. She feared in the cold light of day he could see her for who she really was.

"I didn't know you'd be in Andover," Renwick said with that casual politeness that courtiers were so well versed in—neither enthusiastic nor indifferent, but somewhere in between.

"What's wrong with your witch?" Renwick asked, his eyes staring daggers into Remy. She realized how faint she felt then. Her face must have drained of blood.

Remy straightened herself a bit, summoning that stubbornness and said, "Too much moonshine last night."

"She'll be fine," Hale said dismissively. Renwick laughed.

Good, Remy thought.

Let him think Hale didn't care for her. Let him think she was merely another disposable toy.

"What brings you this far south?" Hale asked, wondering why Renwick would be so close to the road to Yexshire and the Northern Court border.

"It was a sudden trip," Renwick said with bored detachment. "We have some people to deal with a few towns over."

Remy's stomach clenched as he said *deal with*.

"We?" Hale asked, rubbing his thumb down his pointer finger.

Renwick smiled at Remy, his emerald eyes glistening, as he said, "Ah yes, my father accompanies me."

As if on cue, another four Northern guards came galloping around the bend, followed by four shining black horses pulling an ornate carriage with blue and silver filigree. Another four riders took up the rear.

Remy's mind went completely blank as Hale took one step closer to her. Every heartbeat was a hammer to her chest. She sensed Renwick's assessing gaze, missing nothing in the move.

It means nothing. They don't know who I am. They just think I'm a red witch.

But to be mistaken for a red witch was bad enough. The man in that carriage collected the heads of red witches. He enslaved a whole harem of blue witches and tortured them into using magic for his benefit. Remy wanted to vomit.

She counted again. Twelve soldiers accompanied the King and Prince. Too many. There would be no way to fight off that many swords, and on horses they would be impossible to outrun. They trapped her.

The riding party halted in front of them. The carriage window shot open. "What is this delay?" came a booming shout.

Somewhere in her most distant memories Remy remembered his face: Hennen Vostemur, King of the Northern Court. He had a shock of graying red hair and a fading red beard to match. He had watery, bloodshot green eyes that matched his son's. His skin was ruddy and marked with broken blood vessels either from too much drink or too much shouting. He had large cheeks and a portly figure that told her he no longer lifted his sword. He spent his days ordering men to kill for him while he sat back and ate rich food and drank wine. But despite having the body of a jolly drunkard, his green snake-like eyes gave him a predatory countenance. He was too still, too assessing. His eyes had swept over Hale and hitched on Remy.

She could not bear it. It felt like a thousand spiders crawling over her skin as he watched her. A hot poker twisted in her gut. This was the man who had ruined her life. He had slaughtered her entire city out of jealousy and a lust for power. She knew it did not haunt him the way it haunted her: the blood, the smoke, the screaming. He had taken away everything she ever cared about just because he could, just because he wanted it. This man was the reason she had to glamour herself for thirteen years, to live in contemptible backcountry taverns, to never talk to strangers, to never draw the eyes of admirers, to be unremarkable and unnoticed by anyone. It was because of this man.

She wondered for a moment if she were fast enough to kill him. Could she use her magic to impale him on his own sword somehow or throw him under his own carriage? Her magic was still recharging, but she might be able to pull it off . . . and then what? It would spend her magic again, and they'd be facing down a dozen fae guards and Renwick, who would delight in occupying the vacant position that his father had left. Then she noticed the wardings on the carriage. They were so subtle, painted over in the same black hue, getting lost in the intricate metal detailing. A witch had warded the inside of the carriage against magic, like that card room in Ruttmore. She could not use her magic to get to the King. Remy couldn't do it to Hale either way, she realized. She couldn't let him die for her vengeance. Now that she had found him, her Fated mate, she wouldn't be able to sacrifice herself or him for anything. Their fates indelibly tied together as one.

"Look who I ran into, Father," Renwick's voice cut through Remy's murderous plots. "It's Prince Hale of the East."

Remy sent out a silent prayer that Renwick had not acknowledged her.

"Ah yes, Gedwin's bastard," Vostemur said, and Remy had to suppress a snarl. "The Lord of Andover is hosting us this night. Join us."

It was not a request, but Hale said, "It would have been my pleasure, Your Majesty, if only I had come a day sooner. I fear we are making our way west this day."

The King paused, looking at Hale with that predatory stillness, a cobra waiting to strike. Remy felt as though any moment a soldier might draw his sword and ram it through them.

"Pity," he said with a slow cock of his head. He turned his snake eyes to Remy. "Do you have the gift of Sight, witch?"

Remy's entire body went numb with fear as she said, "No, Your Majesty."

Vostemur held out a chubby hand to her and said, "Come, let's see if you can tell the King's fortune."

Remy noted how he said *the* king as though he were the only one, as though he were *their* king. It was his true plan, and they all knew it. He would not stop until he was the only king in Okrith.

Hale went as rigid as a marble statue at the King's request. Remy knew she could not decline. She took a wobbly step forward as Renwick watched her with a barbarous smile. Placing her sweaty palm in the King's hand, she tried not to tremble.

"What do you see?" Vostemur asked in a slow staccato.

"Nothing," Remy whispered. "I'm sorry, Your Majesty."

Vostemur paused, turning her hand over in his and swiping his thumb across the inside of her wrist. His smooth thumb traced each of her freckles.

"No matter," Vostemur said, more to himself than to her. He released her hand with a twisted smile, and Remy retreated to Hale's side.

If Vostemur chose to strike, Remy knew there would be no repercussions to their deaths. No one would avenge them—Vostemur left a bloody trail of such unpredictable violence. No one ever held him in check.

Hale bowed then to the Northern King, and Remy followed. Hale put a guiding hand on her back and moved her down the road.

"Don't run," he whispered as they walked, his warm hand a shining beacon to her in the darkness of her fear.

"Oh, and boy," *boy* the King had called after them, "take good care of that pretty witch of yours."

Remy's entire body seized up at his words, but Hale pushed her to keep moving, one foot after another. The clattering of the carriage and pounding hooves sounded again as the convoy took off, leaving a devastating silence in its wake.

"Keep moving," Hale said softly, continuing to guide her forward. "Just to the bend."

The sound of the horses faded away as they reached the corner. She kept willing her shaky legs to keep moving, even though she couldn't feel her feet anymore. Her whole trembling body chilled as though a sudden snowstorm swirled around them.

"Breathe, Remy," Hale said, his voice so gentle. She had not realized until he said it. She was panting, unable to take a deep breath. They passed the line of sight off the long road to Andover, and Hale guided her to a tree. "Here, sit."

He had to hold on to her arms as she collapsed onto the ground. Her breathing was frantic now, her muscles seizing as her teeth chattered.

"That man," she said as her diaphragm spasmed.

Hale cupped her cold cheek.

"I know." He pulled her in, his arms enveloping her stiff body. "I've got you."

That was all the permission Remy needed before the gasping tears came in a deluge, her body wringing her fear dry as Hale tugged her closer.

"You are not alone, Remy. I'm here," he whispered. "I can take it."

She could pour out every ounce of pain, and he would take it. She knew it wasn't a burden to him, that he welcomed it all, her Fated mate. This is what he did for her, what she did for him. They held all the things together that were impossible to hold alone.

Remy sobbed for a long time until her muscles were fatigued from the straining and shaking. She went limp in Hale's arms. She rested her cheek against his chest and listened to his slow, steady breaths. The sounds of the air filling his lungs, this beating heart, the heart of her Fated, anchored her here in this life. Without it she was sure she would have drifted away from the storms she now faced.

Screwing her eyes shut, she clenched her fists, demanding her body change back into her fae form.

"What are you doing?" Hale murmured into her hair.

Remy scowled down at the snow. "I'm trying to take this bloody glamour off."

She pulled away from him and looked up into those shining pewter eyes. "What does it feel like when you do it?"

Hale rubbed the stubble on his chin, thinking for a moment before he said, "It feels like a relief when I take my glamour off. It feels like releasing a tight muscle."

Remy huffed. She was trying to battle her glamour off instead of releasing it. It was just another one of her failings—just another way she was a hiding coward.

"You will find the right lever to pull. Give it time."

"I don't have time!" she growled.

A snow-laden branch cracked behind them, and Remy jolted. She ran her trembling hands down her face, every sound grating against her jittery nerves. It was just a branch.

"It's over," Hale whispered, enfolding Remy's hands with the warmth of his own.

"It's not over," Remy bit out. "It won't be over until he is dead."

She choked on the words. They filled her with such dread.

She had barely survived the briefest run-in with the Northern King. One look from him had reduced her to a sobbing, shaking puddle. How was she going to kill him?

What that man had done to destroy her life had all flooded back when that carriage window opened. Her secret was a boulder crushing the center of her chest. If Vostemur had known that she was the one standing in the way of his desire to wield the Immortal Blade, he would have sliced her head off. Those snake eyes could stare into her soul.

"You will kill him one day, Remy, and I will be there to watch you do it," Hale said, brushing his lips to hers. "Now, let's get to the inn."

Hale's trick seemed to work all too well, with that kiss taking pride of place in her mind.

CHAPTER TWENTY-THREE

They had stopped at an elegant little inn. They were careful not to pick the fanciest one they feared the Northern fae might stay in. But a human woman ran this inn, and it was still a fine accommodation.

Only one thought stayed lodged in Remy's mind: Ruadora was alive. Rua was through the northern mountain pass, and it was less than a day's ride into Yexshire. Remy's body still buzzed from the excitement of what Baba Morganna had told her.

Remy had lived her entire life thinking she was the last of her family, that she was the only Dammacus sibling to survive the Siege of Yexshire. She wished she had lit that red candle a long time ago, wished she had contacted Baba Morganna as a child. She would have known that Rua was still alive and that there was a safe place in the world for red witches. Remy would have gone to them straight away. She would have saved herself years of working in taverns, hiding.

Hiding, it was all she knew how to do.

As she stood in her nightgown facing the bathroom mirror, her long black hair spilling down her chest, a human woman stared back. She had been hiding in her human form for thirteen years, mistaken for a witch because of her magic. Yes, she would let slip a trickle of her fae power so she could run faster or see more clearly in the dark, but that small step into her fae self was as far as she ever let herself go.

Remy had wanted to ride through the night to see Rua, but she let Hale convince her to rest in the town of Andover. He had given her that pleading look that begged her to take it easy, if only for a day. Watching her die only yesterday, he refused to let her push herself. Remy knew she could say no, she could push Hale harder to relent . . . but she had agreed to stop because of the very reason she stood in front of the bathroom mirror now.

Hale had been right—a fae form would be so much safer in the North. If she changed, she would have the protection of her fae form . . . but she couldn't find that strand of magic that controlled her glamour anymore.

Remy didn't know her true face. This glamour had become who she was. She watched that human reflection, focusing, clenching every muscle in her body so tight and willing the change.

Nothing.

She tried harder, screwing her eyes shut.

"Work, damn it!" she cursed.

Nothing.

Remy couldn't do it. She pictured herself riding into Yexshire in her human body. Riding through the ruins of a castle, the site of her parents' murder, while she was still hiding. She was such a coward. How was she meant to claim her place on the High Mountain throne? How was she meant to lead the resurrection of her people when she hid from her own reflection? How could she face her sister only to see that disappointment on her face? She would let everyone down.

Remy took a deep frustrated breath and clenched her fists, trying again. The buzzing she felt behind her eyes and in her hands was her red witch magic, though, not her fae magic. The entire room was shaking with her effort.

Hale knocked at the bathroom door. "Remy?"

She said nothing. She couldn't face him either. She couldn't let her Fated mate see how broken she was.

Broken. That's what she was—a broken, foolish coward. Her parents would be so disappointed in her too. Her parents were brave and courageous. They had faced the world with all that they were.

She heard the full-length mirror shaking on its frame, but she could not open her eyes.

Remy did not even try to save them. She did not even try to save herself. Letting the world just happen to her, she let everyone tell her what to do and who to be and she had barely fought them. It was a life of nothingness: unnoticed, unremarkable, unworthy of glory or love.

Glass splintered in front of her, but she still would not open her eyes.

That was the truth, wasn't it? She had never fought and her body knew it. What had she done to deserve the love of her parents, her court, her mate? Her human body only knew how to fear and how to hide. She wasn't a princess in any manner of the word, so how could she change into one? She wasn't brave like her parents. Her body knew it.

She had not earned the right to be who she really was.

Shards of glass rained down as Remy collapsed in a heap in front of them. The bathroom door burst open and then Hale was in front of her.

"Are you hurt?" he shouted, running over to her cowering form. He pulled her hands from her face with gentle fingers. "What happened?"

"I'm fine," Remy said, her voice cracking. Her face burned hot with rage as she said, "No. I'm not fine."

"What happened?" She sensed Hale's eyes scanning her body, searching for where the shards of the mirror may have sliced her, but Remy knew she was unharmed.

"I can't do it," Remy murmured, balling her fists.

"Do what?" Hale asked.

"I can't take off the glamour. I can't change." Remy chewed her cheek so hard she was about to draw blood.

"Remy." Hale's voice was a near whisper. She refused to look at the pity he was sure to have on his face. Hale's hands cupped her cheeks. "Look at me."

She kept her eyes shut. How could she face him? How could she disappoint one more person? She felt the hint of Hale's breath before his mouth pressed gently to hers. She still tasted the remnants of her salty tears on his lips. The kiss was so soft, so gentle, as if Hale were telling her in the only way he knew how: she wasn't a disappointment to him.

"I am here. We are here together." He spoke onto her lips, breathing into her. Pulling away, he rested his forehead on hers. "Open your eyes."

Remy gave herself over to her mate's request. Those sparkling gray eyes shone at her, a smile tugging on Hale's lips. His thumbs stroked her cheeks as he gazed at her.

"It is so much, Remy," Hale said softly, brushing his lips to her mouth again as if he could not keep them away. "It is such a big ask. A glamour that has held for *thirteen* years? You are not a failure for not being able to take it off on your first try."

"I . . ." Remy's voice thickened again as she took an angry breath. Her hands still shook by her sides. "I don't think I want to take it off. Not really."

Hale nodded. "It's okay to be scared."

He understood.

"I don't deserve my fae form." Remy trembled. Hale stroked a strong hand down her bare arm. His warmth seeped back into her. "I am a coward."

"No," Hale said, his voice stronger. He had called her a coward once, and it stung even still. She knew Hale directed his anger at himself in the same way she felt for calling him bastard. "Do you think I'm a coward? I didn't stop the way my father treated my mother. I was too afraid to go see her . . ."

"I don't think that. Never," Remy said, cupping his cheek and pulling his forehead back to hers.

"You can't believe that I am not, and yet you are." Hale's eyes burned into hers. "You are so much braver than me, Remy. You are strong and cunning and gutsy and everything that this world needs." Remy shook her head. She couldn't hear it, but Hale squeezed her hand, threading their fingers together, making her meet his eyes again. "No, it is the truth. I wish you could see yourself the way I see you."

It was no distance at all for Remy to press her lips to his, her Fated. She kissed him harder than those first fleeting kisses, his warm mouth pulling her from her despair. Releasing his cheek, she pulled him closer, pressing herself up against him. She licked at the seam of his lips and his mouth opened further, tongue caressing her own.

Her body trembled, not from the anger or the cold this time.

Hale broke the kiss and looked at her, eyes blazing.

"Let me show you who you are," he breathed, his voice edged with pleading, as his mouth hovered over hers. "Let me show you all the ways I can worship you."

Remy's core clenched as she nodded. Smiling, Hale scooped her into his arms and stood like it was no effort at all. Shards of mirror scattered around them as he strode out of the bathroom and to the enormous bed.

He set Remy down, only to pull her into a hot, branding kiss. They stood there at the foot of the bed, breaking apart only long enough to pull off Hale's white undershirt. Remy had seen him shirtless before, but now she could indulge her urge to stroke her hands down his sculpted body. Her hands traced the corded muscles of his arms as he gathered the fabric of her nightdress in his large hands and pulled it over her head, baring her to him.

She leaned backward onto the bed, inching herself up towards the pillows. Hale snarled as he looked over her naked body. Her nipples stiffened against the cool air and the heat of his stare. A hot ache pulsed at her core from Hale's look alone. His molten silver eyes filled with the ferocity of an unspoken promise that he would devour her.

Hale made quick work shucking off his boots and unbuttoning his pants, and it was Remy's turn to go still. Her mouth parted as she looked at him. She had gotten a sense of his size from that night in the woods, but seeing him naked in front of her, the way his abdominal muscles tapered to his thick, hard shaft, had slick wetness pooling between her legs. Hale's nostrils flared, smelling her arousal. The scent made his entire body shudder. Remy vibrated in anticipation. The promise held in those wild gray eyes set her aflame.

Hale prowled on top of her, his mouth meeting back with hers, and Remy was certain he would fulfill that promise. Those kisses were all consuming, a symphony of lips and teeth and tongue, like they were melding their whole beings together. Remy was desperate for that union to be complete, grinding herself with wanton abandon against him. Hale broke the kiss to grin wickedly at her desperate writhing.

"What do you want?" he whispered, skimming his lips across her neck and nipping his way up to her ear.

There was only one thing Remy wanted. She hoped there would be other times, slower times with hands and mouths and casual love-making, but her need for him right in that moment was so over-whelming she needed all of him right away.

"I want you inside me," she breathed even as her hands tried to pull him closer. She spoke with a level of desperation she wasn't even the slightest bit embarrassed of.

Hale smiled that smug, princely smile at her as he nudged himself at her entrance. Upon feeling that wetness between her legs, that smile wiped away. Hale growled again, his lips meeting her once more as he pushed himself in another inch.

He broke the kiss and watched Remy's half-hooded eyes as he pushed himself all the way into her. The feeling of him filling her shattered every thought in her mind other than that pulsing fullness at her core. Every cell in her body homed in to that spot where they became one.

As Hale began slow, testing movements, every sense in her height-ened. She smelled his musky arousal, heard his heart thundering beneath his chest, saw the dilation of his pupils. She tasted his sweat and his ocean air scent. Hale's eyes seemed more flecked with stone and silver, widening as he looked at her, something dawning on his face she couldn't quite name. Did it feel the same for him? Like a door unlocking to another world.

They held each other's stare in awe and wonder for a moment at how right it felt to be united in this way. And then Hale was moving again in a way that had Remy moaning.

"It feels so good," he hissed. "You feel so good."

Her legs shook. Remy bucked her hips up to meet him, demanding more of each thrust. Hale growled, the veins in his arms bulging, as he started moving faster.

"Hale," Remy whimpered, and the sound of his name on her mouth unleashed him.

He pulled all the way out of her and slammed back in, the sensation so good, so overwhelming, Remy cried out. Hale's own desperate groans met her wild sounds as he did it again and again, faster and faster until she was so close to the precipice.

Hale bent down and took her hardened nipple in his mouth and sucked it while continuing his punishing pumps.

Remy's nails bit into his skin as she shattered into a million pieces, screaming his name. One more pump and Hale's body seized as he spilled into her, that climax rolling through them until they were panting and gasping.

Stars danced in Remy's vision.

They held each other for a long while, listening as their breathing slowed, their heartbeats steadying. Eventually, Hale summoned enough energy to drag out of her and roll to his side. His lips skimmed her shoulder, his mind still far away in the memories of ecstasy. Remy closed her eyes, leaning into his touch.

"My Fated mate," she whispered.

When Hale didn't respond, she turned to him and the look of adoration in his eyes made her feel like she was glowing.

"You . . . ," he said with a level of reverence she had never heard from anyone before and never wanted to hear from any other, only him, "you are the most beautiful, stunning, incredible being I have ever laid eyes upon."

He traced idle fingers across Remy's cheek, nose, the lobe of her pointed ear.

"See for yourself," he said.

He reached across to the bedside table. Grabbing a framed portrait, he flipped it to the silver backing, and he held it to her.

Remy furrowed her brow but looked into her distorted reflection . . . but it wasn't her. A female fae looked back. She had shining brown eyes flecked with emerald green, tousled onyx hair and rosy freckled cheeks over smooth tawny brown skin. Her lips were fuller, pinker. Her face was more angular, her skin lit from within with a golden hue. And the tips of her ears tapered into sharp points.

A memory of her mother passed through her mind. She tried not to well up at the thought. She would see Baba in person tomorrow and thank her for all she had done to save her . . . again. Remy blinked at her reflection.

"My mate," Hale echoed, his shining eyes brimming with unshed tears, overcome by what this moment meant for both of them.

They were mated forever and inextricably tied. A part of his soul existed in her and she in him. In their joining, she had revealed her true self to him. She could only ever be her whole real self for her Fated mate. And it made her feel raw and vulnerable, beautiful and worthy all at once. She wanted to stay there, linked to him. She had felt first bound to his eyes and then his lips, and now every part of them had united. The very fabric of their beings had woven so tightly together they would never unravel from each other again.

Remy knelt in the snow in nothing but a black satin robe. Bri had bought it for the warm Southern climate, not the Northern snow. Her long hair wrapped around her like a blanket, shining brighter, the curls tighter in her fae form. Her fae skin felt the cold, but it wasn't as biting. She liked this body . . . her real body, she realized. It felt like she had had a headache for the past thirteen years, and only now that it was gone did she realize what she was meant to feel like. This body felt right. She felt stronger, faster, more resilient even to intangible things. How much easier life would have been if circumstances had permitted her to take off her glamour years ago.

Remy stared at the flickering candle in front of her. She laid her totems bathing in the full moon glow before her. She had discarded her fallen leaf from the last full moon and in its place now was a sprig of pine needles. She added a new one too, one she did not intend on discarding anytime soon: a shard of broken mirror. It would serve as a reminder to her of who she really was, not a witch but a High Mountain fae who could cast red witch magic. She could not shy away from her reflection anymore. Remy and her sister were the last of the High Mountain royals. She had debated whether to do a full-moon ritual at all, wondering if she should leave it behind now that she was in her fae form. But she liked the rhythms of the moon. She liked her prayers and the ritual. The same murmured words every month made her feel steady.

The inn sat to her back, and the whole evergreen forest stretched out before her. She knelt there, staring at her candle. No ancestors could speak on this quiet hunter's moon, but she still felt the echoes of her mother's words. Her mother, the Queen of the High Mountain Court, was wise and strong. She had treated Remy with warmth and love but also a hardness that made sure her daughter wouldn't turn into a simpering princess. Her mother wanted Remy to be strong, cunning, brave, but fair. Remy frowned. She didn't feel like she was any of those things. How could she ever fill the shoes of the fallen Queen? It was an impossible task.

The icy wind blew Remy's hair off her neck, and she heard a soft inhale of breath from far away. Her fae hearing was fine-tuned better than any night-stalking predator. She looked behind her at the window, knowing who she would find leaning on the sill.

"How long have you been there?" she asked, looking up to her Fated love. Hale leaned his shirtless torso out into the chilly air. The moon made his eyes glow even in the shadows.

"As long as you have been down there." The smirk he gave her made her body echo with the pleasure of the last hours. She had waited until he had fallen asleep to sneak out and pray to the moon. Her sneaking skills still needed some work, it seemed. "Only you would dash out into the snow in nothing but a skimpy robe."

She felt the brand of his eyes on all her exposed skin.

"I can take care of myself you know," she said, though her words had no bite.

"I know." Hale grinned, both cheeks dimpling. "But when my Fated is alone with a priceless talisman, it seems wise to have backup." He looked to where the *Shil-de* ring lay in the snow. "Plus, you are half naked, and if any male were to walk by right now, I'd be forced to gouge his eyes out."

"So very even keeled, aren't you?" Remy laughed.

"Yes, I feel very sensible around you. Now, are you coming back to bed?"

She loved that warm, honest grin, those crinkled, happy eyes. She loved every single inch of him.

Remy bit her lip at the thought.

"Yes. I'm done." She whirled with a bit too much eagerness to mumble the last of her prayers and blow out the white candle.

"Good. You have three seconds to climb back up here or else," he said, his voice a playful rasp.

"Or else what?" Remy arched a brow at him, already knowing the answer.

"Or I will jump down there and fuck you in the snow." The low vibration of that threat shook right through Remy, making her thighs clench together.

She was sure the snow was melting under her as she put her totems back into the black bag. She prayed for many nights in the future when they could make love under the stars, but not tonight in the Northern snow. Picking up the candle, she turned to the window a story above. She assessed the outer wall. It would be an impossible climb in her glamoured form, but now . . .

She ran and jumped, pushing herself off one brick that stuck out from the rest and vaulting to the window ledge. Grabbing it one-handed, she clutched her totem bag and candle in the other. She easily lifted herself up and over the ledge, landing in a crouch. Her strength felt amazing.

"You are magnificent." Hale stood before her like a dark god in nothing but a sheet wrapped low across his hips.

His molten eyes watched Remy stand. Remy's robe was split open in a deep V all the way down to where it belted below her hips.

That heat in his eyes made Remy's stomach tighten. With such a sweeping, unexpected urgency, she needed him again. She threw the candle and totem bag onto the floor. Not a single thing mattered anymore. Only him. Only them.

Hale moved the instant the candle hit the floor. His fingers grasped the back of Remy's neck and pulled her to him. He kissed her desperately, that deep, sudden need overcoming him as well. They stood there kissing, in a fire that was unlike anything she had ever felt before. Hot wetness pooled between her legs.

"That scent, your scent." His voice was a deep, rolling purr. "It was made just for me."

He hooked his index finger into Remy's belt and yanked her forward. Inching his way back to the bed, he deftly untied the knotted satin that rested above the apex of Remy's legs. He never broke their gaze, his mouth open and breathless, his eyes dark with wanting. The satin skimmed across Remy's warm brown skin as it fell to the floor.

Hale's hands shook with restraint as he placed his large warm hands on either side of Remy's hips and moved her to the bed. Remy lay back, splayed across the bed, trembling under the predatory gaze of the prince. She shuddered as Hale dropped to his knees and kissed the inside of her ankle.

He trailed slow kisses up her leg. He paused to swirl his tongue on her inner thigh. She shifted, eager for that mouth to move higher. She felt Hale's smile against her flesh. His nose skimming through the coarse black hair between her legs, he took a deep inhale, letting out a growl that was nothing but feral.

His breath tickled the hairs framing Remy's most sensitive spot. She thought she might explode from the anticipation alone.

At the first slide of his fiery tongue, her entire body spasmed. It was already too good. His tongue moved again, slowly up and down. Remy released a heavy, wild moan, crazed by the explosion of sensations.

"You taste even more amazing than you smell," Hale groaned, his hands squeezing her thighs as he spread her wider.

Remy threaded her fingers through Hale's hair as he bent down again. His tongue swirled over her, and she cried out. The sound weakened his restraint, his tongue sweeping faster. Feeling the pad of his finger at her entrance, she could not breathe as he dipped it into her wet depths. Her muscles tightened like a bowstring: she was already on the precipice of release.

"Hale," she moaned. He hummed against her, the vibrations making her gasp. "I want all of you," she gritted out in a voice of a female possessed.

Hale instantly released her from his burning tongue. He crawled up her body like a stalking lion and kissed her deeply. She tasted her musky wetness on his tongue. He pulled back a fraction as his tip brushed against her liquid heat. The sensation made Remy's eyes roll back and flutter closed. It sucked her into a tornado of sensations.

"Open your eyes," Hale's husky voice demanded.

Remy obeyed. Looking into those smoky eyes alone was almost enough to undo her. Hale watched her with everything, every emotion: there were no words for all of existence whirring between their eyes. He fisted the sheet beside Remy's head as he pushed into her. Remy's mouth went slack as she inhaled sharply. He dipped deep inside of her. He held her stare, his eyes filled with wonder.

"I love you, Remy," he said with a deep rawness she had never seen from him before.

"I love you too, Hale." Remy's voice thickened.

This was it. This was the moment she wanted to stretch on for the rest of her life. She wanted this and only this to continue on endlessly.

Slowly, he moved, sweet rolling waves in and out of her. She pulled his head down to hers. His soft lips caressed her own as she swept a hand down his back, settling on his hard backside. She felt the muscles clenching and releasing as he moved into her. This was making love. She had fucked before, but Hale was the first and only person she would ever make love to. Their souls were locking together in the mirror to their bodies. They were right there, on the edge between existing as two separate people and one. The lines blurred as they fell into bliss: one soul in two bodies.

CHAPTER TWENTY-FOUR

The long winter had already reached the Northern Court, but the snow lessened as they rode into the High Mountains. Yexshire had light flurries at this time of year, but the heavy snow was still a month or more away.

Remy felt Hale hard against her ass, even through her thick winter cloak. The rubbing of her leathers on the saddle was driving her mad. It was another two hours south into the High Mountains, and she didn't know if she could make it. The smell of him was intoxicating. Her fae nose relished that musky, scorching arousal wafting from his pores like a heady perfume. She heard Hale inhale and knew he smelled her drenched wanting too.

"Memories of last night?" he whispered, nibbling on the delicate point of her ear. Remy arched into his hot breath with a frustrated mewl. She was so ready for him. Constantly. Endlessly. "Does the sound of my voice make you wet?"

Hale's hand snaked around to her stomach, parting her cloak. His fingers dipped below the tight waist of her leathers. He hissed, his fingers soaked. Remy ground into those fingers shamelessly, desperate for him to touch her.

Hale chuckled in that gravelly way that awakened every nerve ending in her body. His fingers slid down her soft, wet folds and Remy moaned, leaning her head back into his shoulder as her eyes flitted closed.

"Is this what you want?" He slid his teeth across her neck. His other hand had gone slack holding the reins, and the horses trekked on, unguided. The grinding of the saddle, bumping them against each other, made it harder for Remy to hold on to her control. Hale slid two long fingers inside of her, and she cried out.

"What about this?" he purred

"Mm." Remy hummed, the only sound she could make. She gyrated against those fingers, pinning them between her and the saddle. She bucked up as Hale pressed his palm hard over that bundle of nerves. Remy ground against Hale's hard length, making him groan.

"You better hold that gorgeous ass still before it causes any more trouble," he growled even as he moved himself against her.

"I like this kind of trouble," Remy said in a thick voice, her eyes tilting back to see Hale's scorching stare. She ground back against him another time. "What sort of trouble did you have in mind?"

Hale dipped his fingers out and slammed them back into her, causing a moan that shook through them both.

"I am one second away from pulling you off this horse and fucking you against that tree," Hale snarled.

Remy yanked Hale's arm away, pulling his wet fingers out of her leathers. She leapt off the horse in the same way she had on the streets of Wynreach.

She needed him now. All of him.

She looked back at her Fated with a devious smile. He grinned at her viciously as he hooked the horse's reins onto a low branch and dismounted.

His hard shaft strained against his leathers as he prowled toward her. He pounced, spinning her around so her chest pressed against the tree trunk. Ripping down her leathers, he exposed her ass to the cool air.

That gorgeous ass, as he had called it.

Remy barely had time to brace herself as he slammed into her. She screamed out. The sensation of his huge cock filling her was over-whelming. Hale grunted as he pulled himself out and slammed into her again. Remy's palms bit into the tree bark as she braced herself against his fast, deep thrusts. Her pleasure was building as she sank her teeth into her hand to keep from exploding. Hale grabbed her hips tighter as he pounded into her so hard she thought the tree might snap. The sound of their hot, wet flesh slapping together was the only sound in the forest. Hale ramped up to a punishing speed, barreling toward his climax, and Remy couldn't hold on anymore. She shattered with a shout that shook through the forest. Two more pumps and Hale exploded into her, barking out her name.

Remy's body twitched and clenched repeatedly until her teeth at last released the flesh on the back of her hand. She would have a wicked bruise there, and she did not care in the slightest. Her heavy panting breath ebbed.

"You are such trouble, Princess," Hale laughed his heavy breath across her hair. "I think you might be even more wicked than me."

The Yexshiri forests felt eerily familiar. Monopolized by dogwood, buxus, and alder, the leaves and branches allowing for just enough light to scatter through. Rugged purple and golden-hued mountain shrubs erupted from the brittle leaves on the ground below. Thick draping moss clung to the trees, and a hodgepodge of wildflowers tried to claim the last remnants of sunlight. Their brilliant shades of red and blue added some bright touches to the otherwise dark forest floor. A harmony of wild noises, predominantly songbirds, resonated through the air. Remy's sensitive fae ears could hear frog croaks from nearby ponds despite the birdsong.

The forest was alive and thriving, reclaiming the unused road in front of them. The now-quiet highway that led to Yexshire was unrec-ognizable. Fallen trees blocked some of the path. They had to dismount and navigate the horses around the blockages more than once.

As they turned the corner, abandoned houses appeared. Yexshire, once a bustling city and home to many folk, was now a ghost town in the truest sense. A sinister silence had taken over, interrupted only by the cracking of branches in the wind. Even the birds who had made their homes in the many collapsed roofs dared not sing here. Some doors had collapsed, perhaps destroyed by looters or raided by animals as time passed. Most of the rooftops had caved in, sometimes taking the entire building with them. Other houses looked in decent shape and were simply dirty and overgrown with weeds. The fountain in the town square was still full of water, though it had turned green and was overgrown with algae.

Hale's arms tightened around Remy. Her heart pounded in her ears. Snippets of memories flashed through her mind at every corner: the streets decorated for Summer Solstice, the city gathering to wave off the royal family on one of their trips, the lively crowds on market day, selling their wares.

It was all gone.

Street after street of abandoned homes made for a terrifying thought: each house was once a home, a home belonging to a family of Yexshire, and now there was only emptiness. Remy knew even if they could claim the Immortal Blade, this city would never be the same. Many of those families were lost forever.

Her chest clenched tighter as they rode the path up onto the mountainside that towered over the city. The Castle of Yexshire once stood proudly overlooking the High Mountains: now it was only black stone rubble and ash.

Remy could still remember the castle in vivid detail. Black stone towers connected by high walls had surrounded the castle. Around the walls in symmetrical patterns, small windows scattered, along with overhanging lookouts for archers and artillery. It had looked as much a fortress as a castle, for all the good it did them.

The High Mountain fae had the least grand and most practical home, designed for the cold Yexshiri winters. Remy remembered the enormous roaring fireplaces, heavy curtains, and thick rugs. She wondered if it was actually that size or if her childhood imagination had made it bigger.

Heavy metal doors lay discarded on the road, blocking their ride any further into the ruins.

"Do you want to go in?" Hale's voice was a reverent whisper. It felt wrong to speak louder in this place.

"Yes," Remy breathed as though the mountains were listening. "You stay with the horses I won't be a minute."

Hale nodded, knowing this was something she needed to do alone.

Remy dismounted their horse and stalked up the steep hill into the wreckage. She climbed over half-fallen walls and piles of crumbling stone. When the cobblestones beneath her boots gave way to flat gray paving stones, she knew she was standing where the great hall once lay. They had taken everything. Every rug, every flagpole, every golden sconce. There was no chandelier anymore, no tables or chairs. The High Mountain throne was missing from the raised dais before her. The dais, once covered in white marble, was stripped down to the pavers beneath, but she knew that's where it once was. A tall window had once existed in the now-missing far wall. It had cast the perfect beam of light down onto that dais, illuminating the whole royal family. They had timed all of their gatherings for that perfect sunlight, different times in each season so that the light would always shine on the royals. Remy remembered standing in that light, her posture so tall, her chin so high, so proud of her name and her family even at six.

Remy's feet crunched on glass as she walked toward the dais, rubble slipping under her feet, but she continued across the long space and up to where the throne once was. She stood there in the same spot where she had stood as a child, looking out over a grand hall that was no longer there. The road was too steep for her to see Hale, but she knew he was beyond the hill, waiting.

Remy looked over the abandoned city. Flat plains to her right, where lush fields of crops had stretched out to the forest beyond, had provided the Yexshiri with enough food to last them all year round. Now those fields grew over with tall grasses and shrubs and were being reclaimed into the woodland's edge. She looked down at the forested saddle between the city and the mountains beyond.

On the mountainside, parallel with the castle and sitting equal pride of place, was the Temple of Yexshire. Though the castle was in ruins, the temple still stood. Built over 500 years ago, the monolith erupting from the thick forest was a reminder of the alliance between the High Mountain Court and the red witch coven. The placement of the castle and temple signified they were equals, neither looking down upon the other. The seed of the Yexshiri power lay in the union between fae and witch magic.

The Temple of Yexshire was a wide, white stone spire. Crafted and created with lavish materials, it was built from a local quarry's white rock, the color a direct juxtaposition to the black stone castle across the valley.

The massive flagpole still rose from the highest turret, but no red ribbons blew on the wind anymore. The witches had added ribbons each season, a symbol of the prayers of the community. Watching those ribbons flap in the breeze was like watching the beating heart of the people, their dreams and aspirations for the future. But not even a scrap of fabric remained thirteen years later.

Remy swore her eyes snagged on a flash of red from the temple window. She squinted her eyes, narrowing them to thin slits.

She gasped. A hooded red figure stood there: a red witch priestess. Had they moved back into the temple? Baba Morganna had said the red witches gathered in the hills beyond Yexshire. But had they moved into the temple proper? Were there enough of them to reclaim the temple and protect it against any Northern soldiers? Remy blinked again and the red cloak disappeared, the window a black hole once more. She shook her head. Maybe she was seeing ghosts. But Baba Morganna had promised they were there, not far into the woods beyond the temple. Who would think to look there if they didn't know?

Remy was ready. She needed to go find them. She needed to see her sister.

Stepping forward, she snagged her foot on a weed growing

through the cracks in the rock. She threw her arms out to catch herself but regained her balance, staying upright. She glanced at the vine, a thick, thorny plant that wound through the stones. Remy was about to look away when the glint of something beneath the stone caught her eye. She reached down, careful to avoid the thorny vine, and lifted the heavy black stone to the side, freeing what lay underneath. There, beneath the stone, was a crushed pair of golden spectacles. Snapped in two, the metal bent and twisted. Too small, they were half the size of an adult's glasses.

A sob escaped Remy. She knew who these glasses had belonged to.

Her eldest brother, Raffiel, got all the attention for being strong and handsome, and their next eldest sibling quite often got overlooked.

Rivitus. Riv, they called him.

Riv would have been nine on the day of the Siege of Yexshire. He was the smartest person Remy had ever known. Her parents had bragged about his intelligence endlessly, even as the rest of the court all praised Raffiel. Her parents knew Riv would always be there by Raffiel's side when he one day took his place on the High Mountain throne.

Riv had been training with the king's council his whole life. Of his own volition, he would sit in on council meetings and prod their father's advisors with constant questions. He had lived in the library, poring himself into every history and policy book he could get his hands on. His courtly duties, balls, feasts, and entertaining other courts had been the bane of his existence. Her parents had scolded him more times than Remy could count for bringing books into the great hall during ceremonies.

Remy sniffed as she picked up the glasses. Tears spilled down her cheeks. He had probably been frowning and miserable on the night of his death, forced to stand beside their parents while entertaining the Northern King's court. Remy wondered what he saw before he died. She blinked out more tears. She hoped that they had cut him down quickly, judging by his glasses still being on the dais. She prayed he had not suffered.

Remy's breath shuddered. She would never get to hug her brothers again. She would never again get to follow them around like an annoying puppy, peppering them with questions that they were loath to answer. She would never again see their smiles or hear their laughs or know their love. There would be a vast empty hole in her where her siblings had been . . . not all her siblings, though, Remy remembered. Ruadora was still alive, and she was in those woods before Remy.

Remy brushed tears off her cheeks and took a steadying breath. She tucked Riv's glasses into her pocket and left that haunted place. Walking back down the steep road from the palace ruins, she saw Hale waiting beside the horses. Hurt and concern drew his face thin. He held a bouquet of white wildflowers that had been growing along the alpine road in his hands.

He separated the flowers into two bunches and passed half to Remy.

"I believe it's Yexshiri tradition to lay white flowers on the graves of the fallen," he said as Remy took the flowers from his outstretched hand. "These were all I could find."

The tears slipped down Remy's cheeks again, and she nodded. She wanted to tell him it was perfect but couldn't summon the words. She turned back toward the rubble, all that was left of her family's legacy. In the mountains beyond the castle, up a narrow rocky path, were her ancestors, all laid to rest in simple earthen tombs. She remembered laying flowers on the graves of her grandparents, trekking up that hallowed path every Day of the Spirits to honor their ancestors. Their spirits watched over the castle and the city of Yexshire. Eyes scanning the forested summit, she was certain they were looking down on them even now. It steeled her resolve for the obstacles she knew lay ahead. This would not be the end of their legacy.

Hale stepped forward first, dropping to one knee, as he laid the bunch of small white flowers onto the road.

"May their spirits blow freely through the wind. May we see them in the waving grasses and the falling leaves and the mighty ocean waves. Rest in eternal peace."

He stood and took his place at Remy's side.

She had never heard that prayer before. She wondered if it was an Eastern Court prayer.

They stood for a long time. Hale didn't speak or rush her. He stood stoically beside her, an anchor in the storm. She knew he would stand there all night if she needed. He would weather any sorrow beside her, her Fated.

Finally, Remy stepped forward, crouching to the road. She laid the flowers down, touching the earth with her fingertips and then touched her forehead.

She tried to remember the language of her people.

"Immortal creators, guardians of the afterlife, wombs of this world, hear my prayer," she whispered, the Yexshiri words feeling foreign on her tongue, "Guide these spirits into the afterlife. May they know your grace. May they feel your peace. Fill them with your eternal light. Amen."

CHAPTER TWENTY-FIVE

They traveled through the darkened forest and into the sunlight on the other side toward the Temple of Yexshire. Remy's heart was in her throat with anticipation to see Ruadora again. Rua had been four the last time Remy had seen her. Her little sister, less than two years younger, was a faint blur in her mind. She did not know what she would look like all grown up. She'd be eighteen in a few weeks, a grown woman.

The Temple of Yexshire loomed quietly above them as they tied up the horses. A large clearing circled around the temple, overgrown with tall grasses.

Remy craned her neck up to look at the towering white temple.

"Look to the tree line," Hale said. "There must be some clue of which direction their camp is from here."

Remy nodded. "I'll take the far side."

She waded into the chest-high grasses, stumbling a few times over the uneven ground. The meadow was so thick she couldn't see below her thighs. She tried to remember what had once filled this clearing. There had been a low wood fence circling the temple, now either decayed into ruin or lost below the line of golden grass.

Beyond the fence had been a herd of grazing goats. They were gone too. She wondered if one of the many pillagers or witch hunters after the Siege of Yexshire had eaten them.

There had been a giant spiraling herb garden bisecting the gravel path to the temple's front steps. Remy remembered the smells of mint and sage wafting in the air as she walked toward the temple.

She couldn't see any evidence of it. If she dug, maybe she would find it there still. Or maybe looters had taken the holy herbs along with everything else. The years had not been kind. At least a few big storms had blown through, knocking trees into the clearing.

Remy stood directly in front of the temple's open archway. She had climbed over a fallen trunk when she heard a noise. It sounded like a scuffle inside the temple. She wondered if a fox or a bear had found its way inside. The morning frosts, promising winter's impending hand, would have compelled them into the temple's shelter.

Remy looked at the temple and gasped again. She was certain it wasn't a phantom now. A hooded red figure stood in one of the tall windows, looking down on her.

The red witches were here. Remy bolted toward the archway.

The witches must have taken their rightful place in the Temple of Yexshire. Rua would be inside this tower. She was only a few steps from her sister.

Remy scrambled up the disintegrating steps. She had just crossed the threshold when Hale's scream rent the air.

"It's a trap!" he shouted. "Run!"

Remy spun from the threshold of the temple to find Hale, and what she saw . . .

A dozen Northern soldiers had emerged from the tall grass. Two were restraining Hale from where he stood at the forest's edge. How had she missed them? How had she not scented them? Gods, one stood directly in the path in front of her. She must have stepped right over him. Not a fallen tree at all.

"Run!" Hale shouted again as Remy froze in panic. A hard punch to the face cut off Hale's voice.

Remy threw out her magic on instinct, and the two soldiers

holding Hale went flying. She swept out an arc of red magic and flattened the entire field of soldiers before her. Hale was already running toward her. They could run through the temple, out the other side, and into the forest, losing the Northern soldiers before they woke up.

Hale stumbled as he ran but kept himself upright. It wasn't until he was at the base of the steps that his determined stare changed to one of horror. Remy didn't have time to turn as a large arm grabbed her around the middle, hauling her into the darkness of the temple. She scrambled to break free, throwing out her magic in her panic, but it did not land a blow.

An acidic cloth clamped over her nose and mouth. The powerful stench burned her throat. Her limbs felt tingly, her vision spotted with black, as Hale's bellows circled her.

Remy threw out her leg, connecting with the guard's knee, before the dizzying darkness could claim her. He dropped Remy enough so she could grab her dagger on her hip. She didn't stop to think. There was no pausing anymore. As Bri had promised, her instincts took over and in one smooth motion she spun, stabbing directly into the soldier's neck. She didn't wait to see him fall. She yanked back her blade, his blood spraying into the air as she ran.

Her feet remembered the layout of the temple as she instinctively raced up the winding stone steps to her left, taking them two at a time. Her muscles reminding her she was fae, she pushed her legs harder. Remy heard the heartbeat of the soldier up ahead, waiting to strike. Without revealing herself, she stabbed his foot with her dagger. He screamed as Remy ran up the steps, kicking him down into the oncoming soldiers behind her. The falling soldier was not as much of an obstacle for the rest as she had hoped. She ran up the steps faster, but the Northern soldiers were catching up too fast.

They were fae too . . . but . . . they did not have witch magic.

Remy ducked under a white stone archway, slamming out her red magic, crumbling the archway behind her and blocking the staircase upward. She reached the fourth-floor landing and heaved in a breath.

She looked out the keyhole window and saw Hale. He held a sword in each hand, brutal and focused. Four soldiers were coming at him;

another six lay dead all around him. He moved like an avenging god. He pushed some out and pulled others in, pacing their charges, controlling them without them knowing. He cut down every soldier who stepped into reach of his blade instantly. Another dozen soldiers stood in the woods, hesitating to charge.

Gods, how many of them did they bring?

Remy's eyes caught on the red cloak in the woods. It wasn't a red witch wearing it at all. Even at this height her fae eyes could see the face of the woman clearly, those glowing blue hands and painted blue lips. They had brought a blue witch with them.

Remy cursed.

The blue witch's eyes were closed, but her face tilted up to the window where Remy watched. Remy didn't know how honed the witch's Sight was, but if she was powerful, she might have Seen the outcomes of this ambush already. Remy would need to change things up to stay ahead of the blue witch. She could not choose whatever decision came first to her mind. She needed to pick the second option, then the first, then alternate. It was a trick that she had learned from Heather to keep ahead of the blue witches' Sight. But Remy would have to take the blue witch out if they had any hopes of escaping them. Remy could lose the soldiers in the woods, but she wouldn't be able to outrun the blue witch's Sight.

A sudden punishing blow landed at the back of Remy's head as she collided with the stone floor. A guard lifted his sword over her, and she threw out her magic, blasting his weapon out of his hand. Heavy boots shifted behind her. Watching Hale had distracted her. She tried to scramble to her feet, but his heavy boot stomped her down, and she screamed as her arm buckled under the force of the hit. She threw another blast of magic, the pain amplifying her power. The soldier fell backward.

Remy leapt up. Her left arm throbbed with pain. She thanked the Gods it wasn't broken.

She let it hang limply at her side as she looked behind her. A dozen Northern soldiers stood on the landing opposite her, swords in hand, waiting. The one she had toppled stood and smiled at her, wiping blood from his mouth. They trapped her against the wall. Her first instinct was to run up the stairs to her left. So she didn't. She flung out her hand and toppled the archway to the back of the waiting soldiers. Three fell under the heavy rocks, but the others turned. Remy feinted toward the stairs upward, and the soldiers moved in the same direction. Instead, Remy spun, running downward. She knew in one more flight the crumpled stairway below would trap her once more. Heavy armor clanked, following her down as she darted to the left.

She sprinted for the open window, holding her breath, not giving herself a chance to think as she willed her legs faster. And then she leapt into nothing but air.

She free fell, the wind whipping her hair. The world slowed as she calculated her trajectory toward the fir tree out the window. She prayed its branches would hold her as she braced for impact. Pine needles assaulted her as she smacked into the tree. Her injured shoulder screamed at her as she tumbled past several more branches. She caught herself with her one good arm.

She darted a look at the window. The Northern soldiers watched her, mouths gaping. They were all weighted down in heavy armor. None would dare to make that jump.

She clambered across the branches to another tree, deeper into the forest. She decided to cross two more before climbing down. Then she remembered the blue witch and changed her mind, climbing across one more branch and making her way to the forest floor.

She needed to get to Hale and her bow and arrow still with the horses. She needed to get to the amulet too. She wished she had heeded Hale and taken it for herself. Her magic was already fatigued, and she had little left in her.

Circling the temple clearing, she took a deep breath and tiptoed through the woods. She listened to the shouts from the top of the temple. The soldiers were shouting to the ones on the ground that they were clearing the stairwell. That it would take time.

She heard everything: their armor clanking, the branches creaking as more soldiers bashed through the woods ahead, leaves rustling under their feet.

Then she heard a shout: "We've got the prince."

Remy's heart stopped.

Moving on silent feet, she neared the woods behind where they had tied their horses. She ducked behind a spiky shrub and peered above it. Like she was a bloodhound for that ocean scent, she could smell Hale through the forest.

Hale sat bound and gagged against a tree trunk, surrounded by three guards. His head slumped forward, blood trickling down his forehead. Remy zeroed in on the sound of his slow heartbeat and steady breaths. He was unconscious but alive.

Another two Northern fae rummaged through the horses' saddle-bags. Remy's bow and quiver of arrows remained untouched, tied to her pack. Her fingers itched for it. One soldier pulled up the long chain of the amulet of Aelusien.

Remy clenched her teeth together, watching as the soldier whistled to a male standing in the tall grasses by the temple. His silver hair and flowing cerulean cape told Remy he was the unit commander. The commander nodded to the amulet.

"Good. Keep looking for the ring," he ordered. Another soldier stepped up to him. "Let's hear it."

"Twenty-two injured, eight dead," the male said. "We're waiting to hear the final numbers from inside, they're still digging them out."

Remy grimaced. She had done that . . . well, some of it. Most of the death count was Hale's. The enormity of his power confronted Remy once more. He had taken on a complete unit of trained fae soldiers and almost escaped.

"Go get that blue witch. Everything she predicted has been wrong," the commander snarled. "King Vostemur will be most displeased to hear of her failing."

That cruel snarl said enough. They would either kill the witch or make her wish they had killed her, through no fault of her Sight but because Remy knew how to outwit it.

"Have you found the red witch yet?" the commander mused, looking up at the open window Remy had jumped out of.

The witch . . . did they still not know it was her? How could that be? She was in a fae form using red witch magic . . . But people only saw what they wanted to see. The High Mountain fae were gone. They believed it was Raffiel, not Remini, who lived. They were hunting her as a red witch, not as a princess.

"She fled through the trees, but we'll find her, Commander," the soldier replied.

They would start tracking her scent any minute. The soldiers could scent her from there if they thought to try, but they assumed she was long gone. They did not think a little witch would double back on an entire unit of fae soldiers. She probably should have. Hale would have wanted her to. But she could not leave him behind.

Never.

The battle had thoroughly depleted her magic. She wondered if she could get to the amulet. She reached out with a tiny thread of power and felt for the amulet's chain in the pocket of the soldier still digging through the saddlebags. Nothing responded. Not a hint or a tug. They had charmed the amulet against such things. It would have been far too easy to reach it if a red witch could have simply floated the necklace across that poison lake and into their possession. Remy chewed on her cheek. What was her plan? Should she try to grab Hale and drag his limp body on top of a horse, all the while fending off a dozen trained soldiers?

It would be easier if he were conscious. No. She needed her bow and arrows. She could pick them off from the safety of the trees, buy them some time until Hale regained consciousness.

She reached out her thread of power again. It took all her focus to loosen the leather cord around her bow without notice. Her magic held it in place like nothing had happened while she untied the quiver. She closed her eyes, holding the sensation of what she was trying to achieve in her mind. Toppling walls and trees seemed impressive, but making small, intricate movements was much more draining. The weapons hung in the air as if the cord still secured them.

Hale's head moved. He was starting to rouse. Now was the time.

Remy took a deep breath and summoned the last of her magic, making her weapons fly into her hand.

Soldiers shouted, whirling to her as she shouldered her quiver and nocked the first arrow. Her eyes narrowed as she braced her feet and shot straight into a soldier's eye. More shouting erupted as more soldiers spilled out through the woods. Remy did not stop. She shot three more soldiers in rapid succession.

Hale's eyes were fluttering open. She needed to buy them more time.

She grabbed another arrow from her quiver. A blinding pain shot through her forearm and she cried out. They had shot an arrow through her arm. The weapon had come from behind her. She whipped her head around just in time to see another arrow flying toward her. She dropped to the ground, avoiding it.

The archer stood several paces back. Beside him was that blue witch whispering to the archer, whispering what Remy was about to do.

Remy crawled through the underbrush. She crouched, ready to run, when another arrow pierced her thigh. She screeched, trying and failing to run, flopping across the ground like a fish out of water.

Move, move, she urged her body as six fae soldiers ran toward her. She heard another arrow whoosh through the air, and she dropped flat to the ground. She looked up just in time to see a fist swooping toward her face.

CHAPTER TWENTY-SIX

R emy opened her eyes. The pounding in her head was
unbearable. Her mouth and throat felt like sandpaper. She
tasted the metallic tang of blood. She tenderly touched her
eye, now swollen shut. Her left arm throbbed at the slightest movement of her fingers. The wounds where the arrows had struck were
clotted and scabbing. How long had she been out to have healed this
much?

When had that happened? She felt as though she had been
punched many more times than she could remember.

She looked around the darkened room of gray, damp stone. It was
a dungeon. A stench fouler than that of the Rotted Peak assaulted her
nostrils. It smelled of urine, feces, and decaying flesh. Remy retched,
but there was nothing to come up. How long had she been out?

Her thirst tempted her to stick her tongue out and catch the drips
falling along the mossy stones in the corner.

Manacles hung from the far wall, but Remy remained unshackled
in the small cell. Muck covered the dirty stone floor in bat droppings
and pieces of chicken bone . . . Gods, she hoped it was only chicken
bone.

Remy's cloak was missing, stripped off her along with her boots and dagger. She still wore her blood-stained tunic and trousers, though filth soiled them.

Patting her hip, she felt that hidden pocket sewn into her tunic. Tracing the small lump of her totem bag, she still felt the *Shil-de* ring's power vibrating out from beneath her palm.

Remy thought for a moment of putting it on her finger. It would protect her from any death that loomed imminent if she remained in this cell, but . . . what about Hale?

She wanted to save that talisman for him or Ruadora. There were people she loved who needed protecting. It was still a possibility she could find them. She would wait until she confirmed where they were . . . if they were alive.

She shook away that thought.

A gloomy corridor was beyond the wrought iron door, one flickering torch mounted to the wall.

Remy peered into the darkness but could see no one beyond it. She wanted to call out, to hear if Hale was nearby, but she thought twice about calling attention to herself. She knew from her heightened sense of smell and how far she could see down the darkened hall that she was still in her fae form. Did they know who she was? And Hale? Had they captured him for helping her?

She reached out with her senses, searching for him. She smelled his scent, but she realized it was coming from her. His heady aroma still clung to her from their impassioned lovemaking. Gods, she needed to find him.

Reaching out with her witch magic, she focused on turning the lock on the dungeon door.

Nothing.

It didn't even budge. Remy looked closer at the iron bars etched in Mhenbic symbols. They had warded the dungeon against magic. It should not have surprised Remy. The Northern Court had been capturing and torturing witches for thirteen years—they must have learned how to contain them.

Remy's witch magic would give her no advantage . . . but Remy had pretended to be a human woman for most of her life. She had other skills than just her magic and knew there must be another way out of this cell. She could pick the lock.

She looked to the discarded bones on the floor. Grabbing the thickest one, she swallowed the bile rising in her throat.

The courtesans who worked the taverns had taught her more than how to put on makeup. They had Remy picking locks for them at eight years old. She only prayed the chicken bone wouldn't snap as she inserted it into the lock. She jiggled it. Not needing to press her ear to the door the way she had in her witch form, in her fae form she could hear from where she crouched. She twisted the bone a little more.

Listening, listening. There.

She turned the bone with just enough force, producing a loud click as the door unlocked.

Remy paused, waiting to see if anyone responded to the sound. After a minute, she was certain no one was coming.

She opened the door with deliberate slowness, but even still the rusty iron screeched. She paused, listening again. No sounds of footsteps down the hall. She opened the door enough to squeeze through. Closing it behind her, she reached through the bars to grab the chicken bone out of the lock.

She would need the bone to unlock the next door.

She crept down the hallway. Cell after cell lined the wall to her left. She paused at each one. Many were empty, but a few . . . a few had occupants. Some she was sure were dead. Others were so broken they didn't even look up as she passed. Who were they? What had happened to them?

Remy thought to the Temple of Yexshire. Had they found the red witches? Were they still safe in the woods beyond the temple? Where was Ruadora? She had been so close to wrapping her arms around her sister, only to be ripped away again.

As Remy walked past another corpse, a burning anger coursed through her veins. This is what the Northern King did. He destroyed lives. Seeing the abandoned city of Yexshire, the burned-down castle, and now the dark belly of the dungeon, Remy was more determined than ever to slice her dagger across the King's throat. He would pay for what he did to her family.

Remy neared the end of the hallway and the last cell before the giant wooden door. Even above the overwhelming foul stenches, she smelled that summer ocean scent again. Hale, her Fated, was in the cell beyond.

Remy had to choke down her gasp as she looked into the cell. Hale sat there, stripped down to nothing but his trousers. Purple bruises mottled his chest, but it was his face . . . His face was so swollen she could barely make out the location of his eyes. Lip split open, one of his slender fae ears torn and bleeding down his neck. What had they done to him?

She wasn't sure if he scented her or if he felt the sorrow and furious rage burning off of her skin at the sight of him. If she had resolved to kill the King before, the sight of her beaten Fated was his death sentence.

"Remy," Hale whispered. His voice was scratchy and raw.

Remy lifted the chicken bone clenched in her hands. She jiggled it in the lock.

"Remy, what are you doing?" Hale's voice slurred as he spoke. She wondered if he had a concussion. "You need to run, Remy. Now. Before someone comes."

"I told you," Remy said, wiggling the bone some more. "I'm not leaving you behind."

Pain filled his voice. "Remy."

The lock shuddered and gave a little, and she wrenched the bone harder. It snapped beneath her fingers.

"No!" She cursed. She shoved the door, but it remained locked. She tried twisting the fragment, but the sharp splintered bone only sliced into her hand and clattered to the floor.

"Leave me, Remy," Hale pleaded.

"No," Remy snarled, forcing back her tears. "I only just found you. Do not ask me to leave you." She looked around his cell. There was nothing there she could try on the lock. "There's more bones back in my cell . . ."

She heard the stomping of feet to her right.

"Run, Remy," Hale hissed.

Remy turned to run just as the door to her right banged open.

Remy wasn't sure if she had blacked out or not; she was somewhere in between. One of the two burly guards had hit her with enough force to knock her to the ground. She wasn't sure if it was the past injuries or the lack of food, but her eyes went black. Ears still ringing, she heard the faint faraway echoes of Hale screaming her name.

She could not feel her limbs as they hauled her back to her cell. Her limp feet dragged across the floor.

When her body hurtled back into her cell, the putrid smell revived her a bit. Her vision came back, spotted with black patches. She was not sure if it was a blessing or a curse as she felt more in her body again.

Two guards stood in the cell between her and the open door. The Northern guards wore suits of armor, different from the ones she had grown up seeing in other fae courts. They wore much more metal and fewer leathers. Remy assessed her opponents. She could not let one of these towering monsters use their weight against her in a fight—with all that metal, they must weigh a ton.

They had flat-top helmets with a half faceguard shaped like the letter M, a thin shaft of metal protecting their noses. Metal spikes on their rounded shoulders curved towards their backs. The Northern crest was almost unrecognizable. Someone had etched it poorly into the metal of their breastplates. There were enough dents in their armor to let Remy know battle had tested them.

Remy was already eyeing the spaces left unprotected: cheeks, slivers of thighs and calves, and gaps in their armpits. It seemed they didn't wear thick leathers under the suits but a lighter fabric, so if Remy could find an opening she could slice a dagger into them.

It would be her first goal: find a weapon. The guard's swords were her full height. There would be no taking their own weapons to use against them. Still, she wondered if she lured them in close enough if she could stab a piece of chicken bone in one's eye. But then there would be another one coming at her.

No, that wouldn't be a good plan.

The guard who had knocked her to the ground grinned. The color of his icy blue eyes was barely visible under the shadows of his helmet. One eyebrow stung and her eye was already swelling shut again on her left side. When she blinked warm liquid out of her left eye, she knew her eyelid was bleeding.

Remy glared at the sentries, wondering why they stood in her cell and why the door was still open. Her answer came a moment later with the sound of footsteps on the stone.

Turning the corner, holding a plate of food, was Renwick.

He looked so out of place in the filth and gloom of the dungeon. Regal as ever, not a single speck dusting his clothing. He wore a burgundy jacket, the sleeves wide, reaching down well below his fingertips. The rectangular neckline revealed part of his refined bone-white shirt, tied at his throat in an intricate knot. He tied his long, ash-blond hair back with a matching burgundy cord.

He chucked the skin of water in his hand to Remy by way of greeting. She tried to catch it, but with a bruised arm and one swollen eye only beginning to open, she missed and it fell into her lap.

"Look at the state of you," he said. His features seemed even sharper in the flickering torchlight.

Remy sneered as she twisted the top off the waterskin. As she sniffed the water, Renwick laughed.

"You think I'd poison you now?" He chuckled, his cruel smile not meeting his eyes. Remy did not miss that he said now, implying that he may very well poison her later.

Deciding it was worth the risk, she took a long swig. Cool liquid soothed her scratchy throat. She swished more around her mouth before swallowing it, grateful to get the tang of blood out.

Renwick picked a small apple off the silver plate he held. He took a bite of it, proof he had not poisoned it either, before chucking it to Remy. She managed to catch it this time.

"What do you want from me?" Remy asked around a mouthful of apple.

"Forgive me—where are my manners?" Renwick smirked. He sketched an elegant, mocking bow. "Your Highness."

Remy straightened. How had he known?

As if reading the question on her face, Renwick answered, "You look much more beautiful in your fae form, Princess Remini, even in your current sorry state. Even in your witch form, though, you have quite a unique birthmark on your wrist."

He nodded to Remy's hand. She turned it over, looking at the inside of her wrist. A collection of five small freckles dotted the inside of her arm.

"It is nothing. I have freckles all over my body," Remy said.

"You said that to us when you were a child too." Renwick laughed.

Us—him and his father.

Remy remembered that encounter on the high road with the King of the Northern Court. He had brushed Remy's sleeve up when he talked to her and looked at her wrist. She had thought it was strange but didn't understand why.

"Gavialis Minor," Renwick said, snapping her from her spinning thoughts.

"What?"

"It is the name of a constellation. We can see it brightest in the far north. You may have noticed the constellation on the Northern crest?" Renwick said.

She hadn't.

She looked to the Northern crest etched into the guards' breastplates. The prominent part of the crest was a sword crossed with three arrows, a snake coiled around their intersection. She had never given much thought to the five stars scattered in the crest's background.

Remy looked at her wrist. Sure enough, there were two parallel freckles, then another below to the far left, and then the last two sat vertically together on the bottom right. It was the exact same order. How strange for the King to notice all those years ago and still remember such a little detail. That conversation had happened before, and she didn't remember it.

"My father considered taking you that day on the road, but he was more eager to see where you would go. Your actions after weren't particularly illuminating . . . though very entertaining," Renwick said, emerald eyes gleaming as his lips pulled up.

Remy's cheeks burned as she thought about that day on the road to Yexshire. Had there been spies in those woods?

"My father thought your markings were a sign you belonged in the North to the Northern Court," Renwick said. "He tried to arrange a marriage between the two of us because of those constellations alone. He believed it was a sign."

Remy scowled up at Renwick.

"I'd rather die than marry you," she snarled.

"That can be arranged." Renwick laughed, rubbing his finger around his temple. "Besides, the blue oracles had Seen you mated to the Bastard Prince of East . . . though that didn't seem to deter my father's efforts."

"Hale is not a part of this, Witchslayer," Remy hissed. "Release him at once."

"You're still blessed with the ability to make demands like a royal, I see." Renwick smiled. "Your mate," his voice dripped with disgust, "has been hiding you from us. He lied to the Northern King's face. That will not go unpunished. He may still have some information worth bleeding out of him too."

His face twisted into a cruel smile as Remy's eyes widened. He was going to torture information out of Hale.

"He knows nothing that you don't already know yourself," Remy insisted, pleading.

Renwick gave her an assessing look.

"Perhaps not," he said. "But you do, Remini. And keeping your Fated on hand might be the exact right motivation to keep you talking."

"What do you want to know?"

Renwick smiled, gliding over to her. He set the tray of food down beside her and she greedily shoved a whole bread roll into her mouth in one bite.

"Who knew the Dammacus children were so cunning?" Renwick sneered. "Since at least two of you escaped."

Remy looked at Renwick, eyes widening. He knew Rua was alive then? Had they captured her too? She said nothing for fear of giving it away.

"Now tell me, Remini, where is that brother of yours?"

Remy tried to hold in her sigh of relief.

"He's dead," she said. "I am the only one left."

"Now, we both know that's not true." Renwick grinned again. "A blue witch confirmed it for my father only days ago . . . there is more than one Dammacus child alive."

Shit.

Remy shook her head. So that's why they kept her alive. They wanted her to tell them where her brother was. They knew if they killed her, the Dammacus bloodline would still bind the Immortal Blade to the High Mountain Court.

She scowled. "I don't know what you're talking about."

"Are you sure about that?" Renwick asked. He eyed the empty plate of food. "Why don't I give you a few days in this place to think on it. If you'd like another meal, I will expect an answer from you."

"I don't have any answers!" Remy hated the pleading sound in her tone.

Renwick looked her up and down. "Perhaps not. But we will make sure word gets out that we are holding Princess Remini alive, and when Raffiel hears about it, he will come for you, I'm certain of it. And we will be waiting."

With that, Renwick turned and walked out the door. He threw her one last look over his shoulder.

"Try to stay alive down here, Princess," he said and then disappeared down the hallway, the guards locking her cell and following him.

~

The keening rumble of her stomach was her only companion. The darkened dungeon provided no indication of the time. How much time had passed? The cold seeped into her bones. Exhaustion weighed her heavy eyelids, but the silence from the other end of the hall was the worst of all her pain. She didn't know if Hale remained in his cell or if he was even still alive. Kneading her fist into her gnawing, hungry gut, she silently reprimanded herself. She couldn't think like that.

A far door creaked open. Heavy boots and the clanking of armor echoed down the hall. The two knights entered her cell, standing on either side of the open door. When Renwick entered, Remy had to wring her hands together to keep from lurching toward the plate of food in his hands. She did not care if it was poisoned—at least she would die with a full belly.

"You seem much more willing to talk, Princess," Renwick said, pursing his lips as he cocked his head at her.

She would not meet his gaze, her attention devoted wholly to the dish in his hands.

Renwick huffed. "You are worse than the palace dogs."

Armor rattled as the monstrous soldiers laughed. Renwick stepped with a sneer across the muck-covered stones. The dish didn't meet the floor before Remy snatched a chunk of stale bread. She chomped ravenously on the bread as she shoved a wedge of cheese into her mouth. Swallowing the half-chewed food, she shoveled the slices of chicken meat into her mouth, the greasy salt taste sending bolts of relief through her body.

Renwick stood over her, chuckling softly. He watched with his lip curled while she devoured the entire plate.

When she finished, he crouched, careful to not let his clothing touch the filthy floor. His emerald-green eyes bored into her. They seemed to glow in the shadowed light.

"Are you ready to answer my questions?" He narrowed his eyes at her as she licked the salt from her lips.

"I don't know anything about Raffiel," she breathed, wincing as a muscle cramped in her gut. She had eaten too quickly after too many days without food.

"That is not my question."

Remy's pulse hammered in her neck as she looked up to the sentries standing beside the open doorway. If she did not have any answers this time, how many more days could she go without food?

"Where is the *Shil-de* ring, Remini?" His voice was a rough whisper. "We found the amulet of Aelusien in your horses' saddlebag. Not a very clever hiding place for a priceless item, I must say."

"I don't have the ring, Witchslayer," Remy said. She held her chin higher, forcing herself to meet Renwick's violent gaze.

"We both know that's not true." He viciously grinned. "The ring I won in Ruttmore was a fake. You and that Bastard Prince left with the genuine ring. You will not tell me where it is?"

Remy clenched her jaw, staring at him.

"Fine," he said, reaching out and sliding his hand up the hem of her tunic.

Remy moved to pull away, but Renwick gripped her injured forearm. Biting back a cry, she spat in his face. Renwick gaped at her. He yanked his hand out of her tunic to backhand her across the face. Her face stung, the wound opening again from the blow.

"I guess I'll need to check more thoroughly," he snarled, pinning her against the wall with his forearm.

The leering guards at the door chuckled as Remy scrambled to push Renwick back off her. But despite his tall, elegant stature, the Northern Prince was surprisingly strong.

He dipped his free hand down the front of Remy's top, his hand brushing over her breast as she barked out a cry. And then that hand landed on her hip, on that lump in the fabric of the inner pocket.

They both stilled for a moment, Renwick's glowing eyes holding Remy's own as she felt something drop out of his large, belled sleeve. It landed on her belly, inside her tunic. She felt the cool metal against her skin. It was a dagger. Renwick held her eyes for one more fleeting moment and gave her a wink.

Her eyes widened, but she remained unmoving as the Northern Prince stood and straightened his jacket.

He had left a dagger in her clothing for her. Why?

Painting back on that face of disgust, Renwick spat at her feet.

"Stupid bitch," he said as the guards chuckled again. "We will find that ring one way or another, believe you me."

Remy watched, blinking at the incredible act. For a split-second Remy wondered if he did not know she had the ring. But he did. He had felt it there in her hidden totem bag and pretended to ignore it.

"Do you know what tomorrow is, Princess Remini?" Remy hated the sound of her name coming out of him. "It will be fourteen years since that night."

That night. Remy shuddered, the burnt-down ruins of the Castle of Yexshire flashing in her mind. Riv's broken glasses. She tapped her pockets. They must have fallen out during her capture.

"Why did he do it, your father?" Remy asked, drawing her knees up and cradling the hidden dagger against her cramping stomach. "Why did he hate my family so much?"

"The Dammacus King and Queen thought they were the rulers of this land—the favored children of Okrith with their red witch talismans and their fortress of mountain peaks," Renwick snarled. "But they learned." The sentries puffed their chests out as Renwick spoke, but Remy could hear the hollowness in his words. He had probably heard that line spoken most of his life judging by the dull, practiced way it rolled off his tongue. "We took your Immortal Blade, and we dispatched the red witches who could make you another."

Remy's chest seized, a lump hardening in her throat. "You did not *dispatch* them all, Witchslayer."

She clasped her hands together around her knees, fighting the urge to unsheathe the hidden dagger and ram the smug prince straight through. She eyed the looming knights. It would be her death sentence, but Gods would it feel good to twist her blade into the Witchslayer's chest.

His white teeth glinted in the dim light as if reading her train of thought. "The North has more wealth, more ancient talismans, and more powerful witches. If anyone should rule Okrith, it should be us."

"Your father would destroy the world just to claim he was King of the ruins," Remy murmured, watching those green eyes widen.

Renwick held her gaze one more moment, a silent acknowledgement, before turning to the open doorway.

"Where is Hale?" she called after him, causing Renwick to halt. "Is he all right?"

Renwick looked over his shoulder, his sharp features flickering in the torchlight. "The prince lives . . . for now."

Tears sprang to Remy's eyes as she let out a jagged sigh. He was still alive.

The guard grinned at her tear-stained face as he locked the door behind him, Renwick's footsteps already clicking down the hallway.

Remy waited until she could no longer hear their steps and then removed the dagger from her tunic. It was her dagger, the one gifted to her by Bri. As she unsheathed the blade, a small scrap of parchment fell out of the scabbard.

Remy's pulse pounded in her ears as she picked it up. A brief note was scrolled on it that brought more pinpricks to her eyes: *Wait until you have eyes on me to use this. Don't die.—B*

CHAPTER TWENTY-SEVEN

emy didn't realize how cold the dungeon was until they dragged her from the belly of the Northern Court castle. Another day had passed with only one meal and a couple skins of water. Her injuries were healing, but slower than the normal fae speed because of her exhaustion and lack of food. She couldn't seem to sleep enough to fully replenish her red magic either.

She expected sunlight, but darkness greeted her as the two guards dragged her into the throne room. Her dagger's sheath poked into her side as the two guards dropped her into the middle of a grand celebration. People gasped from all around her. The string band stopped their playing. Remy smelled the warm scents of a banquet table of food to her left and the strong aromas of honeyed mead and wine. They had dropped her in her filth into the middle of a party.

From her periphery, Remy saw a crowd gathered in their finery. They wore velvets and furs lined in satin, appropriate for the cold climate. When Remy had imagined the Northern Court, she had imagined it being cold and bleak, and it was . . . but the people. She had never pictured in her mind that there would be a court of people celebrating with a monster like the Northern King. She had never considered that others had supported him in his quest to destroy her family.

Scanning their faces, she could not find Bri. The warm celebrators stood in stark contrast to the fear twisting in her gut. Remy peeked to her side through a strand of greasy hair. White silver braziers sat at the bottoms of alabaster columns, lighting the throne hall in cool, pale streaks. The braziers' flames cast dancing shadows across the walls' banners. Between each banner sat a stone pillar, dripping with white candles.

Through her tousled, knotted hair, Remy saw Hennen Vostemur, the Northern King, lounging on his throne. It was striking silver, topped with an inlaid golden Northern crest, and rested on stubby legs made of pure white stone. Plush, cerulean velvet cushions kept his large body from feeling the icy sting of the metal. Three large wooden seats adjoined the throne. One must be for Renwick, Remy mused, but for the other two she could not think of who would sit on them.

A grand silver chandelier highlighted a long, thin table behind the throne upon which sat two golden crowns. Remy knew those crowns. They belonged to her parents. Beside them lay a blade, its ruby hilt gleaming in the light. The magic emanating from it was so powerful that it bent the surrounding air, like looking through a distorted windowpane.

The Immortal Blade.

It sat right there behind the Northern King. If only she could get to it.

The white marble tiles of the dais sparkled in the light. Something about it looked so familiar to Remy . . . she blanched when she realized it was because she had seen it before. They were the marble slabs stripped from her own court's throne room.

Remy glared at the King in the eyes as he smiled down at her, knowing full well her train of thoughts. Not only had he taken the High Mountain crowns, he also was heartless enough to recreate the dais where he now sat.

Vostemur held a goblet of wine, his cheeks rosy, as he sat casually presiding over his party. He toyed with the pendant of his necklace: a red stone. It was the amulet of Aelusien.

"Welcome to the Northern Court," he grinned, "Princess Remini."

The crowd gasped in unison. Their faces lit with astonished delight. Remy scowled at them.

Where was Hale? She hadn't seen him as she left the dungeons. She couldn't see him in the crowd. Panic gripped her. She prayed he had escaped already. She couldn't see Bri either.

"Do you know what today is, Remini?" King Vostemur glared down at her, mirroring the snake on his crest above him.

"Fourteen years since you slaughtered my family and our whole city." Remy spat at him. The crowd gasped in excitement, like she was the evening's entertainment.

The King laughed in a gratingly unpleasant way, as though they were talking about the spring weather and not a massacre.

"It has been fourteen years this night since I became the most powerful ruler in all of Okrith." He barely got his words out before his court erupted into cheers.

They were *cheering*. The wretched sheep were cheering for a deranged monster and for his desecration of an entire court. Remy lifted her eyes to them, trying to stare each one of them down. Their laughter cooled from the look in her eyes, as if her look alone could curse them. Thinking to how Hale said her mother could command a room with one look, Remy painted her face in a smirk. She would not let them forget who she was.

Remy put one hand in her pocket as she sat back on her heels. Her fingers brushed over the ring. Poised to slip her finger through the ring, she watched to see if the guards standing on either side of her unsheathed their swords.

Even in her grimy state, barefoot on the floor, she tried to hold a regal pose. She sat with a casualness that matched the King's own. She knew it would infuriate him.

"You don't know how to use that necklace, do you?" Remy nodded to the amulet of Aelusien around the King's neck. If he could use it, he would have shown off, but the fact no red power emanated from him told her he had not learned how to summon the magic.

Vostemur's eyes sharpened on her. He was not used to having someone speak down to him.

"I think my guests might be able to help with that." His face twisted into a sadistic grin as he nodded to someone at the great wood doors behind Remy. "Let's bring them in, shall we?"

Remy heard the doors opening, and five guards herded in five hooded red figures. She couldn't contain her gasp.

They had captured five red witches and were parading them through the throne room. They marched across the floor, forced to stand between Remy and the King. The guards turned them to face Remy and, one by one, kicked them into a kneeling position. She heard the soft cry as one hostage's knees crashed into the floor.

The tall, helmeted guards partially obscured the King, only visible from the shoulders up, wearing a violent grin.

King Vostemur looked off to the right of his dais, where heavy blue curtains covered large archways on either side of the throne. Five more soldiers wearing full armor stood in front of each curtain. Remy looked to the back of the great hall. Another ten guards lined the rear of the throne room. They peppered even more around the periphery of the elegant fae crowd.

There was an army in here. Remy's stomach tightened. The dagger at her hip would not be enough to save her.

From behind the thick blue curtain where the King looked, a hooded figure appeared wearing indigo robes. Her hands glowed a faint blue.

The blue witch came to stand at the King's side.

"Now, Princess," the King said, cocking his head to look at Remy. "Tell me where your brother Raffiel is."

"Raffiel is dead." Remy tried to keep the shake out of her voice.

"I was not a child on that night fourteen years ago, girl." Vostemur sneered. "I remember clearly what happened. Your coward elder brother fought his way to a window and jumped out of it."

Coward. Remy shook with rage.

"Then he was cut down by your guards waiting outside," she snarled.

"He was not." The king took another long sip of his wine. "The only members of the Dammacus family I saw die were your parents and that weakling of a son."

Riv. Remy pushed down hard on the lump that was hardening in her throat.

"Just because you did not see his body in the wreckage does not mean he lives," Remy hissed.

The King looked to the hooded figure beside him.

"Tell her," he ordered.

The blue witch raised her glowing blue hands to her hood and pulled it back to reveal her face. Remy contained a shriek at the sight of the witch. She had heard stories of the way the Northern King had tortured the blue witches, but this . . . Burn marks covered her entire head, her skin stretched or loose in an odd patchwork that indicated it was not just one accident that caused the scars, but many over several years. She had no hair or eyebrows, and her eyes were closed. Remy looked closer in horror. They had sewn her eyes shut.

Remy's nostrils flared, and she stifled a gag. The woman's mutilation didn't elicit a single gasp or groan from the crowd. Their silence was a confirmation they had seen these tortured blue witches many times before.

When the witch spoke, her tight leather collar bobbed with her voice.

"I have Seen a vision last night," she said from thin blue lips, "Princess Remini and her elder brother, Prince Raffiel, grown up and standing in this very hall."

Gasps erupted from the crowd behind Remy.

"That is ridiculous." Remy rolled her eyes. "I don't think you can trust the visions of someone you have *tortured*."

"Everything she says comes to pass," Vostemur said, holding his goblet out to be refilled by a scurrying servant. "Unless the Fates are course corrected, that is. Killing you will be part of it . . . but first you will tell me where your brother is."

"Why would I tell you anything if you are going to kill me, anyway?" Remy spat.

"I'm glad you asked." Vostmur's sinister laugh hit her like another blow to the head. "Because if you don't, Remini, I will kill the rest of your witches."

He nodded to the guards standing behind the kneeling red witches, and in unison the guards ripped back their hoods. Two men and three women. Remy's eyes snagged on the last one: Baba Morganna. The old priestess held Remy's eyes with a half-smile on her face, as though she were trying to comfort Remy. Baba Morganna had pulled Remy from death that day below the Rotted Peak, and yet here they were only a few days later facing death once more.

"This is all of them?" Remy worried her lip.

"We found thirty of these witches behind that old Yexshiri temple." Vostemur smiled. "I figured not all thirty were needed to get my message across."

There had been thirty of them, and he had only spared five. Remy scanned the lineup once more and found her mother's golden brown eyes flecked with green staring back at her. The young woman kneeling directly across from her, third in the line, was her sister, Ruadora.

Remy didn't let her face crack as she stared at her little sister, but from the look in Rua's eyes, she knew. Her sister recognized her. Rua had their mother's eyes but their father's warm brown hair, unlike Remy's black. She was a perfect mixture of their two parents. She looked so much like Riv, whereas Raffiel and Remy had both looked like their mother.

Rua was in her human form. No pointed ears or sharp fae features. Remy ached to see what her sister looked like beneath her glamour. She wanted to rush forward and grab her into a hug so desperately her arms shook with restraint. But if she acknowledged Rua in any way, it would put her sister at the end of the King's blade.

With no warning or provocation, the first guard, standing behind the red witch man, unsheathed his sword. In one sudden swoop, he cleaved the man's head from his body. The severed head flew into the crowd.

Screams erupted from the hall. The crowd shrieked in a mixture of delight and horror. Rua flinched and screamed as blood splattered her face.

"Silence!" King Vostemur shouted, and the crowd obeyed. Remy shuddered under his violently excited glare. "Now, Remini, would you like to tell me where your brother is, or shall we continue?"

Remy's eyes widened in horror, her mouth gaping at him.

"Continue, then?" the King said.

Before Remy could scream, the next guard in the line had unsheathed his sword and swung his blade.

The guard yanked on his sword, stuck halfway through the second witch's neck. He failed to sever her head, a horrifying outcome to a poorly swung sword. The guard put his boot to the witch's back, kicking her forward and yanking his bloody sword free. The red witch died, her mouth opening and closing like a caught fish. Remy knew she would never be able to get that image out of her mind. If she lived, she would never be able to scrub away the memory of that witch's body.

Blood dotted Remy's face and body. She tasted the red witch's blood on her lips. Another scream rang out through the devastating silence.

She spotted Rua. Her sister trembled so badly her entire body shook. Tears stained her blood-splattered cheeks. She was next in line, flinching and sobbing in turns, waiting for a sword to strike her.

Remy clenched her fist around the ring in her pocket. She would rush to Rua and slip it on her. She could do that, at least. Remy was about to move when the blue curtain opened once more, and Renwick walked in.

He had that same cold, bored air about him as he sat in the ornate chair at his father's right-hand side.

"The visitors have just arrived, Your Majesty," he said.

Remy frowned at the way he called his father *Your Majesty.*

"Excellent," Vostemur said. He fiddled with the amulet as he spoke. "Bring in the prisoner!" he called across the hall.

The doors creaked open again, and there was Hale, being dragged limply across the floor. His head hung as though he had given up fighting when dumped beside Remy. Two guards loomed on either side of him, waiting for further instructions.

They had given Hale back his dirty tunic, but he was still barefoot. Remy wondered if they gave him his tunic to hide the bruises that had marred his chest.

Hale lifted his head and shook his wavy, brown hair out of his eyes. His face was still purpled with bruises, but he looked mostly recovered, thanks to his fae healing.

"You okay?" he whispered to Remy.

She nodded, choking back tears. She didn't know why that question broke her so much. He was half dead, and he still worried for her. She was not okay, but she wanted to be for him.

"The Bastard Prince." King Vostemur sneered. "Consorting with the enemy."

"Release me at once," Hale demanded, straightening himself so he looked regal even on his knees.

"Or what?" King Vostemur laughed, inciting the crowd to laugh along with him.

"Or you will feel the wrath of the East." Hale's eyes darkened as he glared at the King.

"I see, well . . . I don't think so." King Vostemur smiled so broadly his eyes closed to slits.

"My father will not let this go unpunished," Hale said, his words a biting threat.

King Vostemur's eyes lit up at Hale, white teeth gleaming through a twisted smile.

"Let's ask him then, shall we?" Vostemur said, nodding to the blue curtain to his left.

Hale went still as Gedwin Norwood, King of the Eastern Court, strode out from the far corridor. Prince Belenus walked with him, the spitting image of the Eastern King from the snub nose to the pitch black eyes.

Belenus smirked, looking down his pig nose at the prisoners and sitting beside his father. He was still a complete spoiled brat.

The Eastern King peered at them, unsmiling, from under bushy gray eyebrows. He wore a dark metal crown, the Eastern crest carved into its front peak.

Remy looked to Hale. Horror froze her Fated, paralyzed with an expression of terrible pain. The two beheaded bodies still leaked blood onto the stone floor, though they had stopped moving. It felt terrifyingly strange to carry on with the bodies lying there. Rua kept trembling, waiting for the moment the guard behind her might strike.

"What have you done?" Remy shouted at the Eastern King. She would speak for Hale. "You would sacrifice the life of your son—"

"He is not my son." King Norwood sneered, his lip curling in disgust. Murmured whispers broke out in the crowd.

"How can you even say that?" Remy's fingers twitched to grab her dagger. Where in the Gods' names was Bri?

"Because it is the truth, and it is time he knew it." King Norwood had a thick, syrupy voice. He cleared his throat every few words. He pointed his gnarled finger at Hale. "I did not sire that male. I caught his mother in an affair with another. She was a commoner, and I had been willing to make her a queen, the ungrateful whore."

Hale shook out of his stupor enough to gnash his teeth.

"Why claim me at all?" he said.

"You know why. It's because of her." King Norwood's black eyes darted to Remy. "The oracle proclaimed you were her Fated. You were to be shipped off to the High Mountain Court when she came of age and I would be rid of you, gaining a powerful alliance through the union. So I claimed you," King Norwood darted a look to the half-drunk King Vostemur. "It seemed a wise decision at the time."

"Ha! I am sorry I ruined those calculated plans, Gedwin." The Northern King laughed, lounging back on his arm. "You tried valiantly to rid yourself of the boy, but even the Rotted Peak could not kill him. I am glad you trusted in me, friend, to finish the job."

"You ally with him just to kill me?" Hale balked. "You are a fool."

"My motivations are none of your concern," King Norwood said. "But any *fool* would know that an alliance with the North means security for the future of our court. You think I didn't know when I saw her? She is the spitting image of Rellia Dammacus, raised from the dead! You think I couldn't see it in your eyes, too, that you found your Fated? A mate that would make my King very happy to be in possession of."

Hale gaped as Norwood said *my King*. So the Eastern King bowed to the North then, so as not to get swept into the storm he was brewing.

King Vostemur smiled through wine-stained teeth. His attention darted to the bodies on the floor and back to Remy.

"I will ask you this one last time, Remini. If you do not answer me, I will make you watch as we kill your mate before turning the blade on you. Let Raffiel come to find you in pieces."

"No!" Remy screamed and dove for Hale.

He reached out, grabbing her, crushing her against him in the tightest embrace as he whispered, "I love you."

She only had a second in his arms before they ripped away again from her, but it was all she needed. Hale watched her, wide-eyed for what she had done as a guard dragged her away.

Remy struggled under his grip.

"Stop," the guard whispered.

Remy turned to face him then. She only saw a flash of light blue eyes before he pushed her to the ground. Remy knew those eyes. She had seen them once before across a card table in Ruttmore.

Bern.

The same fae male who warned Remy and Hale that Abalina was after them. What was he doing here?

"How romantic." King Vostemur's voice was lethal and sharp. The Eastern King and Prince watched like birds of prey from their chairs. "Now tell me where your brother is."

Remy shook her head. Unwelcome tears began to stream down her cheeks.

"I don't know," she whispered.

King Vostemur shrugged. *Shrugged*, as if her answer were no great hardship, and nodded to the other guard beside Remy.

Remy screamed as the guard unsheathed his blade. She choked on a sob as Hale looked at her one more time with a grim smile. This may be the end for them.

The guard lifted his sword high in the air as excited "oohs" rang out in the crowd. Everything in Remy clenched, bracing for that sword to swing. But the guard lowered his sword and with his free hand he reached for his helmet, removing it and baring his person to the room.

"If you wanted to talk to me so badly, Hennen, you should have just asked."

Raffiel Dammacus, Crown Prince to the High Mountain Court, stood before the Northern King.

CHAPTER TWENTY-EIGHT

The world halted when Remy saw his face. He looked so much like she remembered him, but he was a man now, growing taller than either of their parents. Raffiel and Remy both looked so much like their mother, warm brown skin and black loose curls. Raffiel used to favor wearing it long when he was twelve, but now he cut it short. His dark hair looked freshly shorn and blended into his short beard. Remy couldn't believe he was capable of growing a beard.

He looked like a king.

In one blink Remy stared at her brother, cherishing the sight of him, and in the next all hell broke loose.

Bern pulled out his sword and took the short blade on his other hip, chucking it to Hale.

"Now!" She heard a barking shout and turned to find Bri, dressed in servant's garb, her golden eyes staring into Remy's. Talhan moved to her side, giving Remy a quick wink even amongst the mayhem before diving back into the throes of battle.

They had come for them.

Remy remembered the dagger hidden in her tunic and grabbed it as guards rushed them from all sides.

The elegant Northern fae morphed into a screaming throng, rushing toward every exit to escape the melee. The room echoed with the thunderous clanging of swords. Commanding shouts came from every direction in Ific, Mhenbic, and Yexshiri.

The shrieking cries of wounded and dying fighters cut above the rest of the noise.

Baba Morganna threw out a flash of red light, and the three guards behind her crumpled. The three red witches ran onto the dais toward the blue curtain, only to be faced head on by five guards. The witches' hands glowed red, preparing to fight.

Remy's vision blurred, trying to take it all in. She saw the whip of blonde braid and knew Carys was there. But the huge guard rushing her was her first concern. Bern and Raffiel fought behind her, so she focused straight ahead. She could not see the guard's entire face, only the menace in his eyes as he advanced. She focused her magic on that heavy punishing sword, and it went clattering to the floor. The guard turned for his sword as Remy rushed in.

She slid on her knees across the blood-slicked floor and plunged her dagger into the back of the soldier's knee. She yanked it free and slashed at the other knee. Not fast enough. As he fell, he backhanded her with a punishing blow to her ear. The room went quiet except for the high-pitched ringing in her ears, but she didn't stop moving.

The guard toppled on his injured knees, dropping like a stone. His head now within reach, Remy moved without thought as she slid her dagger in between the man's helmet and shoulder plate. Remy knew she had struck true when she heard his gurgling grunt.

Remy would add that sound to the list of things she would never be able to scrub out of her mind.

She held tight to her blade and scanned the room to find Rua. Her sister was still on the dais, fighting off what seemed like a never-ending onslaught of guards. Renwick stood behind the throne, sword drawn against no enemy. The two Kings and young prince had moved to the other end of the raised platform, all holding their drawn swords. An impenetrable wall of guards surrounded them. They did not flee the carnage, so certain they would win.

But as Remy looked around, she was not so certain of their victory. She spotted many mini battles happening in every corner of the room, guard against guard, fae courtiers against servants . . . how many people had Raffiel and Bern brought with them?

Remy's eyes snagged on the scarred blue witch. She had not moved an inch since the fighting broke out. Chaos was erupting all around her, but she stood unmoving, waiting for the pandemonium to end, with the faintest smile on her face. It was a horrifying sight.

Rua stood far behind the blue witch, taking on a guard with her witch magic. Still in her witch form, her red hands sputtered with effort, her magic nearly spent. A guard rushed her, slamming her with the blunt end of his sword. Rua cried out, staggering into Renwick.

Remy watched wide-eyed, trapped by the fighting all around her, as Renwick grabbed Rua and moved her behind him, pinning her to the table of antiquities, as he turned his sword on the guard.

His own guard.

Remy only had a chance to blink at them before the bodies of two guards who rushed Rua went flying across the hall.

Baba Morganna's power was burning so brightly it was blinding. Let them never forget she was the witch who moved mountains.

The heavy blue curtain fell, trapping the rushing guards under it, exposing the hallway of more guards, now blocked from running their way. Baba Morgana kept lifting guards with her magic and tossing them to the floor, crushing them in their armor. The remaining guards deserted.

Other guards fled Morganna now as she stacked the crushed bodies in front of all exits. She was blocking them *in*: no more reinforcements would come. This was a fight to the end. Death was in her eyes, promising vengeance for every single fallen witch.

A bellowing scream pierced the air.

Remy whirled to the source of that scream. It was Bern, collapsed on his knees, and in his arms—Raffiel's drooping body. One of Raffiel's eyes was missing, gushing blood where a knife had pierced his skull. Time seemed to freeze, every weapon pausing in mid-air to watch the fallen prince. He was not just one more dead body—he had been the Crown Prince of the High Mountain Court . . . and she didn't see him fall.

Remy's mind shattered into a million pieces. She never got to know him. The glimmer of hope that they would have a happy ending torn cruelly away before it ever began. An hour ago she had not known he was alive, and there he lay, dead once more.

Heart exploding, Remy searched frantically for someone to save him, but every potential ally was far away and outnumbered. Even Bern was forced to drop Raffiel's body and grab his sword again, lest he be cut down too.

Remy stole one more glance at her fallen brother, then returned to the fray.

The guards still gravely outnumbered them. Remy scanned the hall, searching for Hale. There was Hale, fighting his way to the dais. Even as Hale cut down another guard, he fixed his eyes on the man he had once known as his father.

Remy rushed for him, pushing past servants running to cower behind overturned tables and fae courtiers screaming and holding each other. The general din was much quieter now. So many bodies lay strewn across the floors. The room reeked of blood and bile.

Remy reached Hale's side. She jumped straight into his war dance, moving blades and fists. They reached the steps to the dais together. The crush of guards around the royals was too tight for the guards to use their long swords.

Remy ran onto the marble steps. From this angle, she was level with the guards' knees. She sliced through tendons, the guards too distracted by Baba Morganna's magic to notice her until her blade was piercing their skin. She dodged them as they fell, one after the other, down the dais stairs.

Hale reached the top step, slaying the last standing guard between him and his father. Remy stood breathless behind Hale, watching as Belenus stepped in front of his father.

Belenus's sword shook as he pointed it to Hale, but hate filled his eyes.

"You destroy everything you touch, Hale," Belenus snarled, his sour frown deepening. "You were never a part of this family, yet you've always been destroying it."

"Step aside, Bel." Hale heaved a breath, shaking his head. "I don't want to hurt you."

Remy's eyes stung. Despite everything, he still viewed the male before him as his little brother.

In a blur of movement, Belenus swept his sword, knocking Hale's sword wide as he stepped into his brother's body. In the same second, Belenus pulled out a hidden dagger and drove it into Hale's heart.

Remy screamed.

"Bel." Hale sucked in a drag of air.

Anger, horror, despair all seemed to flash across Belenus's face. Remy rushed to Hale, but her Fated stayed standing. Remy couldn't breathe. Her pounding heart deafened all other sounds as she clung to Hale.

But Hale lifted his head.

He pulled the dagger out of his chest and threw it down the steps behind him. Lifting his right hand, he examined the *Shil-de* ring on his ring finger.

"It can't be," Belenus whispered in horror, retreating a step.

"I'm sorry, brother." Hale's voice thickened. Before Belenus could lift his sword in his stupor, Hale swung his blade, slicing open his brother's neck.

Blood poured down Belenus's fine clothes as he choked, grasping for his throat with wide, unseeing eyes.

Hale loosed a heavy sob as he watched Belenus collapse.

"No!" roared the Eastern King. The shock on his face, now, watching gouts of blood pump out of his son's neck, was the first glimmer of emotion on his face since he arrived.

King Norwood bellowed, blind with rage as he charged Hale.

Remy moved to back up Hale when a whipping wind sounded in her fae ears. She had just enough time to duck before a shining thin sword swung over her. She looked to her left and into the watery green eyes of King Vostemur.

"Well, Remini." He smiled, still cold and calm even amongst the bloodshed. "I guess I will have to kill you myself."

Swords clanged as Hale and King Norwood dueled behind her. She adjusted her grip on her dagger, and King Vostemur huffed a laugh.

"Soon it will be Queen Remini, Vostemur," she promised. She knew it the moment she saw Raffiel fall. Her entire life had led her to this point. She could not hide away any longer from who she was. "I will take back everything you have stolen from my family. But you won't live long enough to see it."

Vostemur wiped a spot of blood off his hand, otherwise remaining pristine, unmarred by the bloodbath swirling around him.

"You are going to cut me down with that puny dagger, Princess?" He laughed. "I've been slicing this sword through people since before you were even born."

King Vostemur swung his sword in feigned swipes meant to push Remy backward. She darted out of reach, circling him, but every time she charged, his sword was right there again. For a portly, half-drunk, old man he was damn quick with his weapon.

She ducked under his blade, rushing in once more. This time she made contact, cutting across his leg. It was not a killing blow but would slow him down. The Northern King howled as he kicked her again with his other leg.

Remy rolled backward into a crouch. She held those monstrous green eyes as she stood. She let him see every promise of death in them. As she lifted her hand, her dagger flew from her grip, knocked away by a guard who had sneaked up behind her.

Remy spun—another guard was running up the stairs at her.

Shit.

King Vostemur lifted his sword again, and Remy ducked in toward his body, grasping at the amulet around his neck. Her fingers grazed the red stone, causing it to flare red. Remy was thrown to the side, but it was enough. The amulet of Aelusien gave her a sudden strobe of power, and she threw it out at the three guards at her back, sending them flying across the room.

Vostemur's eyes widened, seeing how readily she absorbed the amulet's power. He hastily grabbed its gold chain and tucked the powerful stone into his jacket. If she wanted a boost of power again, she would have to kill him for it.

Remy dodged as Vostemur attacked again. She searched wildly around her. She needed a weapon.

Hale and King Norwood were still battling behind King Vostemur, and the Eastern King had Hale pinned against the wall. Norwood knew what he was doing. He sneered, knowing the *Shil-de* ring protected Hale. But he could keep him from getting to Remy in time to save her.

Remy scanned the room, searching for aid. She couldn't find any. The witches were still raining hellfire on the remaining guards while Bern, the Eagles, and Carys battled the remaining guards and courtiers through the gory terrain of dead bodies.

Another four guards charged up the stairs to aid their King. Remy dropped toward her dagger, but a guard kicked it out of her reach. Three swords pointed at her from every angle.

The guard to her right gasped, blood spurting from his neck. A loud clanging sounded, and the guard fell face-first to the ground. Behind him stood a servant wielding a dented silver tray and clutching a bloody carving knife. No, not a servant.

Fenrin.

Fenrin stood there in Northern servant garb, panting.

Her relief was short lived as searing-hot pain slashed across her arm. King Vostemur had sliced open her bicep, and Remy spun to face him.

"Goodbye, Princess." He smiled and raised his sword.

Suddenly, Vostemur grunted as the air punched out of him. His eyes went impossibly wide, bulging from his skull. His jacket began flowing with blood, though no wound was visible. Sword clattering to the ground, he looked over Remy's shoulder.

"Impossible." His voice was barely audible over the gurgling of blood from his mouth.

Remy turned, and her heart seized.

Ruadora, Princess of the High Mountain Court, held the Immortal Blade.

An ethereal white glow emanated from the sword, shrouding her little sister. Her hair blew behind her in an invisible wind, her eyes blazing. She smiled, possessed by the power of the Immortal Blade. Rua twisted the glowing sword. The Northern King cried out in agony as he fell to his knees.

"This is for my people and for my family." Her voice like a wildcat, she arced the glowing blade through the air.

King Vostemur cried out, but nothing stopped the landing blow. His severed head volleyed into the shrieking crowd. Remy watched in awe as none other than her little sister finally slew their family's sworn enemy.

The fight was over, or so she thought—a fatal error she realized as she turned her back on the remaining guard. Fenrin screamed her name.

So strange to hear his screams, so many screams of her name coming from every direction.

Why?

The room had slowed, her vision blurred, her ears echoing with muffled sounds like she was under water. She felt warm liquid dripping down her stomach and the legs of her trousers. She looked down and saw it: the tip of a long sword protruded out her middle.

Someone pulled the sword free, and the world sped up again as Remy collapsed to the white marble floor. How fitting to die on the same tiles as the rest of her family.

One by one the screams ended around her, Rua cutting down every remaining guard in easy swoops, the blade never needing to touch its victims.

And then Hale's face appeared over her.

Hale's eyes shone from his blood-speckled face. Blood soaked his hands. *Her* blood, she realized. Remy couldn't feel her legs anymore, only sensing the sticky warmth of her blood pooling beneath her.

Hale's brows twisted and furrowed in pain. The gray of his eyes was almost invisible through his tears. She had died in his arms once before, but this—this was different. He was her Fated now. He was her soul living outside her body. They were so intertwined she knew that even in death she would live on through him.

The agonizing, stabbing pain was all that kept her conscious. The shock had worn off. The brutal acceptance that this was a mortal wound hit her.

Remy's head felt light: everything around her seemed to spin, Hale's tear-stained face blurred, and nausea crept up slowly. She knew the Twin Eagles stood over her, too, and she ached with regret that she couldn't say goodbye.

Why had she thought she could overthrow the Northern King?

Remy's body demanded she rest. Her eyes fluttered closed, only to widen again at the rolling waves of stabbing pain through her chest. She fell into numbness only for the searing pain to mercilessly revive her again and again

Remy whimpered, and Hale's face crumpled. It would not be Remy who had to scrub away all the images of horror from this day. It would be Hale. She knew he would never forget this moment or her dying face.

She reached up a bloody hand and placed it on his cheek. The tremors of her arm barely held it steady.

Remy wanted to tell him she knew this was it. She wanted him to comfort her and tell her it wasn't true. She wanted to beg to be saved and cry that she wasn't ready to die and that there was so much of their life to live together.

But she didn't.

As the tears fell from her eyes into her hair, all she said was, "I love you."

Hale sobbed as he bent to her and placed a tear-covered kiss on her lips. Remy tasted the salt of his tears. When Hale pulled back, the corner of his mouth was bloody. He didn't wipe the blood away.

Remy coughed up more blood. The end was near, then. Remy closed her eyes and relaxed her muscles. She tried to take a deep breath and then another, but every breath was a stabbing pain.

She couldn't breathe.

Her chest felt so heavy as she panted. Then everything went numb. She couldn't feel any more pain or panic to catch a breath, and it was a sweet relief. Soon everything would be over, and she would rest forever.

"Remy." The word was a trembling whisper, but it was not from Hale.

Remy opened her eyes to see Heather hovering over her. Heather wore servants' garb like Fenrin. Tear tracks stained her cheeks, but she smiled down at Remy. And Remy, despite everything, smiled back at her.

To see her mother one last time. Because that's what she was and always had been, her mother. It did not matter if they shared the same blood. They were family.

Then Remy spotted a dagger clenched in Heather's hand, and she knew what was about to happen.

Remy shook her head as more tears fell, mouthing the word "No" though no sound came out of her bloodied mouth.

Heather nodded with a calm, loving smile. This was the last time they'd see each other, sure enough, but it would not be Remy leaving this world.

"I loved you from the moment I first saw you, my Remy," Heather said. So many tears poured down her cheeks as she smiled at her daughter. "I meant it when I said I would give my life for yours."

Remy scrambled to speak, but Heather placed a steadying hand on her shoulder.

"Help lead this world into a better future, Remy. Be brave and kind and strong and clever, as you've always been." Heather's lips quirked up. "Be all the things I tried to teach you to be, but most of all, my Remy, be loved."

With that, she looked up. And with a chant of *"Midon Brik Dzaraas,"* she plunged the dagger into her heart. Remy couldn't move, couldn't scream. Her body and mind numbed as she faded away.

CHAPTER TWENTY-NINE

Beams of sunlight warmed Remy's skin as she opened her eyes. She lay in an enormous bed, a thick azure duvet pulled up to her chest. She must have kicked off another fur blanket in her sleep.

A book thudded shut. Hale sat next to her, leaning against the upholstered velvet headboard.

He beamed at her, relief washing across his face. Remy snuggled further into her soft pillow. Her rumpled white nightdress had slipped off her shoulder in her sleep. Hale traced a finger over her bare shoulder and pulled the strap up.

"This must be the afterlife." She smiled.

"Why, because the bed is too comfortable or because your Fated is too good looking?" Hale grinned.

Remy placed a sleepy hand on his knee.

"My Fated," she whispered, smiling into her pillow.

Hale took her limp hand and kissed it, trailing languid kisses up her forearm.

He paused to say, "Make me a promise, mate."

Remy opened her eyes at that. Hale dropped her hand to cup her cheek instead.

"Promise me I will never have to watch you die again." He said it as if he meant it to be a joke, but there was too much pain in his voice to pull it off.

"You know I can't promise that." Remy stroked her hand down his forearm.

"Lie to me, then," he rasped.

Remy brushed a chestnut lock of his hair off his forehead. She loved this, that she could touch him freely, whenever she wanted, something she had long wished to do.

"I pray we go together, after a lifetime of happiness, in a big comfy bed such as this," she said, stroking her hand across the satin pillow.

"Let it be so," Hale prayed, swiping his thumb across her cheek.

Remy looked to the crackling fireplace, the floor adorned with ornate rugs, the heavy blue velvet curtains that matched the ones in . . . the Northern King's throne room.

"Where are we?" Remy asked, sitting upright.

Someone had left a glass of water on the bedside table. She drained it and then refilled it from the pitcher nearby.

"We have taken control of the Northern palace," Hale said, confirming Remy's fears.

"Is it safe to be staying here? I know the King might be dead, but his people will not so easily bow to the High Mountain Court and . . ."

As if on cue, a knock sounded at the door. Hale looked to Remy and waited for her response.

"Come in," she called.

Remy swept her tangled hair off her face and smoothed her crumpled nightdress. She pulled the fur blanket back over herself, covering her chest as she leaned on the headboard.

The door opened, and there was Bern, standing like a silver snow wolf, smiling through his icy blue eyes. He stood like a warrior, though dressed in his court finery, wearing a waistcoat the color of sea mist that matched his pale eyes.

He stood preternaturally still in the doorway. Remy smiled back, and his throat bobbed, the only sign that he was holding back his emotions.

"It is nice to see you alive." He squeezed out a raw laugh.

He walked to her bedside then. All this time, he had been working for her brother, she thought. It was Bern who tipped off Hale about the red witches and the talismans. Bern had been working for Raffiel.

Remy thought of her brother and of Bern's pained screams as he held Raffiel's body.

"I did not know he was alive," Remy said. Hale wrapped an arm around her shoulder as a sudden wave of grief flooded into her, warring with her disbelief. Raffiel was gone. Heather was gone. A white-hot poker stabbed at her chest. They were gone

"I did not know he lived either. Not for certain." Hale's eyes narrowed at Bern. Hale had been informed by the silver-haired fae about the red witches camping in the mountains, and about the location of the *Shil-de* ring now on his finger . . . but Hale was never told about Raffiel.

"I'm sorry I couldn't tell you everything, friend," Bern said to Hale. "I couldn't let the son of the Eastern King know of what we were up to, just in case." In case Gedwin Norwood was not a true ally to the High Mountain Court as he had shown himself to be.

Bern looked back to Remy. "You did not hear the rumors?"

He faked his usual slyness, but it rang more of sorrow. He had dark circles under his eyes. His face looked weathered, and his hair was disheveled.

"I trust you were the one spreading those rumors," Remy said, her eyes welling at the silver-haired courtier. "So Raffiel was the employer you were playing for at that card game in Ruttmore?"

"We have been gathering forces for some time in the mountains between Yexshire and the Western Court. Baba Morganna told us we'd find a red witch in Harbruck she called Little Sparrow." Bern furrowed his brow. "She did not say it was you. We knew Hale was looking for a red witch, so we tipped him off. But when I went to that card game and saw it was you . . . our plans changed."

Guilt racked her. Their plans changed for her, and now Raffiel was dead. Her capture had forced them to strike before they were ready. Her older brother came to her rescue only to be killed. Remy would never be ready to face that fact. She was responsible for her brother's death.

"You knew who I was as well?" Remy tried to hide her broken heart as she frowned at her wrist. "Was it these bloody freckles again?"

Bern cocked an eyebrow at her. "You mean, I shouldn't have been able to guess just by looking at you?" Bern raised his eyebrows at Remy. "Even in your witch form, the resemblance to your brother is uncanny. If only we had known you were alive, we would have come to find you sooner." His forced smile faded as he looked in her eyes, getting lost in them for a moment. When he spoke, it was a whisper. "You both have those Dammacus eyes . . . as does your sister."

"Rua," Remy breathed, remembering her sister wielding the Immortal Blade. "Is she all right?"

"She is fine," Bern said, albeit a little clipped. "We will send word to her that you are awake."

"Did you know she was alive?" Remy asked.

"Yes, for several years." Bern nodded. "A red witch hiding in the High Mountains told me Baba Morganna lived. She told me that Rua was with them, safe in the mountains across from us. We went to them as soon as we heard. We tried to visit the red witch camps as much as we could, but we had our hands full gathering the survivors of the High Mountain Court."

Remy's hands trembled, and Hale threaded his fingers through hers. Her sister grew up with the coven of their court, in the forests of their own homeland. On the other side of the mountains, Rua had lived this whole time.

"How many are left?" Remy asked.

"Four hundred or so," Bern answered. "The numbers are always changing. Many aren't originally Yexshiri but rather asylum seekers from other courts. We brought the strongest and best fighters with us when we came here."

Four hundred.

It was more than she had hoped to dream, and yet it was devastatingly low compared to the tens of thousands who had once called Yexshire home.

"And the red witches?" Remy asked, remembering all the ones the Northern King had killed before he brought the remaining five before his court.

"We don't know." Bern frowned to the floor. "Baba Morganna and the other red witch left straight after the battle to head back to Yexshire. She said a few dozen witches had fled into the woods when they were captured. More might come out of hiding, those who have scattered to every corner of the realm, now that it is safe to do so."

Remy swallowed. The numbers were disheartening, but there was a spark of hope, a spark she hoped they could coax into a flame.

"The soldiers and I are leaving tonight. We are setting up camp in Yexshire to oversee the rebuilding of the palace and the city. At least, that was Raffiel's plan, but you are the ruler of the High Mountain Court, Your Majesty, should you wish to order the soldiers somewhere else."

"We stick to Raffiel's plan for now." Remy pursed her lips. Bern had called her "Your Majesty." For a fleeting moment, Remy thought she would not have to take the throne. When Raffiel died, that freedom ripped away from her again.

Bern looked to Hale. "I think you should go east to establish your presence in the court there."

"I will not claim the East," Hale said. "It was never mine to claim, nor do I want it now." Bern went to speak, but Hale continued. "I also acknowledge we cannot leave Augustus and the fallen Eastern King's advisors to rule instead. We can ride to the East and arrange an intermediary governance while we plan for a permanent sovereign. I can think of an excellent person to help oversee the selection." Hale smiled.

Bern bobbed his chin. "I can offer you fifty of our soldiers to ride with you, but we will need the rest for the rebuilding of Yexshire."

"I will summon my troops in Falhampton as well," Hale said. "Augustus would be foolish to try to fight us."

"And what of the Northern Court?" Remy asked.

"Renwick will rule the Northern Court," Bern said.

"What? The Witchslayer?" Remy straightened, nearly jumping out of the bed. "You would leave a Vostemur on the throne?"

"I realize it may seem unreasonable, but Renwick has been our ally for some time, Remy," Bern said. "He has had to walk a fine line of allegiances for many years. He is the one who brought me into play. He is the one who slipped you that dagger." Bern cocked his head toward Remy's dagger that lay on her bedside table. "His people will listen to him far more than they would a High Mountain fae too."

"He could be double-crossing us." Remy balked. "He could have just been securing the throne for himself or hedging his bets . . . we cannot trust him."

"I have reason to believe we can . . . ," Bern said, but before Remy could interject, he continued, "I agree we must be cautious, though, which is why Rua is going to stay behind and oversee his transition to power."

"Rua?" Remy protested. "You would leave my little sister behind with our sworn enemy?!"

"She volunteered for the job." Bern laughed. "And I need not remind you that Rua is in possession of the Immortal Blade. She is a fearsome warning, and her presence along with the Immortal Blade will make any Northerner think twice of mutiny."

Remy grimaced. It was true. Keeping the Immortal Blade in the North would be a clever act of intimidation. She hated that her little sister had to stay with it, though. Did Rua even know how to use a sword?

"So you go to the mountains," Remy said looking at Bern, "I go east, and Rua stays in the North. Scattered through the courts once more."

"Hopefully not for long." Bern smiled sadly. He grabbed something out of the pocket of his satin waistcoat. "Here."

He produced a long gold chain holding a heavy glowing red stone: the amulet of Aelusien. Remy shook her head at first, but Bern pressed it into her hands.

"You should have it. You did, after all, nearly die obtaining it."

Remy looked to Hale, smirking at her. He must have told Bern the story of how the amulet of Aelusien came into their possession.

"And it will add a nice bit of pressure on the East too," Bern added, cocking his head.

"Were you his general? Raffiel's?" Remy wondered, looking at Bern. The male's face caved again at the sound of her brother's name.

"No," Bern said. "I was his Fated mate."

Remy exited the bathing chamber and returned into the opulent room. She tied her hair up in a burgundy scarf and wore a fresh golden tunic with red embroidery, fitted trousers, and riding boots. The amulet of Aelusien hung heavily around her neck.

Hale had pushed for them to stay another night in the Northern Court. Remy had denied him, insisting they leave for the East at once. They needed to intervene before Hale's supposed brother, Augustus, and the late King's advisors had time to regroup. Word of what happened the night before would reach them soon enough, and Hale and Remy needed to be right behind the news, ready to take control of the Eastern Court.

Hale had cleaned up as well. He stood over a basin of water, his white shirtsleeves rolled up. He had shaved off the beard from his dungeon days. He looked the princely warrior once more. He shifted his hair out of his eyes. His chestnut brown hair needed a trim too. The sides had gotten long, and the top now stretched past his nose, forcing him to swipe the locks back.

"Ready?" he asked, rolling down his sleeves.

Remy walked to him and wrapped her arms around him. He smiled into her shoulder and gave it a kiss.

"I love you," Remy whispered into his hard chest.

Hale's arms enveloped her, squeezing tighter for a moment before releasing her. He moved his hands to frame Remy's face. Remy didn't think she would ever get used to the way Hale looked at her. She could stare into those smoky gray eyes forever.

"I love you too." His face was so open and beautiful at that moment.

He leaned forward, his lips meeting Remy's in a soft, slow kiss. It was a kiss that promised many sweeter, slow kisses to come. It promised many nights when they could take their time passionately exploring each other's bodies . . . though Remy did not mind their rushed and frantic lovemaking either. She wanted it all with this gorgeous male in front of her. She wanted a lifetime with her Fated.

Hale pulled back from the kiss, leaving Remy wanting. His half-hooded eyes snagged on the *Shil-de* ring on his right hand, resting on Remy's cheek.

"You should not have put this ring on me, Remy." His voice filled with lament. "It belongs to you and your family, and now I cannot take it off."

"You are my family, Hale," Remy whispered.

Hale's eyes darted to hers, raw and vulnerable. His entire family had been a lie. He was just a pawn in his adoptive father's bigger plans. He had never treated him like a son. "I don't really know what family even means."

"Neither do I," Remy said with a sad smile. "I don't know if I'm meant to feel closer to the sister I haven't seen in fourteen years. I don't know how much of a familial bond will carry us through. But I do know something that Heather . . ."

Remy choked on her tears. They sprung up so abruptly when it hit her again: Heather was gone. The grief washed over her anew.

Hale swiped away the tears that fell down Remy's cheek with his thumb. She loved that Hale felt unburdened by her tears. He stood there, letting her feel it all, giving her time to use her voice again.

"Heather was my family." Remy hung her head as her voice shook.

A wave of regret hit her once more. She wished she had been kinder to Heather. Remy wished she hadn't directed her anger at her guardian all the time. She wished she had called her "Mother" because that is who she truly was. Heather was an unknown brown witch who had steadfastly defended Remy and raised her with all of a mother's protection and love. Remy set herself a silent intention that once they returned to Yexshire, she would place Heather's burial stone behind the Castle of Yexshire, along with the rest of the family she lost. And on every Day of the Spirits she would visit both of her mothers.

Resting her hand over his heart, Remy looked to Hale.

"I do not know all that the future will hold, but I know this: I am your Fated, and I am your family." Remy held her mate's eyes as she watched her words crack him open.

His throat bobbed as he nodded. She knew he could not speak.

Before Remy could ask what he was doing, he unknotted that red thread around his wrist. With his teeth he ripped it in two. It had survived a poison lake, imprisonment in a dungeon, and a battle. Yet there it was. She had put it on him and told him he was hers.

"I plan on buying a much nicer ring in the East," Hale said, bending down onto one knee, "but I cannot wait."

Remy's mouth dropped in surprise. Hale held up the two equal lengths of thread. He was her soul mate, the person she intended to live the rest of her life with, and somehow this still came as a surprise.

"Remini Maescia Dammacus, Queen of the High Mountain Court . . . will you marry me?" Hale's smile made Remy want to buckle at the knees. It was a rare smile, so bright and hopeful.

Remy's chest felt like it might burst open.

"Yes." She wasn't sure if it was a laugh or a cry.

Hale leapt to his feet, that beautiful smile widening further as he tied that length of red string around her finger. Remy made quick work of knotting the second length onto his.

Hale pulled her face to him, crashing their mouths together. Remy threaded her fingers through his soft hair, pulling him in closer.

It was a desperate kiss, the horror of all they had seen mixed with the hope of a brighter future. As the chaos of the past collided with what was to come, that kiss was the only thing that mattered.

Hale removed his lips to trail kisses down Remy's neck and collarbone, shifting his hands to her hips, pulling their lower bodies together.

"How did you know my middle name?" she said, recalling his words.

Hale pulled away a mere inch and smiled at her.

"I looked it up in the private libraries of the Eastern Court the last time we were there." His grin turned sinful. "I wanted to know your full name before I proposed to you."

"You were planning on proposing to me even then?" Remy blanched.

Remy remembered that day on the boat, crossing the Crushwold River. She remembered that kiss in that inn in Ruttmore too. She had wanted Hale for a long time as well. But to know he had wanted to marry her for so long . . .

"I have wanted to marry you from the moment you almost crushed me with that pine tree way back in Harbruck," he said in that delicious, rolling purr that made Remy's stomach clench.

It was real. It had always been true and inevitable. Her Fated.

Remy broke her hold on Hale and walked to their bedroom door. She snicked the lock as she looked at him.

"What about leaving at once for the East?" He grinned wickedly.

"The East can wait," Remy said, prowling back to her Fated, her fiancé. The world could wait. The only person that mattered right now was Hale, and she needed him in every way. She needed their bodies as intertwined as their souls.

The caved-in ceiling opened up to a hazy, gray sky. Hale and Remy walked through the snow-filled corridor, navigating around the rubble. The castle was mostly ruins after the wrath of Baba Morganna. They winded toward the front entryway, where a caravan of carriages waited to ride back to Yexshire. The haunted halls were empty, the aftermath of the battle evident every few paces—splatters of brown dried blood, dented armor, abandoned shoes dusted in snow.

"Remy!" a whooping shout came from behind them just as another echoed, "Hale!"

She didn't have time to brace for the impact as three fae warriors barreled into her, squashing her and Hale against the wall, the hood of her cloak flying off. Grabbing the Eagles and Carys, she pulled them into a tight hug, a potent mixture of joy and sorrow coursing through her as she clung to them.

"You were incredible," Talhan exclaimed, looking to Hale. "Did you see her? She fought off five armored soldiers with that one little dagger!"

"I taught her everything she knows," Bri said, clapping her on the shoulder. "You didn't die, Rem."

"I did," Remy muttered as Carys slung her arm around Remy's waist and pulled her into her side.

"I am so sorry about Heather, Remy," she said, her voice cracking as the group sobered. "She was an amazing person and she will be deeply missed."

They pressed in closer, arms tightening around each other, mourning the loss of the brown witch.

"And Raffiel," Talhan said, his golden eyes filled with lament. "They have been washed and dressed, ready to take back to their final resting place."

Remy bit her lips between her teeth to keep the tears from flowing. She would bury them in the hills behind the ruins of the castle in Yexshire. She would give them the burial her parents never received. Fresh white flowers would always adorn their graves. She would make sure their sacrifices were never forgotten.

"The High Mountain crowns have been loaded into the carriages too," Carys said, her blue eyes darting between Remy and Hale. "Your crowns, now."

Bri's gaze dropped to the string on Remy's finger. She smacked her brother hard in the chest. "I told you, didn't I? She was his Fated." She beamed at Remy with her cat-like grin. "I totally guessed it."

Talhan guffawed. "She had no idea."

"So we ride to Yexshire," Remy sighed, looking at Hale and then back to her friends. "And where will you go?"

"Someone needs to head east and get control of Wynreach until a new sovereign is chosen," Carys said. "We will go keep the peace."

"We just got back together," Talhan whined.

"We will come visit you in the East, Tal," Remy said, leaning her shoulder into Hale. "After we lead our people to Yexshire."

"You are free of your oath to me now." Hale's voice dropped an octave as he stared down at his hands. "I am not a Prince of the Eastern Court."

Bri snorted. "No," she said. "You're the future King of the High Mountain Court."

Talhan grinned, looking between Hale and Remy. "We're with you. Always."

Remy swallowed the lump in her throat as she smiled at them.

"Come on, let's get to the carriages." Bri pulled them down the corridor. "I need to take a nap."

"It is mid-morning." Remy chuckled, smelling the lingering scent of ale and moonshine on their breaths.

"Exactly." Talhan wrapped his hefty arm around Remy's shoulder as he guided her down the hall. "Time to sleep."

Their laughter reverberated off the cold stone walls, their joy so at odds with the destruction around them. Remy glanced up at the crumbling wall towering above her. Even through the depths of their losses, there was a feeling of awe too. Against all odds, they had survived.

They had traveled through every court in Okrith together, save for her home court. She hoped there would be nights of drinking and storytelling around the hearth of the rebuilt castle in Yexshire. She hoped they would all go up to the rooftop of Lavender Hall again and sip honey wine in the gardens of Saxbridge. But above all, she hoped that their future adventures would be together more often than apart.

Pulling her fur-trimmed cloak tighter around her, Remy followed Hale out into the blizzard. A carriage waited outside the doorway. Behind them, the Northern castle was all but ruins, only a small part of it remaining untouched by the wrath of Baba Morganna. Two servants from Bern's group were ready to help Remy into the carriage.

Bern sat downhill on horseback. Surrounded by fifty of his soldiers, he readied his troops to march south into Yexshire. Carys,

Talhan, and Bri moved toward the saddled mounts, waiting to head east.

This was her life now—carriages, servants.

Even in the camps of Yexshire while they rebuilt the castle, they would treat her like a queen. She was the queen, though a coronation would have to wait for now.

This was her destiny laid out before her.

For the briefest flicker of time, Remy had thought it wouldn't have to be her, that Raffiel would take the throne and she could relax and live her life with Hale. But that wasn't the truth that had been gnawing into her gut these fourteen years. She knew that, for Yexshire to rise again, she would have to take her place on the throne. She knew no one would come in and do it for her.

The world would not make her, she would make the world.

One soldier broke from the gathering up ahead. He was a head taller than those around him, long and lean, though filling out. Remy's feet were moving before she could stop herself.

Fenrin.

Remy caught the brown witch before he could move into a bow and threw her arms around him. She squeezed him like a vice, willing herself not to cry. All the eyes of her people were on her, but she did not care. Let them see her hugging the witch.

"Don't torture yourself for it, Remy. It was her choice, and she made the right one," Fenrin said, knowing the guilt Remy felt for Heather's death. She didn't have to say one word for him to know from that squeeze that she loved him, appreciated him. "You know she'd always make that choice."

Remy bit her lip so hard she was sure it would draw blood. She would not cry again in front of the people who had risked their lives to save her. She needed to show strength.

They released the hug and surveyed the gathering caravan of people and horses heading to Yexshire.

"It's too much, Fen," Remy said, surveying her people.

"You always were a queen, Remy, always. You just are letting other people see it now too," he said.

"I will have need of a brown witch in Yexshire. I'm sure many of my people will need the help of a palace brown witch. Would you care to take the position?"

"Of course," he said, eyes lighting up. Then he smirked at her. "I have many suggestions of how you can design your palace."

"Excellent." She smiled. They had been imagining building a home in Yexshire since they were twelve. If anyone knew what she wanted in a palace, it would be Fenrin.

The brown witch looked over her shoulder. "Your Fated is a good man, Remy, I'm happy for you."

She loosed a long-held sigh at that. Not knowing how much she needed to hear that, she was grateful that Fenrin had released her from his feelings. She wanted Fenrin's approval of Hale. Remy hoped Heather would have approved of him too.

"Your Majesty." Carys coughed from her horse behind them.

Remy turned and saw, standing in the arched stone doorway of the palace, her sister. She hustled up the hillside, snow sticking to her black hair.

Rua stood stoically in front of her, her hand resting on the ruby hilt of the Immortal Blade. She looked so much like Rivitus. She had the same smattering of dark freckles across her golden-brown skin, green and brown eyes, and highlights of strawberry blonde in her wavy, dark hair. Her looks were willowy and ethereal, but her countenance was rock hard. She stood perfectly, shoulders back, chin up. At eighteen, she looked like she could conquer the world.

Remy hesitated for a moment before hugging her sister. She dropped heavy tears as she hugged Rua. She couldn't contain them, hugging the only member of her family who lived. She never thought she would see Rua again, and here she was, beautiful and strong. Rua lifted one arm and rested it tentatively on Remy's back, the other remaining on her sword.

When they pulled away, Rua's face was unchanged, unaffected by that long embrace. It stung. Remy wondered what had happened in Rua's childhood to make her this way . . . or maybe the sword had done something to her sister.

Renwick appeared, lingering in the archway, as Remy wiped her tears. She narrowed a hateful look at him, and he huffed out a laugh.

She looked back at her sister. "You do not have to stay here. You could come back home with us."

Home. It felt so good to say.

They were going home. Remy and her people would rebuild their homeland. The future of their people was promising once more. Let the realm know what it meant to be a High Mountain fae. She would lead her people back into the light of a new age.

"I will be fine," Rua said. There was no anger or frustration in her voice, only a stoic coldness that worried Remy more than any emotion. This was not the same girl who was shaking and screaming while Northern soldiers cut down witches beside her.

Rua looked back to Renwick with a snarl. Good. At least there was something there, then. "I will let them know the power of the High Mountains."

Remy stared at Rua for another moment. Her little sister was fearsome. Remy wondered what her life had been, growing up with the red witches in hiding. She imagined being raised by red witches in the woods was wholly different from the way Heather raised her in taverns. Whatever her upbringing, it had molded her into the person standing here now. She quaked to think what her sister would do with that blade.

"I will be in touch through fae fires. Regularly. It won't be long until Winter Solstice, which I hope you come home for, you . . . and Renwick," Remy added with a drip of disgust that made her sister smile. At least they could agree to hate him, then. Maybe they could bond over that. "Please contact me whenever you can."

Rua nodded, and that was her only response. Her sister didn't bristle under Remy's sad stare. This was not the reunion Remy had hoped for.

She felt someone standing beside her. A worn leather pack thudded to the ground. She looked over and saw Bri.

"I've had enough of the East," Bri said, looking at Remy. "With your permission, Your Majesty, I'd like to stay behind and offer my protection to Princess Ruadora."

Remy sagged with relief.

She could cry all over again that her friend had offered to stay. She didn't trust any of Bern's soldiers to stay behind. She didn't know any of them. She didn't feel like she could order Hale's warriors around either. She supposed she would have to get used to ordering people around. But Bri had seen her distress and volunteered.

"I do not need your assistance," Rua said.

"I know you don't need it," Remy said to her sister. "You've proven your power and skill," she added, trying to puff her up. "But the North is still rife with those loyal to the fallen King. Even with that sword, you still need to sleep. Let one more pair of eyes guard your back. Please."

Remy hated that she had to beg. She knew she could demand it and her sister could not refuse, but she wasn't willing to throw down that gauntlet, not when they had just found each other again.

So she pleaded. Let her sister think she had a say. This relationship was already more tenuous than Remy had hoped, but with Bri there, at least she would know Rua would be safe.

"Fine." Rua drifted those green-flecked eyes to Bri. The Eagle matched it with her own golden stare. These two were going to be an interesting pairing.

Remy gave one last half smile to her sister and turned. That was that. She plodded to the carriage where Hale waited. He stood proudly, looking at her.

He threaded his warm fingers through her hand. She felt the red thread tied around her ring finger.

"Give her time," he mumbled.

Remy held onto his hand tighter.

Her Fated saw it all, how desperately she wanted her sister's love, how badly she needed that connection.

It would come. Hale was right. Rua had been through an unspeakable trauma. She just needed time. At least, Remy hoped that was all she needed. She hated leaving her in the North, but she didn't want to leave Renwick unchecked either. At least Bri would stay behind.

Remy scanned out over the swirling white blizzard. It would be a long trek through this weather, but she could not wait. She knew her people could not wait either. They would rather trudge through a snowstorm to reach their homeland than to wait another night in the castle of their enemy. It was only the beginning for them. The new day their world had been waiting fourteen years for was dawning. And it would be Remy who would usher in that change, with her King by her side.

CHAPTER THIRTY

They stood on the cliff, overlooking the rugged stone beaches and, beyond that, the ocean. Nothing prepared Remy for the vastness of cerulean waves stretching out before her; the enormity of the giant rolling swells that crashed along the stones, the loud sound of rocks being tumbled as the ocean pulled them back into its watery depths. The scent was so familiar, even though she had never visited the ocean. It was Hale's scent, like the ocean waves had branded themselves on his soul.

Looking out into the mighty, frothy blue that stretched into the horizon, all the world's problems felt incredibly small.

The courts were all a mess; the world had descended into chaos after the slaying of King Vostemur: blue witch uprisings in the North, Augustus Norwood fleeing into the Eastern Mountains with a battalion ready to take back his throne, caravans of displaced Yexshiri and red witch refugees making their way back to the High Mountain Court . . . yet here, everything felt calm.

The wind whipped Remy's pointed ears, muffling the sound of Hale's rapidly beating heart. She looked to her left, to the winding path that led to a cottage carved into the cliff and to the fishing village of Haastmouth Beach.

Ramshackle cottages dotted the narrow paths to a high boardwalk on stilts and a long jetty of tied-up fishing boats, nestled into the harbor to protect from the high winds.

But it was this first cottage that held Hale's gaze. He clutched a bouquet of violet flowers in his hand.

Remy stepped to him and laced her fingers through his free hand.

"I'm here," she said, gripping his hand tighter.

She wouldn't promise that it was going to be okay or make meaningless statements of comfort. But she was there, beside him. Always.

They would walk through these hard moments together.

Hale squeezed her hand back and released it. He faltered down the rickety staircase to the front door.

Remy followed in silence.

The driftwood door looked worn by strong winds. Seagrass covered the weathered walls. From the outside it looked intimate rather than run down. Remy had lived in enough taverns to know the difference. Strings of shells hung above the fogged glass window beside the door, clinking in the breeze.

Hale stood before that door, adjusting the bouquet in his one hand. His other hand hung by his side, his thumb nervously rubbing his pointer finger. He lifted his hand twice and put it back down. Remy stood behind him, trying to emanate love and support.

She would stand here all night if he needed, just as he had stood by her so many times before.

The sun was hanging low on the horizon, lighting the clouds in a pink and gold glow. Remy had never seen the sun setting over the ocean before. The sight was breathtaking. The sound of a final, decisive knock on the door drew her back from her awe.

A slender older woman opened it instantly. She froze for a moment, looking at Hale. She had the same chestnut brown hair, but silver streaked through it. Her locks were wavy and tousled, making her look like she was a mermaid emerging from the ocean waves. She had pale eyes like Hale, but hers had the faintest tinge of sage.

She blinked at Hale one more time and then she was moving, throwing her arms around him. Hale wrapped his arms around her and bowed his head, shoulders caving as he hugged his mother into him.

Remy watched, tears filling her eyes, thinking of Heather and the foggy memories of her mother, the Queen.

The sound of a mewling cat pulled her watery gaze to her feet. She reached down, scratching the black cat arching into her outstretched hand.

Purrs rumbled out from the cat as Remy crouched and whispered, "Hello there." The feline head-butted into her palm in response. "Do you think I'm a witch?"

Remy scratched the cat, watching as the sun began to kiss the horizon and the sky filled with watercolor clouds over the ocean. The mother and son embraced for a long time. The knot in her chest released. Remy whispered goodbye to her doubt and fear—may they set with the sun. When the glowing star rose over the vastness of the ocean tomorrow, she would be ready to be a queen.

Follow Remy's story from the beginning in this FREE prequel novella!

Plus get a FREE BONUS EPILOGUE with the steamy seaside

story *Haastmouth Beach* and more free content when you sign-up to AK Mulford's newsletter at www.akmulford.com

The story continues in The Five Crowns of Okrith Book 2: *The Witches' Blade.*

If you enjoyed this story, please consider leaving a review!

ABOUT THE AUTHOR

AK Mulford lives in the perfect place for a fantasy author: New Zealand! Mulford grew up craving seeing herself represented in the world of fantasy and is inspired to create diverse and LGBTQ+ fantasy stories that transport readers to new realms of imagination, helping them to fall in love with fantasy for the first time, or, all over again. A former primatologist, Mulford has now swapped raising monkeys for writing fantasy. She lives in Wellington with her husband and two wonderful young  kids. In her down time (what is this mythical "down time"?), she spends time with her cat and dog, and makes ridiculous and fun Tiktok videos.

www.akmulford.com

ACKNOWLEDGMENTS

First and foremost I want to thank my wonderful husband, Glen. Thank you for supporting my dreams, for putting up with my minor (and major) freak outs, and for holding down the fort while I wrote this story. You are a wonderful husband and father and I am forever grateful that I met you all those many years ago in Guatemala.

Thank you to the bright, shining, vibrant lights that are my children, I love you with all of my heart. Thank you for being patient with me (or at least trying valiantly) while I chase after my dreams. You are probably reading this many years in the future, if not: wow, congratulations, you can read!

To my mom and dad; thank you for always encouraging me to write and continuing to cheer me on even now. I am so thankful that you believed in my storytelling and supported my creativity from a young age.

And to my brother, thanks for daydreaming up fantastical stories with me. You and I always had the souls of storytellers. (Also, what's up? Call me sometime so we can hang!)

To the amazing community of friends I have made on Tiktok: thank you for all of your support and welcoming me into the best bookish community around! I am grateful for each and every one of you. Right, okay, back to lip-syncing and goofing off. #Ily

To my amazing beta team, thank you for all of your support and feedback making this book the best it could be! I so appreciate all of your notes and reactions to this story!

Thank you to all of my ARC readers! I so appreciate you sharing this story far and wide!

To Hayley, thank you for beta reading for me and being the self-appointed president of my fan club. I am so grateful to have you in my life. Love you babe.

To my crispy taco delights, thanks for always being in my corner and getting me through the tough days! I don't know what I would do without you.

Thank you to Hannah Close from Reedsy for her amazing editing services and for elevating my story with her editorial assessment.

Thank you Carolyn Bahm for being an amazing editor and for helping me make this story the best it could be!

Thank you to Norma Gambini from Normas Nook Proofreading for all of your support and amazing proofreading skills!

To my podcast wifey, K. Elle Morrison, thank you for cheering me on and keeping from melting down so many times during the production of this story! I love hosting *Indies Fully Booked* with you!

Thank you to Kelli from KDL editing for your eagle eyes in proofreading!

Thank you to Kristen Timofeev for the beautiful map!

Thank you to Bianca Bordianu *www.bbordianudesign.com* for the amazing book cover.

And lastly, I'd like to thank Ziggy, my gorgeous labradoodle, for being the most patient, loving dog in the world and for not getting mad at me those times when I was too deep in a story and made him wait for breakfast.